𝔊𝔬𝔥𝔫 𝔊𝔞𝔯𝔱𝔢𝔯:
𝔗𝔥𝔢 𝔐𝔬𝔳𝔦𝔢
𝔑𝔬𝔳𝔢𝔩𝔦𝔷𝔞𝔱𝔦𝔬𝔫

(John Carter: The Movie Novelization)

Also includes:

𝔞
𝔓𝔯𝔦𝔫𝔠𝔢𝔰𝔰
𝔬𝔣
𝔐𝔞𝔯𝔰

(A Princess of Mars)

ᎣᎥᎦᏃ ᏟᏗᎯᎫᎧᎠ: ᎧᏃᎦ ᎦᎥᏎᏇᎦ ᏃᎥᎦᎧᎦᎴᎵᏇᎧᎧ

(John Carter: The Movie Novelization)

BY STUART MOORE

BASED ON THE SCREENPLAY BY
ANDREW STANTON & MARK ANDREWS
AND MICHAEL CHABON

BASED ON THE STORY *A PRINCESS OF MARS* BY
EDGAR RICE BURROUGHS

PRODUCED BY
JIM MORRIS, COLIN WILSON
AND LINDSEY COLLINS

DIRECTED BY
ANDREW STANTON

Also includes:

Ꭷ ᏟᏇᏃᎦᏟᏗᎵᏳ ᎧᏃ ᎦᎯᎦᏃ

(A Princess of Mars)

BY EDGAR RICE BURROUGHS

DISNEY EDITIONS • New York

(Contents)

A PRINCESS OF MARS

TO THE READER OF THIS WORK:

In submitting Captain Carter's strange manuscript to you in book form, I believe that a few words relative to this remarkable personality will be of interest.

My first recollection of Captain Carter is of the few months he spent at my father's home in Virginia, just prior to the opening of the Civil War. I was then a child of but five years, yet I well remember the tall, dark, smooth-faced, athletic man whom I called Uncle Jack.

He seemed always to be laughing; and he entered into the sports of the children with the same hearty good fellowship he displayed toward those pastimes in which the men and women of his own age indulged; or he would sit for an hour at a time entertaining my old grandmother with stories of his strange, wild life in all parts of the world. We all loved him, and our slaves fairly worshipped the ground he trod.

He was a splendid specimen of manhood, standing a good two inches over six feet, broad of shoulder and narrow of hip, with the carriage of the trained fighting man. His features were regular and clear cut, his hair black and closely cropped, while his eyes were of a steel gray, reflecting a strong and loyal character, filled with fire and initiative. His manners were perfect, and his courtliness was that of a typical southern gentleman of the highest type.

His horsemanship, especially after hounds, was a marvel and delight even in that country of magnificent horsemen. I have often heard my father caution him against his wild recklessness, but he would only laugh, and say that the tumble that killed him would be from the back of a horse yet unfoaled.

When the war broke out he left us, nor did I see him again for some fifteen or sixteen years. When he returned it was without warning, and I was much surprised to note that he had not aged apparently a moment, nor had he changed in any other outward way. He was, when others were with him, the same genial, happy fellow we had known of old, but when he thought himself alone I have seen him sit for hours gazing off into space, his face set in a look of wistful longing and hopeless misery; and at night he would sit thus looking up into the heavens, at what I did not know until I read his manuscript years afterwards.

He told us that he had been prospecting and mining in Arizona part of the time since the war; and that he had been very successful was evidenced by the unlimited amount of money with which he was supplied. As to the details of his life during these years he was very reticent, in fact he would not talk of them at all.

He remained with us for about a year and then went to New York, where he purchased a little place on the Hudson, where I visited him once a year on the occasions of my trips to the New York market—my father and I owning and operating a string of general stores throughout Virginia at that time. Captain Carter had a small but beautiful cottage, situated on a bluff overlooking the river, and during one of my last visits, in the winter of 1885, I observed he was much occupied in writing, I presume now, upon this manuscript.

He told me at this time that if anything should happen to him he wished me to take charge of his estate, and he gave me a key to a compartment in the safe which stood in his study, telling me I would find his will there and some personal instructions which he had me pledge myself to carry out with absolute fidelity.

After I had retired for the night I have seen him from my window standing in the moonlight on the brink of the bluff overlooking the Hudson with his arms stretched out to the heavens as though in appeal. I thought at the time that he was praying, although I never had understood that he was in the strict sense of the term a religious man.

Several months after I had returned home from my last visit, the first of March, 1886, I think, I received a telegram from him asking me to come to him at once. I had always been his favorite among the younger generation of Carters and so I hastened to comply with his demand.

I arrived at the little station, about a mile from his grounds, on the morning of March 4, 1886, and when I asked the livery man to drive me out to Captain Carter's he replied that if I was a friend of the Captain's he had some very bad news for me; the Captain had been found dead shortly after daylight that very morning by the watchman attached to an adjoining property.

For some reason this news did not surprise me, but I hurried out to his place as quickly as possible, so that I could take charge of the body and of his affairs.

I found the watchman who had discovered him, together with the local police chief and several townspeople, assembled in his little study. The watchman related the few details connected with the finding of the body, which he said had been still warm when he came upon it. It lay, he said, stretched full length in the snow with the arms outstretched above the head toward the edge of the bluff, and when he showed me the spot it flashed upon me that it was the identical one where I had seen him on those other nights, with his arms raised in supplication to the skies.

There were no marks of violence on the body, and with the aid of a local physician the coroner's jury quickly reached a decision of death from heart failure. Left alone in the study, I opened the safe and withdrew the contents of the drawer in which he had told me I would find my instructions. They were in part peculiar indeed, but I have followed them to each last detail as faithfully as I was able.

He directed that I remove his body to Virginia without embalming, and that he be laid in an open coffin within a tomb which he previously had had constructed and which, as I later learned, was well ventilated. The instructions impressed upon me that I must personally see that this was carried out just as he directed, even in secrecy if necessary.

His property was left in such a way that I was to receive the entire income for twenty-five years, when the principal was to become mine. His further instructions related to this manuscript which I was to retain sealed and unread, just as I found it, for eleven years; nor was I to divulge its contents until twenty-one years after his death.

A strange feature about the tomb, where his body still lies, is that the massive door is equipped with a single, huge gold-plated spring lock which can be opened only from the inside.

Yours very sincerely,
EDGAR RICE BURROUGHS.

ꜱᴏɴᴇ ᴄᴀʀᴛᴇʀ: ᴀ ɴᴏᴠᴇʟɪᴢᴀᴛɪᴏɴ

(John Carter: A Novelization)

ᘓ𝔍⑂𐤈⑂𐤈𝔍⑂𐤈: 𐤊𝔥𐤈 ⚹ᘏ𝔥⚹

(prologue: Sab Than*)*

"Light," Sab Than yelled, leaning forward into the swirling dust of the airship's bridge. "I need *clean light!*"

The men hunched forward over their controls, struggling to steer the ship upward into the dust cloud. Sand blew in through the open portals of the semi-enclosed bridge. One crewman, an old man who'd served Sab's father, coughed harshly.

"I said clean light," Sab continued. "Full loft!"

"Full loft, aye!" the man repeated.

Sab Than, ruler of the predator city of Zodanga, grabbed hold of the waist-high bridge walls and staggered out onto the open deck, waving the deadly sand away with a swipe of his mailed gauntlet. The ship lurched, nosed upward. Outside, teams of airmen worked furiously to deploy the ship's solar vanes . . . the long, waferlike metal constructs that made air travel possible on the red planet of Barsoom—otherwise known as Mars.

Sab gazed upward, past the waving red flag of Zodanga, into the looming cloud. Then he turned to peer behind the ship. He couldn't see the pursuers through the blinding dust, but he knew they were still on his tail. Two ships of Helium, the only kingdom that still dared to defy Zodanga's supremacy. And now they had the ruler of Zodanga cornered in a sandstorm.

Despite the danger, Sab's blood thrilled to the challenge. His thoughts flickered to the proudest, most powerful moment of his life: the day he'd first assumed Zodanga's throne. Zodanga, the devourer—the moving city, trampling the sands of Barsoom beneath its hundreds of legs, draining this world of all energy and life. To rule Zodanga was to wield true power such as no other man had ever known.

As the ship climbed higher into the storm, the dust grew thick and dark. All around Sab Than, airmen coughed and sputtered despite their masks. Sab stood firm, blinking only slightly as he stared into the furious Martian sky.

Then the ship tilted to the left, angling around in a sharp curve. The air began to lighten. The sandstorm receded below the ship . . . and was replaced by the blinding light of the sun.

Sunlight struck the ship's deck, wing tiles, and solar vanes. The airmen cheered, working their ropes to aim the tiles toward the light.

Flush with triumph, Sab strode back inside just as

sunlight flooded into the bridge. The crew jumped into action, dashing from wheel to wheel, instrument to instrument.

Light danced along the multilensed controls of the ship's Light Master. "Intensity full!" he cried.

"Ten points ascending," the Navigator said.

The Plotter's hands were a blur on the controls. "Facing new plot—"

"No time," Sab said. "Hard turn. *Now!*"

The Plotter grimaced, then nodded and obeyed. Sab held tight to a half-wall as the ship banked hard, doubling back over the exact spot where they'd emerged from the dust storm.

Sab ran back out to the deck just as the gunmen were taking their places at weapons stations. They grabbed hold of the big mounted guns, swiveling them up, down, and around. They couldn't yet see their targets.

"Aim below," Sab yelled against the wind, just as the two Helium airships burst into view, breaking upward out of the dust cloud. The gunmen prepared to fire—

"*Shadow!*"

It was the worst possible warning call on an airship.

Shocked, Sab whipped his head upward to see a *third* Helium ship hovering above, blocking the light to the Zodangans' sails. Sab felt the ship beneath him slow, the hum of its mighty engines fade as their precious sun power was abruptly cut off.

Everything happened quickly then. The first two Helium ships wafted upward, opening fire as they drifted into place alongside Sab's vessel. Cannon bursts rained down on the Zodangan deck. The third ship began to drop boarding parties down on long ropes.

Sab Than's warriors needed no orders, no command from their leader. They drew swords and engaged the invaders in open combat on the lurching, chaotic deck of the airship. Cannon fire fell deafeningly all around. Sab's gunmen struggled to return fire, but the deck soon became a blur of Zodangans in red and Heliumites in their cursed blue capes. Some fell to the deck as they died while others tumbled over the side, dropping to the Martian sands below.

Sab gritted his teeth, unsheathed his sword, and immediately drew blood. One, two, three blue-garbed soldiers. But he knew it wouldn't be enough. He could stand against a single Helium ship, perhaps two. But these three had him boxed in without sufficient power to escape. Already the Helium soldiers were storming the bridge.

Sab Than's rule, he knew, was over. Along with his life.

And then something happened. Something that changed the destiny of the planet Barsoom.

As Sab staggered back momentarily against a rail, a strange blue light caught his eye. It emanated from the nearest Helium ship, hovering mere yards away across open sky. The ship seemed engulfed in blue flame, an eerie cold fire unlike anything Sab had ever seen. As he watched, the flame burned bright, encircling the Helium ship—which then winked out of existence.

Gone.

Sab turned his gaze upward just in time to see the same flame touch the ship hovering above. That vessel too vanished, disappearing in a bright blue flash and revealing the blinding sun above. All around Sab, the warriors—Zodangan and Helium alike—pointed and stared, shocked and afraid, as the third Helium ship suffered the same fate, dissolving into a wisp of blue ash.

But the blue flame didn't die out. It moved nearer, closing in from all sides. Shockingly, it left Sab's deck plates and instruments untouched. But as the ruler watched, stunned, it incinerated one warrior after another, each one vanishing in a flash of deadly fire. Zondangans and Heliumites, gunmen and navigators—no one was spared.

Finally only Sab Than remained.

Still the flame grew closer. Gritting his teeth, Sab raised his sword—a futile gesture, he knew. But to his surprise, the fire stopped at the tip of the sword and dissolved in a shimmer of blue.

A burst of sunlight struck Sab full on, blinding him momentarily. He shaded his eyes, peered up at the sun. Three robed figures dropped smoothly down out of the glaring light, coming easily to rest on the open deck— where no trace remained now of neither Sab Than's crew nor of the Helium invaders.

The figures were tall and hairless, their pale robes patterned with intricate, ancient designs. The leader held a strange weapon, a combination of gauntlet and gun that enveloped his hand in a web of blue lace. As Sab Than watched, the leader approached and handed him the device.

Sab stared down at the weapon for a long moment. In the months to come, he would learn the word *nanotechnology* as well as the leader's name, Matai Shang, and the name of his race: the Therns. But right now—

Sab aimed at Matai Shang and fired.

The blast struck an energy field and dissipated harmlessly. Matai raised a hand and waved casually, knocking Sab off his feet with some invisible force. The gun struck the deck with a surprisingly soft thud.

"Being a fool is a great luxury, Sab Than," Matai said in a deep, ancient voice. "Get up."

Sab staggered to his feet. "Who—what are you?"

"We serve the Goddess," Matai said. "And she has chosen you to receive this weapon."

He waved his hand again and the weapon levitated off the deck, returning to Sab's hands.

Sab ran his hands over the gun, its odd texture firm but soft beneath his touch. And suddenly he felt the old power, that sense of imminent conquest—just as he had on the day he'd first taken the throne.

His life, he now knew, was not over. It was only just beginning.

"Do as we command," Matai continued, "and you will rule all Barsoom. With none to defy you and nothing to stand in your way."

Alone on the deck of his airship, with but three godlike Therns as his judge, Sab Than nodded and prepared to embrace his destiny.

CHAPTER 1

MY NAME is Edgar Rice Burroughs, and by trade I am a writer of popular fiction. When one makes one's living in this way, one *reads* a lot as well: books, popular magazines, instruction manuals, even advertisements. But nothing I'd ever read disturbed me quite so much as the telegram I received on that fateful day in 1881:

> DEAR NED
> SEE ME AT ONCE
> JOHN CARTER

It was terse, uninformative, and yet it chilled me with its implications. My Uncle Jack had never been a man to ask for help, and I knew him well enough to sense the desperation hiding behind his words. By the time my train pulled into Croton-on-Hudson station, I had read the telegram a dozen times, searching in vain for clues.

Then I saw the grave, downcast older man standing on the platform, calling my name. And I knew.

"Mister Burroughs? I'm Thompson, Captain Carter's butler. I'm afraid I bring sad tidings . . ."

After a quiet carriage ride, we pulled up at Uncle Jack's sober granite mansion. Thompson helped me down, and I shook hands with a squat, business-suited gentleman who introduced himself as Noah Dalton, my uncle's attorney.

"My deepest sympathies, Mister Burroughs." Dalton ushered me inside. "Your uncle's death came as a shock to all of us. He was a model of health and vigor."

Standing in the immaculately kept foyer, I could scarcely believe the news. "How did he . . ."

"A stroke. Just dropped dead in his study, not five minutes after sending for me and the doctor. When I arrived he was already . . . gone."

We entered the front hall and I stopped short, staring at the scene before me. Artifacts filled the room: relics, maps, charts, documents, photographs from architectural sites representing all the ancient cultures of the world. They were spread haphazardly around a central desk—not like a museum display, but as if they were all vital parts of some massive research project.

"The man never stopped exploring," Dalton continued. "All over the world. No sooner'd start in digging one hole than he was off to Java or the Orkney Islands to dig another. He said it was pure research, but it always seemed to me like he was searching for something." He cast a pious gaze heavenward. "God grant that he has found it now."

I was barely listening. My attention had been drawn to a large world map stabbed with dozens of tiny pins, all interlinked by multicolored threads. And beside it: a portrait of my uncle, fierce and powerful, but with a hint of sadness in his eyes. He was a very vigorous man who'd seemed to stop aging at a certain point. He looked no older than my earliest memories of him.

Dalton gestured at the portrait. "Every inch a cavalryman, to the very end."

"My mother said Jack never really came back from the war," I said. "That it was only his body that went west. I always suspected something happened to him in those days, when he was young."

"Many men bear scars from that conflict," Dalton said softly.

"He used to tell me the most wondrous stories." My breath caught briefly, and I wiped away a tear. "I'd like to pay my respects."

Dalton led me outside and across the grounds to a plain stone mausoleum, standing free amid the green-fringed paths. It was barely large enough for a single body, and above the door were etched the words INTER MUNDOS.

"Between worlds," I whispered, running a hand over the perfectly smooth door.

"You won't find a keyhole," Dalton said. "Thing only opens from the *inside*. He insisted. Open coffin; no embalming, no funeral."

I walked around the clean, almost featureless stone tomb. Still searching for clues.

Dalton smiled wryly. "You don't acquire the kind of wealth your uncle commanded by behaving like the rest of us, eh?"

That evening, I sat in a small annex of the front hall as Dalton recited my uncle's will. My attention kept straying to the artifacts: small statues, obscure maps, strange carvings from cultures I'd never seen before . . .

". . . hereby direct that my estate shall be held in trust for twenty-five years, the income to benefit my beloved nephew, Edgar Rice Burroughs, at the end of which term the principal will revert to him in full."

I snapped my head around in shock. "What?"

Dalton nodded. "In full," he repeated.

"I . . . of course I always adored him. But it's been so long. Why . . . ?"

"He never offered an explanation, and I never asked for one."

Dalton reached into his briefcase and pulled out a worn, leather-covered journal fastened shut by a large clasp. He pushed it across the desk to me.

"His private journal," Dalton said. "He was most explicit that you, and only you, were to read its contents. You might find some kind of explanation in there, I suppose."

I touched the book, ran my fingers across its soft leather cover.

"I'll leave you now." Dalton stood. "Again, my condolences."

Staring at the book, I was scarcely aware of Dalton's departure. With trembling hands, I reached for the clasp, pulled it open. And began to read, with tears and wonder in my eyes.

My dear Edgar. I remember how I used to take you on my knee and tell you wild tales, which you always did me the great courtesy of believing. Now you are grown; time and space have parted us. But I reach out across that distance to that same wide-eyed boy and ask him to believe me once more.

This wild tale begins in 1868, thirteen years ago, in the Arizona Territory between the Pinaleño Mountains and the backside of Hell . . .

CHAPTER 2

BY THE TIME John Carter hauled himself back to Fort Grant Outpost, he was barely a human being. His beard was long and insect-ridden, his buffalo skins stank of sweat and dust. His saddlebags hung practically in tatters; his mule was half dead. His eyes glinted with the fire of madness.

But none of that was the reason Dix, the general store keeper, rolled his eyes and turned away when Carter shambled inside.

Two thick-bodied roughnecks sat drinking at the counter. One of them turned to smirk at him. "Come to stock up on spider bait, Carter?"

Carter ignored him, strode up to Dix, and dropped two heavy saddlebags on the bar. Dix just shook his head.

"No more, Carter."

Carter smoothed his beard, peered at the shopkeeper. "There a problem, Mister Dix?"

"Yeah. You're a loon."

The roughnecks laughed and slapped the bar. But Dix's face was deadpan serious, even angry.

"I done took all your money, Carter. Your tab's a hundred dollars in arrears."

"I'll pay," Carter replied. "I'm close. This old Yavapai I met, he said he'd seen the cave up near—"

"Stop." Dix held up a hand. "Not one more word about your cave of gold."

"Now, now," one of the roughnecks said. "Show some respect, Dix. It's the *evil spider* cave of gold."

The roughnecks howled again and clinked their glasses.

"You're cut off, Carter." Dix's stare didn't waver. "Now get on home."

Carter didn't move.

Slowly the roughnecks rose to their feet. The first one pulled out a knife and stuck his face up very close to Carter's. "I believe he done told you to get out of here."

The second roughneck put a hand on his Colt.

"I'll leave when these bags are full," Carter said.

The first roughneck twitched. Carter grabbed a lid from a jar on the counter, blocking the knife thrust easily. The man grunted and dropped his knife, but Carter was already whirling around to grab the second man's Colt barrel. Carter jammed both gun and hand up into the man's own face, breaking his nose. Then in one swift motion he jabbed the jar lid up into the first man's jaw with a sickening crack.

Both men went down, unconscious.

Carter grabbed the roughneck's Colt and whipped around, sticking it right in Dix's face. He knew what the shopkeeper kept hidden under the counter.

"Drop the shotgun, Dix."

Dix swallowed. His gun clattered to the floor.

Keeping the Colt trained on Dix's head, Carter reached into his pocket with his other hand. He fished out a small object and tossed it to the stunned shopkeeper.

"Found that two days ago, up by Bonita. Ought to cover my tab and then some."

Dix's eyes widened. He stared at the object, a small Apache figurine about two inches tall. A nine-legged spider worked in shiny, glistening gold.

Dix raised his head to Carter, staring in shock. "Whyn't you just show me this first?"

"Didn't care for your attitude." Carter lowered his gun, slammed a grocery list down on the counter. "Beans. First item is beans."

"John Carter?"

Carter didn't turn around, but he recognized the

tone. Cavalrymen—more than one, by the sound of it. He swore under his breath. He'd been so preoccupied with the locals that he'd failed to watch his back.

"Your presence is requested up at the fort. I suggest you come peaceably."

Carter's hand tightened on his pistol. "Do you, now." He spun around—right into the butt of an army Remington.

He had just enough time to register the disgusted face of a sergeant, flanked by three privates. Then he sank into a sleep of spiders, pain, and regret.

"You're a difficult man to find."

Afterward, Carter couldn't remember which had come first: the sharp words or the splash of cold water in his face. He sputtered back to the living in a wooden chair, dead center of a spare, makeshift military office. Two guards gripped his shoulders in meaty hands. A gruff, weary, middle-aged colonel stood before him holding a dossier full of papers.

"Captain John Carter," the colonel continued. "First Virginia Cavalry, Army of Northern Virginia. Confederate States of America." He bent down to face Carter directly. "I'm Colonel Powell. Welcome to the Seventh Cavalry of the *United* States of—"

Carter lunged forward, head-butting Powell with all his might. The colonel's head snapped back, trailing blood. Carter sprang to his feet but lurched off balance, still groggy. The two guards moved in, grabbed him expertly, and threw him to the ground. As Powell dabbed blood from his nose, grimacing in disappointment, Carter fell beneath the guards' blows.

Twenty minutes later, Carter stood handcuffed to the bars of the fort's stockade cell. His face was bruised, his eye still bleeding. Powell stood outside, calmly reading from the dossier as if nothing had happened.

". . . excellent horseman, fine swordsman. Decorated six times, including the Southern Cross of Honor. At Five Forks, the company under your command nearly turned the tide."

Carter sniffed contemptuously, then winced at the pain. Everything hurt.

"In short," Powell continued, "a born fighter. And in the eyes of Uncle Sam, a necessary man for the defense of the Arizona territory—"

"No."

Powell looked up from the dossier, his eyes hard. "We're up to our chinstraps in Apache, son."

"Ain't my concern," Carter said.

"I believe it *is* your concern, Captain. Folks are being

attacked in their homes. Slain. They need protection."

"You all started it. You finish it."

"Gone native, have we?"

"The Apaches can go to hell, too." Carter rattled his cuffs, felt the old anger growing inside him. "Mankind's a savage, warlike species. I want no part of it."

"You're a cavalryman. That makes you valuable to our country and our cause."

"Colonel Powell. Sir." Carter pushed his bruised face through the bars as far as he could. "Whatever it is you *suppose* I owe you, our country, or any other beloved cause, I have already paid. In full."

He spat through the bars. Powell faced him down, impassive.

"But I tell you what I *will* do," Carter continued. "I'll get me out of this cell, claim my gold, trade it in for a fortune in filthy money, and then *buy* your righteous flat blue behind just so's I can kick it around the block all damn day long."

Suddenly, savagely, Powell gut-punched Carter through the bars. Carter fell back onto the floor of the cell, coughing.

Powell stared down contemptuously at his prisoner. "Captain," he said slowly, "I am finding it difficult to reconcile the man in my dossier with the one I'm looking at. I suggest you find the horse sense to accept my offer before I give in to my better judgment."

The door slammed and Powell was gone. Carter swooned, on his knees, thinking, *Don't pass out. And if you do, for God's sake don't dream of Sarah.*

But of course he did.

Next morning at dawn, Carter tricked a guard, snatched the colonel's horse, and was five miles up in the Arizona hills before they caught up with him.

He steered the horse up a steep hillside and took a quick glance back. Six mounted soldiers led by Powell himself, gaining fast. And the colonel didn't look happy. Carter swore, urged his horse forward faster. He'd stolen the guard's coat and hat, and now the hot sun was making him sweat. But the guard's gun might still come in handy.

As Carter approached the crest of the hill, the thunder of hooves grew stronger behind him. They had him, he knew. Unless there was something unexpected over this ridge . . .

There was. A dozen Apache warriors, dressed in full war regalia. And heavily armed, with modern rifles.

Carter swiveled his horse to a halt, held up both hands in surrender. The Apache moved toward him, suspicious. Then they heard the sounds of Carter's pursuers and snapped back to alert.

Slowly, carefully, Carter addressed the Apache in their own language. He explained that this was an exercise, a game the white men were playing among themselves—*not* an attack against the natives. The Apache leader, a man called Domingo, listened warily, but his men's guns didn't waver from Carter's head.

Domingo seemed to have a beef with the local white men. Carter could relate. There were lots of white men he didn't care for himself.

By the time Powell's cavalrymen charged over the ridge, Carter had *almost* talked Domingo into not killing them all.

Then a twitchy corporal called out. "Sir!"

The Apache moved to charge him.

"Shut your damn mouth, Corporal," Powell said. He trotted over toward Carter and Domingo, whose men kept their guns trained on him.

Powell's men fanned out slowly, guns also raised. Apache and cavalrymen watched each other's every move, fingers quivering on triggers.

"What's he saying, Carter?"

Carter grimaced, held up his hand for silence. But Domingo was already growing agitated, accusing Carter of leading the Apache into a trap. Carter kept his voice low, calm, but insistent, explaining to Domingo that this was purely a matter between Carter and Colonel Powell.

"Carter, what the hell are they—"

One shot rang out—Carter never was sure who started it—and that was all it took. The ridge exploded in gunfire.

Carter's horse bolted down the hill, almost throwing him off. He struggled with the reins, trying to get control. He watched the cavalrymen fall—one, two, all six in the end, their horses running wild back over the ridge. And just behind him—

"Carter!"

Powell was in pursuit, his eyes red with rage. Then a stray shot hit the colonel. He screamed and slumped forward on his horse, which panicked, racing up even with Carter's.

Carter reached out and grabbed the horse's reins, thinking, *I must be crazy.*

Grimacing, Carter struggled to maintain control of

both mounts. Domingo was shouting obscenities, but Carter and Powell had a pretty good lead. Still, the Apache would be after them soon enough.

Powell grimaced, clutching his bleeding shoulder. "I thought—you didn't care."

"Shut up."

Up ahead, the sparse desert terrain narrowed into a thin canyon winding upward between high hills. It was their only chance. Carter pulled hard on both sets of reins, aiming the horses toward the canyon.

He knew the Apache were already in pursuit. Silent as coyotes.

Carter yanked the horses to a halt at a large cave mouth and quickly dismounted. Then he eased the groggy Powell from his horse. Powell glared briefly when Carter took his guns, but said nothing. Carter dragged him inside the cave and sat him up against the wall.

The cave was dark, but there was only one entrance. Carter doubted he could bring down a dozen Apache singlehanded, but at least he'd be able to see them coming.

From outside, the faint clopping of horses.

Powell stirred, grimaced up at Carter. "Gimme a gun, Carter."

Carter nodded and handed the colonel a pistol. He raised his own rifle and cocked it back. The Apache rode into view in full force, framed in the opening of the cave mouth—and stopped dead, their mouths open in horror.

Their horses whinnied in fear.

Domingo locked frightened eyes with Carter for just a moment, shook his head. Then he gestured, and the Apaches turned and rode swiftly away.

Carter turned to Powell, who shrugged. Slowly, his rifle still raised, Carter crept toward the cave opening. He stepped outside, eyeing the last dust raised by the Apache as they disappeared over the ridge. Then he turned to look up at the mouth of the cave, and his heart seemed to skip a beat.

Carved over the entrance was a circle with nine lines radiating from it.

The nine-legged spider.

A few minutes later, deep inside the cave, Carter lit a match and drew in a sharp breath.

Artifacts filled the room: a rotting canoe, pieces of old arrows. But an eerie, complex lattice of lines stretched all along the walls, apparently carved long, long ago. And at the far wall stood a stone platform, a large, carven rock with the same nine-legged spider pattern on it.

Behind Carter, Powell grunted. "This place for sure ain't Apache."

Carter fanned the match around slowly—and something on the wall reflected its glow. Eyes wide, Carter followed a shiny vein upward along the wall to the ceiling, which glimmered bright against the match flame.

"Gold," he whispered.

"Carter!"

Carter whirled to see a strange robed figure advancing toward him. It wore a medallion with the nine-legged spider design. As Carter watched, a deadly black dagger seemed to appear in its hand from nothing at all.

Carter fired. The figure clutched its chest and fell backward.

Powell limped into the room, staring at the figure. "He wasn't there. And then he *was*—"

The figure struggled to rise, but Carter could see it was dying. It lifted its medallion, which glowed bright blue now, and began to chant. *"Och Ohem, Och Tay, Wyees—"* A gasp of pain. *"Och Ohem, Och Tay, Wyees B—"*

As the medallion slipped from the creature's limp fingers, Carter snatched it up.

"Wyees—Barsoom," the figure finished.

Carter stared at the glowing artifact. "Barsoom?"

He had just enough time to see Powell reach toward him, crying out in alarm.

And then John Carter was gone.

Chapter 3

THE LEGS of the spider seemed to stretch out in all directions, fracturing space and time in an infinite web of light. Carter was falling, falling forever, unable even to reach out and grab one of the light strands that might lead back home. Then the strands seemed to compress, weaving together into a single thick, shining cord of light. It tugged at him, pulling him to it with an irresistible gravitational force. Carter fell into it, blind and helpless . . .

Then he lifted his head and spat crimson sand.

He looked around, blinking in disbelief. He definitely wasn't in the cave anymore. Pale red sands stretched away in all directions as far as Carter could see. Yellow moss covered scarlet rocks; strange, bulbous rock formations dotted the desert landscape. Carter shook his head, sprang to his feet.

And pinwheeled through the air. Twenty feet, then thirty, finally crashing back down on a bed of the strange yellow moss.

Stunned, he crawled slowly to his feet. Took another

tentative step—and soared upward, corkscrewing like a high diver.

Over the next half hour, Carter tried skipping, creeping, frog hopping, treading water in air, and bunny hopping. Every move ended in a painful return to the desert floor. In desperation, he squatted down and tried to crab walk himself along the sand safely. The process was slow and humiliating, but it worked. Frustrated, he accelerated his pace and shot back up into the air, narrowly missing a rock formation as he crashed back down again.

Enraged, Carter picked up a stone and hurled it with all his might. It took off like a missile, flying away as far as he could see. Carter's eyes went wide. He crouched down and threw *himself* into the air, just like the stone. Twisted in mid-air and managed to land safely, on his feet.

Four or five jumps later, he was almost having fun.

He executed a complex arc through the air, barely avoiding a ring of jagged rocks. Then he noticed, just ahead, a strange octagonal structure like a corral with featureless, opaque sides and a faceted glass top. Carter crept up to it, hoisted himself up to peer in through the top.

And gasped.

Large eggs filled the floor of the enclosure, quivering like Mexican jumping beans. As Carter watched, spellbound with horror, a wiry green arm punched its way out of a cracked egg. Another crack, and another arm. Then a pair of green legs.

One of the eggs shattered open, and a thin, monstrous baby blinked and glared up at Carter. Its skin was green all over. Two small, stubby tusks protruded from its smooth, newborn cheeks.

Carter couldn't look away. *It's an incubator*, he realized.

Another egg hatched, and then a third. Soon the incubator was filled with a writhing stew of angry green babies. One of them started to wail and the others joined in, forming a horrible blare of noise. Carter winced.

Then came an answering howl from behind Carter, followed by a roar of massive hooves. A herd of gigantic beasts thundered into view, kicking up a red dust cloud. Enormous creatures, each one the size of a small stable house, with gray tusks, four legs on each side, and odd, flat tails. Carter had never seen anything like them.

But when he spotted the beasts' riders, Carter felt a new kind of fear.

They were vaguely human-shaped but green in color, with elongated, spiderlike bodies. They stood ten feet tall at least, with four arms instead of the normal two. They wore ceremonial warrior garb and carried an impressive array of spears, guns, and unfamiliar weapons. Like their mounts—and like the babies Carter had just seen hatched—each rider sported two sharp, curved tusks curling up from the lower half of his face.

What had Powell said back in the cave?

This place for sure ain't Apache.

The lead rider yelled something, aimed a sharp lance at Carter, and charged. Not even thinking, Carter leaped straight upward and sailed far over the rider's head. The beast slammed into a boulder, tossing its rider free. The green man crashed down hard, then lay sprawled in the dirt.

Carter landed easily, just as the first shot rang out.

The riders charged, firing their long rifles. Carter dove and rolled behind a pile of boulders. Bullets chewed into the stones, eating away at his cover. Old war instincts took over, and he started a zigzag, hopscotching series of short leaps from rock to rock, edging toward higher ground.

He glanced back just in time to see the leader—now recovered from his fall—slap away the rifle barrel of a warrior with a broken tusk.

"Katom! Tet mu yat Jeddak hok ta!"

As Carter watched warily from behind a boulder, the lead warrior ordered his men back with a severe, imperious hand motion. The broken-tusked warrior glared briefly, then reluctantly joined the others in forming a perimeter around Carter's position.

Then the leader moved in toward Carter. *"Kaor!"* he called. *"Jah mu tet!"*

Carter tensed as the green warrior approached him—slowly, deliberately, his eyes never leaving Carter's. The leader laid down his lance, unstrapped his sidearm, and unsheathed each blade in turn, stacking the weapons in a neat pile on the ground. When he spoke again, his tone was calm, almost soothing.

"Jah mu tet. Satav . . . satav."

Carter stepped out and raised his hand, palms forward. "All right, you got me. I surrender."

"Jeddak." The creature pointed toward itself. *"Tars Tarkas."*

"Jeddak?" Carter repeated.

"Tars. Tars Tarkas."

The creature grinned, an awful, terrifying grin. Carter tried not to wince. "Captain John Carter. Virginia."

"Vir-gin-ya," the creature said slowly, then pointed sharply to Carter. "Virginia!"

"No, no. John Carter. I'm *from* Virginia."

Then Carter grinned, and it was the creature's turn to wince. While he was distracted, Carter vaulted clear over him, landing neatly next to the pile of discarded alien weapons. The four-armed being stared at Carter in a stunned silence. Clearly, he had never seen anyone with Carter's abilities before.

"*Vir-gin-ya!*" The leader whirled and took off at a run toward Carter, his eight arms pinwheeling almost comically. "*Tet! Tet saal! Tet saal!*"

Carter glanced at the ring of warriors and spotted the broken-tusked one drawing a bead on him. Frantically, Carter snatched up the leader's enormous pistol from the pile. He fumbled with it, struggling with its firing mechanism. Then the leader slammed into him, knocking him aside—just as a bullet sliced into Carter's left buttock before exploding in the sand. Carter screamed in pain.

Somehow he knew his ordeal was just beginning.

The next part passed almost as if in a dream. The creatures gathered up the newborns from the incubator, trussed and swaddled them, and hung them from the flanks of two of the largest pack creatures. At the leader's insistence, they dressed Carter's wound with one of the diapers. Vaguely Carter was aware that he should be humiliated. But all he could think about was the pain in his hindquarters.

After the babies had been gathered, a small number of eggs remained unhatched: a dozen, perhaps two. The broken-tusked warrior cocked his rifle, and the leader—Tars Tarkas—looked over at him sharply. Then Tars nodded and joined the broken-tusked one over at the incubator.

Tars issued a short, regretful-sounding order. Then, together, the two warriors opened fire into the incubator, shattering and obliterating the unhatched eggs.

Much later, when he had gotten to know these creatures, Carter would learn that they were called Tharks and their beasts, thoats. And then he would know the meaning of Tars Tarkas's hesitant command: *leave nothing for the white apes.*

CHAPTER 4

BARSOOM. A world on the brink . . .

She shook her head, started over. Rehearsing the words in her mind.

Zodanga's newfound power threatens to destroy our city of Helium. And if Helium falls, so falls Barsoom . . .

No. Too strong!

Dejah Thoris, Princess of Helium, stood alone in the grandly appointed throne room, frowning at a long table. Her life's work lay upon that table, draped in a silk cover, concealed from view. She tugged at the cloth nervously.

Your Highness—no, My Lord. My . . . Jeddak. My Jeddak, after years of tireless research, I present to you . . . the answer.

Aloud, she added: "I hope."

Dejah was tall, regal, and very beautiful. Half the men of Helium had asked for her hand in marriage at one time or another. One particularly florid suitor had described her haunted eyes as the blue of vanished oceans. Her skin, he'd said, was tinged with the rich crimson of Barsoom itself.

But Dejah Thoris had no time for romance. She understood the precipice her city—her very world—stood at the brink of. Her every waking moment was devoted to saving her people.

A clamor of voices, and Dejah snapped to attention. Her father burst in: Tardos Mors, Jeddak of Helium. He looked agitated, tired. Kantos Kan, the Jeddak's battle-stained admiral, followed, and then the other members of the High Council.

Tardos Mors glanced briefly at the covered object on the table, then frowned. Avoided Dejah's gaze.

"My Jeddak." She bowed. "After years of tireless research, I present to you—"

"I'm sorry, Princess." He swept right past her. "Your presentation will have to wait."

"Father? What's happened?"

Kantos shot her a look: *not now.*

Tardos Mors ascended to his throne and sank heavily into it. The council members swarmed around him, all talking at once in low voices. Something had happened with Zodanga . . . Dejah caught the words "last chance" more than once.

Finally Tardos spoke up. "I know the terms set by Sab Than! What I want to know is, can we afford to reject them?"

"The eastern border is a wasteland," Kantos said grimly. "Sab Than has burned through our defenses with his new weapon. The borderfolk have been massacred."

Dejah's eyes grew wide. Urgently, she swept the cover off the table, revealing a complex, sophisticated machine.

Her father and the Council paid her no heed. "Our best troops and fleetest ships have proven useless," Kantos Kan continued. "And now comes word that our last remaining squadron has been lost."

Tardos lowered his head. "*Helium* is lost. My people, my world . . . I have failed them all."

"No, my Jeddak. You haven't."

All eyes turned, then, to Dejah. She reached for the device, powered it up with a hum.

Kantos frowned. "My lady, you have not seen the Zodangan weapon. It radiates the most intense, baleful—"

"Blue light?"

As she spoke the words, Dejah flicked the final switch . . . and a beam of pure blue light stabbed down to the floor, glinting harmlessly off the ornate tiles.

Tardos rose from the throne. The council members moved with him, toward Dejah and her machine. They stared at the blue beam, keeping a cautious distance from it.

Dejah cleared her throat. "When I read our reports on Sab's weapon, I knew: somehow that idiotic brute had discovered it first."

"Discovered what?"

"The Ninth Ray. Unlimited power."

The blue beam began to flicker, to play against the tiles, illuminating dust motes in the air. Hope filled Tardos's eyes. Even Kantos began to nod.

"Sab uses it only for slaughter," Dejah continued. "But think what *we* might accomplish with such power. Transforming the deserts . . . restoring the seas . . ."

The council members crowded closer, examining the machine, peering at the beam from different angles. Tardos turned to the admiral. "Is that what you saw, Kantos?"

"It looks very close."

"Give it time," Dejah said. "It *will* work."

Then something strange happened. From the corner of her eye, Dejah thought she saw a quick movement in the group of council members—almost like a flash of blue lace, arcing out to strike the machine. She turned in alarm—just as a surge ran through the device, shorting it out. Sparks flew. The blue beam swung wildly for a moment, and everyone shrank back in fear. Then the beam died, and the machine sat silent, smoking slightly.

The council members all turned their attention to Dejah, their expressions a mixture of disappointment and confusion. She closed her eyes in despair.

"Everyone leave us," Tardos Mors said. "Now."

Kantos left last, throwing Dejah a pitying look. The giant doors slammed shut.

Dejah stood across the smoking device from her father. She tried not to cringe as he touched a severed wire, fidgeted with it briefly.

"It was *working*, Father." She struggled to keep the quaver from her voice. "And then something happened . . . some sort of sabotage . . . ?"

She trailed off. Even to her own ears, it sounded like a weak excuse.

"Dejah," Tardos said slowly. "Ever since you were a little girl, you—you've always met the expectations placed on you. Exceeded them, in fact . . ."

She looked up at him sharply. Something else was bothering him. She reached out, took his quivering hand, and forced him to look her in the eye.

"Sab's terms," he whispered.

"What are they?"

He clapped his other hand over hers.

"He will spare Helium if you accept his hand in marriage."

"Sab Than?" She yanked her hand away. "He's a monster!"

"Dejah—"

"Father, you have to refuse him."

"He's already on his way here."

"But—all my work—" She gestured frantically at the ruined machine. "I just need more time! You can't just—how can you bow down to Zodanga?"

"A wedding will save this city."

"Perhaps. But it could destroy Barsoom."

He turned away, glaring.

Dejah kept after him. "With no one to stop Zodanga, it will be the beginning of the end. You are the Jeddak of Helium. You must find another way—"

"There is no other way!"

She turned away, stung. Immediately Tardos softened, placed a hand on her shoulder.

"My child . . . you know if there were another choice, I would risk anything to seize it. *This* is the chance we've been given. Perhaps . . . perhaps it is the Will of the Goddess."

"No. It's your will."

He flinched at her tone.

"When I was little," she continued, "we would look up at the stars, and you'd tell me about the heroes whose glory was written in the sky. You'd say there was a star up there just for me. Is this what you imagined would be written on it?"

Kantos Kan reentered the room, cleared his throat. "Sab Than's corsair approaches the city, my Jeddak. They've signaled for permission to land."

For a long moment, Tardos and Dejah stood together. Eyes locked, neither one willing to budge.

"Grant permission," Tardos said. "And let us all prepare for a wedding."

Then he strode out of the room, leaving Dejah Thoris—Princess of Helium, possible future queen of all Barsoom—with the smoking wreckage of her life's work.

LATE THAT NIGHT, John Carter sat chained to a wall alongside rows of diapered Thark babies. The Thark nursery resembled a dungeon: filthy walls, rusted chains, a hard clay floor.

Female Tharks moved gently along the row of green-skinned hatchlings, tipping kettles of a strong, foul brew into the tiny, hungry mouths. They murmured words, the harsh, unknown language of the Tharks.

The female called Sola approached Carter, hesitantly at first. Then she grabbed hold of his head. When he struggled, she vaulted on top of him, pinning his arms with two of her four hands. Sola was wiry but tall, and she outweighed Carter by a good measure. With her third hand, she forced open his mouth, and with the fourth she poured the brew. He gagged, swallowed, and coughed.

Sola was speaking, too . . . and as Carter sputtered, he realized he was beginning to understand her words. *"Drink . . . good . . ."*

He blinked, shook his head. "What's in that stuff?"

Her strange eyes bored into his. When she spoke again, he heard every word clearly.

"The voice of Barsoom."

After he had consumed the potion, Carter was able to remember and translate the words the Tharks had spoken earlier that day. And then their customs made sense . . . as much sense, at least, as anything he'd seen in this strange place.

They'd ridden into the city as a troop. Carter, tied to a pack thoat along with the newborns, had watched as a settlement of ruined buildings loomed into view. The troop passed along the ramparts of a seawall and in through a crumbling gate.

A horde of Tharks seemed to materialize, creeping out of every portal, every building's doorway. Hundreds of them swarmed around the returning troop, welcoming their warriors home. Carter noticed that every Thark carried weapons, even the children.

As the warriors came to an open square, the female Tharks—dozens of them—stepped forward. One giant scowling female, whom Carter would come to know as Sarkoja, ordered them into two lines facing each other, roughly five feet apart.

Then Tars Tarkas, leader of the Thark warriors, slashed out, cutting the baskets free from the pack thoat. The babies tumbled to the ground along with Carter, who grunted and lay still for a moment, dazed and stiff. As he watched, the babies reeled, staggered to their feet, and scampered into the gauntlet between the two lines of females.

The females moved in, reaching for the babies. Some of the hatchlings squirmed and dodged away, scuttling and squirming with their four arms, while others allowed themselves to be scooped up. Several times, two females reached for the same baby and began to fight, grappling until one either fell or abandoned the struggle, turning her attention to a different child.

Not for the first time, Carter wondered, *where on Earth am I?*

One female—Sola—held back and failed to catch a child. The other women shouted at her, some of them holding out their newly adopted charges to taunt her. Sarkoja strode over to Sola, shoved her backward, and slapped her.

Tars Tarkas stepped forward. "Sarkoja," he called, in words that Carter would soon come to understand. "Enough!"

Sarkoja glared at Tars. The other women stood in their lines watching the drama. One of them scooped up the last stray child.

Then Sarkoja broke from the line and crossed to Carter, who still lay sprawled on the ground. She scooped him up and hurled him into the gauntlet. Helpless, he landed on the dirt in front of Sola, who had just pulled herself back to her feet.

"Sola can take the little white worm," Sarkoja said.

Sola looked down at Carter, her expression unreadable. Then she bent down, picked him up, and released him from his bindings. Her touch was softer than he'd expected. Her arms bore an intricate pattern of scars, a chaos of symbols burned and calloused over. The other Tharks, he'd noticed, all bore scarification, but Sola's was by far the most extensive.

"What happened to you?" he asked.

"Be still."

Sarkoja snorted and led the other women away. Sola followed sheepishly, carrying Carter like a baby, past the assembled Tharks. Something metallic and shiny hung from one young warrior's belt—

The medallion. The ancient-looking artifact that had brought Carter to this strange land. He'd lost his grip on it, he realized, when he'd first tumbled down onto these red sands. This Thark warrior must have found it out near the incubator and snatched it up just before harvesting the babies.

Carter leaped free of Sola's grasp and slammed into the surprised warrior, knocking him into several of the others. As they howled in anger, Carter reached out and grabbed the medallion, snapping it free.

Then, incredibly fast, three green arms grasped hold of him, pinning him to the ground. A fourth arm flashed a blade up under Carter's neck, and the grim face of the grizzled, broken-tusked warrior glared down at him.

The medallion slipped from Carter's fingers.

"Now we kill it," the warrior said. A drop of spittle flecked his chipped tusk.

"Step away, Tal Hajus."

Carter recognized Tars Tarkas's voice by now, if not his words.

Tal Hajus hauled Carter roughly to his feet. "You prize *this* more highly than my judgment?"

The towering figure of Tars Tarkas appeared above Carter, right in Tal's face. As Carter watched, their tusks locked together in a clear gesture of challenge, with Carter directly between them.

"Step away," Tars said slowly.

Tal turned cold with anger. He pressed the blade against Carter's neck. "I claim the right of challenge."

"And who supports your challenge?"

Still holding the blade to Carter's throat, Tal disengaged his tusks from Tars's and turned to address the assembled Tharks. "Who will pledge their metal to mine?"

Silence.

Tars Tarkas stepped forward and grabbed Carter like a rag doll. "You will not be Jeddak this day, Tal. Perhaps tomorrow."

Tal Hajus glared back at Tars for a long moment.

"Tomorrow, then."

Tal whirled and strode off into the crowd. Carter let out a sigh of relief—then coughed as Tars Tarkas dragged him toward the crowd.

"See the prize your Jeddak has found!"

The Tharks gathered around, staring with undisguised curiosity. "Is it a baby white ape?" one asked.

"No," Tars replied proudly. "It is a rare and valuable animal. It is called a Virginia."

"Vir-gin-ya," the Tharks repeated, haltingly.

"Watch. Step back, everyone." Tars released Carter, who staggered free. "Show them, Virginia. Jump."

Carter still didn't understand Tars's words, but the

meaning of the Thark's gesture was clear. And inside Carter, something snapped. He'd been tossed around, swaddled like an infant, treated like a pet and a slave. He was damned if he'd perform tricks on command.

Tars mimed a jumping motion with three of his hands. "Jump," he repeated.

Sola stepped forward, gestured encouragingly.

"No," Carter said.

Tars whacked Carter on the back of the knees. Carter sprawled forward, his face landing just inches from the fallen medallion. The Tharks burst into a storm of laughter, baring their monstrous teeth.

"Sola," Tars said, "chain him. Initiate him with the other hatchlings."

Grimacing, Sola clamped a metal collar onto Carter's neck. As the Thark females dragged him to his feet, he heard Tars Tarkas hiss, "By Issus, you will jump tomorrow, Virginia."

That night Carter was shaved, swabbed, cleaned, and powdered along with the other newborns. No Thark woman seemed to know which of the children was her biological spawn. They just adopted whichever ones they could grab, and then all the hatchlings were put through the same rough process of initiation into Thark society. To Carter, it seemed a cold, inhuman system.

But then, he reminded himself, these people were not human.

After Sola fed him the translation potion, Carter collapsed in exhaustion. He woke in a sweat and looked around at the crowded floor carpeted with snoring babies. Slowly he rose and began to creep toward the entrance. A long chain still tethered him to the wall, rattling as if to remind him of his helplessness.

A fearsome creature barred Carter's way, staring at him with beady eyes. Half lizard, half bulldog, an enormous mouth crammed with rows of sharp teeth. As Carter approached, it rose up on ten stumpy legs.

"Easy, boy," Carter said softly. "Nice, ugly . . . dog?"

The creature settled back down again. Past it, the nursery opened onto a clear spiral ramp leading upward. An easy jump—except for the chain. Carter tugged on his shackle, felt a link begin to give way. The creature opened one eye, then closed it again.

The next tug broke Carter's chain. He sprang up and out, vaulting over the surprised animal. He lit easily on top of the spiral ramp, turned to exit—but the animal stood right in front of him. Snuffling.

"How in the world?" Carter asked.

The creature grunted, tried to nudge Carter back

down into the nursery. He leaped over it again—and this time he saw it follow in a blur of dust. Carter landed farther up the ramp, a few steps closer to freedom.

The animal didn't seem to want to hurt Carter. In fact, he had the odd feeling it was concerned for his safety. But it sure was slowing him down.

A final jump carried Carter out into the heart of the Thark settlement. Tents lay scattered all around the ruins, filled with sleeping Tharks. Carter landed in a crouch, then stopped to gather his thoughts.

He still had no idea where he was. He'd heard tales of Africa and South America, of remote villages untouched by modern civilization. But none of those accounts had mentioned ten-foot-tall, green-skinned warriors with tusks.

Carter's first instinct was to run for it, to leap for the edge of the settlement and just keep going. But there was nothing around for miles. How long could he survive, alone, in an unfamiliar desert?

The animal from the nursery crept up behind him and growled softly.

"Shoo," Carter said. "Go away. Git!"

No, he realized, the Tharks were his best option. Now that Carter understood their language, he was in a better position to negotiate with Tars Tarkas. But a weapon would improve his chances even further.

Quietly, followed closely by the gruff animal, Carter crossed the central square to a huge, partly destroyed building. Up on a high terrace, firelight flickered, and the sound of drums and voices wafted down. An armed sentry crossed the terrace.

Carter leaped straight up to the terrace and grabbed the surprised sentry around the neck. As the Thark's four arms flailed about, Carter jabbed him hard on the head and took his long, tapered sword. The sentry went down.

Beyond the terrace, a large pavilion tent stood within the ruined walls of an ancient throne room. Carter crossed silently to the edge of the tent, stopping in the shadows. Through the open side, he could see Tars Tarkas surrounded by his clansmen, eating. A few Tharks pounded on ceremonial drums.

Carter took a deep breath and raised his sword.

Then the animal burst past him, roaring. It slammed clumsily into a group of Tharks, knocking their dishes to the stone floor. Turning to face Carter, it roared again.

The Tharks were upon the creature in an instant, raining down blows on its thick hide.

Carter's first instinct was to protect the animal.

He dove forward, sword upraised, calling out, "That's enough!" He pulled a Thark off the creature and punched him hard, knocking the warrior back a dozen feet into a tent pole. The pole cracked, knocking the tent wall down, and the Thark slammed hard against a stone wall. Dead.

The other Tharks stopped in shock, staring at Carter. He held up his own fist, amazed at his strength.

Tars Tarkas stood now, gazing down at the dead Thark. Slowly he straightened and turned cold eyes on Carter. "You killed him with one blow."

"I—I didn't mean to—"

Carter realized he now understood Tars's words. But even as the thought flitted through his mind, Tars gestured to the others, and they all set upon Carter with their hands, furious and eager to avenge their fallen comrade.

Carter was still too stunned to fight back. He went limp, wincing as green fists pummeled him into unconsciousness. His last thought was to wonder if he would die here . . . without ever knowing where *here* really was.

Chapter 6

SLOWLY, Sarkoja raised the white-hot iron out of the flame. She smiled the horrific grin of the Tharks. Then she brought the iron down firmly onto Sola's heavily scarred arm.

Sola's flesh sizzled. She struggled against the bonds that held her fast. But she didn't cry out.

"For the love of God!" Carter screamed.

He stood chained in the plaza square, watching helplessly as the Tharks performed their barbaric scarification ritual. Tars Tarkas and the others had blamed Sola for Carter's escape. This was her punishment. Her arms were lashed to an X-shaped frame, and Sarkoja crouched over her, relishing every second of Sola's pain. Under the hot sun, the assembled Tharks watched, hungry for blood or perhaps just for a diversion.

As the brand burned into Sola's flesh again, Carter leaned forward. "It was *my* fault—"

Tal Hajus strode forward and slapped Carter hard in the face. "Silence!"

"Do that again and I'll—"

Tal slapped him again.

"Enough!"

All eyes followed Tars Tarkas as he pulled Sarkoja away from her captive. Sarkoja snarled and waved the iron in the air, but Tars ignored her. He raised his knife and cut Sola loose.

Sola's arms were covered with welts. "There is no room for another mark, Sola," Tars said. "Your next offense will be your last."

Something in the Thark's tone made Carter look away. Then he felt a tugging and turned to see Tars holding his chain like a leash.

"Jump, Virginia."

Carter glared at Tars briefly. He wanted nothing more to do with these savages . . . whoever they were, wherever they came from.

"You will jump, Virginia. *Now.*"

From behind Tars Tarkas, Sola fixed pleading eyes on Carter.

"Fliers!"

Everyone looked up. High on a battered rooftop was a Thark scout pointing wildly at the sky.

"You are the stones," Tars Tarkas said. "The sand!"

The Tharks scattered silently, slipping like ghosts into the doorways and arcades, the holes and windows and hiding places they'd carved out in the ruins. A few burrowed into drifts of sand, leaving only the nostrils on top of their heads exposed.

Tars yanked sharply on Carter's chain, pulling him toward a collapsed outpost tower. Carter glanced skyward again and heard the first faint rumbling from above. Hurriedly, he turned to follow the Thark leader.

Tharks crowded the collapsed battlements, staring at the sky. A bookmaker moved among them collecting armbands, torques, and other valuables into a bowl. "Helium," a Thark said. Another sneered at him. "Zodanga!" A third dropped a necklace into the bowl. "Helium."

Carter stretched his limbs, struggling to peer up into the sky. Tars had loosened his chains, but his muscles still ached. Up above, three vicious looking, red-colored airships pursued a single, ornate one flying a blue flag.

"Zodanga are the red flag," Tars said. "Helium, the blue."

Carter pointed at the lead Zodangan ship. A deadly looking black weapon gripped its side, tendrils reaching into the hull. The weapon looked out of place, like a living creature stitched to a machine. "What is that?"

Tars peered through a spyglass for a moment, then shrugged.

"Flying ships," Carter whispered.

The lead Zodangan ship pulled almost directly overhead. Its eerie blue weapon began to glow bright, then fired a bolt of blue energy directly at the Helium vessel. When it struck, the Helium ship glowed, listed, and sparked. Carter thought he saw a man on the side stiffen, cry out, and vanish in the blue light.

The Helium ship stopped dead in the air, hovering just above the ruins. The Tharks cheered.

Carter turned to Tars. "Your people root for Zodanga?"

"Zodanga is winning the war. But it makes no difference to us. I say let red men kill red men until only Tharks remain."

Above, the blue beam flashed out again. "That don't look like a fair fight," Carter said.

Tars stared grimly through the spyglass. "Zodanga never fights fair."

Sab Than watched with satisfaction as his crew marched the last of the Helium prisoners onto the deck of his airship. A prisoner stumbled as he stepped off the gangplank, almost falling into the open air between the two ships.

The Heliumites fell passively into a line, facing their captors. Their faces were hidden by protective helmets, but Sab Than could almost smell their fear. They'd just seen dozens of their fellow crewmen disintegrate, wiped from existence by the blue ray. And now they were prisoners of Zodanga.

Sab Than smiled. Encasing his hand, the Thern pistol pulsed like a living thing.

He strode down the line, flipping open the first prisoner's helmet. Sab scanned the young face and frowned. He moved to the second prisoner, then the third.

He stopped at the fourth, an older man with slate-dark eyes set against reddish skin. "Where is she?"

The man said nothing.

Sab Than raised his hand and fired the Thern weapon. The prisoner screamed, flashed blue, and vanished.

The next prisoner's eyes were wide with fear when Sab pulled up his helmet. Sab raised the weapon and held its glowing tip right before the man's face. "Where is sh—"

"Sire!"

Sab Than whirled to see a crewman pointing toward the captive Helium ship. The gangway between the ships lurched, jerking violently up and to the side. Zodangan soldiers, caught on the gangway, flailed wildly, struggling to maintain their balance.

The Helium corsair was pulling away, spreading its vanes to gather power. Trying to break free.

"Who's on that ship?" Sab Than demanded.

"Only our own men," the boarding party leader replied. "We left no Heliumites alive, sire. I swear!"

"To the bridge. Move!" Sab turned, pointed, saw one of the Heliumites give a signal—and then the prisoners were upon them. They swarmed over their captors, and a brawl began.

"Finish them!" Sab Than screamed, firing his hand weapon. Another Heliumite dissolved in blue fire.

The gangplank snapped. Zodangans screamed and toppled off into the open air.

Sab Than raced for the bridge, dodging both his own soldiers and the rebel Heliumites. This was not the end, he vowed. Before this day was out, he would possess the Helium princess's hand in marriage—and Barsoom would be united under his iron rule.

Sab stopped just before the bridge entrance and glanced over the side of the deck. His sister ship was arcing in toward the runaway Helium corsair, moving to intercept it. But the corsair was moving too fast . . .

Zodangan soldiers rained down among the Tharks, their necks snapping and heads crunching as they struck the stone ruins. The Tharks pointed with each impact, groaning in glee and mock sympathy.

"Those ships are gonna collide," Carter said.

As he and Tars watched, the Helium corsair picked up speed and struck the second Zodangan ship with a sickening crunch. The corsair listed sharply to one side, its solar vanes cracked and damaged. More Zodangans spilled off the deck, dropping to their deaths among the uncaring Tharks.

But Carter's eye was caught by another motion on the corsair's deck. He snatched the spyglass away from Tars, ignoring the Thark's protest. Through it he saw an armored, visored figure, dressed very differently from the red-garbed Zodangans, tumble across the deck to pitch over the side. The figure sailed through the air for a moment, then managed to catch hold of the ship's gunwale projecting off the side. The figure's helmet flipped off, and long brown hair spilled out.

Carter's first thought was: *she's beautiful.*

His second: *she's human.*

The woman was tall and lush, with full lips, strong arms, and a rich red hue to her skin. She hung desperately from the airship, her deep blue eyes searching wildly. For an instant they seemed to lock on Carter's, through the spyglass.

Faintly, he heard her cry out for help.

Carter tossed the spyglass to Tars and took off with a leap, soaring high up into the air. His chain unspooled behind him. Tars reached for it, but the Thark was too late.

Carter arced down toward a rooftop, almost missing it; the chain's weight was throwing him off. As he landed, he heard the woman's cry, clearer this time. He glanced up at her thrashing figure, then around at the various buildings. Only a few roofs stood higher than his current position. Gathering up his chain, he jumped again, gaining a few more feet. If the ship kept drifting . . . and if he could just get a little bit closer to it . . .

For the first time since the Apache cave, Carter felt a sense of purpose—maybe, he realized with a shock, for the first time since the war.

I won't fail you, he thought. And leaped again, ever closer to the strange red woman with the flowing hair.

Down on the ground, the Thark bookmaker continued his rounds. He stepped over a fallen Zodangan soldier, cocked his head at Tars Tarkas. "Zodanga or Helium?"

Grimacing, Tars dropped an amulet into the bookmaker's bowl.

"I bet Virginia," he said.

CHAPTER 7

THE THARK settlement had once been a great port city. Now its stonework stood weathered and chipped, towers and temples torn down by sand, time, and scavenging hordes.

Carter sprang from rooftop to rooftop, cupola to crumbling parapet, zigzagging his way up toward the listing Helium airship. He paused, darted a glance ahead. Only one thin-ledged cupola stood higher now, and it was at least fifty feet away. He hesitated.

Then the Helium airship lurched over, tipping onto its side in mid-air. The woman lost her grip, cried out, and began to fall.

Grimacing, Carter crouched and sprang as high as he could.

He rose. She fell. Carter stretched in mid-air until he caught her flailing body. She grabbed tight to him and he twisted again, managing to land on the cupola. His chain unspooled down off the platform, almost toppling him from the ledge. He staggered for a second, then recovered, still clutching her in his arms.

Time seemed to stop as they stared into each other's eyes. For an instant, he felt that sense of purpose that had been missing for so long.

Then a gangplank slammed down onto the cupola's ledge. Carter looked up and saw one of the Zodangan airships hovering just above. Red-garbed soldiers poured down the gangplank, swords and guns drawn.

Carter set Dejah down on her feet. "Beg your pardon, ma'am." As she watched in surprise, he grabbed the sword out of her hilt. "If you'll kindly stay behind me . . . this might get dangerous."

The soldiers swarmed off the gangplank. Carter grabbed the chain still leashed to his body and cracked it like a whip, slamming into the first two soldiers.

With his other hand, Carter swung the woman's sword in a wide arc, marveling at how light and flexible it was. One soldier screamed and grabbed his slashed chest. The other was less fortunate—the blade stabbed straight into his heart.

Carter had done well so far. But as he caught his breath, the last remaining Zodangan swung his gun like a club, knocking the blade clean out of Carter's hand. Stunned, Carter watched it fly . . . straight toward the woman. She grabbed it expertly by the hilt, tumbled acrobatically down in front of Carter, and impaled the Zodangan with a single quick, neat motion.

Carter stared down at the dead man, then up at the fierce woman. "Maybe I ought to stay behind *you*," he said.

She smiled; it was a warm smile, very unlike the monstrous grins of the Tharks. "Let me know when it gets dangerous," she said.

She reached down and wiped her blade clean on Carter's baby garment. Only then did he realize he was still wearing the loincloth Sola had dressed him in the night before. He felt briefly embarrassed.

Then a great shadow fell on them both, and Carter looked up to see the other two Zodangan warships converging on their position. One of them, the highest, bore the strange black weapon he'd seen before. The Helium ship still hung next to it, smoking and listing on its side.

Aboard the nearest Zodangan ship, a fresh contingent of soldiers appeared at the top of the gangplank. Their leader pointed, and they started down toward Carter and the woman at a run.

"I've had about enough of these boys," Carter said. He pointed to a spiral ramp leading down the far side of the cupola to the settlement below. "Ma'am, may I suggest you run?"

Without waiting for her reply, Carter charged the gangplank and vaulted over the astonished soldiers, landing just above them. Another leap took him onto the deck of their ship, where more surprised Zodangans whirled to face him, drawing their swords. But Carter was already airborne again, springing to the roof of the ship's bridge. He gazed out toward the second airship and hissed in a deep breath.

Then he jumped through empty air toward the second ship. He banked off its deck, then leaped up to that ship's roof in turn. Without letting himself think, Carter sprang up again toward the biggest ship, aiming straight for its weapons deck.

The startled gun crew saw him coming, pointed, and struggled to swivel their weapons in his direction. Too late. Carter arced down like a missile, landing with a flurry of punches and kicks. He knocked the gunmen off the deck, not even turning to watch as they fell. Then he grabbed a mounted gun, pivoted it, and aimed it downward.

The mechanism was unfamiliar, but simple enough. Carter peered through the gun's sight, centered it on the airship directly below, and fired. Once, twice, three times.

The second Zodangan airship lurched, cracked in half, and burst into flames. It began to plummet, towing the still-tangled Helium ship in its wake.

For a sick moment, Carter thought the two ships might strike the Thark settlement. The Tharks' ways were barbaric, and they'd treated him like a child. But he didn't want them slaughtered.

He sighed in relief as the ships swung wide, striking the sand just beyond the settlement where, in centuries gone by, the sea had once been. The ground shook with the tremendous crash.

Carter thought he heard something else from below, too: the cheering of the Tharks.

Then he turned to see a fierce warrior facing him. Cruel human eyes, a golden breastplate fringed with fur, and the red cape of Zodanga. Carter reached for his weapon, realized he had none.

The warrior raised a hand. It was covered in a strange, glowing blue weapon unlike anything Carter had ever seen.

"I am Sab Than, ruler of Zodanga," the man said. "And I sentence you to . . ."

He trailed off and seemed to cock his head at some unknown voice. The weapon's glow faded, and Sab Than looked down at his own hand in dismay. "What? Take him *alive*?"

A trio of soldiers swarmed Carter. He swung his chain, knocking them back, slashing deep.

Sab Than cried out. "Leave him!"

Then Sab stepped forward, drawing his sword. He smiled, almost a leer. "This should be fun."

Carter snatched up a sword from one of the fallen Zodangans, raising it just in time. The two blades clashed, glancing off each other with a bright spark. Sab Than pulled back, grinned, and thrust forward. Carter parried, but just barely.

"What are you?" the Zodangan asked. "You aren't a red man. You aren't *quite* a white ape . . ."

Carter had trained with blades, but the weapon was unfamiliar, and Sab Than was clearly a master swordsman. Slowly, the Zodangan backed him up against the gunwale.

"Whatever you are," Sab Than hissed, "you will bleed like a—"

The Zodangan stopped, gaping over the deck past Carter. *"Tharks!"*

Carter turned, looked down, and caught a split-second glimpse: the green horde stood massed atop the ruins, heavily armed. Every weapon aimed straight up at the airships.

Carter slashed out wildly, forcing Sab Than back. Then he leaped, bouncing off the remaining airship's roof just as the Tharks opened fire.

The airship burst into flame, exploding in a huge conflagration. Carter felt the heat on his back as he soared through the air, swimming and flailing, trying to aim for a soft area on the sand below. It was a long way down.

Above him, the sole remaining airship—Sab Than's vessel—took hit after hit, but remained aloft. Sab's gunners recovered, firing a few rounds back down at the Tharks. But the ship was clearly damaged.

Carter braced himself for a hard landing, looked down . . . and saw a small red figure, followed by a flash of green, running out on the sand away from the Thark settlement. It was the red woman, the one from the Helium ship. He crashed down on a sand dune directly in front of her.

The woman watched him land and held up her hands.

Carter looked past her and saw her pursuer: Sola. The Thark female stopped in her tracks, unsure.

In the distance, the wreckage of three airships burned, filling the air with a charred smell of wood and human flesh.

The Helium woman handed her sword to Sola, but her eyes never left Carter. She spoke with the terse confidence of a commanding officer. "You may take me captive now."

Sab Than burst onto his bridge. Soldiers lay dead everywhere, slumped over smoking equipment. As the ship lurched beneath him, Sab heaved the Light Master's body off the light meter and checked the readings. He moved from one station to another, slamming levers hastily.

The surviving Navigator stared at him with frightened eyes.

"Prepare to turn about," Sab said. "We're going after the princess."

Then he felt the familiar tingling in his mind, and Matai Shang was there again. In his thoughts, on his bridge, always with him. Always in control.

The price Sab Than paid for unlimited power.

"*No*," Matai Shang said. "*The Tharks have her. This opportunity has been lost.*"

"Why did you want him alive? The white ape—man—whatever he is?"

"Go home, Sab Than. Another chance will present itself."

"How will you find them again?"

Matai Shang smiled a thin smile, and Sab Than winced at a brief, sharp stabbing in his brain.

"We can find anyone."

HER NAME was Dejah Thoris, and Carter had never met a woman like her. Strong arms, dancing blue eyes, full lips that curled in a smile. Her skin was tinged with red, a savage hue that matched the alien sands beneath their feet.

They stood together for a long moment as the airships smoked and the Thark woman, Sola, watched uneasily. Then a wild chant rang out, and Carter whirled around to see the entire Thark horde charging straight toward them.

"Did I not tell you he could jump?" Tars Tarkas demanded.

Carter crouched to leap, but something held him back. He looked down to see the faithful doglike animal, Woola, gripping his leg in playful affection.

Carter patted Woola's head—"Let go!"—but it was too late. The Tharks swarmed around him, pulling him away from Dejah Thoris, slapping him roughly on the back.

Tars Tarkas pushed through the crowd. He grabbed Carter up in all four of his arms, beaming like a proud father. "You are ugly, but you are beautiful. And you fight like a Thark!"

Carter sputtered, but before he could speak Tars set him down in front of the warriors. One by one they lined up, handing him their gear and weapons, dressing him up like a Christmas tree.

Tars Tarkas himself removed his baldric, draping it around Carter. And Carter spotted something hanging around the leader's neck: the medallion, the object that had brought him to this strange place.

Tars frowned at him, and Carter realized he was staring. He pointed at the medallion, started to speak—

"Jeddak of the Tharks!"

Everyone turned at the sound of Dejah's voice. Sola stood guarding her at gunpoint.

"I am Dejah Thoris," she continued, "Regent of the Royal Helium Academy of Science. My research vessel was attacked. I managed to restart its Eighth Ray drive, but I was unable to save my—"

Tars stepped up roughly, shoved Dejah into Carter's arms. "Your share of the spoils," Tars said.

The Tharks laughed, a horrible sound. Dejah turned even redder.

"Sola," Tars said, "tend to Virginia's property."

"Yes, my Jeddak." Sola grabbed the struggling Dejah

in all four arms. Carter watched, helpless and unsure.

"You know," Dejah snarled, "once Sab Than has conquered me, he will turn his weapon on you."

"I know that Zodanga has found a way to defeat you," Tars replied. "And now you seek a weapon of your own. But Virginia fights for us! He will fight the Torquas in the south, the Warhoons in the north. And he will be called 'Dotar Sojat'! My good right arms!"

The Tharks raised their weapons in a mighty cheer. Tars turned to Carter, grinning his horrific Thark grin.

"No," Carter said.

Tars's face fell.

"I don't fight for anyone. Not anymore."

Exhausted, Carter began to strip off the Thark gifts: a belt, a rifle, a large amulet. The adrenaline rush had worn off, and the reality of the situation began to wash over him. This was not his home; these were not his people. They were barely people at all.

Tars moved toward him, grinning again.

"Virginia," he said, low. "Reject this honor, and I cannot guarantee the safety of your red girl."

Carter stared at Tars, eyes dropping once again to the spider-patterned medallion around the Jeddak's neck. Then he looked past Tars at Sola's scars, the barbaric markings that covered her arms. He scanned the faces of the Tharks. Sarkoja and Tal Hajus stood watching, eager for Carter to make the wrong decision. They would be only too happy to see him exiled or killed.

And lastly there was Dejah. Still proud, still haughty, but with a hint of fear in her eyes.

Grimacing, Carter pumped his fist . . . weakly at first, then with as much vigor as he could manage.

"I . . . I am Dotar Sojat," he said.

The Tharks erupted in madness, whooping and cheering louder than ever.

Tars Tarkas pointed to the wrecked airships. "To the plunder!" Still cheering, the Tharks took off at a run toward the wreckage. Sarkoja and Tal Hajus paused to glower briefly at Carter. Then they too followed.

Carter moved toward Dejah, still held firm in Sola's grasp. But the Helium woman gave him a dark look and turned away.

Hours later, a bleak sun set over the wreckage of Helium's airship. The fires had died down, but Tharks still swarmed over the ship's splintered decks like an army of giant green ants. Carter stood a few feet away on the sands, watching as the Tharks tossed Helium corpses aside carelessly.

Dejah stood next to him, biting her lip to hold back tears at the fate of her countrymen. A crude leash, held by Sola, encircled her neck.

"War," Carter said. "Shameful thing."

The words sounded weak, inadequate.

"Not when a noble cause is taken up by those who can make a difference." Dejah turned to him, serious. "You made a difference today, Virginia."

"The name's John Carter. Virginia is where I'm *from.*"

She circled him slowly, her leash trailing behind. "How did you learn to jump that way?" Scientific curiosity gleamed in her eyes.

"Don't know." Carter shrugged. "How'd you learn to fly?"

"Your ships cannot sail on light? In 'Virginia'?"

"No, Professor. Our ships sail the seas." From her blank look, he could see that she barely grasped the concept. He gestured around at the barren sands. "Water. Endless water, everywhere."

She nodded patronizingly, then grabbed his arm and squeezed. "Skeletal structure seems normal. Perhaps the density of your bones . . ." She smacked his leg. "Jump for me."

"No!"

"Enough." Sola gave a tug on Dejah's leash. "There will be time for playfulness later."

Dejah tugged back, defiant. "I want no playfulness from him. I want his help." She turned back to Carter. "Explain to me how you do it—the jumping! If it's a skill, I will pay you to teach it to Helium. Name your price."

"I'm not for hire. Got a cave of gold all my own." Carter walked away. "Somewhere."

He glanced at the sun's weak orb just vanishing over the horizon. The light was fading now, sand shifting from red to brown. A Thark sentry patrolled in the distance, his spidery green form dwarfed by the huge thoat beneath him.

I want to go home, Carter realized. Suddenly nothing was more important . . . not even this alluring, frustrating woman who'd fallen out of the sky.

"There are no seas on this planet," Dejah called to him. "Not anymore. Only a madman would rave about the Time of Oceans."

He turned to look back. "That your expert view? I'm mad?"

"Or a liar."

Sola gave a tiny Thark smirk. "She is well matched to you, Dotar Sojat."

"Don't call me that—" He stopped, snapped his head to face Dejah. "You said 'planet.'"

Dejah stared at him, a strange look in her eyes. Walking to the end of her leash, she knelt down, picked up a stick, and drew a single circle in the sand.

"Sun," she said.

Then she drew a ring around it, and another. Nine circles in all, surrounding the "sun." As Carter watched, Dejah marked a dot along each circle, beginning with the innermost.

"Rasoom," she counted off.

"Mercury," Carter said softly.

"Cosoom."

"Venus. Then Earth—that's us."

She looked up at him, a strange light of discovery in her eyes. "That is Jasoom." Then she placed a dot in the fourth ring out from the sun.

"You are on *Barsoom*, John Carter."

He turned away, shaking his head. The sun had set; darkness was falling swiftly. Carter cast his eyes upward . . . and saw not one but two bright moons shining in the night sky.

"Cluros and Thuria," Dejah said. "The Heavenly Lovers. Paired, like the bands you wear on your finger."

Carter fingered his wedding rings. Suddenly he

felt a deep sorrow, as vast as the distance between here and . . . and *Jasoom*.

"I'm on Mars," he whispered.

"So your home is Jasoom—sorry, 'Earth.'" Dejah's tone was skeptical. "Did you come here in one of your sailing ships? Across millions of karads of empty space?"

Carter was too shell-shocked even to rise to her taunting. "No," he said. "A medallion brought me here. The same one that now hangs around Tars Tarkas's neck."

"A medallion . . ." Dejah straightened. "Ah! Well, that explains everything."

"It does?"

"Yes. You're a Thern . . . and you wish to return to your rightful home. Is that it?"

"I don't know what a Thern is."

"We can sort this out right now. Come on."

Grabbing hold of her leash, Dejah started off away from the wreckage, toward the Thark settlement. Sola frowned, looked to Carter. He shrugged, and together they followed.

"I don't like her tone," Sola said.

Carter had to admit: he didn't either.

"You cannot enter here," Sola protested. "It is forbidden!"

But Dejah Thoris paid her no heed. The Helium

woman ran into the ruined temple, waving a torch to illuminate toppled pillars and walls made of jumbled stone.

Carter and Sola followed her into a huge, echoing chamber. An ancient statue of a goddess loomed above them, several stories high.

"*You* insisted I unleash her," Sola said. Carter nodded, grimacing.

Dejah lifted her torch, lighting up a window made of dusty, rose-colored glass. In its intricate stone mullions shone a nine-legged pattern identical to the one on the medallion.

"Look familiar?" she asked.

Sola knelt. She raised two hands to cover her head, two to her heart.

"Sure," Dejah sneered, "kneel before the Holy Thern." She turned angrily to Carter. "You can cloak yourself in religion to fool savage Tharks, but not me. I see what you're doing."

Carter shrugged, baffled.

"You waste my time with fantasies of 'Earth' while my city lies on the verge of defeat."

"You called me a—a Thern." Carter pointed to the statue. "Is that what *she* is?"

"She is Issus!" Sola cried. "Her temple stands at

the heart of every city on Barsoom. All worship the Goddess."

"Not quite all," Dejah said.

But Carter had stopped listening. He was staring up at a bas-relief, intertwined with an unknown, ancient script, running around the base of the temple ceiling. A geometric pattern wove in and out of it.

He'd seen that pattern before. In the cave, in Arizona. Back home.

"What does that say?"

"Forgotten your own scripture? How convenient."

Carter grabbed Dejah and sprang upward, enjoying her yelp of surprise. He landed on a tottering pillar just below the bas-relief.

Dejah struggled in his grip, almost dropping her torch. "Put me down!"

"As soon as you read this to me."

Grimacing, she handed him the torch. He held it up to the wall, and she pointed at the first in a row of images: human or near-human figures wearing medallions, standing above a vast mountain range.

"'In the time of oceans, all Barsoom was lawlessness and chaos.'" She paused, struggling to read. "'There came . . . the Therns. Holy messengers of the Goddess Issus . . . they took the firstborn and divided the red men from the green. To each they gave the gifts of knowledge . . .'" Her finger passed over a series of blurred, overlapping images of godlike Therns.

"The doubled faces," Carter said. "What do they mean?"

"Supposedly the Therns once walked among us as guardians. Taking any form they wished . . . speaking directly to men, in their minds. Guiding them, protecting . . ."

"Like angels."

Once again he grabbed up Dejah, then leaped to a ledge on the opposite side of the temple. Dejah glared at him and turned back to the wall. She ran her finger along an image of a long, snaking river.

"'The Therns' final gift of knowledge,'" she read, "'was the Way of the Goddess—'"

Carter stabbed out a finger to touch the far end of the river's image. Another medallion was depicted there within an upside-down pyramid. "There's the medallion again. What does it mean?"

"Don't rush me. '. . . that those who seek the solace of eternity may journey down the River . . . to pass through the sacred Gates of Iss and find everlasting peace in the bosom of Issus.'"

Carter followed her gaze to a carving of huge,

ornate gates. "'The Gates of Iss . . .' Do you think the answer is there?"

She hesitated. "Yes. I'm certain of it." Then she cast a glance down at Sola, on the ground, and lowered her voice. "What if I could take you there?"

He frowned. "What if I don't trust you?"

"Then we'd be even."

He smiled.

"I can lead you to the Gates," Dejah continued. "To the answers you seek. A way back to Jasoom."

"Earth."

"Earth." She looked around conspiratorially. "Assuming you can get us out of here."

They locked eyes for a long moment. Then he stuck out his hand. "Deal."

She stared at the hand, puzzled.

"You shake it," he said.

A very awkward handshake ensued. Carter smiled again, despite himself. "Now I just need to get that medallion off of Tars. I don't suppose he'll just—"

"Dotar Sojat?"

They looked down to see Sola struggling in the grip of Sarkoja's four strong arms. Five Tharks raised rifles in warning, aiming them straight at Carter and Dejah.

"I told you it was forbidden," Sola said.

TARS TARKAS burst into the holding tent, sweeping the flap open with all four arms. "What in the name of Issus is going on?"

Four Tharks held Carter, who struggled in tight bindings. Sarkoja stood above the kneeling Sola and Dejah Thoris, brandishing a sword in triumph.

"Issus has been profaned," Sarkoja said. "We found these ones plotting in the temple."

Tars stared down at Dejah Thoris. "In the temple?"

"Sola led them there."

Carter watched as Tars's gaze turned to Sola, and a horrible, pained look crossed the Jeddak's face.

"No," Carter said. "Sola tried to stop us. I meant no disrespect to your goddess, Tars."

Sarkoja pressed her blade against Carter's neck. "Your 'right arm' was planning to rob you of the medallion, my Jeddak. He planned to take it down the River Iss to use it for greater blasphemy."

"I'm just tryin' to get home!" Carter cried.

Tal Hajus came up behind Tars Tarkas, surveying the scene coldly. "They must all die," he said. "In the arena."

Tars reached forward with one arm and shoved Sarkoja aside. He hoisted Carter up in the air with two more arms and carried the Earthman away from the others, to a corner of the tent.

"How could you do this?" Tars's fourth hand clamped down hard on Carter's throat and began to strangle him. "I spared your life, made you Dotar Sojat. Yet *her* life means nothing to you!"

The Thark's voice was bitter, disgusted . . . and tinged with an odd, hopeless sadness.

"You knew," Tars continued. "You knew she had no room for another mark. Now Sola will die because of you."

"She's—" Carter gasped for breath. "She's your daughter, isn't she?"

The Jeddak's face lit up with shock and guilt. He hefted Carter again, moved him even farther away from the others, and slammed him up against a rock. Still bound, Carter was helpless to resist.

"Who told you that?" Tars kept his voice low. "A Thark has no parent but the horde."

"Call it a father's intuition." Carter glanced down at the bands on his own, bound hand. "But how do you know? That she's your daughter, I mean?"

"Her mother kept her egg. Sola is the last flicker of our ancient greatness."

Carter pointed to Tars's medallion. "Then you can't just stand by and let her be killed—"

Suddenly Tars grabbed Carter up by the throat again. When the Thark whirled around, Carter saw why: Tal Hajus and Sarkoja had crept up behind them, straining to hear the hushed exchange.

Tars Tarkas faced Sarkoja directly. "You are correct. My right arms have offended me. It falls to me to cut them off."

Then he leaned forward and spoke with all the force of a Thark Jeddak. *"Leave us."*

Tal and Sarkoja filed out, casting suspicious glances back.

When they were gone, Tars Tarkas pulled out his knife. As he raised it, Carter had a horrible moment of fear and doubt. Had he overplayed his hand? Would the Jeddak really kill Carter to keep secret the truth about Sola?

Then Tars cut his bonds. Carter was free.

Sola and Dejah moved in to join them. "You must hurry," Tars said, pointing to the tent's rear flap.

Dejah took Carter's arm. "Thank you, Jeddak—"

"One condition." Tars unhooked the medallion, handing it to Carter. "Take Sola with you down the River Iss."

Sola gasped. When Tars turned to her, his voice was oddly . . . human.

"I'd rather you died in the arms of the Goddess than become food for wild banths in a Thark arena." Tars turned solemnly to Carter. "From this moment, Sola serves under Dotar Sojat. Where you go, she goes."

Carter nodded, then gestured toward the tent's front flap. "What about Sarkoja and Tal Hajus? What will they do to you?"

"Leave a Thark his head and his hand, and he may yet conquer." Tars grinned then, the ghastly Thark smile. "Now go!"

As Carter started running, followed by Dejah and Sola, he realized in surprise: *I'm almost getting used to that grin.*

The three figures galloped across the sands, each astride a swift thoat. Carter heard a noise and turned swiftly, expecting pursuers. But a familiar figure whooped along after them, kicking up a cloud of dust.

"Woola!" Carter exclaimed. "How in the world—"

"You belong to him," Sola said. "Woola would find you anywhere on Barsoom."

Dejah Thoris pointed ahead. "Follow me!"

They rode for many miles, past trackless wastes dotted with a startling variety of ruins. Once, Dejah explained, this had been a lush sea covered with islands, settlements, and ports. But the waters had dried up long ago, and the moving, predatory city of Zodanga had soaked up most of the planet's remaining resources. Barsoom had become a shadow of a world, a barren desert fallen largely into savagery.

Carter was captivated by Dejah's beauty, her energy, and her passion to save her people. But more and more he came to realize she wasn't telling him everything.

On the second day, as Dejah rode ahead under the hot sun, Sola frowned up at the sky. Then she pulled her thoat over alongside Carter's.

"Dotar Sojat," she said. "I mean, *Carter*. I do not think she leads us to the Iss."

Carter nodded grimly. "Play along."

Then he galloped up fast behind Dejah. As she turned in surprise, he reached out and grabbed the reins of her thoat. "What did you think I'd do when I saw your city?"

"What?"

"You're supposed to be taking us to the river."

Sola trotted up alongside and pointed to the twin moons in the sky. "Cluros and Thuria. They should be at our backs by now. You lead us toward Helium."

Dejah grimaced and moved to slow her thoat—but Carter tugged on its reins, urging it forward. "Once we reached Helium," she said, "I knew you would see the virtue of our cause."

"Everyone thinks their cause is virtuous, Professor."

With a swift motion, he yanked at her saddlebag. Its contents spilled out onto the sand. When Dejah turned in surprise, Carter shoved her roughly off the beast and released its reins.

Dejah tumbled to the ground. The thoat dashed off, riderless, disappearing quickly over a rise. Carter and Sola broke to the side, riding off together in the opposite direction.

"No," Dejah cried. "John Carter, you can't!"

"I like this plan better," Sola said.

Carter motioned the Thark to silence.

"You mad fool!" Dejah ran after them on foot, gasping for breath. "You're not from Earth—and there are no Therns! I only told you what you wanted to hear so you'd help us—so you'd help *me*."

Sola looked over at Carter questioningly.

"Wait for the truth," he said, too softly for Dejah to hear.

"Stop," Dejah called. "I can't—*I cannot marry him!*"

Carter reined in his thoat and wheeled it around to face Dejah.

"Can't marry who?" he asked.

She glared up at him. "Sab Than. The Zodangan Jeddak you fought aboard the airship. He offered a truce in exchange for my hand. My father fears the Zodangans' new weaponry, so he consented, but I—I could not."

"Your father?"

"Tardos Mors."

"The Jeddak of Helium?" Sola rode up, her voice sharp with shock. "She is a princess!"

"A princess of Mars." Carter pulled up alongside Dejah, began to circle around her. "A princess who didn't want to get married, so she ran away."

He suddenly felt angry. She'd used him, lied to him, placed hundreds of lives in peril. And for this?

He turned and trotted away.

Dejah kept after him. "I didn't run. I escaped."

He swung his thoat around. "Why don't you just marry him and help your people?"

"I can't do that to them."

"Do what? Let them live?"

"A life of oppression? That is not living."

"*Death* is not living."

"But they don't have to die."

"Right. You can marry Sab Than."

"Or *you* can help us—*uhhh!*"

He heard Dejah trip and turned to see her sprawled face down on the sand. Swearing, he pulled his thoat to a halt, then jumped down to help her.

He reached out a hand, but she slapped it away.

Sola circled on her own thoat, keeping her distance.

Slowly Dejah stood up and stared at the ground. When she spoke, there was steel in her voice.

"If you had the means to save others—to save those you cared most about—would you not take any action to do that?"

"No good will come of me fighting your war."

"I would lay down my life for Helium. But I will not sell my soul." She looked down again. "Yes, I ran away. I was afraid, weak. Maybe I should have just married him. But I feared it would mean the end of Barsoom."

She took both his shoulders in her firm, lovely hands.

"I tell you true, John Carter of Earth. There are no Gates of Iss. They are not real."

"I'm sorry, Princess." He held up the medallion, almost apologetically. "But *this* is real, and it brought me here. If it can bring me home again . . . I've got to try."

They looked into each other's eyes for a long moment. A strange thought came to Carter: *if she can understand my sorrow, then maybe I can understand hers.*

Together, hand in hand, they walked back to his thoat.

CHAPTER 10

THE CITY of Zodanga was on the move. Stalking along on countless gigantic legs, shaking the desert beneath a thousand tons of iron and stone. Crushing all that lay before it, leaving a deep trench in its wake.

Sab Than strode across the open-air expanse of the Royal Hangar. To the airmen preparing his personal flier he looked fearless, almost as powerful as the Therns themselves. But Matai Shang's consciousness still buzzed within Sab's mind, constantly reminding him who held the true power here.

A general approached, nervous. "Sire. Prudence demands you take an escort with you."

"*No,*" Matai Shang said in Sab's mind. His tone of voice brooked no argument.

"I will go alone," Sab said aloud.

"But Jeddak—"

"In one stroke, I can end a thousand years of civil war and bring Helium to her knees forever. But my *general,* in his superior wisdom, objects?"

The general withdrew, mumbling apologies.

As Sab Than mounted the flier, he whispered to

Matai Shang. "I'm even starting to talk like you."

The Thern made no reply.

The flier rose up into the sky, leaving the spires of Zodanga behind. "I have doubts about this plan," Sab said. "The princess is still missing. And that white ape . . ."

"Don't concern yourself with them."

Then a switch seemed to open in Sab Than's brain, and suddenly he saw what Matai Shang saw. A dozen images at once: the city of Zodanga on its scuttling legs. Sab Than's own flier, seen from the ground as it climbed into the sky. Tardos Mors, his eyes dark as he prepared for a royal wedding. A long view of the blue-spired city of Helium, twin halves divided by a deep, unbridgeable chasm.

And then, just for a moment, an image of the open desert: Dejah Thoris, a Thark female, and the white ape called Carter winding their way down a deep trench toward the River Iss.

They're everywhere, Sab realized, *the Therns. And whatever one of them sees, all the others see too, through their brothers' eyes.*

Matai Shang broke the connection. Sab blinked, startled and disoriented. The flier lurched beneath him, and he struggled to right it.

"They will not reach the Gates," Matai said. *"Wherever they are, I am already there."*

By the time they reached the River Iss, the thoats were parched. Carter led his mount down to the black water and left it to drink. He stood taking in the scene as Sola and Dejah Thoris rode up behind him and dismounted. Faithful Woola had found them again too and galloped up to join them at river's edge.

Carter had expected to see signs of life around the river—bodies of water were very rare on Barsoom. But the shore held no people, red or green. Only canoes, some wrecked and some whole, all littered with abandoned food and offerings. A fatal stillness hung over the landscape.

Sola gestured at the offerings. "Here, pilgrims must leave behind all they have, all they know. Never to return." She lowered her head, spoke more softly. "May the Goddess find me worthy."

Carter glanced briefly at her. Sola had been very quiet for the past day. Carter wished, not for the first time, that he understood the Tharks better.

He knelt down, scooped up a handful of water—and pitched over as Woola slammed into him, whimpering and licking his face.

"Woola!"

Then Dejah gasped. Carter looked up, followed her gaze, and saw his thoat lying dead on the riverbank a few feet away. Foam oozed out of its muzzle.

"The water is poisonous." Thoroughly, Carter shook the water off his hands and wiped them clean. He turned to Woola, who sat panting next to him. "Good boy!"

Then he spied Sola, beginning a solemn march down to the river.

"Wait!"

Carter leaped up and landed on the riverbank between Sola and the water. She reached out to push him aside, but he stood firm. "What do you think you're doing?"

"It is my way, Dotar Sojat. Not yours." Her voice was flat. "I must honor my Jeddak, and redeem my unworthiness."

"You want to honor your father? Then stay alive and help me."

"My *father*?"

Too late, Carter realized what he'd just said.

"What do you mean?" she continued.

"Sola . . . that's what drives your compassion. The blood of your father, of Tars Tarkas. Of all the Tharks, you're the only one worthy of him."

Carter watched her for a moment, saw her struggle with this new knowledge. He felt the urge to reach out to her and realized something very strange. As inhuman—as alien—as she was, Sola was the closest thing to a mother he'd known for a long, long time.

He turned away and crossed to one of the intact canoes.

"And your duty to your father demands that you see me through." He held out an oar, gesturing to the canoe. "Just help me find the Gates. Then you can decide what your honor requires."

Sola stared at the oar. Dejah Thoris walked up behind Carter and laid a gentle hand on his shoulder.

"Just to the Gates, then." Sola took the oar and climbed into the canoe.

When Carter looked over at Dejah, she was smiling at him. The most tender, human smile he'd yet seen on this world.

They left poor Woola on the riverbank, whimpering and fidgeting, to guard the remaining thoats. The water was thick but flowing with a strong current that pushed them downstream toward their destination.

Sola kept watch, eyeing the water carefully for omens. Once she gestured, and Carter paddled the canoe over to the bank. A flatboat glided by bearing three gaunt, unmoving Tharks. Two of them knelt in the bow, chanting low, while the third stood aft, poling the boat like some eerie gondolier of death.

"Other pilgrims," Sola said.

They paddled for the better part of a day, past broken piers and abandoned boats. Finally they drifted around a sharp bend, and Carter reached for Dejah with sudden excitement.

The Gates of Iss loomed before them, an inverted pyramid that seemed to grow up out of the river: a massive, sandblasted structure that dwarfed everything around it, like a madman's vision of an earthly water dam.

Sola whispered a chant and began making signs in the air with all four of her arms.

Dejah shook her head, eyes wide. "Impossible," she said.

Carter peered closer. Every inch of the Gates' surface was covered with the strange lattice of lines he'd seen in the Arizona cave and again in the Thark temple. But those etchings, he now realized, had been crude carvings, primitive imitations. This was the real thing, a pulsing web of living machinery built for some powerful, specific purpose.

The current guided them straight to the narrow foot of the Gates. They struck it with a slight bump, coming to a stop as the river flowed around the structure on both sides.

Dejah reached out a hand, touching the intricate line work. "I've never seen this material before . . ."

"I want to get a better look." Carter scooped up Dejah in his arms and leaped. She cried out, burying her head in his chest.

They soared up a hundred feet, clearing the top of the Gates, then came to a landing on its flat, wide roof. Below, in the canoe, Sola continued to chant.

Dejah was staring at him. He set her down.

"Carter," she said. "Your feet."

He glanced down. A blue aura spread out from him, forming a glowing pattern against the latticework on the roof of the Gates. Tentatively, he took a step. When his foot touched down again, a flare of blue energy rose up.

Carter raised the medallion in surprise. It too glowed blue, its forked lines seeming to come alive in the Gates' presence.

Then the surface of the Gates seemed to open up in front of them, stone falling away like sand rushing down an hourglass. A stairway wove itself into being, leading down into the heart of the structure.

Together they began their descent. The walls of the Gates surrounded them, the staircase constantly forming new steps just ahead of their feet. Carter couldn't tell how far down they walked—at least to the level of the river's surface, probably deeper.

When they reached the bottom, the medallion flared bright.

Ahead, a portal opened in the blue stone. A corridor knitted itself into existence just as the stairway had done before. Carter peered ahead but the passageway was dim, lit only by the blue glow of the medallion.

He glanced over at Dejah, and she returned his gaze. Once again he felt that bond between them, the sense that he was born to meet this woman. This strange, willful, infuriating, unspeakably beautiful princess of Mars.

They drew their swords as one, in a single fluid motion. And stepped forward into the dark.

CHAPTER 11

CARTER AND DEJAH had only taken a few steps when the corridor sparked to life. An eerie, diffuse light filled the air, seeming to follow them as they walked. At its edges up ahead they could still see the corridor weaving itself into existence, forming new stone and mortar work before their eyes.

Dejah Thoris shook her head in disbelief. "This is not the work of gods. These are *machines*."

Abruptly the corridor stopped. Carter stepped forward toward the wall—and again his foot began to glow. An intricate lattice of energy rose up into the air, glowing and twisting all around them. The walls began to melt away, shaping and swirling, expanding outward to form a new, much larger chamber.

When the energy faded, Dejah and Carter found themselves standing in a cylindrical, high-ceilinged room. Faint lights danced along the rock walls, glowing in the now-familiar lattice pattern.

Almost in a trance, Dejah ran her fingers along the blue-lit wall. She glanced at the floor, then held out her hand to Carter.

"Your medallion."

He passed it to her. She knelt and placed it atop a softly glowing mark on the floor. The medallion flared again, seething briefly with light. Dejah snatched her hand away—and the medallion rose up, stopping to hover just a few inches above the floor.

Carter grabbed Dejah's hand, and together they stepped back as the floor beneath them came alive, glowing with luminous text and symbols. Abstract shapes connected by radiant lines, arcs, circles. When it was done, Carter stared in awe at the final pattern.

The nine-legged spider. Its legs stretched outward from their common origin point: the mark directly beneath the hovering medallion.

"Nine," Dejah whispered. "Nine rays."

He looked at her, puzzled.

"Carter, the Ninth Ray is real. It can be harnessed! Don't you see?" She darted around the floor, pointing and gesturing at the grid of lines. "This entire structure runs on Ninth Ray isolates. I was right! Mother Issus—" She stopped, whirled around. "The Therns. They're real. And you . . . you really are John Carter of *Earth*?"

He grinned at her excitement. "Yes, ma'am."

"And the ships that sail the sea . . . you've seen them. It must be a beautiful sight."

"It truly is." He moved toward her. "But I'm not sure I'd trade it for the look on your face right now."

Carter stepped on another disk of light—and that mark too expanded under his feet, eclipsing the first pattern with its own. A central glowing spot with nine concentric circles fanning out around it. Various-size dots swelled along each line, completing a model of the solar system. Just as Dejah had etched it out in the sand back in the Thark settlement.

But the pattern didn't stop there. As Carter and Dejah stared, eight more lines sprouted from the third dot, the one representing Earth. The lines spread out, crossing the concentric circles, forming links to every other planet in the diagram. Along each line, glyphs appeared in the ancient language of Barsoom.

Together they knelt down next to "Earth" and began tracing the lines with their fingers. Carter turned to Dejah. "What's it say?"

"I'm not sure." She ran a hand over the glyphs. "It appears to be a . . . a kind of technical diagram. This line links Jasoom to Barsoom, and the glyph here . . . it's like our symbol for a transcription. A copy sent along these lines between the worlds. Like—"

"Like a telegram." Carter shook his head, struggling with the concept. "You're saying I got *telegraphed* here? I'm a copy of myself?"

"Possibly. These words could be the command for travel." She frowned. "I don't like guessing. I need more information . . . charts, codices . . ."

Carter's pulse quickened. Could this be his way home?

"These charts. Where could we find them?"

"In the Hall of Science. In Helium."

"Oh yes. Let's just turn around and head on back to Helium." Suddenly angry, he lifted her up into the air. "What do you take me for?"

She looked down into his eyes for a long moment.

"I take you for a man who's lost," she said.

"I won't be lost if you tell me how to work this thing."

"I'll tell you what I can. But everything I need to understand that medallion is in Helium."

He pulled her closer, staring into her eyes. Was she telling the truth? Or was this just another trick to lure him to her city?

"I'm trying to help you," she continued. "To get you back to your cave of gold. Isn't that what you want?"

"Yes," he said. But even to him, the answer seemed weak. Hollow.

"No," she replied, firmer now. "I don't believe that. We were born worlds apart, but I *know* you, John Carter." He tried to look away but her blue eyes held him fast. "From the first moment you leaped into the sky and caught me, I knew. When we stood together atop that tower, swords drawn, I—I felt the heart of a good man. A man willing to lay down his life for others."

He said nothing.

"To fight for a cause." She moved even closer, until their eyes were only inches apart. "*Here*. On Barsoom."

Then the space between them collapsed, as easily as the space between Earth and Barsoom. They kissed, a hot, passionate melding of lips. She smelled of blood and fire, like the ancient sands covering her proud, warrior world.

Carter closed his eyes and, despite himself, a memory flooded into his mind: the last time he'd known such a passionate kiss. Dressed in his rebel grays, out on the steps of the old house in Virginia. Sarah's lips warm on his, her tousled hair framed against the green trees, the lilacs in bloom. Carter's hand resting firm on their daughter's head as the girl clung to Sarah's skirts.

"Don't you see, Carter?"

His eyes snapped open.

"I fled Helium to find another way," Dejah continued. She raised a hand, caressed his cheek. "*You* are that other way."

He shook his head, guilt and passion warring within him. Opened his mouth to speak . . . then whirled at the sound of gunfire.

"Outside!" Dejah cried. She took off at a run down the corridor.

Still dazed, Carter took a last look around at the majestic solar system model covering the floor. Then he snatched up the floating medallion and took off after Dejah.

Behind him, the room dissolved into atoms.

From atop the Gates, Carter stared down at a grim sight. Sola stood alone in the canoe, rifle raised, firing round after round at the bluffs above the river . . . which teemed with Warhoons.

Tars Tarkas had described the Warhoons to Carter: snarling, savage, piratical cousins of the Tharks, with deadly gnarled teeth and sharply hooked tusks. Hundreds of them stood massed on the bluff, firing off an almost solid wall of spears and arrows. Some Warhoons sat astride thoats while others rode banths, eight-legged beasts with rat tails and sharp lionlike claws.

Sola was holding her own, and the Warhoons were keeping their distance from the poison river. But the Thark was badly outnumbered. Sooner or later, a spear would strike her down.

Barely thinking, Carter snatched up Dejah and jumped. They landed hard in the canoe, splashing deadly black water up all around. Sola whirled in surprise, almost dropping her rifle. "Dotar Sojat!"

"Are they from Helium?" Carter asked.

Dejah shook her head emphatically. A volley of arrows whizzed between them, and she shrank back.

"Sola," Carter said, "get Dejah out of here."

"Carter?" Dejah asked.

He took her by the shoulders, looked deep into her eyes. "I was too late once. I won't be again."

Then he tensed his muscles and leaped again—toward the shore.

Dejah called after him. "Carter! *No!*"

He landed just as a piercing horn blast rang out, assaulting his senses. The Warhoon horde charged, bearing straight down on him. A hundred howling, slavering beast warriors, each of them four times his size, spears and arrows cocked and flying.

As he faced certain death, a memory once again flashed into Carter's mind. The horrible moment when he'd returned home from war, bloodied and limping, kept alive only by the hope of seeing Sarah and his little girl again. He'd ridden that horse till it dropped—in front of a burned-out farm, every bit of it destroyed by fire. Sobbing, exhausted, he'd scrabbled with his bare hands through the wreckage . . . till he found it.

Sarah's body curled in death around a tiny, swaddled, unmoving form.

I was too late once. I won't be again.

Inside Carter, something snapped. He let out a savage cry, funneling all the horror and rage of his past into this one moment, this battle that would probably be his last. He vaulted into the air away from the river and dove into the seething mass of Warhoons. Whirling, slashing, drawing blood and springing up again.

Arrows struck him, spears pierced his flesh, but Carter felt nothing. All he saw was the memory of his own hand dribbling a handful of earth onto his daughter's tiny grave. The hand that now bore two wedding bands in memory of all he'd lost.

Through his rage, through his grief and pain, the thought came to Carter: *I've found something worth fighting for.* But was it Dejah Thoris? Sarah's memory? Or just the hope of returning home? As a dozen Warhoon fists pummeled him, as his blood fell and mixed with the blood of the Warhoon horde he decimated, Carter realized that he still didn't know. And no matter the answer, even as the horde overwhelmed him, he knew he would never stop fighting.

CHAPTER 12

DEJAH THORIS watched with horror as the Warhoon horde flooded over Carter. One monster after another piled atop him, stabbing and punching, forcing him slowly but surely to the ground.

"He'll be dead in minutes," she said. "We have to help him!"

Sola gave her a sharp look. "No. You heard Dotar Sojat's orders."

Dejah moved to grab the paddle, planning to row the canoe toward shore. But then a huge explosion rocked the river, sending the poison waters swirling perilously close to the canoe's lip. Up on the bluff, Warhoons and thoats flew through the air. The survivors scattered and ran for cover. A second blast struck the shore, then a third.

A shadow loomed over the canoe. Dejah cast her eyes upward and pointed with excitement. "The *Xavarian*! It's the *Xavarian*!"

The majestic Helium airship hovered above, raining down barrage after barrage on the panicking Warhoons. On the deck, expert swivel-gunners targeted the creatures surgically, isolating the largest fighters and separating them from their fellows.

As Dejah paddled the boat to the riverbank, the *Xavarian* glided in to an easy landing beside the scattered Warhoon corpses. The blue standard of Helium waved proudly from its flagpoles. The few remaining Warhoons ran, scurrying for the hills.

Warriors spilled down the airship's ramp, moving to greet Dejah Thoris as she stepped up onshore. Sola followed her warily.

The Heliumite warriors parted, revealing a familiar, imposing figure.

"Father!" Dejah cried.

"Dejah!" Tardos Mors swept her up into his arms. "Thank Issus!"

For a split second, Dejah buried her face in her father's shoulder. Then she pulled away urgently. "Carter?"

Tardos led her to a heaped pile of Warhoon corpses. One by one, Helium soldiers rolled away the dead Warhoons, revealing Carter's body half crushed beneath.

Heart pounding, Dejah dropped to his side. She checked his pulse: faint but steady.

"Thank Issus," she breathed.

"Who is he?" Tardos Mors asked.

"His name is John Carter. He saved my life. And . . . he is from Jasoom."

"From Jasoom? You believe that?"

She smiled. "Yes. I do."

Tardos started to argue but a deep, commanding voice rang out from the direction of the airship. "We'll take him to Zodanga. It's closer than Helium."

Dejah turned to see Sab Than striding toward them, proud and tall. His red dress uniform stood out against the sea of Helium blue. He bowed deeply before Dejah, gestured casually at Carter. "He'll have my personal physician, I promise."

Snarling, Dejah whirled away from the Zodangan ruler. Before Tardos Mors could protest, she grabbed his pistol from its holster and aimed it straight at Sab Than. Her hands were steady, calm.

"Daughter!" Tardos cried.

"He shot me out of the sky," Dejah said.

Sab Than eyed her calmly.

Tardos moved between them, holding Dejah back. "Daughter, listen to me. Sab Than admitted to every-thing. He came to *me*—alone, without an escort. I could have killed him easily. Yet it was clear he cared only about your safety."

"I feared you might be tortured by the Tharks," Sab

JOHN CARTER: A NOVELIZATION

said. "Condemned to die in their arena. I could not live with that on my conscience." He smiled at her, an easy smile. "I do have a conscience, Princess."

"Really?" Dejah lowered the gun but kept her eyes trained on Sab. "I heard you had it removed along with your—"

"Daughter!"

Sab Than held up a hand. "She does not trust me, Jeddak. And why should she? There has never been trust between Zodanga and Helium. Therefore, I offer this token of my good will."

He unsheathed his sword, held it upright—and a hundred Helium soldiers drew their blades in response. In a quick, easy motion, Sab Than flipped his sword around and held out the hilt to Dejah Thoris.

"My life," he said.

Dejah felt herself in the grip of great forces, passions that would transform the history of Barsoom. Nodding, she reached out and grasped the sword. She pointed it at Sab Than's throat, ignoring her father's protests.

"You hold the power, Princess." Sab's voice remained calm. "The power of life over me and over all our world. With our cities united, all is possible. All you have to do is marry me."

Sab was right: she held his life in her hands. Yet

suddenly, Dejah felt exhausted, defeated. She cast her eyes around from her grimacing father to the dead Warhoons to the proud, blue-garbed warriors of Helium.

And, finally, to the unmoving form of John Carter.

Slowly, she lowered the sword and nodded sadly.

Carter woke in a spartan jail cell. A sharp-tongued Helium officer named Kantos Kan quickly spirited him out of his cell, tricking the guards assigned to watch him. Before Carter could catch his breath he found himself atop a palace roof, casting his eyes over the spires of an unfamiliar city.

"Is this Helium?" Carter asked.

"Zodanga," Kantos replied. "Where the men are as limited as the menu and the women as hard as the beds."

Carter had no idea how to reply to that.

"We must rejoin Princess Dejah," Kantos continued, looking back at the stairwell—which now clattered with the pursuing Zodangan guards.

"Dejah!" Carter said.

"From what she tells me, you'll be able to get us . . . *there*."

Kantos pointed to a turreted tower fifty feet below the palace and twice as far away. Carter swallowed. "She said I could make that?"

Kantos smirked, "Would you dare call Her Highness a liar?"

The guards reached the roof and pointed toward them.

Carter grabbed Kantos and jumped into the air, as high and far as he could. He reached the top of his arc and began to descend toward the tower. With a sick feeling, he realized they weren't going to make it. He reached out with his free hand, stretched as far as he could, and managed to grab a window ledge. He dangled for a second, still holding tight to Kantos, who regarded him with amused disdain and a bit of fear.

Then the stone ledge crumbled, and the two men plummeted down. Carter relaxed his legs and aimed for another, wider ledge. He landed, bounced, and rebounded upward.

He smiled. He had what the Yankees called his "sea legs" again. Deftly he leaped from spire to spire, catwalk to catwalk, rebounding once off the deck of a passing flier. Kantos pointed, and Carter carried him in through a stone window . . . to the royal dressing room. A group of handmaidens shrieked at the men's arrival. Startled, Carter tripped, released Kantos, and fell to the floor. Quickly he picked himself up, scrambling to his feet.

Princess Dejah Thoris stood before him in full

wedding regalia. A gown of serpentine gold wound around her tall body, accentuating her curves and leaving her shoulders, stomach, and legs bare. She looked stunning, radiant, and imperious, her ritual tattoos proudly displayed. The rightful queen of Barsoom.

Carter could barely speak. "Excuse me, ma'am . . ."

Her lip twisted in a half smirk. "You are expected to bow in my presence, *Captain* Carter."

He tried to bow, wincing at the injuries he'd suffered at the Warhoons' clawed hands. The handmaidens giggled.

"I fetched him as you commanded," Kantos said. "Alas, he seems to have suffered some kind of blow to the head."

"Thank you, Kantos. I wish to speak to Captain Carter alone. Keep watch outside."

Kantos saluted and withdrew. The handmaidens hesitated, their eyes on Carter. *I'm exotic to them*, he realized.

The matron of the chamber—a stern, lanky woman— shooed the maidens out. "*Now*, ladies. Off you go!"

Dejah fastened the door bolt behind them and turned to face Carter. Waited for him to speak.

"You look beautiful," he said. The word wasn't nearly strong enough.

She gestured at the gown. "Traditional Zodangan. Worn by the groom's mother at *her* wedding, I'm told. A little vulgar by my standards, but then, my opinions are about to become irrelevant."

"Not if I can help it." In a quick motion, he grabbed her under his arm and sprang to the window. He leaned out, prepared to jump—and then, to his shock, she pulled free, clocking him on the jaw.

He realized she was furious. "Have you so little regard for my situation?" she demanded.

"I'm rescuing you!"

"No. *I* am rescuing *Helium*."

He shook his head, baffled. "You told me—back in the desert. You said you could not marry him."

"I have no other choice." She glared at him, furiously radiant in her wedding dress. "You told *me* that."

He turned away, fists clenched.

"Give me a reason," she said, her voice cracking suddenly. "A reason not to marry him. Will you—will you stay and fight for Helium?"

As he turned toward her, he saw hope blossom in her eyes. Hope for herself and for her people. Hope that Helium might find a champion and that she might not have to marry a man who saw her only as a possession.

Carter opened his mouth to speak. Then a glint of

gold caught his eye, and he glanced down at his own hand. At the twin wedding rings wound around his finger.

"Dejah . . ."

"We have a saying on Barsoom." Her voice was dead now, flat. "A warrior may change his metal, but not his heart."

She stepped in close to him, reached into her robe. Pulled out the medallion.

"You were right," she continued. "I could decipher the script—read the command. I can give you what you want."

He stared at the medallion. His heart quickened.

"It's a simple phrase—a sequence of sounds. Repeat after me." She placed the medallion in his hands. *"Och Ohem. Och Tay."*

Suddenly there was a clatter from outside the room. Carter could hear the voices through the door.

Kantos Kan: "Her Highness has demanded not to be disturbed."

Sab Than: "With that freak on the loose? Step aside, you preening she-calot."

Kantos: "With all due respect, O Mighty Magnificence, I cannot."

A knock at the door.

Sab: "Dejah! Are you all right?"

Dejah leaned in urgently to Carter. "Say this. *Och Ohem. Och Tay.*"

Carter's throat was dry. "*Och Ohem. Och Tay.*"

The medallion began to glow in his hand. Energy pulsed along the legs of the spider.

"*Wyees,*" Dejah continued. "*Jasoom.*"

"*Wyees* . . ." He hesitated.

"*Jasoom,*" she repeated.

The knock at the door became a pounding, then a loud crack.

"*Jasoom.* Say it!" She was practically screaming at him. "*Say it!*"

Carter stared at the medallion, its glow almost blinding now. He could feel the rush of space, the immense distance between worlds beginning to call him back again. He opened his mouth, began to form the final word.

"Jasoo—"

The door erupted inward in an explosion of wood. Dejah Thoris shielded her face, turning away. The Zodangan guardsmen rushed in, followed by the curious matron and handmaidens.

Sab Than swept past all of them and strode straight toward Dejah. He seized her by both shoulders, admiring, proud, and possessive all at the same time. "Are you alone?"

Together they scanned the room. Bathtub, bed, regal furnishings, and trunks full of silks.

But no John Carter.

"Yes," Dejah said quietly. "I am alone."

CHAPTER 13

HIGH UP NEAR the vaulted ceiling, perched in the shadows of the eaves, Carter watched silently as Sab Than led Dejah out of the room, one arm wrapped possessively around her waist. The guardsmen and maidens followed. The matron took a quick, suspicious look around the room, then exited last, pulling the heavy door shut behind her.

Alone now, Carter dropped to the floor.

He'd made his decision, he realized. Earth had been no more than a syllable away; he'd felt its pull, almost *smelled* the sweet grass of Virginia calling. But in the end, it was all nothing next to Dejah Thoris. She meant the world to him.

Unfortunately, he had no idea what to do next. Carter was free but hunted, in a hostile, alien city. And Dejah was less than a day away from marrying that city's tyrant ruler.

Helium and Zodanga had made their pact. Carter's only hope was the Tharks.

He slipped out of the room, eyes darting around the empty corridor. He turned a corner toward a winding staircase and came face to face with Dejah's matron.

The old woman held up a strange bracelet weapon. A web of glimmering blue energy spat out from it, striking Carter's chest and growing like instant moss. It expanded up to his neck and down over his legs, stretching out to cover his arms, his clothing. Then it turned rigid, hard as stone, locking his body in place.

"What is this—?"

The web snaked up around his throat, wrapping around his jaw to form a gag.

The matron raised a finger to her mouth. *"Shh."* With a graceful motion, she plucked the medallion from Carter's hand. Then she circled behind him, leaned over his shoulder . . . and her face shifted and changed. Became harder, more angular, more masculine. She seemed to grow taller as well, and a timeless, ancient look appeared in her eyes.

"I am Matai Shang," the figure said. "And I assure you, we will have plenty of time to talk."

Then the energy web spread up over Carter's eyes and the world went black. He made a muffled, panicky noise, but Matai Shang's firm arm pulled him forward. Carter heard sounds, voices. The stagnant indoor air gave way to a warm breeze, and he felt the jostle of a crowd around him. He almost tripped over a short flight of steps, and then a firm hand shoved him into a seated position.

When the Thern energy weapon receded from his eyes, Carter found himself sitting in a Zodangan battle-wagon. He managed to turn his neck far enough to see out the window: a crowded street lined with pedestrians and market stalls. And statues of Sab Than.

"The Avenue of Warriors," Matai Shang said.

Matai sat directly across from him, dressed now in an ethereal, shifting beige robe and metallic wristbands. He studied Carter like a cat with an injured mouse.

Carter struggled but the Thern device held his limbs tight. Matai touched his wristband, and a tendril receded from Carter's throat. Carter gagged, coughed.

"Now," Matai said. "Let's have that talk."

"Who are you?"

"Ah. American."

Carter frowned. "Who *are* you, sir?"

"'Sir.' Definitely the South." Shang cocked his head, almost amused. "The Carolinas? Virginia? It's Virginia, isn't it. Lovely place."

"You know it?"

"Not well, yet. But I will."

The wagon lurched, jolted to a stop. Matai slid open a small panel behind his head. Then he placed a finger to his throat and spoke in a completely different voice. The voice of a Zodangan military officer.

"Padwar, what's the holdup?"

From up front, the driver's muffled reply. "Sorry, sir. Streets are blocked. It's the wedding procession."

Matai closed the panel, mildly annoyed. He turned back around, smiling at Carter's futile struggles.

"Increased strength and agility. A simple matter of gravitation and anatomy . . . we should have foreseen it."

"We?"

"No apparent intelligence increase—unfortunately for you. Still, this will not do at all." Matai held up the medallion, dangled it close to Carter. "We can't have Earthmen projecting themselves to Barsoom, leaping about and causing all manner of disruption."

Carter frowned. This man or creature, whatever he was, had enormous weaponry and power at his command—and he seemed to know all about Carter and Earth as well. Suddenly Carter recalled Dejah's words back in the Thark settlement.

"You're a Thern," he said.

"Therns are a myth," Matai replied.

Then Matai touched his throat again and spoke in the officer's voice. "Padwar, we'll go on foot."

The battlewagon's rear doors swung open. Carter

felt a lightening sensation in his legs and discovered he could stand. When he looked up again, Matai Shang had transformed wholly, body and clothing, into a young Zodangan officer.

They hurried out of the wagon and into the crowd. Zodangan citizens massed around them, dressed in celebratory red. There were too many, packed too tightly, for Carter to make a run for it. And his arms were still bound.

"The Therns do not exist," Matai said in a low voice. "*I* do not exist. Indeed, I work very hard at that."

The crowd grew even thicker, jostling and bumping against Carter. When he looked up, Matai's officer form had been replaced by the figure of a smiling elderly woman.

"Excuse me," Matai was saying. "Many pardons . . . the blessings of Issus be upon you . . ."

As the crowd thinned, Carter looked up to see the royal float approaching, gliding above the wide street. Sab Than and Dejah Thoris stood atop its roof, waving down at the adoring citizens.

"It's a shame, really," Matai said in his old lady's voice. "She is a remarkable creature. And she came very close indeed."

"You mean the Ninth Ray," Carter said.

"It's of no consequence now. Tonight, when the two moons meet and vows are exchanged, there will be a grand ceremony. And then she, and anyone else with knowledge of the Ninth Ray, will be eliminated." Matai turned to Carter and smiled a cruel, inhuman smile. "Shame there's no one to warn her."

Carter whipped around, back toward the float—and the web snaked its tendrils up, covering his mouth again. A muffled cry died in his throat.

The royal float slid by. Of all the cheering crowd, only Carter could see the sadness behind Dejah Thoris's stoic smile.

Matai waved as the float passed by. "The balance must be restored."

Then he grasped Carter's arm roughly, leading him off through the crowd again. Up ahead, Carter saw the elevated space of the Zodangan Hangar Deck with its multiple levels of skycraft, pilots, and mechanics.

The web receded again. Carter gasped for breath.

"What—what gives you the right to interfere?"

"Why do you care?" Matai seemed honestly curious. "This is not your home; you have no obligation to these people. How would they say it in Virginia? You have no dog in this fight. You're a man without a cause."

As they approached the base of the Hangar Deck,

Matai shifted casually back into the form of an officer. He saluted the guards and led Carter swiftly onto an open-air elevator platform.

As the platform started to rise, Matai shifted back into his true, robed form.

"What is *your* cause?" Carter asked.

"Oh, we have none. We are not haunted by mortality as you are. We are eternal."

"The wedding—this little stroll. Why not just kill me? Kill Dejah?"

"Don't question our motives, Earthman." Matai gestured out past the open platform, at the city of Zodanga laid out below. "What must happen will happen. Tonight Dejah Thoris will say her vows, drink from the chalice, and seal the fate of Barsoom. Our agents have spent decades preparing for this: they ply their trade in the Council of Helium, in the highest spires of Zodanga, in the lowest slums of Barsoom.

"We are everywhere. We've been playing this game since before the birth of this world, and we will play it long after the death of yours."

Carter gazed out over the city's spires. He could just make out the royal float receding into the distance down the crowd-choked Avenue of Warriors.

"You see," Matai continued, "we don't actually cause

the destruction of a world. We simply *manage* it . . . feed off it, if you like. But on every host world, it plays out the same way. Populations rise, societies divide, wars rage. And all the while, the neglected planet slowly dies."

The platform reached the elevated Hangar Deck. Matai Shang, in officer form again, snapped out an order. "Prisoner transport. Prep a two-man flier immediately."

The flier was a frightening contraption: barely more than a large cylinder with instrument controls, a windscreen, and metal "wings" fanning out from the sides to collect solar energy. As the Thern anchored him to the rear seat, throttling the engine to life, Carter felt a deep sense of despair. The unearthly web held him fast, responding to Matai Shang's every slight command. Carter was utterly helpless.

But more than that. The Therns held this world in a vise, and they seemed all-powerful. No man from Earth, no Thark, Zodangan, or Heliumite, could possibly stand against them. No creature on either world . . .

Before they could take off, the flier suddenly slammed over onto its side. Matai was thrown free, but Carter went down with the flier. He struggled to turn his head and managed to see a snarling, bulky figure spring through the air, landing atop the Thern with a clamping of powerful jaws.

"Woola!" Carter cried.

Matai struggled beneath the animal's bulk. Woola snapped out and crunched Matai's bracelet, crushing it against the Thern's arm. Matai cried out in pain.

With the bracelet destroyed, Carter's shackles crumbled to dust. He jumped to his feet, then knelt down next to the trapped, squirming Thern.

"Immortal ain't bulletproof," Carter said, petting Woola absently. "I shot one of you back on Earth. Remember that."

Carter grabbed the medallion, shoving it quickly into his boot. Then he turned to see the Zodangan guards pointing and running toward him. Woola whimpered urgently.

Carter turned his attention to the two-man flier, still humming with power. He hopped onto it, fumbled with its controls. And tried not to think about what he had to do now.

Captain John Carter, veteran of nineteenth-century ground combat, was about to make his first solo flight.

CHAPTER 14

FOR CARTER, the next hour passed in a blur of instinct and action. He managed to guide the flier up, lost control, and righted it again. He heard Matai Shang shout something, and then a loud buzzing rose up behind him: guards on mounted fliers taking off in pursuit. Carter panicked, plummeted his flier over the side of the Hangar Deck, then pulled up just in time to see the palace looming ahead.

He banked sharply, lost control, and dove again—into the mazelike pipework of the city's refineries, the steaming brass network that fed power to its streets. Two Zodangan fliers were right on his tail now. Carter dodged thick, scalding-hot pipes, pulling up hard on the flier's stick as he'd seen the pilots of Barsoom do.

Every slight twitch made the flier lurch sharply beneath him. *This ain't no horse*, he thought.

He banked, swerved, shot to the side—and suddenly found himself beneath the city, weaving through its rows of gigantic moving legs. They pressed down into the sand like oil derricks, like pile drivers. Carter grimaced, tightening his grip on the flier's controls.

One of the Zodangans was too slow and slammed right into a leg. His flier exploded in a burst of fire.

But as Carter slowed, disoriented, the second Zodangan pressed his advantage. He swerved to the side, pulling up even with Carter, then banked back hard, aiming his grapnel gun straight at his prey. Carter grimaced.

A shot rang out. The Zodangan spun off his flier, trailing blood. Carter looked around frantically. He was almost clear of the city now, and he could see the empty trench left behind in its wake. The last few legs clomped past him, and he spotted the shooter standing on the flat sand below.

Sola, with her Thark rifle. Woola stood next to her, yapping excitedly.

Carter bumped his way down to an uneasy landing. Behind him, the city lumbered slowly onward through the trackless desert.

When he dismounted, Sola swept him up like a mother reunited with her child.

"Easy now!" he said. "Sola—"

"I told you Woola could find you anywhere," she replied.

He smiled down at the beast, which was hopping up and down with joy. Then he turned away, started back toward his flier.

"Where are you going?" Sola asked.

"To save Dejah. And I'm going to need an army to do it." He kicked the flier to life. "Get on."

"No." Sola hesitated. "It is unnatural. Tharks do not fly."

Again Carter smiled. "They do now."

They made quite a sight: Carter in the pilot's seat, Sola perched behind, clasping four arms painfully around his chest—and Woola stretched out like a hood ornament on the front of the flier. At first the animal seemed dubious, but soon he was howling with excitement into the onrushing wind.

When they reached the Thark settlement, Carter discovered that landing the flier was even more difficult with passengers. He collided with a dune, sending a wave of sand spitting up into the air. They skidded noisily to a halt, blinded by dust.

When the dust cleared, they found themselves staring into the barrels of two Thark rifles.

"Take me to the Jeddak," Carter said. "Now!"

The guards led them through the maze of tents. Sarkoja sneered at them as they passed. Sola cringed, turning quickly away.

When they reached the Jeddak's tent, Carter pushed straight through the flap. "Tars! They're gonna kill Dejah—"

But the Thark sitting in the Jeddak's chair was not Tars Tarkas. Tal Hajus jerked his head up from a platter of food, a dark grin forming on his face.

"Issus truly rewards the just," he said.

They dumped Carter through a grate and he dropped twenty feet or more down to a ruined dungeon. A heavy rock fell after him, chained to his leg.

Tal Hajus smirked down at him, then replaced the grate and walked away.

Carter's eyes struggled to adjust to the darkness. Tall, elongated Thark skeletons filled the corners of the dark, foul-smelling space . . . and something else, too. Another figure . . .

"I see the dead."

The voice was raspy but familiar. Carter squinted. "Tars?"

The former Jeddak slumped against a wall, naked and battered. Dozens of tiny wounds covered his body.

He seemed more dead than alive and only half aware of his surroundings.

"The Virginia I knew," Tars said, "he traveled the Iss—"

"Virginia has returned, my friend." Carter bent to examine him. "What have they done to you?"

Tars looked up, seeming to focus on Carter for the first time. "Your once great Jeddak now battles starved banths in the arena." He coughed blood. "When I saw you I wished to believe it was a sign that something new could come into this world. No matter. My daughter is with her mother in paradise. I take comfort in that."

Carter hesitated. "Ah, Tars . . . actually, Sola came back here. With me."

Tars reared up, amazingly fast, and struck Carter full strength. Carter flew across the room, slamming hard against the far wall. The chain and rock followed, almost hitting him.

With a murderous look, Tars Tarkas rose to his full height and began advancing toward the Earthman.

"Tars. No—wait!" Carter held up a hand. "Dejah, Helium. They're about to—"

"*This* is how you repay your debt to me?"

Tars reached out with all four hands and began to choke the life out of the Earthman. Carter gasped, struggled to speak. "Tars—don't—Helium! They're—"

But it was no use. Even wounded, the Thark was far stronger than Carter. Carter felt the iron grip of green hands, saw the dungeon begin to fade into a death haze. His eyes settled on one of the skeletons: *that'll be me soon.*

Then the hands went slack on his neck, and Tars Tarkas passed out from exhaustion.

A huge door swung open and three Thark guards stormed in. They prodded Carter with spears, poking Tars until his eyes snapped open.

"Up. Now!" the first guard said. "We go!"

Carter swatted the spears away, no longer caring what the guards did to him. To his surprise, they backed off and let him help Tars Tarkas to his feet.

"We are finished," Tars said quietly.

"Nonsense." Carter forced a smile. "Leave a Thark his head and one hand and he may yet conquer. Right?"

"Your spirit annoys me."

As the guards led them out, Carter felt a sudden, irrational hope. With Tars Tarkas at his side, he might yet escape.

But not, he knew, without a battle.

Light washed over Carter—glaring, blinding light—as the huge stone wall lifted up, revealing the Thark arena beyond. Beside him, Tars Tarkas tensed for battle.

Crumbling grandstands filled with cheering, chanting Tharks lined the huge amphitheater. A high wall topped with iron spikes separated the arena from the spectators. The arena itself was littered with dry bones and the huge, putrefying carcasses of a half dozen banths.

Carter gestured at the carnage. "This your work?"

Tars nodded wearily.

Behind them the stone wall slammed down, trapping them in the arena. No escape.

High above, in the grandstand, a single figure rose from the wreckage of a carved throne. Tal Hajus raised his arms, and the crowd instantly fell silent.

"Weakness. Sentiment." Tal gestured down at Carter. "Allowing abominations like this white worm to contaminate the horde!"

Again the Tharks cheered.

"We are united because we cull our freaks," the new Jeddak continued. "We are strong because we despise weakness." He glared down the stands at Sola, who sat collared and chained like a dog. Sarkoja, cruel as ever, held her leash.

"Let them be crushed like our unhatched eggs!"

The crowd jeered and began to throw rubble down

into the arena. Tars flinched under the pelting, falling to his knees. Carter moved to protect him but came up short against the chain still bound to his leg. He looked back and saw that the Thark guards had anchored the other end of his chain to a large boulder near the door. Restrained this way, Carter would only be able to reach the center of the arena.

Then a scream rang out—a nightmare cry of predatory hunger, unlike anything Carter had ever heard before. Its near-human fury chilled him on a base, instinctive level.

"Was that a banth?" he asked.

"No." Tars shook his head slowly, eyes filled with dread. "It is a white ape."

On the far side of the arena, an iron gate creaked upward. The white ape burst free: gigantic, four-armed, twice the height and three times the bulk of a Thark, with no visible eyes. It stopped in the center of the arena and sniffed the air blindly, then turned slowly toward Tars and Carter.

The Tharks cheered.

"God almighty," Carter whispered.

The ape howled and charged. Carter reached out to protect the weakened Tars Tarkas—too late. The ape struck out blindly with flailing arms and flung Tars clear across the arena. When Tars crashed down, the ape turned and began trudging back toward him, abandoning Carter for the moment.

Carter took off at a run after the creature. But once again the chain stopped him in his tracks. As he watched, helpless, the ape closed in on the former Jeddak, roaring and thumping the ground.

The Tharks rose to their feet, howling with excitement. Carter caught a quick glimpse of Sola pressing her face between the barrier spikes, eyes wide as she watched Tars's plight. Sarkoja still held tightly to her leash.

Carter tugged at his chain, frustrated beyond belief. He couldn't help Sola, and he couldn't help Tars. Tal Hajus ruled the Tharks now, and Sab Than would soon rule the rest of Barsoom. And Dejah . . . Dejah Thoris . . .

No. He could not let it all fall apart. Not for him, not for the Tharks who'd become his comrades in battle. And especially not for *her*.

Gritting his teeth, Carter reached out and grabbed his chain in both hands. He whipped it up and down, slapping it against the ground as hard as he could. Once, twice, four and five times.

The white ape paused above Tars Tarkas's unmoving body and turned at the noise.

Then it charged Carter.

The ape was upon him quicker than he'd expected. Carter sprang up, sailing over the creature's head, then jerked to a halt in mid-air as the chain reached its end. He slammed hard to the ground, momentarily dazed.

Again the ape charged. Again, Carter leaped.

In the crowd, Tal Hajus turned to a guard and coldly demanded: "Release the other one."

As he landed, the second ape charged him. Carter stared at it for a moment, then whirled around to see the first ape approaching from the other side. He could leap again, but there was no escape now. He looked around frantically, eyes straying from the dead banths to the cheering Tharks—and then Sola flipped herself into the arena, vaulting over the spiked wall.

Sarkoja—still holding Sola's leash—let out a yelp as the leash went taut, flinging Sarkoja up into the air after the younger female. Sarkoja's armor snagged on the spikes, catching her on the wall above the arena. She cursed, waving her sword wildly.

Sola landed in the center of the arena. The apes turned, sniffing the air.

On the floor, Tars Tarkas roused himself. "Sola! Are you mad?"

"No," Sola cried. "The blood of my father drives me!"

Sarkoja wriggled free of the spikes and glared down into the arena. *"Father?"*

Sola gave a sharp tug on the chain, and Sarkoja tumbled down into the arena. Right into the arms of the first white ape.

It howled once, then ripped her in half.

The crowd jeered and booed.

As Carter watched, Sola helped Tars Tarkas to his feet. Barely looking around, Tars reached behind him and plucked a discarded spear from a banth carcass. He hurled it at the second ape, landed it firmly in the beast's chest.

The ape yanked the spear out, howling and bleeding, then took off in a fury after Tars and Sola.

Carter smiled. This was more like it.

He began circling around the first ape, winding his chain around its fearsome body. The ape howled and jerked free, yanking out an entire chunk of the stone wall at the end of the chain. Straining his muscles to the limit, Carter whirled the chain around above his head, with boulder and stone attached, and struck the ape square in the face.

There was a sickening crack, and the ape fell to the ground. Dead.

The other ape was howling in agony, still chasing Sola and Tars around the arena. As they ran past Sarkoja's broken body, Carter called out: *"Sola!"*

Sola ducked sideways, snatched up Sarkoja's sword, and tossed it to Carter, just as the ape began to descend on Sola and Tars.

Carter sprang into action, plucking the sword out of the air. He landed near the two Tharks just as the white ape crushed them all. For a long series of seconds, the arena was still. And then, the point of the sword pierced through the back of the ape. Carter cut his way through the beast, covered in its blood, and the crowd erupted.

When he emerged, sword held high, the Tharks cheered.

"Virginia! Virginia! Virginia!"

Sola led her father away, limping, from the ape's twitching carcass.

Coated with gore, Carter strode boldly toward the grandstand. With a single thrust, he hacked his chain in two, then pointed his sword straight up at Tal Hajus. The Tharks grew silent.

"I claim the right of challenge!" Carter cried.

The crowd gasped.

Tal Hajus stood slowly. He glared down at Carter, but his tone was less confident now. "You have no right of challenge. You are not Thark."

"He *is* Thark!" Tars Tarkas shook his fist. "He is Dotar Sojat!"

Sola started up a new chant: "Do-tar So-jat! Do-tar So-jat!"

Soon the entire crowd was on their feet. "Do-tar So-jat! Do-tar So-jat! Do-tar So-jat!"

A flicker of fear crossed Tal Hajus's face.

Carter swept his sword around, taking in the whole arena. "Who will pledge their metal to mine?"

The Tharks cheered even louder. Tars Tarkas and Sola moved in to join Carter but he waved them back. His attention—and his sword—were focused solely on Tal Hajus.

Tal made his move. He grabbed four swords from the guards attending him, one with each hand. Then he vaulted easily over the spiked wall and into the arena, a fierce war cry on his green lips.

Carter tensed and leaped in response. As he passed Tal Hajus in mid-air, Carter reached out with his sword and sliced. Earth muscles strained as the sword cut into . . . something. It was all happening too fast to see.

Carter landed, catlike, and turned to see Tal Hajus

sneering back at him. For a moment, Carter thought his sword stroke had missed, struck some flying debris by mistake.

Then Tal's perfectly sliced head slid off his torso, falling to land on the arena floor.

Carter looked to the stunned crowd. Once again they began to chant. "Do-tar So-jat! Do-tar So-jat!"

Sola placed a hand on his shoulder, and Tars gave him a weary Thark smile. Carter smiled back . . . then he leaped again, soaring up over the wall to land atop Tal's abandoned throne. Carter scanned the crowd, raised his sword. The Tharks fell back into an obedient silence.

"The Jeddak of Zodanga means to crush Helium this very night," Carter said. "And if Helium falls, so falls Barsoom. We must throw off the yoke of old hatreds. Tharks did not begin this, but by Issus, *Tharks will end it!*"

The crowd went berserk. In the arena below, Tars's eyes shone with pride.

"We ride," Carter screamed, "for Zodanga!"

CHAPTER 15

SAB THAN felt oddly restless as he watched the wedding party file into the Palace of Light. This was his goal, the culmination of everything he'd been working toward. Yet even now, Matai Shang's consciousness squatted on his brain, intruding into his thoughts.

Even this, he thought, *is not mine.*

The cream of Zodangan royalty filed in through one entrance, resplendent in red. From the opposite side, the Heliumites marched in, a sea of blue. The two groups crossed to staircases on either side, climbing to a common balcony beneath the shimmering dome. The wedding would take place on the central dais, where Sab now stood with his five groomsmen and a single bodyguard.

On the other side of the dais, Dejah Thoris approached her father, Tardos Mors. He handed her one end of a ceremonial chain, and they began to speak in low tones.

"Would you like to hear their words?" Matai Shang asked in Sab's mind. Sab nodded, and suddenly he was privy to every word of Tardos and Dejah's conversation. No doubt Matai had another spy planted in the

Helium royal party and was sharing the Thern group consciousness again.

"I know," Tardos said, "this is not the fate you would have chosen, daughter. For yourself, or for Helium. But choice is a luxury, even for a Jeddak of Barsoom. Your heart—"

"A heart is a luxury too," Dejah replied.

Then they turned and began to walk toward the center of the dais. Sab Than stepped toward her, forcing a smile. Dejah's face was hard, emotionless.

"*Easy,*" Matai Shang said to him alone. "*Remember that she is not the prize.*"

The groomsmen moved in on Sab's side, and Dejah's maidens joined her. Sab fell in beside his bride-to-be, and the priestess took up her officiating position before them.

High above, a mirror mounted at the top of the dome flipped over. A beam of moonlight stabbed down to a receptor on the dais—and the dais began to levitate, rising slowly up into the air. When it reached the level of the balcony, the ceremony would begin.

"*The prize is Barsoom,*" Matai said.

Zodanga was easy to find. It hadn't traveled far since Carter's escape, and its path of destruction was visible miles away. When its spires came into view, the Earthman let out a rebel yell, and several hundred mounted Tharks stormed the city's gates.

At Tars Tarkas's command, the Tharks fired off a volley, shattering the main gate to scrap. Tharks poured into the streets, whooping and roaring. Carter tensed himself for resistance, pulling hard on his thoat's reins. He looked around, past the old stone buildings and guard barracks, and saw . . .

Nothing. No crowds, no wedding party, no defenses. No army. Only a few Zodangan guards and civilians running hastily for cover from the green horde.

The Thark charge slowed to a bewildered crawl. Tars Tarkas rode up beside Carter, and they exchanged puzzled glances.

Sola spotted a Zodangan guard hiding in a doorway. She leaped off her thoat and snatched him up, holding him close to her sharp tusks. "Why is Zodanga undefended?" she asked. "Where is everyone?"

"The army's been repositioned outside Helium! Only a small contingent remains." The man squirmed, terrified. "I beg you—have mercy—"

Carter rode up next to them. "Sab and Dejah Thoris. Where are they?"

"At the wedding."

Carter, frustrated beyond belief, drew his sword.

"In *Helium!*" the man cried.

Tars Tarkas rode up behind Carter. "We're in the wrong city?" He smacked the Earthman on the back of the head, a painful blow.

I deserve that, Carter thought.

"It's the only way to get there in time," Carter insisted.

Tars Tarkas fixed him with a steely glare. "Tharks. Do. Not. Fly."

They stood together on the Zodangan Hangar Deck. Tharks loitered around the edges, eyeing the assembled airships warily. Normally the green Martians were fearless, eager to rush into any new situation at their Jeddak's command. But this seemed to be a leap too far.

Carter opened his mouth to argue, then stopped. Time was running out.

"Okay," he said. He gestured to a Thark guard, who tossed him an extra pistol. He strapped on another sword, then hopped onto a one-man flier and kicked it to life.

Woola, faithful Woola, roared in protest. Sola held the beast back. Tars Tarkas approached Carter cautiously. "This is madness, Dotar Sojat. You'll die."

"Then I'll see you down the River Iss!" Carter yelled, over the noise of the flier.

Sola touched his arm. "Follow the canal," she said. "And be careful. Moonlight will force you to fly low."

He nodded, smiled, and shook her off. Lifted his flier into the night sky.

And began his one-man assault on the forces of Helium *and* Zodanga.

As the dark wasteland sped beneath him, Carter realized a startling fact. Since he'd come to Barsoom, this was the first time he'd been alone. And despite the urgency of his mission, he found himself growing pensive.

His former life, back on Earth, seemed unimaginably distant now. He felt a twinge of guilt at the thought, and for just a moment he felt Sarah next to him, her long hair soft against his neck. Silently, sadly, he bade her a final good-bye.

In that moment, he knew what mattered to him. Barsoom—and Dejah Thoris most of all. Carter's old war, his old pain, was gone. Now he had something new to fight for, something worth a man's life. He flicked the flier's light controls, feeding more stored power into the motor. The rush of acceleration forced him back against the seat.

Helium loomed ahead, a glowing jewel in an ocean of dead sand. Carter frowned and banked his flier to the side, scanning the desert before him. Sure enough—it was hard to make out, but a vast fleet of Zodangan ground troops lay scattered on the desert floor ahead, just now fanning out to surround the city. The troops carried no lights, no torches. That would have given them away.

Just as he'd thought. Zodanga was planning to use the royal wedding as a distraction to invade and conquer Helium with overwhelming force. That was why they'd left their own city almost undefended.

Carter grimaced as his flier approached the Zodangan army. A trooper pointed up at him, swiveling a rifle quickly in his direction. But a big officer quickly slapped his hand down.

Carter exhaled in relief. He'd hoped they wouldn't risk giving away their presence by firing. Besides, Carter was riding a Zodangan flier. They probably assumed he was one of their own scouts.

Still, he knew that this was the easy part.

Carter glided over the city walls, cutting his motor to silence. He scanned the spires quickly, spotted a domed palace blazing with light.

Gangway, boys, he thought. *I'm late to the chapel.*

Chapter 16

"LIKE OUR ANCESTORS before us, we gather under the mingled light of Barsoom's first lovers . . . Cluros and Thuria . . ."

For Dejah Thoris, all hope was lost. She stood ramrod-straight on the elevated dais, listening as the priestess sealed her marriage vows. And her doom.

". . . as the moons are joined in celestial union, so do we unite Sab Than and Dejah Thoris. So do we unite Zodanga . . . and Helium."

Sab Than's eyes flickered to hers. But Dejah just stared straight ahead, painfully aware of the hundreds of eyes fixed on her from the balconies. More spectators watched from the floor below, along with half of Helium's royal guard.

The priestess poured clear liquid into a crystal goblet. "In the Time of Oceans, the celestial lovers rose from the sea each night to consummate their love in the sky." She handed the goblet to Sab Than. "Drink now of this holy water, and be wed."

Sab Than drew himself up to full height, held out the goblet in a toast to the congregation. "So may it be again." He turned to Dejah, his eyes seeming to take possession of her. "I am yours forever."

Sab took a long, full drink, then offered the goblet to Dejah. She stared at it for a moment, then took it in both hands.

"And I am yours. Forever."

She lifted the goblet to her lips . . .

Carter burst through the dome, raining shattered glass down on the crowd. Helium guards scurried up and down the balconies, drawing swords and pistols. Carter swooped his flier down and around, circling above the floating dais.

He cried out to Dejah Thoris, who stood shielding her eyes from the falling glass. She lowered her hand and called back, "Carter!"

The ceremonial goblet slipped from her hand, shattering on the dais.

"It's a trap!" he yelled. "Zodanga is at your walls!"

Sab Than stepped in front of Dejah, followed by his retinue of groomsmen. He glared up at Carter, then stopped as his bodyguard grabbed his arm.

When the "bodyguard" spoke, Carter recognized the deep voice of Matai Shang.

"The nanoblade," Matai said to Sab Than. "Now!"

Grimacing, Sab Than pulled a disk from his belt. As Carter watched from above, the familiar blue energy leaped up out of it, weaving itself into a sharp, glowing sword.

Carter sprang off his flier, letting it crash into the balcony. He landed on the far side of the dais, momentarily disoriented. Dejah made a run toward him, but Sab Than grabbed her by the hair, stopping her in her tracks.

Then, as Carter watched, Sab Than levitated upward in a stream of blue energy, dragging the screaming Dejah with him by her hair. He soared all the way up to the very top of the cracked dome, to the mirror that fed power down to the dais's receptor.

Sab held up the blue sword, and for a moment Carter thought he was going to slit Dejah's throat. Then Sab reached out with its blade and flipped the mirror upward, sending a bright beam of reflected moonlight shooting up into the night sky.

"Helium falls!" Sab Than cried.

It was the sign, Carter knew. The signal for Zodanga to invade in force.

But it was more than that. Deprived of its power source, the dais plummeted downward, crashing to the floor below. Carter lost his balance, toppling into an elderly Heliumite couple scrambling to avoid the falling platform. He muttered apologies, then threw them to safety as the first wave of Zodangan soldiers poured in the door.

The room erupted in chaos. Zodangans opened fire, mowing down stunned Heliumites. Carter drew his sword and glanced back upward to see Sab Than and his five groomsmen suspended in mid-air, held aloft by the crackling blue Thern energy. Dejah Thoris still hung by her hair in Sab's grip, struggling but held fast. The hovering groomsmen pulled out their own blue disks and morphed them into fiery blue guns. They rained down fire on the soldiers and scientists of Helium. Carter dodged to the side, barely escaping the deadly barrage.

Then Dejah Thoris pulled out her jeweled hair comb and stabbed it into Sab's hand. He screamed, released her.

Carter leaped, arcing over the fallen, shattered dais. He caught Dejah in both arms, swooping past the floating groomsmen. They turned, momentarily startled, as Carter and Dejah sailed by.

When they landed, she gave him a brief, intense look. "So you have changed your metal."

He nodded. "And my heart."

"If you'll just get behind me, sir."

She grabbed his sword and thrust it through an attacking Zodangan, impaling him. Then she swung wide, slicing into two more men.

Carter smiled as he dodged two other Zodangan swordsmen. He elbowed one into the other, knocking them off balance, and grabbed both their blades as they fell.

From the balcony, Tardos Mors cried out as blue fire assaulted him. Dejah Thoris broke away from Carter to help her father. As she ran, she fired at the five floating groomsmen. Carter watched her with pure admiration. He turned quickly to follow her—and then Sab Than was upon him, furious, swinging his deadly blue nanoblade. Carter ducked behind a pillar, and Sab's blade sliced through it like butter. The next stroke made contact with Carter's first sword, chipping off the tip. Carter stumbled backward, edging down a small flight of stairs.

Sab Than smiled, cruel and confident.

Carter parried the next blow, but the nanoblade sliced his sword in half. Carter gasped, barely managing to raise his remaining sword in time.

He realized grimly that whatever Thern science or magic was at play here, mere swordsmanship wasn't going to defeat it. Sab had him, and the Zodangan knew it. Meticulously, one stroke at a time, Sab whittled Carter's blades down to blunt nubs.

At last Sab backed him up against a wall. Sab leveled his black glowing blade against Carter's throat, his hot breath foul on the Earthman's face.

"When you are dead," Sab hissed, "when Helium is mine . . . *she* will be mine too."

Carter darted a glance past him to the balcony, where Tardos Mors, Kantos Kan, and Dejah Thoris crouched behind a pillar, making their last stand against several regiments of red-clad Zodangan troops swarmed through the palace, making short bloody work of the remaining Helium forces.

No, Carter thought, squirming back from Sab's hot blade on his throat. *It can't end this way.*

Then the palace itself seemed to implode. People screamed, Zodangans and Heliumites alike running for cover as the dome's framework toppled inward. Sab stumbled but maintained his grip on Carter. Together they watched as a heavy Zodangan personnel transport wobbled, toppled, and crashed down to the floor stern first, cracking the ancient stonework.

Time seemed to stand still as the transport's hatch

creaked open. Then Tars Tarkas climbed out, looking a bit dazed.

"Thank the Goddess that's over with," he said.

Sola appeared behind him, and then a hundred more Tharks spilled out of the transport. At the sight of the green warriors, both the Zodangans and the Heliumites panicked. *"Tharks!"*

Even Sab Than gasped, momentarily surprised. Seizing the moment, Carter dove and jabbed his sword's blunt nub into Sab's leg, impaling him by sheer force. Sab roared in pain, hacking and slashing wildly at Carter. But Carter was already leaping free.

"Virginia!" Tars Tarkas cried.

Carter turned as Tars flung his sword. Carter caught it by the hilt and, in one fluid motion, sliced off Sab Than's entire sword arm. Sab howled, a blood-curdling cry of pain that mingled with the buzz of one-man fliers ridden by the remaining Tharks. They swooped down into the roofless dome, firing mounted guns. Three of the floating groomsmen fell before their fury.

Maybe Tharks never flew before, Carter thought. *But they sure learn fast.*

He whirled toward Dejah, saw that the two remaining groomsmen still held her and her father pinned under fire. Carter crouched to spring to her aid—and then Sola and Woola swooped past him on a one-man flier heading straight for the groomsmen. Sola held out her sword, impaling one assassin in mid-air. Woola bounded, roaring, and chomped down hard on the other's torso. They landed in a ball, Woola whooping and yowling over his prey.

Dejah grinned upward, and Sola grinned back.

"The Tharks," Tardos Mors said, amazed. "By Issus, they're fighting *with* us!"

And so they were. Throughout the palace Tharks swarmed, firing and slashing—but only at the red-caped Zodangans. A Heliumite flashed his blue uniform at Tars Tarkas, and the Thark grinned in response, moving on to his next target.

Carter whipped his head down to see Sab Than moaning, clutching his bleeding arm-stump. Carter jabbed his sword at the Zodangan's throat.

"The Therns," Carter said. "You're gonna spit out everything you know about them."

Sab Than flinched in pain, nodded. "Spare me and I will tell you—"

Then Sab stopped, eyes flicking in fear to his own severed arm, lying nearby. The nanoweb of the weapon was crawling off of it, oozing across the floor toward

Sab himself. "No," the Zodangan said. "No, you can't. I've done everything. I've—I've served the Goddess . . ."

But as Carter watched in horror, the web reached Sab and crept up over his face, into his mouth and nose. Sab began to choke, to spasm, gasping hopelessly for air—strangled by his own unearthly weapon.

When Sab Than lay dead, the web seemed to recede, moving away—toward Carter. The Earthman turned to leap, but it was too late. The web oozed onto Carter's sword and up his arm. He shook his sword, eyes casting around frantically as the eerie substance crawled slowly toward his face . . . and then he saw it. A green Thark, up on the balcony, manipulating a Thern bracelet. Medallion around his neck.

As if from nowhere, Dejah Thoris's well-aimed sword struck the fake Thark's bracelet. The instant it shattered, the nanoweb evaporated from Carter's body, dissipating into the air.

Up on the balcony, Dejah pointed her sword at the Thark. He grinned, shape-shifted—and then Matai Shang stood before her.

Dejah had not seen Matai's transformations before; she stepped back in amazement. Matai Shang took immediate advantage, transforming into a duplicate of Dejah herself. "Your Highness," he said. As she stood, astonished, he reached out and snatched her sword away.

"Dejah!" Carter called. All around him, Tharks still sparred with Zodangans, but all he could see was *her*. In one smooth motion, he sprang up onto the balcony—just as Matai-Dejah brought the sword up around the real Dejah's neck.

"A fitting solution to your setback, wouldn't you say, Captain?" The Thern smiled with Dejah's face. "Dejah Thoris survives her assassins, but fails to prove her misguided theory of the Ninth Ray."

"You don't have to do this," Carter said.

"Oh, I know. But I think she—I mean, *I*—will enjoy playing out this particular scenario."

Teeth gritted, the real Dejah ripped the medallion off her captor's neck and tossed it to Carter. He caught it handily, smiling as Matai's eyes went wide.

"You want it?" Carter asked, then hurled the medallion into the seething fray below. It vanished into the battling mob of Zodangans, Tharks, and Heliumite guards.

Sneering back, Matai threw Dejah off the balcony.

Carter leaped immediately and caught her in midair. Dejah pointed downward. "He's—I'm—no, *he's* getting away!"

Carter landed on the lip of the balcony, placing

Dejah down gently. When he turned to look, Matai was already floating down toward the floor. The Thern morphed several times in rapid succession: Zodangan, Heliumite, Zodangan again. Then he disappeared into the crowd.

"The medallion," Dejah said.

Carter nodded, turned, and vaulted off the balcony. He landed on a piece of jagged debris between two brawling groups of Zodangans and Tharks. Then an oddly familiar voice rang out.

"Tars. The medallion!"

Carter turned to see *himself* reaching out toward Tars Tarkas. Tars stood holding the medallion, hesitating.

"Give it to me, my Jeddak."

Carter yelled to Tars, leaping over the crowd toward the Thark. He saw Tars's eyes dart from the real John Carter, arcing toward him in mid-air, to the disguised Matai Shang, still holding out his hand for the medallion.

Tars made his decision. He swung his sword straight at Matai-Carter just as the real Carter soared down out of the air, also swinging.

And then Matai was gone. Tars Tarkas's sword sliced through open air, nicking the real Carter on the neck. The Thark jumped back, his eyes darting around warily.

Carter mopped blood off his neck and looked around. The last of the Zodangans were being marched off by a dual force of Heliumites and Tharks—the red and green people of Barsoom, working together at last.

No trace remained of the blue energy, or the Thern weapons.

Tars Tarkas crossed to Carter and placed a hand on his shoulder. "You are my Jeddak now. And you have won." He grinned. "All is finished."

Carter turned as Dejah ran down from the balcony toward him, her arms spread wide. Her face was bruised, her wedding dress shredded, her hair smeared with blood. An Earthman would have recoiled at the sight of her.

She was the most beautiful thing Carter had ever seen.

"No," he said. "Not quite finished."

They embraced with a fire and a passion unique on two worlds. And in the ruined Palace of Helium, all eyes turned, with great curiosity, to learn the meaning of their new Jeddak's words.

Chapter 17

". . . WE GATHER under the mingled light of Barsoom's first lovers, Cluros and Thuria . . ."

Once again the words rang out under the shattered palace dome. But this time, Tardos Mors spoke them with joy and pride. And the lovers who stood on the broken dais, amid dust and rubble and spilled blood, were Princess Dejah Thoris and Captain John Carter.

Carter smiled at Dejah, raising the goblet to drink. Then he stopped and glanced down at the twin rings on his finger. He pulled them off, held them up to the light, and studied them one last time. Then he placed them down tenderly on a silver tray and allowed Sola to take them away.

Carter drank deep, then handed the goblet to Dejah. She drained it, sealing their union.

"By the ancient rite of moon and water," Tardos continued, "you are bound together. Husband and wife."

They kissed like long-lost lovers, like worlds reunited after centuries apart. The palace erupted in a thunderous cheer.

• • •

But that night, Carter found himself restless. He rose from their wedding bed, taking care not to wake Dejah Thoris, and strode out onto the balcony. Helium lay spread out below, battered but unbroken, a many-faceted jewel of life and light.

"John?"

Dejah walked up behind him, wrapping her silk-covered arms around him. She felt warm, comforting.

"Homesick for the Thark nursery?"

He smiled. "I'm sorry. I just had that feeling you get, suddenly . . . that you've left a light burning. Or a door open, maybe."

She cocked her head at him, questioningly.

"Go back to bed." He stroked her cheek. "I won't be long."

She took his hand and kissed it. "Don't be, John Carter of Earth."

After she was gone, he left the chamber, strolling up several flights of stairs. Up here, a small terrace overlooked the vast chasm dividing the two halves of Helium. Woola scampered up to join him, yelping, startling the lone guard at his post.

Carter stared up into the night sky. A blue-green star caught his eye: Earth. He reached into his boot and pulled out the medallion. Six simple words could transport him all the way across that distance . . .

"John Carter of Earth," he whispered.

With all his strength, he hurled the medallion out over the terrace. Woola barreled to the balcony's edge to fetch it, then stopped, staring down into the blackness of the chasm. He turned and grunted at Carter.

"You're right." Carter rubbed the animal's muzzle. "John Carter of *Mars* sounds much better."

When they returned to the bottom of the stairs, the guard bowed low, dropping to one knee.

"Sire, I must express the deepest of gratitude. You saved all Helium—"

"Please." Carter held up a hand. "The honor's mine."

He bent down, helped the guard to rise—and Woola growled.

"Fair enough, Earthman."

The guard gripped Carter's hand tight. Too late, Carter watched as he morphed into the deadly shape of Matai Shang.

"My people play this game in moves that last for centuries," Matai said. "Did you think one setback would drive us from Barsoom forever?"

Then Carter saw the medallion in Matai's hand.

The Thern shot out his other hand, touching Carter's bare chest. *"Och Ohem,"* Matai recited. *"Och Tay. Wyees Jasoom."*

The medallion pulsed. Woola yowled. Matai Shang sneered in triumph.

Carter felt a deep shudder ripple through his body, a wrenching sensation he'd only felt once before.

No, he tried to say. *No, not now!* But he was paralyzed, unable to speak. The medallion flared bright, nine legs of light spreading out like hot blue mandibles. And in a burst of light, John Carter vanished.

In the cave, a lone shaft of moonlight danced across the vein of gold.

Carter shot upright—and pain lanced through his stiff body. Old, decaying clothes cracked and ripped, shredding to powder. He coughed, shaking dust off his face. Every muscle ached, atrophied after years of stasis.

Then he saw the skeleton that had been Colonel Powell. A few shreds of Union braid still hung from the rags of his uniform.

Carter lurched to his feet, fighting the pain. He searched the remains of his pockets, his shirt, and then dropped to his knees and began scrabbling in the dirt. "No," he whispered. "No. No . . ."

Nothing. No medallion.

He lurched over to the large rock, the one with the nine-legged spider carved across its surface. He slapped a hand against it frantically, desperately.

"*Och Ohem*," he gasped. "*Och Tay, Wyees Barsoom. Och Tay! Wyees BARSOOM!*"

Weathered fingers dug into the rock, clutched frantically at the etching. Traced its pattern beneath his hand.

"Barsoom," Carter said weakly. But it was no use.

Captain Carter was back on Earth.

CHAPTER 18

. . . FIFTY *million miles apart, and no way to bridge the gap. No way to telegraph myself back, to return my body and soul to their true home. Like a fool, I had thrown away my medallion back on Barsoom.*

I stepped outside the cave and stared into the dark Arizona sky, so familiar and yet so cold. So alien, now.

And then I thought of Matai Shang, of his knowledge of Earth and our history. That meant the Therns were a presence on this world as well as on Mars. This cave in Arizona, its carvings and the Thern I'd killed there, were proof of that.

There might be other places. Other Thern way stations, hidden somewhere on Earth.

As soon as I realized that, I knew what my gold must be used for.

For ten bitter years, dear nephew, I searched. I followed every possible trail of rumor and legend, from darkest Africa to the Arctic wastelands. At times I despaired of ever locating the Therns again.

And then, in the Orkney Islands of Scotland, I found them.

I shall spare you the tedious details, but suffice it to say: I managed to obtain a medallion. But before I could return to Barsoom, there were many plans I had to make in secret. And the Earthbound Therns were now following my movements closely, plotting to reclaim the property I had taken from them.

I can trust no one. Except you.

No doubt much of this is puzzling to you. But I promise that soon you will understand the cause of my sudden death, my bizarre funeral instructions, and the reason the mausoleum door can only be opened from the inside. One thing I have learned from the Therns: if my body dies on Earth, then its "copy" shall also perish on Mars.

Know this: you are the key, Edgar. This is the task I entrust to you, along with all my worldly fortune. Protect my body, for the Therns will attempt to destroy it. Indeed, in the time it has taken you to read these pages, they may already have done so.

I slammed my uncle's journal shut and leaped up, the implications of his words ringing in my mind. I rushed out of the study and outside, dashing through the night air across the pathways and hedgerows.

In the dark, I almost slammed up against the mausoleum. I ran my hands all along its surface, searching frantically. Nothing. No indentation, no keyhole, no depression of any kind.

You are the key, Uncle Jack had written. *The key.* But where was the lock?

Then I noticed the epitaph written above the door: INTER MUNDOS. My eyes darted to the letter E, then to D. E-D. Edgar.

I pressed the two letters in succession.

Nothing.

I stood frustrated for a long moment. Then I remembered the telegram, the strange missive that had brought me here in the first place. I fished it out of my vest pocket and smoothed its crumpled surface.

DEAR NED
SEE ME AT ONCE

"Ned," I said aloud. And I remembered one of Uncle Jack's quirks: he never called me Edgar.

I reached back up to the inscription on the tomb and pressed the letters N-E-D in succession.

The door rolled open on well-oiled gears.

I stepped forward, peering into the dark. And stopped short at the sight that greeted me.

An empty casket. In an empty tomb.

A sudden movement caught my attention, and I whirled around just in time to avoid a plunging dagger. A wiry man in black suit and bowler hat reared back and raised the dagger again, aiming straight for my chest. I cringed, knowing this was my doom. I have never been a fighter.

Then a gunshot rang out, and the man fell to the ground.

Behind him stood my uncle, Captain John Carter. His revolver still smoking.

"Good lord," I said, stunned. "It's you."

Carter smiled. "Hello, Ned."

He pulled a small vial from his pocket, tossed it to me.

"Toxin derived from the puffer fish," he said. "Simulates death."

He knelt down and began to examine the assassin's body.

I stared at the vial, beginning to understand. "You never found a medallion. In the Orkneys or anywhere else."

"No. But I was right about the Therns." He ripped

open the bowler-hat man's shirt to reveal a Thern medallion, adorned with the nine-legged spider design. "That's why I'm so grateful to you for bringing me one."

"I was just . . . bait?"

"No, no." He stood, moved tenderly toward me. "You're far more than that. I really do need a protector . . . that is, if you're willing."

Suddenly I was overwhelmed by emotion. I clasped my uncle in a fierce bear hug, almost knocking him over. He returned the embrace, then patted me firmly on the back and handed me his pistol.

Then, as I watched, he stepped into the mausoleum. The medallion seemed to glow slightly in his hand.

"Good-bye, Ned," he said. "Oh, and Ned? You should take up a cause. Fall in love. Write a book, maybe."

"Can't you stay a bit longer?" I asked.

He shook his head, straining at the heavy door from inside. "It's time I went home."

The door slammed shut.

Write a book, he'd said. And so I have.

There's one more thing. As I stood outside the tomb, pistol heavy in my hand, I could just make out my uncle's muffled voice from within. *"Och Ohem. Och Tay . . . Wyees . . ."*

And then—for just a second—I thought I heard

a woman's voice entwine with his. A rich, deep voice, born of a world where savage women fought alongside men for a cause greater than themselves. The voice of a true princess of Mars, welcoming her warrior husband home.

". . . Barsoom," she said.

"Barsoom," he echoed.

Within the tomb, there was a brief flash of light. And for the last time, John Carter was gone.

END

(A Princess of Mars)

Chapter I

𝄐𝄐 𝄐𝄐𝄐 𝄐𝄐𝄐𝄐𝄐 𝄐𝄐𝄐𝄐𝄐

(On the Arizona Hills)

I AM A VERY OLD MAN; how old I do not know. Possibly I am a hundred, possibly more; but I cannot tell because I have never aged as other men, nor do I remember any childhood. So far as I can recollect I have always been a man, a man of about thirty. I appear today as I did forty years and more ago, and yet I feel that I cannot go on living forever; that some day I shall die the real death from which there is no resurrection. I do not know why I should fear death, I who have died twice and am still alive; but yet I have the same horror of it as you who have never died, and it is because of this terror of death, I believe, that I am so convinced of my mortality.

And because of this conviction I have determined to write down the story of the interesting periods of my life and of my death. I cannot explain the phenomena; I can only set down here in the words of an ordinary soldier of fortune a chronicle of the strange events that befell me during the ten years that my dead body lay undiscovered in an Arizona cave.

I have never told this story, nor shall mortal man see this manuscript until after I have passed over for eternity. I know that the average human mind will not believe what it cannot grasp, and so I do not purpose being pilloried by the public, the pulpit, and the press, and held up as a colossal liar when I am but telling the simple truths which some day science will substantiate. Possibly the suggestions which I gained upon Mars, and the knowledge which I can set down in this chronicle, will aid in an earlier understanding of the mysteries of our sister planet; mysteries to you, but no longer mysteries to me.

My name is John Carter; I am better known as Captain Jack Carter of Virginia. At the close of the Civil War I found myself possessed of several hundred thousand dollars (Confederate) and a captain's commission in the cavalry arm of an army which no longer existed; the servant of a state which had vanished with the hopes of the South. Masterless, penniless, and with my only means of livelihood, fighting, gone, I determined to work my way to the southwest and attempt to retrieve my fallen fortunes in a search for gold.

I spent nearly a year prospecting in company with another Confederate officer, Captain James K. Powell of Richmond. We were extremely fortunate, for late in the winter of 1865, after many hardships and privations, we located the most remarkable gold-bearing quartz vein that our wildest dreams had ever pictured. Powell, who was a mining engineer by education, stated that we had uncovered over a million dollars worth of ore in a trifle over three months.

As our equipment was crude in the extreme we decided that one of us must return to civilization, purchase the necessary machinery and return with a sufficient force of men properly to work the mine.

As Powell was familiar with the country, as well as with the mechanical requirements of mining we determined that it would be best for him to make the trip. It was agreed that I was to hold down our claim against the remote possibility of its being jumped by some wandering prospector.

On March 3, 1866, Powell and I packed his provisions on two of our burros, and bidding me good-bye he mounted his horse, and started down the mountainside toward the valley, across which led the first stage of his journey.

The morning of Powell's departure was, like nearly all Arizona mornings, clear and beautiful; I could see him and his little pack animals picking their way down the mountainside toward the valley, and all during the morning I would catch occasional glimpses of them as they topped a hog back or came out upon a level plateau. My last sight of Powell was about three in the afternoon as he entered the shadows of the range on the opposite side of the valley.

Some half hour later I happened to glance casually across the valley and was much surprised to note three little dots in about the same place I had last seen my friend and his two pack animals. I am not given to needless worrying, but the more I tried to convince myself that all was well with Powell, and that the dots I had seen on his trail were antelope or wild horses, the less I was able to assure myself.

Since we had entered the territory we had not seen a hostile Indian, and we had, therefore, become careless in the extreme, and were wont to ridicule the stories we had heard of the great numbers of these vicious marauders that were supposed to haunt the trails, taking their toll in lives and torture of every white party which fell into their merciless clutches.

Powell, I knew, was well armed and, further, an experienced Indian fighter; but I too had lived and fought for years among the Sioux in the North, and I knew that his chances were small against a party of cunning trailing Apaches. Finally I could endure the suspense no longer, and, arming myself with my two Colt revolvers and a carbine, I strapped two belts of cartridges about me and catching my saddle horse, started down the trail taken by Powell in the morning.

As soon as I reached comparatively level ground I urged my mount into a canter and continued this, where the going permitted, until, close upon dusk, I discovered the point where other tracks joined those of Powell. They were the tracks of unshod ponies, three of them, and the ponies had been galloping.

I followed rapidly until, darkness shutting down, I was forced to await the rising of the moon, and given an opportunity to speculate on the question of the wisdom of my chase. Possibly I had conjured up impossible dangers, like some nervous old housewife, and when I should catch up with Powell would get a good laugh for my pains. However, I am not prone to sensitiveness, and the following of a sense of duty, wherever it may lead, has always been a kind of fetich with me throughout my life; which may account for the honors bestowed upon me by three republics and the decorations and friendships of an old and powerful emperor and several lesser kings, in whose service my sword has been red many a time.

About nine o'clock the moon was sufficiently bright for me to proceed on my way and I had no difficulty in following the trail at a fast walk, and in some places at a brisk trot until, about midnight, I reached the water hole where Powell had expected to camp. I came upon the spot unexpectedly, finding it entirely deserted, with no signs of having been recently occupied as a camp.

I was interested to note that the tracks of the pursuing horsemen, for such I was now convinced they must be, continued after Powell with only a brief stop at the hole for water; and always at the same rate of speed as his.

I was positive now that the trailers were Apaches and that they wished to capture Powell alive for the fiendish pleasure of the torture, so I urged my horse onward at a most dangerous pace, hoping against hope that I would catch up with the red rascals before they attacked him.

Further speculation was suddenly cut short by the faint report of two shots far ahead of me. I knew that Powell would need me now if ever, and I instantly urged my horse to his topmost speed up the narrow and difficult mountain trail.

I had forged ahead for perhaps a mile or more without hearing further sounds, when the trail suddenly debouched onto a small, open plateau near the summit of the pass. I had passed through a narrow, overhanging gorge just before entering suddenly upon this table land, and the sight which met my eyes filled me with consternation and dismay.

The little stretch of level land was white with Indian tepees, and there were probably half a thousand red warriors clustered around some object near the center of the camp. Their attention was so wholly riveted to this point of interest that they did not notice me, and I easily could have turned back into the dark recesses of the gorge and made my escape with perfect safety. The fact, however, that this thought did not occur to me until the following day removes any possible right to a claim to heroism to which the narration of this episode might possibly otherwise entitle me.

I do not believe that I am made of the stuff which constitutes heroes, because, in all of the hundreds of instances that my voluntary acts have placed me face to face with death, I cannot recall a single one where any alternative step to that I took occurred to me until many hours later. My mind is evidently so constituted that I am subconsciously forced into the path of duty without recourse to tiresome mental processes. However that may be, I have never regretted that cowardice is not optional with me.

In this instance I was, of course, positive that Powell was the center of attraction, but whether I thought or acted first I do not know, but within an instant from the moment the scene broke upon my view I had whipped out my revolvers and was charging down upon the entire army of warriors, shooting rapidly, and whooping at the top of my lungs. Singlehanded, I could not have pursued better tactics, for the red men, convinced by sudden surprise that not less than a regiment of regulars was upon them, turned and fled in every direction for their bows, arrows, and rifles.

The view which their hurried routing disclosed filled me with apprehension and with rage. Under the clear rays of the Arizona moon lay Powell, his body fairly bristling with the hostile arrows of the braves. That he was already dead I could not but be convinced, and yet I would have saved his body from mutilation at the hands of the Apaches as quickly as I would have saved the man himself from death.

Riding close to him I reached down from the saddle, and grasping his cartridge belt drew him up across the withers of my mount. A backward glance convinced me that to return by the way I had come would be more hazardous than to continue across the plateau, so, putting spurs to my poor beast, I made a dash for the opening to the pass which I could distinguish on the far side of the table land.

The Indians had by this time discovered that I was alone and I was pursued with imprecations, arrows, and rifle balls. The fact that it is difficult to aim anything but imprecations accurately by moonlight, that they were upset by the sudden and unexpected manner of my advent, and that I was a rather rapidly moving target saved me from the various deadly projectiles of the enemy and permitted me to reach the shadows of the surrounding peaks before an orderly pursuit could be organized.

My horse was traveling practically unguided as I knew that I had probably less knowledge of the exact location of the trail to the pass than he, and thus it happened that he entered a defile which led to the summit of the range and not to the pass which I had hoped would carry me to the valley and to safety. It is probable, however, that to this fact I owe my life and the remarkable experiences and adventures which befell me during the following ten years.

My first knowledge that I was on the wrong trail came when I heard the yells of the pursuing savages suddenly grow fainter and fainter far off to my left.

I knew then that they had passed to the left of the jagged rock formation at the edge of the plateau, to the right of which my horse had borne me and the body of Powell.

I drew rein on a little level promontory overlooking the trail below and to my left, and saw the party of pursuing savages disappearing around the point of a neighboring peak.

I knew the Indians would soon discover that they were on the wrong trail and that the search for me would be renewed in the right direction as soon as they located my tracks.

I had gone but a short distance further when what seemed to be an excellent trail opened up around the face of a high cliff. The trail was level and quite broad and led upward and in the general direction I wished to go. The cliff arose for several hundred feet on my right, and on my left was an equal and nearly perpendicular drop to the bottom of a rocky ravine.

I had followed this trail for perhaps a hundred yards when a sharp turn to the right brought me to the mouth of a large cave. The opening was about four feet in height and three to four feet wide, and at this opening the trail ended.

It was now morning, and, with the customary lack of dawn which is a startling characteristic of Arizona, it had become daylight almost without warning.

Dismounting, I laid Powell upon the ground, but the most painstaking examination failed to reveal the faintest spark of life. I forced water from my canteen between his dead lips, bathed his face and rubbed his hands, working over him continuously for the better part of an hour in the face of the fact that I knew him to be dead.

I was very fond of Powell; he was thoroughly a man in every respect; a polished southern gentleman; a staunch and true friend; and it was with a feeling of the deepest grief that I finally gave up my crude endeavors at resuscitation.

Leaving Powell's body where it lay on the ledge I crept into the cave to reconnoiter. I found a large chamber, possibly a hundred feet in diameter and thirty or forty feet in height; a smooth and well-worn floor, and many other evidences that the cave had, at some remote period, been inhabited. The back of the cave was so lost in dense shadow that I could not distinguish whether there were openings into other apartments or not.

As I was continuing my examination I commenced to feel a pleasant drowsiness creeping over me which I attributed to the fatigue of my long and strenuous ride, and the reaction from the excitement of the fight and the pursuit. I felt comparatively safe in my present location as I knew that one man could defend the trail to the cave against an army.

I soon became so drowsy that I could scarcely resist the strong desire to throw myself on the floor of the cave for a few moments' rest, but I knew that this would never do, as it would mean certain death at the hands of my red friends, who might be upon me at any moment. With an effort I started toward the opening of the cave only to reel drunkenly against a side wall, and from there slip prone upon the floor.

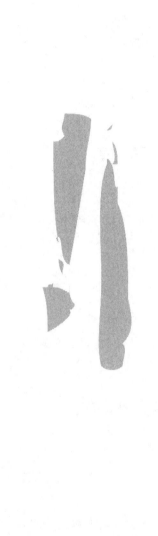

Chapter II
⚹𝄃 𝄃𝄃𝄃𝄃𝄃 𝄃𝄃 ⚹𝄃 𝄃𝄃𝄃

(The Escape of the Dead)

A SENSE OF DELICIOUS dreaminess overcame me, my muscles relaxed, and I was on the point of giving way to my desire to sleep when the sound of approaching horses reached my ears. I attempted to spring to my feet but was horrified to discover that my muscles refused to respond to my will. I was now thoroughly awake, but as unable to move a muscle as though turned to stone. It was then, for the first time, that I noticed a slight vapor filling the cave. It was extremely tenuous and only noticeable against the opening which led to daylight. There also came to my nostrils a faintly pungent odor, and I could only assume that I had been overcome by some poisonous gas, but why I should retain my mental faculties and yet be unable to move I could not fathom.

I lay facing the opening of the cave and where I could see the short stretch of trail which lay between the cave and the turn of the cliff around which the trail led. The noise of the approaching horses had ceased, and I judged the Indians were creeping stealthily upon me along the little ledge which led to my living tomb. I remember that I hoped they would make short work of me as I did not particularly relish the thought of the innumerable things they might do to me if the spirit prompted them.

I had not long to wait before a stealthy sound apprised me of their nearness, and then a war-bonneted, paint-streaked face was thrust cautiously around the shoulder of the cliff, and savage eyes looked into mine. That he could see me in the dim light of the cave I was sure for the early morning sun was falling full upon me through the opening.

The fellow, instead of approaching, merely stood and stared; his eyes bulging and his jaw dropped. And then another savage face appeared, and a third and fourth and fifth, craning their necks over the shoulders of their fellows whom they could not pass upon the narrow ledge. Each face was the picture of awe and fear, but for what reason I did not know, nor did I learn until ten years later. That there were still other braves behind those who regarded me was apparent from the fact that the leaders passed back whispered word to those behind them.

Suddenly a low but distinct moaning sound issued from the recesses of the cave behind me, and, as it reached the ears of the Indians, they turned and fled in terror, panic-stricken. So frantic were their efforts to escape from the unseen thing behind me that one of the braves was hurled headlong from the cliff to the rocks below. Their wild cries echoed in the canyon for a short time, and then all was still once more.

The sound which had frightened them was not repeated, but it had been sufficient as it was to start me speculating on the possible horror which lurked in the shadows at my back. Fear is a relative term and so I can only measure my feelings at that time by what I had experienced in previous positions of danger and by those I have passed through since; but I can say without shame that if the sensations I endured during the next few minutes were fear, then may God help the coward, for cowardice is of a surety its own punishment.

To be held paralyzed, with one's back toward some horrible and unknown danger from the very sound of which the ferocious Apache warriors turn in wild stampede, as a flock of sheep would madly flee from a pack of wolves, seems to me the last word in fearsome predicaments for a man who had ever been used to fighting for his life with all the energy of a powerful physique.

Several times I thought I heard faint sounds behind me as of somebody moving cautiously, but eventually even these ceased, and I was left to the contemplation of my position without interruption. I could but vaguely conjecture the cause of my paralysis, and my only hope lay in that it might pass off as suddenly as it had fallen upon me.

Late in the afternoon my horse, which had been standing with dragging rein before the cave, started slowly down the trail, evidently in search of food and water, and I was left alone with my mysterious unknown companion and the dead body of my friend, which lay just within my range of vision upon the ledge where I had placed it in the early morning.

From then until possibly midnight all was silence, the silence of the dead; then, suddenly, the awful moan of the morning broke upon my startled ears, and there came again from the black shadows the sound of a moving thing, and a faint rustling as of dead leaves. The shock to my already overstrained nervous system was terrible in the extreme, and with a superhuman effort I strove to break my awful bonds. It was an effort of the mind, of the will, of the nerves; not muscular, for I could not move even so much as my little finger, but none the less mighty for all that. And then something gave, there was a momentary feeling of nausea, a sharp click as of the snapping of a steel wire, and I stood with my back against the wall of the cave facing my unknown foe.

And then the moonlight flooded the cave, and there

before me lay my own body as it had been lying all these hours, with the eyes staring toward the open ledge and the hands resting limply upon the ground. I looked first at my lifeless clay there upon the floor of the cave and then down at myself in utter bewilderment; for there I lay clothed, and yet here I stood but naked as at the minute of my birth.

The transition had been so sudden and so unexpected that it left me for a moment forgetful of aught else than my strange metamorphosis. My first thought was, is this then death! Have I indeed passed over forever into that other life! But I could not well believe this, as I could feel my heart pounding against my ribs from the exertion of my efforts to release myself from the anaesthesis which had held me. My breath was coming in quick, short gasps, cold sweat stood out from every pore of my body, and the ancient experiment of pinching revealed the fact that I was anything other than a wraith.

Again was I suddenly recalled to my immediate surroundings by a repetition of the weird moan from the depths of the cave. Naked and unarmed as I was, I had no desire to face the unseen thing which menaced me.

My revolvers were strapped to my lifeless body which, for some unfathomable reason, I could not bring myself to touch. My carbine was in its boot, strapped to my saddle, and as my horse had wandered off I was left without means of defense. My only alternative seemed to lie in flight and my decision was crystallized by a recurrence of the rustling sound from the thing which now seemed, in the darkness of the cave and to my distorted imagination, to be creeping stealthily upon me.

Unable longer to resist the temptation to escape this horrible place I leaped quickly through the opening into the starlight of a clear Arizona night. The crisp, fresh mountain air outside the cave acted as an immediate tonic and I felt new life and new courage coursing through me. Pausing upon the brink of the ledge I upbraided myself for what now seemed to me wholly unwarranted apprehension. I reasoned with myself that I had lain helpless for many hours within the cave, yet nothing had molested me, and my better judgment, when permitted the direction of clear and logical reasoning, convinced me that the noises I had heard must have resulted from purely natural and harmless causes; probably the conformation of the cave was such that a slight breeze had caused the sounds I heard.

I decided to investigate, but first I lifted my head to fill my lungs with the pure, invigorating night air of the mountains. As I did so I saw stretching far below me the beautiful vista of rocky gorge, and level, cacti-studded flat, wrought by the moonlight into a miracle of soft splendor and wondrous enchantment.

Few western wonders are more inspiring than the beauties of an Arizona moonlit landscape; the silvered mountains in the distance, the strange lights and shadows upon hog back and arroyo, and the grotesque details of the stiff, yet beautiful cacti form a picture at once enchanting and inspiring; as though one were catching for the first time a glimpse of some dead and forgotten world, so different is it from the aspect of any other spot upon our earth.

As I stood thus meditating, I turned my gaze from the landscape to the heavens where the myriad stars formed a gorgeous and fitting canopy for the wonders of the earthly scene. My attention was quickly riveted by a large red star close to the distant horizon. As I gazed upon it I felt a spell of overpowering fascination—it was Mars, the god of war, and for me, the fighting man, it had always held the power of irresistible enchantment. As I gazed at it on that far-gone night it seemed to call across the unthinkable void, to lure me to it, to draw me as the lodestone attracts a particle of iron.

My longing was beyond the power of opposition; I closed my eyes, stretched out my arms toward the god of my vocation and felt myself drawn with the suddenness of thought through the trackless immensity of space. There was an instant of extreme cold and utter darkness.

Chapter III

ᔕᔦ ᕋᔕᔖᣔᐸᔓᔥ ᕆᔦᔖ ᔕᔥᔐᕆ

(My Advent on Mars)

I OPENED MY EYES upon a strange and weird landscape. I knew that I was on Mars; not once did I question either my sanity or my wakefulness. I was not asleep, no need for pinching here; my inner consciousness told me as plainly that I was upon Mars as your conscious mind tells you that you are upon Earth. You do not question the fact; neither did I.

I found myself lying prone upon a bed of yellowish, moss-like vegetation which stretched around me in all directions for interminable miles. I seemed to be lying in a deep, circular basin, along the outer verge of which I could distinguish the irregularities of low hills.

It was midday, the sun was shining full upon me and the heat of it was rather intense upon my naked body, yet no greater than would have been true under similar conditions on an Arizona desert. Here and there were slight outcroppings of quartz-bearing rock which glistened in the sunlight; and a little to my left, perhaps a hundred yards, appeared a low, walled enclosure about four feet in height. No water, and no other vegetation than the moss was in evidence, and as I was somewhat thirsty I determined to do a little exploring.

Springing to my feet I received my first Martian surprise, for the effort, which on Earth would have brought me standing upright, carried me into the Martian air to the height of about three yards. I alighted softly upon the ground, however, without appreciable shock or jar. Now commenced a series of evolutions which even then seemed ludicrous in the extreme. I found that I must learn to walk all over again, as the muscular exertion which carried me easily and safely upon Earth played strange antics with me upon Mars.

Instead of progressing in a sane and dignified manner, my attempts to walk resulted in a variety of hops which took me clear of the ground a couple of feet at each step and landed me sprawling upon my face or back at the end of each second or third hop. My muscles, perfectly attuned and accustomed to the force of gravity on Earth, played the mischief with me in attempting for the first time to cope with the lesser gravitation and lower air pressure on Mars.

I was determined, however, to explore the low structure which was the only evidence of habitation in sight, and so I hit upon the unique plan of reverting to first principles in locomotion, creeping. I did fairly well at this and in a few moments had reached the low, encircling wall of the enclosure.

There appeared to be no doors or windows upon the side nearest me, but as the wall was but about four feet high I cautiously gained my feet and peered over the top upon the strangest sight it had ever been given me to see.

The roof of the enclosure was of solid glass about four or five inches in thickness, and beneath this were several hundred large eggs, perfectly round and snowy white. The eggs were nearly uniform in size being about two and one-half feet in diameter.

Five or six had already hatched and the grotesque caricatures which sat blinking in the sunlight were enough to cause me to doubt my sanity. They seemed mostly head, with little scrawny bodies, long necks and six legs, or, as I afterward learned, two legs and two arms, with an intermediary pair of limbs which could be used at will either as arms or legs. Their eyes were set at the extreme sides of their heads a trifle above the center and protruded in such a manner that they could be directed either forward or back and also independently of each other, thus permitting this queer animal to look in any direction, or in two directions at once, without the necessity of turning the head.

The ears, which were slightly above the eyes and closer together, were small, cup-shaped antennae, protruding not more than an inch on these young specimens. Their noses were but longitudinal slits in the center of their faces, midway between their mouths and ears.

There was no hair on their bodies, which were of a very light yellowish-green color. In the adults, as I was to learn quite soon, this color deepens to an olive green and is darker in the male than in the female. Further, the heads of the adults are not so out of proportion to their bodies as in the case of the young.

The iris of the eyes is blood red, as in Albinos, while the pupil is dark. The eyeball itself is very white, as are the teeth. These latter add a most ferocious appearance to an otherwise fearsome and terrible countenance, as the lower tusks curve upward to sharp points which end about where the eyes of earthly human beings are located. The whiteness of the teeth is not that of ivory, but of the snowiest and most gleaming of china. Against the dark background of their olive skins their tusks stand out in a most striking manner, making these weapons present a singularly formidable appearance.

Most of these details I noted later, for I was given but little time to speculate on the wonders of my new discovery. I had seen that the eggs were in the process of hatching, and as I stood watching the hideous little monsters break from their shells I failed to note the approach of a score of full-grown Martians from behind me.

Coming, as they did, over the soft and soundless moss, which covers practically the entire surface of Mars with the exception of the frozen areas at the poles and the scattered cultivated districts, they might have captured me easily, but their intentions were far more sinister. It was the rattling of the accouterments of the foremost warrior which warned me.

On such a little thing my life hung that I often marvel that I escaped so easily. Had not the rifle of the leader of the party swung from its fastenings beside his saddle in such a way as to strike against the butt of his great metal shod spear I should have snuffed out without ever knowing that death was near me. But the little sound caused me to turn, and there upon me, not ten feet from my breast, was the point of that huge spear, a spear forty feet long, tipped with gleaming metal, and held low at the side of a mounted replica of the little devils I had been watching.

But how puny and harmless they now looked beside this huge and terrific incarnation of hate, of vengeance and of death. The man himself, for such I may call him, was fully fifteen feet in height and, on Earth, would have weighed some four hundred pounds. He sat his mount as we sit a horse, grasping the animal's barrel with his lower limbs, while the hands of his two right arms held his immense spear low at the side of his mount; his two left arms were outstretched laterally to help preserve his balance, the thing he rode having neither bridle or reins of any description for guidance.

And his mount! How can earthly words describe it! It towered ten feet at the shoulder; had four legs on either side; a broad flat tail, larger at the tip than at the root, and which it held straight out behind while running; a gaping mouth which split its head from its snout to its long, massive neck.

Like its master, it was entirely devoid of hair, but was of a dark slate color and exceeding smooth and glossy. Its belly was white, and its legs shaded from the slate of its shoulders and hips to a vivid yellow at the feet. The feet themselves were heavily padded and nailless, which fact had also contributed to the noiselessness of their approach, and, in common with a multiplicity of legs, is a characteristic feature of the fauna of Mars. The highest type of man and one other animal, the only mammal existing on Mars, alone have well-formed nails, and there are absolutely no hoofed animals in existence there.

Behind this first charging demon trailed nineteen others, similar in all respects, but, as I learned later, bearing individual characteristics peculiar to themselves; precisely as no two of us are identical although we are all cast in a similar mold. This picture, or rather materialized nightmare, which I have described at length, made but one terrible and swift impression on me as I turned to meet it.

Unarmed and naked as I was, the first law of nature manifested itself in the only possible solution of my immediate problem, and that was to get out of the vicinity of the point of the charging spear. Consequently I gave a very earthly and at the same time superhuman leap to reach the top of the Martian incubator, for such I had determined it must be.

My effort was crowned with a success which appalled me no less than it seemed to surprise the Martian warriors, for it carried me fully thirty feet into the air and landed me a hundred feet from my pursuers and on the opposite side of the enclosure.

I alighted upon the soft moss easily and without mishap, and turning saw my enemies lined up along the further wall. Some were surveying me with expressions which I afterward discovered marked extreme astonishment, and the others were evidently satisfying themselves that I had not molested their young.

They were conversing together in low tones, and gesticulating and pointing toward me. Their discovery that I had not harmed the little Martians, and that I was unarmed, must have caused them to look upon me with less ferocity; but, as I was to learn later, the thing which weighed most in my favor was my exhibition of hurdling.

While the Martians are immense, their bones are very large and they are muscled only in proportion to the gravitation which they must overcome. The result is that they are infinitely less agile and less powerful, in proportion to their weight, than an Earth man, and I doubt that were one of them suddenly to be transported to Earth he could lift his own weight from the ground; in fact, I am convinced that he could not do so.

My feat then was as marvelous upon Mars as it would have been upon Earth, and from desiring to annihilate me they suddenly looked upon me as a wonderful discovery to be captured and exhibited among their fellows.

The respite my unexpected agility had given me permitted me to formulate plans for the immediate future and to note more closely the appearance of the warriors, for I could not disassociate these people in my mind from those other warriors who, only the day before, had been pursuing me.

I noted that each was armed with several other weapons in addition to the huge spear which I have described. The weapon which caused me to decide against an attempt at escape by flight was what was evidently a rifle of some description, and which I felt, for some reason, they were peculiarly efficient in handling.

These rifles were of a white metal stocked with wood, which I learned later was a very light and intensely hard growth much prized on Mars, and entirely unknown to us denizens of Earth. The metal of the barrel is an alloy composed principally of aluminum and steel which they have learned to temper to a hardness far exceeding that of the steel with which we are familiar. The weight of these rifles is comparatively little, and with the small caliber, explosive, radium projectiles which they use, and the great length of the barrel, they are deadly in the extreme and at ranges which would be unthinkable on Earth. The theoretic effective radius of this rifle is three hundred miles, but the best they can do in actual service when equipped with their wireless finders and sighters is but a trifle over two hundred miles.

This is quite far enough to imbue me with great respect for the Martian firearm, and some telepathic force must have warned me against an attempt to escape in broad daylight from under the muzzles of twenty of these death-dealing machines.

The Martians, after conversing for a short time, turned and rode away in the direction from which they had come, leaving one of their number alone by the enclosure. When they had covered perhaps two hundred yards they halted, and turning their mounts toward us sat watching the warrior by the enclosure.

He was the one whose spear had so nearly transfixed me, and was evidently the leader of the band, as I had noted that they seemed to have moved to their present position at his direction. When his force had come to a halt he dismounted, threw down his spear and small arms, and came around the end of the incubator toward me, entirely unarmed and as naked as I, except for the ornaments strapped upon his head, limbs, and breast.

When he was within about fifty feet of me he unclasped an enormous metal armlet, and holding it toward me in the open palm of his hand, addressed me in a clear, resonant voice, but in a language, it is needless to say, I could not understand. He then stopped as though waiting for my reply, pricking up his

antennae-like ears and cocking his strange-looking eyes
still further toward me.

As the silence became painful I concluded to hazard
a little conversation on my own part, as I had guessed
that he was making overtures of peace. The throwing
down of his weapons and the withdrawing of his troop
before his advance toward me would have signified a
peaceful mission anywhere on Earth, so why not, then,
on Mars!

Placing my hand over my heart I bowed low to
the Martian and explained to him that while I did not
understand his language, his actions spoke for the peace
and friendship that at the present moment were most
dear to my heart. Of course I might have been a bab-
bling brook for all the intelligence my speech carried to
him, but he understood the action with which I immediately followed my words.

Stretching my hand toward him, I advanced and
took the armlet from his open palm, clasping it about
my arm above the elbow; smiled at him and stood waiting. His wide mouth spread into an answering smile,
and locking one of his intermediary arms in mine we
turned and walked back toward his mount. At the
same time he motioned his followers to advance. They
started toward us on a wild run, but were checked by a

signal from him. Evidently he feared that were I to be really frightened again I might jump entirely out of the landscape.

He exchanged a few words with his men, motioned to me that I would ride behind one of them, and then mounted his own animal. The fellow designated reached down two or three hands and lifted me up behind him on the glossy back of his mount, where I hung on as best I could by the belts and straps which held the Martian's weapons and ornaments.

The entire cavalcade then turned and galloped away toward the range of hills in the distance.

Chapter IV
𝔥 𝒯𝔰𝒬𝔳𝔢𝒵𝔦𝒯
(A Prisoner)

WE HAD GONE PERHAPS ten miles when the ground began to rise very rapidly. We were, as I was later to learn, nearing the edge of one of Mars' long-dead seas, in the bottom of which my encounter with the Martians had taken place.

In a short time we gained the foot of the mountains, and after traversing a narrow gorge came to an open valley, at the far extremity of which was a low table land upon which I beheld an enormous city. Toward this we galloped, entering it by what appeared to be a ruined roadway leading out from the city, but only to the edge of the table land, where it ended abruptly in a flight of broad steps.

Upon closer observation I saw as we passed them that the buildings were deserted, and while not greatly decayed had the appearance of not having been tenanted for years, possibly for ages. Toward the center of the city was a large plaza, and upon this and in the buildings immediately surrounding it were camped some nine or ten hundred creatures of the same breed as my captors, for such I now considered them despite the suave manner in which I had been trapped.

With the exceptions of their ornaments all were naked. The women varied in appearance but little from the men, except that their tusks were much larger in proportion to their height, in some instances curving nearly to their high-set ears. Their bodies were smaller and lighter in color, and their fingers and toes bore the rudiments of nails, which were entirely lacking among the males. The adult females ranged in height from ten to twelve feet.

The children were light in color, even lighter than the women, and all looked precisely alike to me, except that some were taller than others; older, I presumed.

I saw no signs of extreme age among them, nor is there any appreciable difference in their appearance from the age of maturity, about forty, until, at about the age of one thousand years, they go voluntarily upon their last strange pilgrimage down the river Iss, which leads no living Martian knows whither and from whose bosom no Martian has ever returned, or would be allowed to live did he return after once embarking upon its cold, dark waters.

Only about one Martian in a thousand dies of sickness or disease, and possibly about twenty take the voluntary pilgrimage. The other nine hundred and seventy-nine die violent deaths in duels, in hunting, in aviation and in war; but perhaps by far the greatest death loss comes during the age of childhood, when vast numbers of the little Martians fall victims to the great white apes of Mars.

The average life expectancy of a Martian after the age of maturity is about three hundred years, but would be nearer the one-thousand mark were it not for the various means leading to violent death. Owing to the waning resources of the planet it evidently became necessary to counteract the increasing longevity which their remarkable skill in therapeutics and surgery produced, and so human life has come to be considered but lightly on Mars, as is evidenced by their dangerous sports and the almost continual warfare between the various communities.

There are other and natural causes tending toward a diminution of population, but nothing contributes so greatly to this end as the fact that no male or female Martian is ever voluntarily without a weapon of destruction.

As we neared the plaza and my presence was discovered we were immediately surrounded by hundreds of the creatures who seemed anxious to pluck me from my seat behind my guard. A word from the leader of the party stilled their clamor, and we proceeded at a trot across the plaza to the entrance of as magnificent an edifice as mortal eye has rested upon.

The building was low, but covered an enormous area. It was constructed of gleaming white marble inlaid with gold and brilliant stones which sparkled and scintillated in the sunlight. The main entrance was some hundred feet in width and projected from the building proper to form a huge canopy above the entrance hall. There was no stairway, but a gentle incline to the first floor of the building opened into an enormous chamber encircled by galleries.

On the floor of this chamber, which was dotted with highly carved wooden desks and chairs, were assembled about forty or fifty male Martians around the steps of a rostrum. On the platform proper squatted an enormous warrior heavily loaded with metal ornaments, gay-colored feathers and beautifully wrought leather trappings ingeniously set with precious stones. From his shoulders depended a short cape of white fur lined with brilliant scarlet silk.

What struck me as most remarkable about this assemblage and the hall in which they were congregated was the fact that the creatures were entirely out of proportion to the desks, chairs, and other furnishings;

these being of a size adapted to human beings such
as I, whereas the great bulks of the Martians could
scarcely have squeezed into the chairs, nor was there
room beneath the desks for their long legs. Evidently,
then, there were other denizens on Mars than the wild
and grotesque creatures into whose hands I had fallen,
but the evidences of extreme antiquity which showed
all around me indicated that these buildings might have
belonged to some long-extinct and forgotten race in the
dim antiquity of Mars.

Our party had halted at the entrance to the building, and at a sign from the leader I had been lowered
to the ground. Again locking his arm in mine, we had
proceeded into the audience chamber. There were few
formalities observed in approaching the Martian chieftain. My captor merely strode up to the rostrum, the
others making way for him as he advanced. The chieftain rose to his feet and uttered the name of my escort
who, in turn, halted and repeated the name of the ruler
followed by his title.

At the time, this ceremony and the words they
uttered meant nothing to me, but later I came to
know that this was the customary greeting between
green Martians. Had the men been strangers, and
therefore unable to exchange names, they would have

silently exchanged ornaments, had their missions been peaceful—otherwise they would have exchanged shots, or have fought out their introduction with some other of their various weapons.

My captor, whose name was Tars Tarkas, was virtually the vice-chieftain of the community, and a man of great ability as a statesman and warrior. He evidently explained briefly the incidents connected with his expedition, including my capture, and when he had concluded the chieftain addressed me at some length.

I replied in our good old English tongue merely to convince him that neither of us could understand the other; but I noticed that when I smiled slightly on concluding, he did likewise. This fact, and the similar occurrence during my first talk with Tars Tarkas, convinced me that we had at least something in common; the ability to smile, therefore to laugh; denoting a sense of humor. But I was to learn that the Martian smile is merely perfunctory, and that the Martian laugh is a thing to cause strong men to blanch in horror.

The ideas of humor among the green men of Mars are widely at variance with our conceptions of incitants to merriment. The death agonies of a fellow being are, to these strange creatures, provocative of the wildest hilarity, while their chief form of commonest amusement is to inflict death on their prisoners of war in various ingenious and horrible ways.

The assembled warriors and chieftains examined me closely, feeling my muscles and the texture of my skin. The principal chieftain then evidently signified a desire to see me perform, and, motioning me to follow, he started with Tars Tarkas for the open plaza.

Now, I had made no attempt to walk, since my first signal failure, except while tightly grasping Tars Tarkas' arm, and so now I went skipping and flitting about among the desks and chairs like some monstrous grasshopper. After bruising myself severely, much to the amusement of the Martians, I again had recourse to creeping, but this did not suit them and I was roughly jerked to my feet by a towering fellow who had laughed most heartily at my misfortunes.

As he banged me down upon my feet his face was bent close to mine and I did the only thing a gentleman might do under the circumstances of brutality, boorish-ness, and lack of consideration for a stranger's rights; I swung my fist squarely to his jaw and he went down like a felled ox. As he sunk to the floor I wheeled around with my back toward the nearest desk, expecting to be overwhelmed by the vengeance of his fellows, but deter-mined to give them as good a battle as the unequal odds would permit before I gave up my life.

My fears were groundless, however, as the other Martians, at first struck dumb with wonderment, finally broke into wild peals of laughter and applause. I did not recognize the applause as such, but later, when I had become acquainted with their customs, I learned that I had won what they seldom accord, a manifestation of approbation.

The fellow whom I had struck lay where he had fallen, nor did any of his mates approach him. Tars Tarkas advanced toward me, holding out one of his arms, and we thus proceeded to the plaza without further mishap. I did not, of course, know the reason for which we had come to the open, but I was not long in being enlightened. They first repeated the word "sak" a number of times, then Tars Tarkas made several jumps, repeating the same word before each leap; then, turning to me, he said, "sak!" I saw what they were after, and gathering myself together I "sakked" with such marvelous success that I cleared a good hundred and fifty feet; nor did I this time, lose my equilibrium, but landed squarely upon my feet without falling. I then returned by easy jumps of twenty-five or thirty feet to the little group of warriors.

My exhibition had been witnessed by several

hundred lesser Martians, and they immediately broke into demands for a repetition, which the chieftain then ordered me to make; but I was both hungry and thirsty, and determined on the spot that my only method of salvation was to demand the consideration from these creatures which they evidently would not voluntarily accord. I therefore ignored the repeated commands to "sak," and each time they were made I motioned to my mouth and rubbed my stomach.

Tars Tarkas and the chief exchanged a few words, and the former, calling to a young female among the throng, gave her some instructions and motioned me to accompany her. I grasped her proffered arm and together we crossed the plaza toward a large building on the far side.

My fair companion was about eight feet tall, having just arrived at maturity, but not yet to her full height. She was of a light olive-green color, with a smooth, glossy hide. Her name, as I afterward learned, was Sola, and she belonged to the retinue of Tars Tarkas. She conducted me to a spacious chamber in one of the buildings fronting on the plaza, and which, from the litter of silks and furs upon the floor, I took to be the sleeping quarters of several of the natives.

The room was well lighted by a number of large

windows and was beautifully decorated with mural paintings and mosaics, but upon all there seemed to rest that indefinable touch of the finger of antiquity which convinced me that the architects and builders of these wondrous creations had nothing in common with the crude half-brutes which now occupied them.

Sola motioned me to be seated upon a pile of silks near the center of the room, and, turning, made a peculiar hissing sound, as though signaling to someone in an adjoining room. In response to her call I obtained my first sight of a new Martian wonder. It waddled in on its ten short legs, and squatted down before the girl like an obedient puppy. The thing was about the size of a Shetland pony, but its head bore a slight resemblance to that of a frog, except that the jaws were equipped with three rows of long, sharp tusks.

CHAPTER V

𝓲 𝕂⩫⟩⧊𝕂 𝔰⫫ 𝕎⩩⩰ℂ⧈ 𝔷⦿𝕆

(I Elude My Watch Dog)

SOLA STARED INTO the brute's wicked-looking eyes, muttered a word or two of command, pointed to me, and left the chamber. I could not but wonder what this ferocious-looking monstrosity might do when left alone in such close proximity to such a relatively tender morsel of meat; but my fears were groundless, as the beast, after surveying me intently for a moment, crossed the room to the only exit which led to the street, and lay down full length across the threshold.

This was my first experience with a Martian watch dog, but it was destined not to be my last, for this fellow guarded me carefully during the time I remained a captive among these green men; twice saving my life, and never voluntarily being away from me a moment.

While Sola was away I took occasion to examine more minutely the room in which I found myself captive. The mural painting depicted scenes of rare and wonderful beauty: mountains, rivers, lake, ocean, meadow, trees and flowers, winding roadways, sun-kissed gardens— scenes which might have portrayed earthly views but for the different colorings of the vegetation. The work had evidently been wrought by a master hand, so subtle the atmosphere, so perfect the technique; yet nowhere was there a representation of a living animal, either human or brute, by which I could guess at the likeness of these other and perhaps extinct denizens of Mars.

While I was allowing my fancy to run riot in wild conjecture on the possible explanation of the strange anomalies which I had so far met with on Mars, Sola returned bearing both food and drink. These she placed on the floor beside me, and seating herself a short ways off regarded me intently. The food consisted of about a pound of some solid substance of the consistency of cheese and almost tasteless, while the liquid was apparently milk from some animal. It was not unpleasant to the taste, though slightly acid, and I learned in a short time to prize it very highly. It came, as I later discovered, not from an animal, as there is only one mammal on Mars and that one very rare indeed, but from a large plant which grows practically without water, but seems to distill its plentiful supply of milk from the products of the soil, the moisture of the air, and the rays of the sun. A single plant of this species will give eight or ten quarts of milk per day.

After I had eaten I was greatly invigorated, but

feeling the need of rest I stretched out upon the silks and was soon asleep. I must have slept several hours, as it was dark when I awoke, and I was very cold. I noticed that someone had thrown a fur over me, but it had become partially dislodged and in the darkness I could not see to replace it. Suddenly a hand reached out and pulled the fur over me, shortly afterwards adding another to my covering.

I presumed that my watchful guardian was Sola, nor was I wrong. This girl alone, among all the green Martians with whom I came in contact, disclosed characteristics of sympathy, kindliness, and affection; her ministrations to my bodily wants were unfailing, and her solicitous care saved me from much suffering and many hardships.

As I was to learn, the Martian nights are extremely cold, and as there is practically no twilight or dawn, the changes in temperature are sudden and most uncomfortable, as are the transitions from brilliant daylight to darkness. The nights are either brilliantly illumined or very dark, for if neither of the two moons of Mars happen to be in the sky almost total darkness results, since the lack of atmosphere, or, rather, the very thin atmosphere, fails to diffuse the starlight to any great extent; on the other hand, if both of the moons are in the heavens at night the surface of the ground is brightly illuminated.

Both of Mars' moons are vastly nearer her than is our moon to Earth; the nearer moon being but about five thousand miles distant, while the further is but little more than fourteen thousand miles away, against the nearly one-quarter million miles which separate us from our moon. The nearer moon of Mars makes a complete revolution around the planet in a little over seven and one-half hours, so that she may be seen hurtling through the sky like some huge meteor two or three times each night, revealing all her phases during each transit of the heavens.

The further moon revolves about Mars in something over thirty and one-quarter hours, and with her sister satellite makes a nocturnal Martian scene one of splendid and weird grandeur. And it is well that nature has so graciously and abundantly lighted the Martian night, for the green men of Mars, being a nomadic race without high intellectual development, have but crude means for artificial lighting; depending principally upon torches, a kind of candle, and a peculiar oil lamp which generates a gas and burns without a wick.

This last device produces an intensely brilliant

far-reaching white light, but as the natural oil which it requires can only be obtained by mining in one of several widely separated and remote localities it is seldom used by these creatures whose only thought is for today, and whose hatred for manual labor has kept them in a semi-barbaric state for countless ages.

After Sola had replenished my coverings I again slept, nor did I awaken until daylight. The other occupants of the room, five in number, were all females, and they were still sleeping, piled high with a motley array of silks and furs. Across the threshold lay stretched the sleepless guardian brute, just as I had last seen him on the preceding day; apparently he had not moved a muscle; his eyes were fairly glued upon me, and I fell to wondering just what might befall me should I endeavor to escape.

I have ever been prone to seek adventure and to investigate and experiment where wiser men would have left well enough alone. It therefore now occurred to me that the surest way of learning the exact attitude of this beast toward me would be to attempt to leave the room. I felt fairly secure in my belief that I could escape him should he pursue me once I was outside the building, for I had begun to take great pride in my ability as a jumper. Furthermore, I could see from the shortness of his legs that the brute himself was no jumper and probably no runner.

Slowly and carefully, therefore, I gained my feet, only to see that my watcher did the same; cautiously I advanced toward him, finding that by moving with a shuffling gait I could retain my balance as well as make reasonably rapid progress. As I neared the brute he backed cautiously away from me, and when I had reached the open he moved to one side to let me pass. He then fell in behind me and followed about ten paces in my rear as I made my way along the deserted street.

Evidently his mission was to protect me only, I thought, but when we reached the edge of the city he suddenly sprang before me, uttering strange sounds and baring his ugly and ferocious tusks. Thinking to have some amusement at his expense, I rushed toward him, and when almost upon him sprang into the air, alighting far beyond him and away from the city. He wheeled instantly and charged me with the most appalling speed I had ever beheld. I had thought his short legs a bar to swiftness, but had he been coursing with greyhounds the latter would have appeared as though asleep on a door mat. As I was to learn, this is the fleetest animal on Mars, and owing to its intelligence, loyalty, and ferocity is used in hunting, in war, and as the protector of the Martian man.

I quickly saw that I would have difficulty in escaping the fangs of the beast on a straightaway course, and so I met his charge by doubling in my tracks and leaping over him as he was almost upon me. This maneuver gave me a considerable advantage, and I was able to reach the city quite a bit ahead of him, and as he came tearing after me I jumped for a window about thirty feet from the ground in the face of one of the buildings overlooking the valley.

Grasping the sill I pulled myself up to a sitting posture without looking into the building, and gazed down at the baffled animal beneath me. My exultation was short-lived, however, for scarcely had I gained a secure seat upon the sill than a huge hand grasped me by the neck from behind and dragged me violently into the room. Here I was thrown upon my back, and beheld standing over me a colossal ape-like creature, white and hairless except for an enormous shock of bristly hair upon its head.

Chapter VI

ᚠ ᚠᚢᚾᛋᚴ ᚴᛋᚾᛉ ᚡᛁᚠ ᚠᛝᛃᛚᛋᛉᚢ

(A Fight That Won Friends)

THE THING, WHICH MORE nearly resembled our earthly men than it did the Martians I had seen, held me pinioned to the ground with one huge foot, while it jabbered and gesticulated at some answering creature behind me. This other, which was evidently its mate, soon came toward us, bearing a mighty stone cudgel with which it evidently intended to brain me.

The creatures were about ten or fifteen feet tall, standing erect, and had, like the green Martians, an intermediary set of arms or legs, midway between their upper and lower limbs. Their eyes were close together and non-protruding; their ears were high set, but more laterally located than those of the Martians, while their snouts and teeth were strikingly like those of our African gorilla. Altogether they were not unlovely when viewed in comparison with the green Martians.

The cudgel was swinging in the arc which ended upon my upturned face when a bolt of myriad-legged horror hurled itself through the doorway full upon the breast of my executioner. With a shriek of fear the ape which held me leaped through the open window, but its mate closed in a terrific death struggle with my preserver, which was nothing less than my faithful watch-thing; I cannot bring myself to call so hideous a creature a dog.

As quickly as possible I gained my feet and backing against the wall I witnessed such a battle as it is vouchsafed few beings to see. The strength, agility, and blind ferocity of these two creatures is approached by nothing known to earthly man. My beast had an advantage in his first hold, having sunk his mighty fangs far into the breast of his adversary; but the great arms and paws of the ape, backed by muscles far transcending those of the Martian men I had seen, had locked the throat of my guardian and slowly were choking out his life, and bending back his head and neck upon his body, where I momentarily expected the former to fall limp at the end of a broken neck.

In accomplishing this the ape was tearing away the entire front of its breast, which was held in the vise-like grip of the powerful jaws. Back and forth upon the floor they rolled, neither one emitting a sound of fear or pain. Presently I saw the great eyes of my beast bulging completely from their sockets and blood flowing from its nostrils. That he was weakening perceptibly was evident, but so also was the ape, whose struggles were growing momentarily less.

Suddenly I came to myself and, with that strange instinct which seems ever to prompt me to my duty, I seized the cudgel, which had fallen to the floor at the commencement of the battle, and swinging it with all the power of my earthly arms I crashed it full upon the head of the ape, crushing his skull as though it had been an eggshell.

Scarcely had the blow descended when I was confronted with a new danger. The ape's mate, recovered from its first shock of terror, had returned to the scene of the encounter by way of the interior of the building. I glimpsed him just before he reached the doorway and the sight of him, now roaring as he perceived his lifeless fellow stretched upon the floor, and frothing at the mouth, in the extremity of his rage, filled me, I must confess, with dire forebodings.

I am ever willing to stand and fight when the odds are not too overwhelmingly against me, but in this instance I perceived neither glory nor profit in pitting my relatively puny strength against the iron muscles and brutal ferocity of this enraged denizen of an unknown world; in fact, the only outcome of such an encounter, so far as I might be concerned, seemed sudden death.

I was standing near the window and I knew that once in the street I might gain the plaza and safety before the creature could overtake me; at least there was a chance for safety in flight, against almost certain death should I remain and fight however desperately.

It is true I held the cudgel, but what could I do with it against his four great arms? Even should I break one of them with my first blow, for I figured that he would attempt to ward off the cudgel, he could reach out and annihilate me with the others before I could recover for a second attack.

In the instant that these thoughts passed through my mind I had turned to make for the window, but my eyes alighting on the form of my erstwhile guardian threw all thoughts of flight to the four winds. He lay gasping upon the floor of the chamber, his great eyes fastened upon me in what seemed a pitiful appeal for protection. I could not withstand that look, nor could I, on second thought, have deserted my rescuer without giving as good an account of myself in his behalf as he had in mine.

Without more ado, therefore, I turned to meet the charge of the infuriated bull ape. He was now too close upon me for the cudgel to prove of any effective assistance, so I merely threw it as heavily as I could at his advancing bulk. It struck him just below the knees, eliciting a howl of pain and rage, and so throwing him off his balance that he lunged full upon me with arms wide stretched to ease his fall.

Again, as on the preceding day, I had recourse to earthly tactics, and swinging my right fist full upon the point of his chin I followed it with a smashing left to the pit of his stomach. The effect was marvelous, for, as I lightly sidestepped, after delivering the second blow, he reeled and fell upon the floor doubled up with pain and gasping for wind. Leaping over his prostrate body, I seized the cudgel and finished the monster before he could regain his feet.

As I delivered the blow a low laugh rang out behind me, and, turning, I beheld Tars Tarkas, Sola, and three or four warriors standing in the doorway of the chamber. As my eyes met theirs I was, for the second time, the recipient of their zealously guarded applause.

My absence had been noted by Sola on her awakening, and she had quickly informed Tars Tarkas, who had set out immediately with a handful of warriors to search for me. As they had approached the limits of the city they had witnessed the actions of the bull ape as he bolted into the building, frothing with rage.

They had followed immediately behind him, thinking it barely possible that his actions might prove a clew to my whereabouts and had witnessed my short but decisive battle with him. This encounter, together with my set-to with the Martian warrior on the previous day and my feats of jumping placed me upon a high pinnacle in their regard. Evidently devoid of all the finer sentiments of friendship, love, or affection, these people fairly worship physical prowess and bravery, and nothing is too good for the object of their adoration as long as he maintains his position by repeated examples of his skill, strength, and courage.

Sola, who had accompanied the searching party of her own volition, was the only one of the Martians whose face had not been twisted in laughter as I battled for my life. She, on the contrary, was sober with apparent solicitude and, as soon as I had finished the monster, rushed to me and carefully examined my body for possible wounds or injuries. Satisfying herself that I had come off unscathed she smiled quietly, and, taking my hand, started toward the door of the chamber.

Tars Tarkas and the other warriors had entered and were standing over the now rapidly reviving brute which had saved my life, and whose life I, in turn, had rescued.

They seemed to be deep in argument, and finally one of them addressed me, but remembering my ignorance of his language turned back to Tars Tarkas, who, with a word and gesture, gave some command to the fellow and turned to follow us from the room.

There seemed something menacing in their attitude toward my beast, and I hesitated to leave until I had learned the outcome. It was well I did so, for the warrior drew an evil-looking pistol from its holster and was on the point of putting an end to the creature when I sprang forward and struck up his arm. The bullet striking the wooden casing of the window exploded, blowing a hole completely through the wood and masonry.

I then knelt down beside the fearsome-looking thing, and raising it to its feet motioned for it to follow me. The looks of surprise which my actions elicited from the Martians were ludicrous; they could not understand, except in a feeble and childish way, such attributes as gratitude and compassion. The warrior whose gun I had struck up looked inquiringly at Tars Tarkas, but the latter signed that I be left to my own devices, and so we returned to the plaza with my great beast following close at heel, and Sola grasping me tightly by the arm.

I had at least two friends on Mars; a young woman

who watched over me with motherly solicitude, and a dumb brute which, as I later came to know, held in its poor ugly carcass more love, more loyalty, more gratitude than could have been found in the entire five million green Martians who rove the deserted cities and dead sea bottoms of Mars.

Chapter VII

(ᘓᕋᕐᒣ)ᔭᕐᔭᖕᗴᖑᕋᔭᒣᔭ ᐁᔭ ᕐᖑᔭᐅ
(Child-Raising on Mars)

After a breakfast, which was an exact replica of the meal of the preceding day and an index of practically every meal which followed while I was with the green men of Mars, Sola escorted me to the plaza, where I found the entire community engaged in watching or helping at the harnessing of huge mastodonian animals to great three-wheeled chariots. There were about two hundred and fifty of these vehicles, each drawn by a single animal, any one of which, from their appearance, might easily have drawn the entire wagon train when fully loaded.

The chariots themselves were large, commodious, and gorgeously decorated. In each was seated a female Martian loaded with ornaments of metal, with jewels and silks and furs, and upon the back of each of the beasts which drew the chariots was perched a young Martian driver. Like the animals upon which the warriors were mounted, the heavier draft animals wore neither bit nor bridle, but were guided entirely by telepathic means.

This power is wonderfully developed in all Martians,

and accounts largely for the simplicity of their language and the relatively few spoken words exchanged even in long conversations. It is the universal language of Mars, through the medium of which the higher and lower animals of this world of paradoxes are able to communicate to a greater or less extent, depending upon the intellectual sphere of the species and the development of the individual.

As the cavalcade took up the line of march in single file, Sola dragged me into an empty chariot and we proceeded with the procession toward the point by which I had entered the city the day before. At the head of the caravan rode some two hundred warriors, five abreast, and a like number brought up the rear, while twenty-five or thirty outriders flanked us on either side.

Every one but myself—men, women, and children—were heavily armed, and at the tail of each chariot trotted a Martian hound, my own beast following closely behind ours; in fact, the faithful creature never left me voluntarily during the entire ten years I spent on Mars. Our way led out across the little valley before the city, through the hills, and down into the dead sea bottom which I had traversed on my journey from the incubator to the plaza. The incubator, as it proved, was the terminal point of our journey this day, and, as the entire cavalcade broke into a mad gallop as soon as we reached the level expanse of sea bottom, we were soon within sight of our goal.

On reaching it the chariots were parked with military precision on the four sides of the enclosure, and half a score of warriors, headed by the enormous chieftain, and including Tars Tarkas and several other lesser chiefs, dismounted and advanced toward it. I could see Tars Tarkas explaining something to the principal chieftain, whose name, by the way, was, as nearly as I can translate it into English, Lorquas Ptomel, Jed; jed being his title.

I was soon appraised of the subject of their conversation, as, calling to Sola, Tars Tarkas signed for her to send me to him. I had by this time mastered the intricacies of walking under Martian conditions, and quickly responding to his command I advanced to the side of the incubator where the warriors stood.

As I reached their side a glance showed me that all but a very few eggs had hatched, the incubator being fairly alive with the hideous little devils. They ranged in height from three to four feet, and were moving restlessly about the enclosure as though searching for food.

As I came to a halt before him, Tars Tarkas pointed over the incubator and said, "Sak." I saw that he wanted me to repeat my performance of yesterday for the edification of Lorquas Ptomel, and, as I must confess that my prowess gave me no little satisfaction, I responded quickly, leaping entirely over the parked chariots on the far side of the incubator. As I returned, Lorquas Ptomel grunted something at me, and turning to his warriors gave a few words of command relative to the incubator. They paid no further attention to me and I was thus permitted to remain close and watch their operations, which consisted in breaking an opening in the wall of the incubator large enough to permit of the exit of the young Martians.

On either side of this opening the women and the younger Martians, both male and female, formed two solid walls leading out through the chariots and quite away into the plain beyond. Between these walls the little Martians scampered, wild as deer; being permitted to run the full length of the aisle, where they were cap-tured one at a time by the women and older children; the last in the line capturing the first little one to reach the end of the gauntlet, her opposite in the line captur-ing the second, and so on until all the little fellows had left the enclosure and been appropriated by some youth or female. As the women caught the young they fell out of line and returned to their respective chariots, while those who fell into the hands of the young men were later turned over to some of the women.

I saw that the ceremony, if it could be dignified by such a name, was over, and seeking out Sola I found her in our chariot with a hideous little creature held tightly in her arms.

The work of rearing young, green Martians consists solely in teaching them to talk, and to use the weapons of warfare with which they are loaded down from the very first year of their lives. Coming from eggs in which they have lain for five years, the period of incubation, they step forth into the world perfectly developed except in size. Entirely unknown to their own mothers, who, in turn, would have difficulty in pointing out the fathers with any degree of accuracy, they are the common children of the community, and their education devolves upon the females who chance to capture them as they leave the incubator.

Their foster mothers may not even have had an egg in the incubator, as was the case with Sola, who had not commenced to lay, until less than a year before she became the mother of another woman's offspring. But this counts for little among the green Martians, as parental and filial love is as unknown to them as it is common among us. I believe this horrible system which has been carried on for ages is the direct cause of the loss of all the finer feelings and higher humanitarian instincts among these poor creatures. From birth they know no father or mother love, they know not the meaning of the word home; they are taught that they are only suffered to live until they can demonstrate by their physique and ferocity that they are fit to live. Should they prove deformed or defective in any way they are promptly shot; nor do they see a tear shed for a single one of the many cruel hardships they pass through from earliest infancy.

I do not mean that the adult Martians are unnecessarily or intentionally cruel to the young, but theirs is a hard and pitiless struggle for existence upon a dying planet, the natural resources of which have dwindled to a point where the support of each additional life means an added tax upon the community into which it is thrown.

By careful selection they rear only the hardiest specimens of each species, and with almost supernatural foresight they regulate the birth rate to merely offset the loss by death. Each adult Martian female brings forth about thirteen eggs each year, and those which meet the size, weight, and specific gravity tests are hidden in the recesses of some subterranean vault where the temperature is too low for incubation. Every year these eggs are carefully examined by a council of twenty chieftains, and all but about one hundred of the most perfect are destroyed out of each yearly supply. At the end of five years about five hundred almost perfect eggs have been chosen from the thousands brought forth. These are then placed in the almost air-tight incubators to be hatched by the sun's rays after a period of another five years. The hatching which we had witnessed today was a fairly representative event of its kind, all but about one percent of the eggs hatching in two days. If the remaining eggs ever hatched we knew nothing of the fate of the little Martians. They were not wanted, as their offspring might inherit and transmit the tendency to prolonged incubation, and thus upset the system which has maintained for ages and which permits the adult Martians to figure the proper time for return to the incubators, almost to an hour.

The incubators are built in remote fastnesses, where there is little or no likelihood of their being discovered by other tribes. The result of such a catastrophe would mean no children in the community for another five years. I was later to witness the results of the discovery of an alien incubator.

The community of which the green Martians with

whom my lot was cast formed a part was composed of some thirty thousand souls. They roamed an enormous tract of arid and semi-arid land between forty and eighty degrees south latitude, and bounded on the east and west by two large fertile tracts. Their headquarters lay in the southwest corner of this district, near the crossing of two of the so-called Martian canals.

As the incubator had been placed far north of their own territory in a supposedly uninhabited and unfrequented area, we had before us a tremendous journey, concerning which I, of course, knew nothing.

After our return to the dead city I passed several days in comparative idleness. On the day following our return all the warriors had ridden forth early in the morning and had not returned until just before darkness fell. As I later learned, they had been to the subterranean vaults in which the eggs were kept and had transported them to the incubator, which they had then walled up for another five years, and which, in all probability, would not be visited again during that period.

The vaults which hid the eggs until they were ready for the incubator were located many miles south of the incubator, and would be visited yearly by the council of twenty chieftains. Why they did not arrange to build their vaults and incubators nearer home has always

JOHN CARTER. Carter reluctantly begins a journey to rediscover his humanity while at the same time saving his newfound world.

TARS TARKAS. A fierce green Martian warrior who is king of the Tharks, he becomes John Carter's most trusted ally.

TARDOS MORS. King of Helium, he is a tough and pragmatic ruler. He must find a way to save his beloved Helium—no matter the cost.

KANTOS KAN. A captain of the Helium air navy, Kantos will do anything in his power to fight for his country.

MATAI SHANG. Leader of the powerful and mysterious Therns.

SAB THAN. The impulsive and arrogant king of Zodanga's scavenger city, he will try to make a deal with the devil to destroy Helium and rule all of Barsoom.

DEJAH THORIS. A scientist and heir to the throne of Helium, Dejah is a fierce Barsoomian princess.

WOOLA. A loyal, ten-legged doglike creature. Woola accompanies and protects John Carter across Barsoom.

A FORBIDDEN TEMPLE. John Carter and Dejah Thoris explore Barsoom's past in an abandoned temple.

A NEW WORLD. Dejah explains to John Carter that he is on the solar system's fourth planet, Barsoom, which he knows as the planet Mars.

SAB THAN'S CORSAIR. The Zodangan airship Sab Than uses for transport and attack.

JOHN CARTER. After his adventures across a new landscape, he embraces his destiny and becomes John Carter of Mars.

been a mystery to me, and, like many other Martian mysteries, unsolved and unsolvable by earthly reasoning and customs.

Sola's duties were now doubled, as she was compelled to care for the young Martian as well as for me, but neither one of us required much attention, and as we were both about equally advanced in Martian education, Sola took it upon herself to train us together.

Her prize consisted in a male about four feet tall, very strong and physically perfect; also, he learned quickly, and we had considerable amusement, at least I did, over the keen rivalry we displayed. The Martian language, as I have said, is extremely simple, and in a week I could make all my wants known and understand nearly everything that was said to me. Likewise, under Sola's tutelage, I developed my telepathic powers so that I shortly could sense practically everything that went on around me.

What surprised Sola most in me was that while I could catch telepathic messages easily from others, and often when they were not intended for me, no one could read a jot from my mind under any circumstances. At first this vexed me, but later I was very glad of it, as it gave me an undoubted advantage over the Martians.

Chapter VIII
ᚠ ᚱᚾᚢᛈ ᚳᚻᚱᚥᛢᚢᛇᛁᚳ ᛁᚱᚦᚻᛂ ᛉᚦᛁᚳ ᚻᛋᛈ

(A Fair Captive from the Sky)

THE THIRD DAY after the incubator ceremony we set
forth toward home, but scarcely had the head of the
procession debouched into the open ground before the
city than orders were given for an immediate and hasty
return. As though trained for years in this particular
evolution, the green Martians melted like mist into the
spacious doorways of the nearby buildings, until, in less
than three minutes, the entire cavalcade of chariots,
mastodons and mounted warriors was nowhere to be
seen.

Sola and I had entered a building upon the front of
the city, in fact, the same one in which I had had my
encounter with the apes, and, wishing to see what had
caused the sudden retreat, I mounted to an upper floor
and peered from the window out over the valley and the
hills beyond; and there I saw the cause of their sudden
scurrying to cover. A huge craft, long, low, and gray-
painted, swung slowly over the crest of the nearest hill.
Following it came another, and another, and another,
until twenty of them, swinging low above the ground,
sailed slowly and majestically toward us.

Each carried a strange banner swung from stem to stern above the upper works, and upon the prow of each was painted some odd device that gleamed in the sunlight and showed plainly even at the distance at which we were from the vessels. I could see figures crowding the forward decks and upper works of the air craft. Whether they had discovered us or simply were looking at the deserted city I could not say, but in any event they received a rude reception, for suddenly and without warning the green Martian warriors fired a terrific volley from the windows of the buildings facing the little valley across which the great ships were so peacefully advancing.

Instantly the scene changed as by magic; the foremost vessel swung broadside toward us, and bringing her guns into play returned our fire, at the same time moving parallel to our front for a short distance and then turning back with the evident intention of completing a great circle which would bring her up to position once more opposite our firing line; the other vessels followed in her wake, each one opening upon us as she swung into position. Our own fire never diminished, and I doubt if twenty-five percent of our shots went wild. It had never been given me to see such deadly accuracy of aim, and it seemed as though a little figure on one of the craft dropped at the explosion of each bullet, while the banners and upper works dissolved in spurts of flame as the irresistible projectiles of our warriors mowed through them.

The fire from the vessels was most ineffectual, owing, as I afterward learned, to the unexpected suddenness of the first volley, which caught the ship's crews entirely unprepared and the sighting apparatus of the guns unprotected from the deadly aim of our warriors.

It seems that each green warrior has certain objective points for his fire under relatively identical circumstances of warfare. For example, a proportion of them, always the best marksmen, direct their fire entirely upon the wireless finding and sighting apparatus of the big guns of an attacking naval force; another detail attends to the smaller guns in the same way; others pick off the gunners; still others the officers; while certain other quotas concentrate their attention upon the other members of the crew, upon the upper works, and upon the steering gear and propellers.

Twenty minutes after the first volley the great fleet swung trailing off in the direction from which it had first appeared. Several of the craft were limping perceptibly, and seemed but barely under the control of their depleted crews. Their fire had ceased entirely and all their energies seemed focused upon escape. Our warriors then rushed up to the roofs of the buildings which we occupied and followed the retreating armada with a continuous fusillade of deadly fire.

One by one, however, the ships managed to dip below the crests of the outlying hills until only one barely moving craft was in sight. This had received the brunt of our fire and seemed to be entirely unmanned, as not a moving figure was visible upon her decks. Slowly she swung from her course, circling back toward us in an erratic and pitiful manner. Instantly the warriors ceased firing, for it was quite apparent that the vessel was entirely helpless, and, far from being in a position to inflict harm upon us, she could not even control herself sufficiently to escape.

As she neared the city the warriors rushed out upon the plain to meet her, but it was evident that she still was too high for them to hope to reach her decks. From my vantage point in the window I could see the bodies of her crew strewn about, although I could not make out what manner of creatures they might be. Not a sign of life was manifest upon her as she drifted slowly with the light breeze in a southeasterly direction.

She was drifting some fifty feet above the ground, followed by all but some hundred of the warriors who had been ordered back to the roofs to cover the possibility of a return of the fleet, or of reinforcements. It soon became evident that she would strike the face of the buildings about a mile south of our position, and as I watched the progress of the chase I saw a number of warriors gallop ahead, dismount and enter the building she seemed destined to touch.

As the craft neared the building, and just before she struck, the Martian warriors swarmed upon her from the windows, and with their great spears eased the shock of the collision, and in a few moments they had thrown out grappling hooks and the big boat was being hauled to ground by their fellows below.

After making her fast, they swarmed the sides and searched the vessel from stem to stern. I could see them examining the dead sailors, evidently for signs of life, and presently a party of them appeared from below dragging a little figure among them. The creature was considerably less than half as tall as the green Martian warriors, and from my balcony I could see that it walked erect upon two legs and surmised that it was some new and strange Martian monstrosity with which I had not as yet become acquainted.

They removed their prisoner to the ground and then commenced a systematic rifling of the vessel. This operation required several hours, during which time a number of the chariots were requisitioned to transport the loot, which consisted in arms, ammunition, silks, furs, jewels, strangely carved stone vessels, and a quantity of solid foods and liquids, including many casks of water, the first I had seen since my advent upon Mars.

After the last load had been removed the warriors made lines fast to the craft and towed her far out into the valley in a southwesterly direction. A few of them then boarded her and were busily engaged in what appeared, from my distant position, as the emptying of the contents of various carboys upon the dead bodies of the sailors and over the decks and works of the vessel.

This operation concluded, they hastily clambered over her sides, sliding down the guy ropes to the ground. The last warrior to leave the deck turned and threw something back upon the vessel, waiting an instant to note the outcome of his act. As a faint spurt of flame rose from the point where the missile struck he swung over the side and was quickly upon the ground. Scarcely had he alighted than the guy ropes were simultaneously released, and the great warship, lightened by the removal of the loot, soared majestically into the air, her decks and upper works a mass of roaring flames.

Slowly she drifted to the southeast, rising higher

and higher as the flames ate away her wooden parts and diminished the weight upon her. Ascending to the roof of the building I watched her for hours, until finally she was lost in the dim vistas of the distance. The sight was awe-inspiring in the extreme as one contemplated this mighty floating funeral pyre, drifting unguided and unmanned through the lonely wastes of the Martian heavens; a derelict of death and destruction, typifying the life story of these strange and ferocious creatures into whose unfriendly hands fate had carried it.

Much depressed, and, to me, unaccountably so, I slowly descended to the street. The scene I had witnessed seemed to mark the defeat and annihilation of the forces of a kindred people, rather than the routing by our green warriors of a horde of similar, though unfriendly, creatures. I could not fathom the seeming hallucination, nor could I free myself from it; but somewhere in the innermost recesses of my soul I felt a strange yearning toward these unknown foemen, and a mighty hope surged through me that the fleet would return and demand a reckoning from the green warriors who had so ruthlessly and wantonly attacked it.

Close at my heel, in his now accustomed place, followed Woola, the hound, and as I emerged upon the street Sola rushed up to me as though I had been the object of some search on her part. The cavalcade was returning to the plaza, the homeward march having been given up for that day; nor, in fact, was it recommenced for more than a week, owing to the fear of a return attack by the air craft.

Lorquas Ptomel was too astute an old warrior to be caught upon the open plains with a caravan of chariots and children, and so we remained at the deserted city until the danger seemed passed.

As Sola and I entered the plaza a sight met my eyes which filled my whole being with a great surge of mingled hope, fear, exultation, and depression, and yet most dominant was a subtle sense of relief and happiness; for just as we neared the throng of Martians I caught a glimpse of the prisoner from the battle craft who was being roughly dragged into a nearby building by a couple of green Martian females.

And the sight which met my eyes was that of a slender, girlish figure, similar in every detail to the earthly women of my past life. She did not see me at first, but just as she was disappearing through the portal of the building which was to be her prison she turned, and her eyes met mine. Her face was oval and beautiful in the extreme, her every feature was finely chiseled and exquisite, her eyes large and lustrous and her head surmounted by a mass of coal black, waving hair, caught loosely into a strange yet becoming coiffure. Her skin was of a light reddish copper color, against which the crimson glow of her cheeks and the ruby of her beautifully molded lips shone with a strangely enhancing effect.

She was as destitute of clothes as the green Martians who accompanied her; indeed, save for her highly wrought ornaments she was entirely naked, nor could any apparel have enhanced the beauty of her perfect and symmetrical figure.

As her gaze rested on me her eyes opened wide in astonishment, and she made a little sign with her free hand; a sign which I did not, of course, understand. Just a moment we gazed upon each other, and then the look of hope and renewed courage which had glorified her face as she discovered me, faded into one of utter dejection, mingled with loathing and contempt. I realized I had not answered her signal, and ignorant as I was of Martian customs, I intuitively felt that she had made an appeal for succor and protection which my unfortunate ignorance had prevented me from answering. And then she was dragged out of my sight into the depths of the deserted edifice.

Chapter IX
𝔶 ꞏ)ꞁ꜀ꞵꞩꞛ꜀ ꜀ꞡꞁ꜀ ꞏ)ꞕꞛꞩ꜀ꞵ꜀ꞕꞁ꜀

(I Learn the Language)

As I CAME BACK to myself I glanced at Sola, who had witnessed this encounter and I was surprised to note a strange expression upon her usually expressionless countenance. What her thoughts were I did not know, for as yet I had learned but little of the Martian tongue; enough only to suffice for my daily needs.

As I reached the doorway of our building a strange surprise awaited me. A warrior approached bearing the arms, ornaments, and full accouterments of his kind. These he presented to me with a few unintelligible words, and a bearing at once respectful and menacing.

Later, Sola, with the aid of several of the other women, remodeled the trappings to fit my lesser proportions, and after they completed the work I went about garbed in all the panoply of war.

From then on Sola instructed me in the mysteries of the various weapons, and with the Martian young I spent several hours each day practicing upon the plaza. I was not yet proficient with all the weapons, but my great familiarity with similar earthly weapons made me an unusually apt pupil, and I progressed in a very satisfactory manner.

The training of myself and the young Martians was conducted solely by the women, who not only attend to the education of the young in the arts of individual defense and offense, but are also the artisans who produce every manufactured article wrought by the green Martians. They make the powder, the cartridges, the firearms; in fact everything of value is produced by the females. In time of actual warfare they form a part of the reserves, and when the necessity arises fight with even greater intelligence and ferocity than the men.

The men are trained in the higher branches of the art of war; in strategy and the maneuvering of large bodies of troops. They make the laws as they are needed; a new law for each emergency. They are unfettered by precedent in the administration of justice. Customs have been handed down by ages of repetition, but the punishment for ignoring a custom is a matter for individual treatment by a jury of the culprit's peers, and I may say that justice seldom misses fire, but seems rather to rule in inverse ratio to the ascendency of law. In one respect at least the Martians are a happy people; they have no lawyers.

I did not see the prisoner again for several days

subsequent to our first encounter, and then only to catch
a fleeting glimpse of her as she was being conducted to
the great audience chamber where I had had my first
meeting with Lorquas Ptomel. I could not but note
the unnecessary harshness and brutality with which her
guards treated her; so different from the almost mater-
nal kindliness which Sola manifested toward me, and
the respectful attitude of the few green Martians who
took the trouble to notice me at all.

I had observed on the two occasions when I had
seen her that the prisoner exchanged words with her
guards, and this convinced me that they spoke, or at
least could make themselves understood by a common
language. With this added incentive I nearly drove Sola
distracted by my importunities to hasten on my education, and within a few more days I had mastered the
Martian tongue sufficiently well to enable me to carry
on a passable conversation and to fully understand practically all that I heard.

At this time our sleeping quarters were occupied by
three or four females and a couple of the recently hatched
young, beside Sola and her youthful ward, myself, and
Woola the hound. After they had retired for the night
it was customary for the adults to carry on a desultory
conversation for a short time before lapsing into sleep,

and now that I could understand their language I was always a keen listener, although I never proferred any remarks myself.

On the night following the prisoner's visit to the audience chamber the conversation finally fell upon this subject, and I was all ears on the instant. I had feared to question Sola relative to the beautiful captive, as I could not but recall the strange expression I had noted upon her face after my first encounter with the prisoner. That it denoted jealousy I could not say, and yet, judging all things by mundane standards as I still did, I felt it safer to affect indifference in the matter until I learned more surely Sola's attitude toward the object of my solicitude.

Sarkoja, one of the older women who shared our domicile, had been present at the audience as one of the captive's guards, and it was toward her the questioners turned.

"When," asked one of the women, "will we enjoy the death throes of the red one? Or does Lorquas Ptomel, Jed, intend holding her for ransom?"

"They have decided to carry her with us back to Thark, and exhibit her last agonies at the great games before Tal Hajus," replied Sarkoja.

"What will be the manner of her going out?" inquired Sola. "She is very small and very beautiful; I had hoped that they would hold her for ransom."

Sarkoja and the other women grunted angrily at this evidence of weakness on the part of Sola.

"It is sad, Sola, that you were not born a million years ago," snapped Sarkoja, "when all the hollows of the land were filled with water, and the peoples were as soft as the stuff they sailed upon. In our day we have progressed to a point where such sentiments mark weakness and atavism. It will not be well for you to permit Tars Tarkas to learn that you hold such degenerate sentiments, as I doubt that he would care to entrust such as you with the grave responsibilities of maternity."

"I see nothing wrong with my expression of interest in this red woman," retorted Sola. "She has never harmed us, nor would she should we have fallen into her hands. It is only the men of her kind who war upon us, and I have ever thought that their attitude toward us is but the reflection of ours toward them. They live at peace with all their fellows, except when duty calls upon them to make war, while we are at peace with none; forever warring among our own kind as well as upon the red men, and even in our own communities the individuals fight amongst themselves. Oh, it is one continual, awful period of bloodshed from the time we break the shell until we gladly embrace the bosom of the river of mystery, the dark and ancient Iss which carries us to an unknown, but at least no more frightful and terrible existence! Fortunate indeed is he who meets his end in an early death. Say what you please to Tars Tarkas, he can mete out no worse fate to me than a continuation of the horrible existence we are forced to lead in this life."

This wild outbreak on the part of Sola so greatly surprised and shocked the other women, that, after a few words of general reprimand, they all lapsed into silence and were soon asleep. One thing the episode had accomplished was to assure me of Sola's friendliness toward the poor girl, and also to convince me that I had been extremely fortunate in falling into her hands rather than those of some of the other females. I knew that she was fond of me, and now that I had discovered that she hated cruelty and barbarity I was confident that I could depend upon her to aid me and the girl captive to escape, provided of course that such a thing was within the range of possibilities.

I did not even know that there were any better conditions to escape to, but I was more than willing to take my chances among people fashioned after my own mold rather than to remain longer among the hideous and bloodthirsty green men of Mars. But where to go, and how, was as much of a puzzle to me as the age-old search for the spring of eternal life has been to earthly men since the beginning of time.

I decided that at the first opportunity I would take Sola into my confidence and openly ask her to aid me, and with this resolution strong upon me I turned among my silks and furs and slept the dreamless and refreshing sleep of Mars.

Chapter X
ᏫᎦᎻᏚᏕᏴᎻᎨᎾ ᏚᏘᎦ ᏫᎦᏴᎢᏟ
(Champion and Chief)

Early the next morning I was astir. Considerable freedom was allowed me, as Sola had informed me that so long as I did not attempt to leave the city I was free to go and come as I pleased. She had warned me, however, against venturing forth unarmed, as this city, like all other deserted metropolises of an ancient Martian civilization, was peopled by the great white apes of my second day's adventure.

In advising me that I must not leave the boundaries of the city Sola had explained that Woola would prevent this anyway should I attempt it, and she warned me most urgently not to arouse his fierce nature by ignoring his warnings should I venture too close to the forbidden territory. His nature was such, she said, that he would bring me back into the city dead or alive should I persist in opposing him; "preferably dead," she added.

On this morning I had chosen a new street to explore when suddenly I found myself at the limits of the city. Before me were low hills pierced by narrow and inviting ravines. I longed to explore the country before me, and, like the pioneer stock from which I sprang, to view what the landscape beyond the encircling hills might disclose from the summits which shut out my view.

It also occurred to me that this would prove an excellent opportunity to test the qualities of Woola. I was convinced that the brute loved me; I had seen more evidences of affection in him than in any other Martian animal, man or beast, and I was sure that gratitude for the acts that had twice saved his life would more than outweigh his loyalty to the duty imposed upon him by cruel and loveless masters.

As I approached the boundary line Woola ran anxiously before me, and thrust his body against my legs. His expression was pleading rather than ferocious, nor did he bare his great tusks or utter his fearful guttural warnings. Denied the friendship and companionship of my kind, I had developed considerable affection for Woola and Sola, for the normal earthly man must have some outlet for his natural affections, and so I decided upon an appeal to a like instinct in this great brute, sure that I would not be disappointed.

I had never petted nor fondled him, but now I sat upon the ground and putting my arms around his heavy neck I stroked and coaxed him, talking in my newly acquired Martian tongue as I would have to my hound at

home, as I would have talked to any other friend among
the lower animals. His response to my manifestation of
affection was remarkable to a degree; he stretched his
great mouth to its full width, baring the entire expanse
of his upper rows of tusks and wrinkling his snout until
his great eyes were almost hidden by the folds of flesh.
If you have ever seen a collie smile you may have some
idea of Woola's facial distortion.

He threw himself upon his back and fairly wallowed
at my feet; jumped up and sprang upon me, rolling me
upon the ground by his great weight; then wriggling
and squirming around me like a playful puppy presenting its back for the petting it craves. I could not resist
the ludicrousness of the spectacle, and holding my sides
I rocked back and forth in the first laughter which had
passed my lips in many days; the first, in fact, since the
morning Powell had left camp when his horse, long
unused, had precipitately and unexpectedly bucked him
off headforemost into a pot of frijoles.

My laughter frightened Woola, his antics ceased
and he crawled pitifully toward me, poking his ugly
head far into my lap; and then I remembered what
laughter signified on Mars—torture, suffering, death.
Quieting myself, I rubbed the poor old fellow's head
and back, talked to him for a few minutes, and then

in an authoritative tone commanded him to follow me, and arising started for the hills.

There was no further question of authority between us; Woola was my devoted slave from that moment hence, and I his only and undisputed master. My walk to the hills occupied but a few minutes, and I found nothing of particular interest to reward me. Numerous brilliantly colored and strangely formed wild flowers dotted the ravines and from the summit of the first hill I saw still other hills stretching off toward the north, and rising, one range above another, until lost in mountains of quite respectable dimensions; though I afterward found that only a few peaks on all Mars exceed four thousand feet in height; the suggestion of magnitude was merely relative.

My morning's walk had been large with importance to me for it had resulted in a perfect understanding with Woola, upon whom Tars Tarkas relied for my safe keeping. I now knew that while theoretically a prisoner I was virtually free, and I hastened to regain the city limits before the defection of Woola could be discovered by his erstwhile masters. The adventure decided me never again to leave the limits of my prescribed stamping grounds until I was ready to venture forth for good and all, as it would certainly result in a curtailment of my liberties, as well as the probable death of Woola, were we to be discovered.

On regaining the plaza I had my third glimpse of the captive girl. She was standing with her guards before the entrance to the audience chamber, and as I approached she gave me one haughty glance and turned her back full upon me. The act was so womanly, so earthly womanly, that though it stung my pride it also warmed my heart with a feeling of companionship; it was good to know that someone else on Mars beside myself had human instincts of a civilized order, even though the manifestation of them was so painful and mortifying.

Had a green Martian woman desired to show dislike or contempt she would, in all likelihood, have done it with a sword thrust or a movement of her trigger finger; but as their sentiments are mostly atrophied it would have required a serious injury to have aroused such passions in them. Sola, let me add, was an exception; I never saw her perform a cruel or uncouth act, or fail in uniform kindliness and good nature. She was indeed, as her fellow Martian had said of her, an atavism; a dear and precious reversion to a former type of loved and loving ancestor.

Seeing that the prisoner seemed the center of

attraction I halted to view the proceedings. I had not long to wait for presently Lorquas Ptomel and his retinue of chieftains approached the building and, signing the guards to follow with the prisoner, entered the audience chamber. Realizing that I was a somewhat favored character, and also convinced that the warriors did not know of my proficiency in their language, as I had pleaded with Sola to keep this a secret on the grounds that I did not wish to be forced to talk with the men until I had perfectly mastered the Martian tongue, I chanced an attempt to enter the audience chamber and listen to the proceedings.

The council squatted upon the steps of the rostrum, while below them stood the prisoner and her two guards. I saw that one of the women was Sarkoja, and thus understood how she had been present at the hearing of the preceding day, the results of which she had reported to the occupants of our dormitory last night. Her attitude toward the captive was most harsh and brutal. When she held her, she sunk her rudimentary nails into the poor girl's flesh, or twisted her arm in a most painful manner. When it was necessary to move from one spot to another she either jerked her roughly, or pushed her headlong before her. She seemed to be venting upon this poor defenseless creature all the hatred, cruelty, ferocity, and spite of her nine hundred years, backed by unguessable ages of fierce and brutal ancestors.

The other woman was less cruel because she was entirely indifferent; if the prisoner had been left to her alone, and fortunately she was at night, she would have received no harsh treatment, nor, by the same token would she have received any attention at all.

As Lorquas Ptomel raised his eyes to address the prisoner they fell on me and he turned to Tars Tarkas with a word, and gesture of impatience. Tars Tarkas made some reply which I could not catch, but which caused Lorquas Ptomel to smile; after which they paid no further attention to me.

"What is your name?" asked Lorquas Ptomel, addressing the prisoner.

"Dejah Thoris, daughter of Mors Kajak of Helium."

"And the nature of your expedition?" he continued.

"It was a purely scientific research party sent out by my father's father, the Jeddak of Helium, to rechart the air currents, and to take atmospheric density tests," replied the fair prisoner, in a low, well-modulated voice.

"We were unprepared for battle," she continued, "as we were on a peaceful mission, as our banners and the colors of our craft denoted. The work we were doing was as much in your interests as in ours, for you know full well that were it not for our labors and the fruits of our scientific operations there would not be enough air or water on Mars to support a single human life. For ages we have maintained the air and water supply at practically the same point without an appreciable loss, and we have done this in the face of the brutal and ignorant interference of your green men.

"Why, oh, why will you not learn to live in amity with your fellows, must you ever go on down the ages to your final extinction but little above the plane of the dumb brutes that serve you! A people without written language, without art, without homes, without love; the victim of eons of the horrible community idea. Owning everything in common, even to your women and children, has resulted in your owning nothing in common. You hate each other as you hate all else except yourselves. Come back to the ways of our common ancestors, come back to the light of kindliness and fellowship. The way is open to you, you will find the hands of the red men stretched out to aid you. Together we may do still more to regenerate our dying planet. The granddaughter of the greatest and mightiest of the red jeddaks has asked you. Will you come?"

Lorquas Ptomel and the warriors sat looking silently

and intently at the young woman for several moments after she had ceased speaking. What was passing in their minds no man may know, but that they were moved I truly believe, and if one man high among them had been strong enough to rise above custom, that moment would have marked a new and mighty era for Mars.

I saw Tars Tarkas rise to speak, and on his face was such an expression as I had never seen upon the countenance of a green Martian warrior. It bespoke an inward and mighty battle with self, with heredity, with age-old custom, and as he opened his mouth to speak, a look almost of benignity, of kindliness, momentarily lighted up his fierce and terrible countenance.

What words of moment were to have fallen from his lips were never spoken, as just then a young warrior, evidently sensing the trend of thought among the older men, leaped down from the steps of the rostrum, and striking the frail captive a powerful blow across the face, which felled her to the floor, placed his foot upon her prostrate form and turning toward the assembled council broke into peals of horrid, mirthless laughter.

For an instant I thought Tars Tarkas would strike him dead, nor did the aspect of Lorquas Ptomel augur any too favorably for the brute, but the mood passed, their old selves reasserted their ascendency, and they smiled. It was portentous however that they did not laugh aloud, for the brute's act constituted a side-splitting witticism according to the ethics which rule green Martian humor.

That I have taken moments to write down a part of what occurred as that blow fell does not signify that I remained inactive for any such length of time. I think I must have sensed something of what was coming, for I realize now that I was crouched as for a spring as I saw the blow aimed at her beautiful, upturned, pleading face, and ere the hand descended I was halfway across the hall.

Scarcely had his hideous laugh rang out but once, when I was upon him. The brute was twelve feet in height and armed to the teeth, but I believe that I could have accounted for the whole roomful in the terrific intensity of my rage. Springing upward, I struck him full in the face as he turned at my warning cry and then as he drew his short-sword I drew mine and sprang up again upon his breast, hooking one leg over the butt of his pistol and grasping one of his huge tusks with my left hand while I delivered blow after blow upon his enormous chest.

He could not use his short-sword to advantage because I was too close to him, nor could he draw his pistol, which he attempted to do in direct opposition to Martian custom which says that you may not fight a fellow warrior in private combat with any other than the weapon with which you are attacked. In fact he could do nothing but make a wild and futile attempt to dislodge me. With all his immense bulk he was little if any stronger than I, and it was but the matter of a moment or two before he sank, bleeding and lifeless, to the floor.

Dejah Thoris had raised herself upon one elbow and was watching the battle with wide, staring eyes. When I had regained my feet I raised her in my arms and bore her to one of the benches at the side of the room.

Again no Martian interfered with me, and tearing a piece of silk from my cape I endeavored to staunch the flow of blood from her nostrils. I was soon successful as her injuries amounted to little more than an ordinary nosebleed, and when she could speak she placed her hand upon my arm and looking up into my eyes, said:

"Why did you do it? You who refused me even friendly recognition in the first hour of my peril! And now you risk your life and kill one of your companions for my sake. I cannot understand. What strange manner of man are you, that you consort with the green men, though your form is that of my race, while your color is little darker than that of the white ape? Tell me, are you human, or are you more than human?"

"It is a strange tale," I replied, "too long to attempt to tell you now, and one which I so much doubt the credibility of myself that I fear to hope that others will believe it. Suffice it, for the present, that I am your friend, and, so far as our captors will permit, your protector and your servant."

"Then you too are a prisoner? But why, then, those arms and the regalia of a Tharkian chieftain? What is your name? Where your country?"

"Yes, Dejah Thoris, I too am a prisoner; my name is John Carter, and I claim Virginia, one of the United States of America, Earth, as my home; but why I am permitted to wear arms I do not know, nor was I aware that my regalia was that of a chieftain."

We were interrupted at this juncture by the approach of one of the warriors, bearing arms, accouterments and ornaments, and in a flash one of her questions was answered and a puzzle cleared up for me. I saw that the body of my dead antagonist had been stripped, and I read in the menacing yet respectful attitude of the warrior who had brought me these trophies of the kill the same demeanor as that evinced by the other who had brought me my original equipment, and now for the first time I realized that my blow, on the occasion of my first battle in the audience chamber had resulted in the death of my adversary.

The reason for the whole attitude displayed toward me was now apparent; I had won my spurs, so to speak, and in the crude justice, which always marks Martian dealings, and which, among other things, has caused me to call her the planet of paradoxes, I was accorded the honors due a conqueror; the trappings and the position of the man I killed. In truth, I was a Martian chieftain, and this I learned later was the cause of my great freedom and my toleration in the audience chamber.

As I had turned to receive the dead warrior's chattels I had noticed that Tars Tarkas and several others had pushed forward toward us, and the eyes of the former rested upon me in a most quizzical manner. Finally he addressed me:

"You speak the tongue of Barsoom quite readily for one who was deaf and dumb to us a few short days ago. Where did you learn it, John Carter?"

"You, yourself, are responsible, Tars Tarkas," I replied, "in that you furnished me with an instructress of remarkable ability; I have to thank Sola for my learning."

"She has done well," he answered, "but your education in other respects needs considerable polish. Do you know what your unprecedented temerity would have cost you had you failed to kill either of the two chieftains whose metal you now wear?"

"I presume that that one whom I had failed to kill, would have killed me," I answered, smiling.

"No, you are wrong. Only in the last extremity of self-defense would a Martian warrior kill a prisoner; we like to save them for other purposes," and his face bespoke possibilities that were not pleasant to dwell upon.

"But one thing can save you now," he continued. "Should you, in recognition of your remarkable valor, ferocity, and prowess, be considered by Tal Hajus as worthy of his service you may be taken into the community and become a full-fledged Tharkian. Until we reach the headquarters of Tal Hajus it is the will of Lorquas Ptomel that you be accorded the respect your acts have earned you. You will be treated by us as a Tharkian chieftain, but you must not forget that every chief who ranks you is responsible for your safe delivery to our mighty and most ferocious ruler. I am done."

"I hear you, Tars Tarkas," I answered. "As you know I am not of Barsoom; your ways are not my ways, and I can only act in the future as I have in the past, in accordance with the dictates of my conscience and guided by the standards of mine own people. If you will leave me alone I will go in peace, but if not, let the individual Barsoomians with whom I must deal either respect my rights as a stranger among you, or take whatever consequences may befall. Of one thing let us be sure, whatever may be your ultimate intentions toward this unfortunate young woman, whoever would offer her injury or insult in the future must figure on making a full accounting to me. I understand that you belittle all sentiments of generosity and kindliness, but I do not, and I can convince your most doughty warrior that these characteristics are not incompatible with an ability to fight."

Ordinarily I am not given to long speeches, nor ever before had I descended to bombast, but I had guessed at the keynote which would strike an answering chord in the breasts of the green Martians, nor was I wrong, for my harangue evidently deeply impressed them, and their attitude toward me thereafter was still further respectful.

Tars Tarkas himself seemed pleased with my reply, but his only comment was more or less enigmatical—"And I think I know Tal Hajus, Jeddak of Thark."

I now turned my attention to Dejah Thoris, and assisting her to her feet I turned with her toward the exit, ignoring her hovering guardian harpies as well as the inquiring glances of the chieftains. Was I not now a chieftain also! Well, then, I would assume the responsibilities of one. They did not molest us, and so Dejah Thoris, Princess of Helium, and John Carter, gentleman of Virginia, followed by the faithful Woola, passed through utter silence from the audience chamber of Lorquas Ptomel, Jed among the Tharks of Barsoom.

Chapter XI
𝕨𝕚⋇𝕤 𝕤𝕚𝕔𝕤𝕙𝕤 ⋇𝕤𝕙𝕡𝕙𝕚𝕝

(With Dejah Thoris)

As we reached the open the two female guards who had been detailed to watch over Dejah Thoris hurried up and made as though to assume custody of her once more. The poor child shrank against me and I felt her two little hands fold tightly over my arm. Waving the women away, I informed them that Sola would attend the captive hereafter, and I further warned Sarkoja that any more of her cruel attentions bestowed upon Dejah Thoris would result in Sarkoja's sudden and painful demise.

My threat was unfortunate and resulted in more harm than good to Dejah Thoris, for, as I learned later, men do not kill women upon Mars, nor women, men. So Sarkoja merely gave us an ugly look and departed to hatch up deviltries against us.

I soon found Sola and explained to her that I wished her to guard Dejah Thoris as she had guarded me; that I wished her to find other quarters where they would not be molested by Sarkoja, and I finally informed her that I myself would take up my quarters among the men.

Sola glanced at the accouterments which were

carried in my hand and slung across my shoulder.

"You are a great chieftain now, John Carter," she said, "and I must do your bidding, though indeed I am glad to do it under any circumstances. The man whose metal you carry was young, but he was a great warrior, and had by his promotions and kills won his way close to the rank of Tars Tarkas, who, as you know, is second to Lorquas Ptomel only. You are eleventh, there are but ten chieftains in this community who rank you in prowess."

"And if I should kill Lorquas Ptomel?" I asked.

"You would be first, John Carter; but you may only win that honor by the will of the entire council that Lorquas Ptomel meet you in combat, or should he attack you, you may kill him in self-defense, and thus win first place."

I laughed, and changed the subject. I had no particular desire to kill Lorquas Ptomel, and less to be a jed among the Tharks.

I accompanied Sola and Dejah Thoris in a search for new quarters, which we found in a building nearer the audience chamber and of far more pretentious architecture than our former habitation. We also found in this building real sleeping apartments with ancient beds of highly wrought metal swinging from enormous gold chains depending from the marble ceilings. The decoration of the walls was most elaborate, and, unlike the frescoes in the other buildings I had examined, portrayed many human figures in the compositions. These were of people like myself, and of a much lighter color than Dejah Thoris. They were clad in graceful, flowing robes, highly ornamented with metal and jewels, and their luxuriant hair was of a beautiful golden and reddish bronze. The men were beardless and only a few wore arms. The scenes depicted for the most part, a fair-skinned, fair-haired people at play.

Dejah Thoris clasped her hands with an exclamation of rapture as she gazed upon these magnificent works of art, wrought by a people long extinct; while Sola, on the other hand, apparently did not see them.

We decided to use this room, on the second floor and overlooking the plaza, for Dejah Thoris and Sola, and another room adjoining and in the rear for the cooking and supplies. I then dispatched Sola to bring the bedding and such food and utensils as she might need, telling her that I would guard Dejah Thoris until her return.

As Sola departed Dejah Thoris turned to me with a faint smile.

"And whereto, then, would your prisoner escape should you leave her, unless it was to follow you and crave your protection, and ask your pardon for the cruel thoughts she has harbored against you these past few days?"

"You are right," I answered, "there is no escape for either of us unless we go together."

"I heard your challenge to the creature you call Tars Tarkas, and I think I understand your position among these people, but what I cannot fathom is your statement that you are not of Barsoom.

"In the name of my first ancestor, then," she continued, "where may you be from? You are like unto my people, and yet so unlike. You speak my language, and yet I heard you tell Tars Tarkas that you had but learned it recently. All Barsoomians speak the same tongue from the ice-clad south to the ice-clad north, though their written languages differ. Only in the valley Dor, where the river Iss empties into the lost sea of Korus, is there supposed to be a different language spoken, and, except in the legends of our ancestors, there is no record of a Barsoomian returning up the river Iss, from the shores of Korus in the valley of Dor. Do not tell me that you have thus returned! They would kill you horribly anywhere upon the surface of Barsoom if that were true; tell me it is not!"

Her eyes were filled with a strange, weird light; her

voice was pleading, and her little hands, reached up upon my breast, were pressed against me as though to wring a denial from my very heart.

"I do not know your customs, Dejah Thoris, but in my own Virginia a gentleman does not lie to save himself; I am not of Dor; I have never seen the mysterious Iss; the lost sea of Korus is still lost, so far as I am concerned. Do you believe me?"

And then it struck me suddenly that I was very anxious that she should believe me. It was not that I feared the results which would follow a general belief that I had returned from the Barsoomian heaven or hell, or whatever it was. Why was it, then! Why should I care what she thought? I looked down at her; her beautiful face upturned, and her wonderful eyes opening up the very depth of her soul; and as my eyes met hers I knew why, and—I shuddered.

A similar wave of feeling seemed to stir her; she drew away from me with a sigh, and with her earnest, beautiful face turned up to mine, she whispered: "I believe you, John Carter; I do not know what a 'gentleman' is, nor have I ever heard before of Virginia; but on Barsoom no *man* lies; if he does not wish to speak the truth he is silent. Where is this Virginia, your country, John Carter?" she asked, and it seemed that this fair name of my fair land had never sounded more beautiful than as it fell from those perfect lips on that far-gone day.

"I am of another world," I answered, "the great planet Earth, which revolves about our common sun and next within the orbit of your Barsoom, which we know as Mars. How I came here I cannot tell you, for I do not know; but here I am, and since my presence has permitted me to serve Dejah Thoris I am glad that I am here."

She gazed at me with troubled eyes, long and questioningly. That it was difficult to believe my statement I well knew, nor could I hope that she would do so however much I craved her confidence and respect. I would much rather not have told her anything of my antecedents, but no man could look into the depth of those eyes and refuse her slightest behest.

Finally she smiled, and, rising, said: "I shall have to believe even though I cannot understand. I can readily perceive that you are not of the Barsoom of today; you are like us, yet different—but why should I trouble my poor head with such a problem, when my heart tells me that I believe because I wish to believe!"

It was good logic, good, earthly, feminine logic, and if it satisfied her I certainly could pick no flaws in it. As a matter of fact it was about the only kind of logic that could be brought to bear upon my problem. We fell into a general conversation then, asking and answering many questions on each side. She was curious to learn of the customs of my people and displayed a remarkable knowledge of events on Earth. When I questioned her closely on this seeming familiarity with earthly things she laughed, and cried out:

"Why, every school boy on Barsoom knows the geography, and much concerning the fauna and flora, as well as the history of your planet fully as well as of his own. Can we not see everything which takes place upon Earth, as you call it; is it not hanging there in the heavens in plain sight?"

This baffled me, I must confess, fully as much as my statements had confounded her; and I told her so. She then explained in general the instruments her people had used and been perfecting for ages, which permit them to throw upon a screen a perfect image of what is transpiring upon any planet and upon many of the stars. These pictures are so perfect in detail that, when photographed and enlarged, objects no greater than a blade of grass may be distinctly recognized. I afterward, in Helium, saw many of these pictures, as well as the instruments which produced them.

"If, then, you are so familiar with earthly things,"

I asked, "why is it that you do not recognize me as identical with the inhabitants of that planet?"

She smiled again as one might in bored indulgence of a questioning child.

"Because, John Carter," she replied, "nearly every planet and star having atmospheric conditions at all approaching those of Barsoom, shows forms of animal life almost identical with you and me; and, further, Earth men, almost without exception, cover their bodies with strange, unsightly pieces of cloth, and their heads with hideous contraptions the purpose of which we have been unable to conceive; while you, when found by the Tharkian warriors, were entirely undisfigured and unadorned.

"The fact that you wore no ornaments is a strong proof of your un-Barsoomian origin, while the absence of grotesque coverings might cause a doubt as to your earthliness."

I then narrated the details of my departure from the Earth, explaining that my body there lay fully clothed in all the, to her, strange garments of mundane dwellers. At this point Sola returned with our meager belongings and her young Martian protege, who, of course, would have to share the quarters with them.

Sola asked us if we had had a visitor during her

absence, and seemed much surprised when we answered in the negative. It seemed that as she had mounted the approach to the upper floors where our quarters were located, she had met Sarkoja descending. We decided that she must have been eavesdropping, but as we could recall nothing of importance that had passed between us we dismissed the matter as of little consequence, merely promising ourselves to be warned to the utmost caution in the future.

Dejah Thoris and I then fell to examining the architecture and decorations of the beautiful chambers of the building we were occupying. She told me that these people had presumably flourished over a hundred thousand years before. They were the early progenitors of her race, but had mixed with the other great race of early Martians, who were very dark, almost black, and also with the reddish yellow race which had flourished at the same time.

These three great divisions of the higher Martians had been forced into a mighty alliance as the drying up of the Martian seas had compelled them to seek the comparatively few and always diminishing fertile areas, and to defend themselves, under new conditions of life, against the wild hordes of green men.

Ages of close relationship and intermarrying had

resulted in the race of red men, of which Dejah Thoris was a fair and beautiful daughter. During the ages of hardships and incessant warring between their own various races, as well as with the green men, and before they had fitted themselves to the changed conditions, much of the high civilization and many of the arts of the fair-haired Martians had become lost; but the red race of today has reached a point where it feels that it has made up in new discoveries and in a more practical civilization for all that lies irretrievably buried with the ancient Barsoomians, beneath the countless intervening ages.

These ancient Martians had been a highly cultivated and literary race, but during the vicissitudes of those trying centuries of readjustment to new conditions, not only did their advancement and production cease entirely, but practically all their archives, records, and literature were lost.

Dejah Thoris related many interesting facts and legends concerning this lost race of noble and kindly people. She said that the city in which we were camping was supposed to have been a center of commerce and culture known as Korad. It had been built upon a beautiful, natural harbor, landlocked by magnificent hills. The little valley on the west front of the city, she explained, was all that remained of the harbor, while the pass through the hills to the old sea bottom had been the channel through which the shipping passed up to the city's gates.

The shores of the ancient seas were dotted with just such cities, and lesser ones, in diminishing numbers, were to be found converging toward the center of the oceans, as the people had found it necessary to follow the receding waters until necessity had forced upon them their ultimate salvation, the so-called Martian canals.

We had been so engrossed in exploration of the building and in our conversation that it was late in the afternoon before we realized it. We were brought back to a realization of our present conditions by a messenger bearing a summons from Lorquas Ptomel directing me to appear before him forthwith. Bidding Dejah Thoris and Sola farewell, and commanding Woola to remain on guard, I hastened to the audience chamber, where I found Lorquas Ptomel and Tars Tarkas seated upon the rostrum.

Chapter XII
ఈ ౬ఇ౪౧౿ఽ౿ఌ ౶౪*ఽ ౿౪౶౿ఌ
(A Prisoner with Power)

As I entered and saluted, Lorquas Ptomel signaled me to advance, and, fixing his great, hideous eyes upon me, addressed me thus:

"You have been with us a few days, yet during that time you have by your prowess won a high position among us. Be that as it may, you are not one of us; you owe us no allegiance.

"Your position is a peculiar one," he continued; "you are a prisoner and yet you give commands which must be obeyed; you are an alien and yet you are a Tharkian chieftain; you are a midget and yet you can kill a mighty warrior with one blow of your fist. And now you are reported to have been plotting to escape with another prisoner of another race; a prisoner who, from her own admission, half believes you are returned from the valley of Dor. Either one of these accusations, if proved, would be sufficient grounds for your execution, but we are a just people and you shall have a trial on our return to Thark, if Tal Hajus so commands.

"But," he continued, in his fierce guttural tones, "if you run off with the red girl it is I who shall have to account to Tal Hajus; it is I who shall have to face Tars Tarkas, and either demonstrate my right to command, or the metal from my dead carcass will go to a better man, for such is the custom of the Tharks.

"I have no quarrel with Tars Tarkas; together we rule supreme the greatest of the lesser communities among the green men; we do not wish to fight between ourselves; and so if you were dead, John Carter, I should be glad. Under two conditions only, however, may you be killed by us without orders from Tal Hajus; in personal combat in self-defense, should you attack one of us, or were you apprehended in an attempt to escape.

"As a matter of justice I must warn you that we only await one of these two excuses for ridding ourselves of so great a responsibility. The safe delivery of the red girl to Tal Hajus is of the greatest importance. Not in a thousand years have the Tharks made such a capture; she is the granddaughter of the greatest of the red jeddaks, who is also our bitterest enemy. I have spoken. The red girl told us that we were without the softer sentiments of humanity, but we are a just and truthful race. You may go."

Turning, I left the audience chamber. So this was the beginning of Sarkoja's persecution! I knew that none other could be responsible for this report which had reached the ears of Lorquas Ptomel so quickly, and now I recalled those portions of our conversation which had touched upon escape and upon my origin.

Sarkoja was at this time Tars Tarkas' oldest and most trusted female. As such she was a mighty power behind the throne, for no warrior had the confidence of Lorquas Ptomel to such an extent as did his ablest lieutenant, Tars Tarkas.

However, instead of putting thoughts of possible escape from my mind, my audience with Lorquas Ptomel only served to center my every faculty on this subject. Now, more than before, the absolute necessity for escape, in so far as Dejah Thoris was concerned, was impressed upon me, for I was convinced that some horrible fate awaited her at the headquarters of Tal Hajus.

As described by Sola, this monster was the exaggerated personification of all the ages of cruelty, ferocity, and brutality from which he had descended. Cold, cunning, calculating; he was, also, in marked contrast to most of his fellows, a slave to that brute passion which the waning demands for procreation upon their dying planet has almost stilled in the Martian breast.

The thought that the divine Dejah Thoris might fall into the clutches of such an abysmal atavism started the cold sweat upon me. Far better that we save friendly bullets for ourselves at the last moment, as did those brave frontier women of my lost land, who took their own lives rather than fall into the hands of the Indian braves.

As I wandered about the plaza lost in my gloomy forebodings Tars Tarkas approached me on his way from the audience chamber. His demeanor toward me was unchanged, and he greeted me as though we had not just parted a few moments before.

"Where are your quarters, John Carter?" he asked.

"I have selected none," I replied. "It seemed best that I quartered either by myself or among the other warriors, and I was awaiting an opportunity to ask your advice. As you know," and I smiled, "I am not yet familiar with all the customs of the Tharks."

"Come with me," he directed, and together we moved off across the plaza to a building which I was glad to see adjoined that occupied by Sola and her charges.

"My quarters are on the first floor of this building," he said, "and the second floor also is fully occupied by warriors, but the third floor and the floors above are vacant; you may take your choice of these.

"I understand," he continued, "that you have given up your woman to the red prisoner. Well, as you have said, your ways are not our ways, but you can fight well enough to do about as you please, and so, if you wish to give your woman to a captive, it is your own affair; but as a chieftain you should have those to serve you, and in accordance with our customs you may select any or all the females from the retinues of the chieftains whose metal you now wear."

I thanked him, but assured him that I could get along very nicely without assistance except in the matter of preparing food, and so he promised to send women to me for this purpose and also for the care of my arms and the manufacture of my ammunition, which he said would be necessary. I suggested that they might also bring some of the sleeping silks and furs which belonged to me as spoils of combat, for the nights were cold and I had none of my own.

He promised to do so, and departed. Left alone, I ascended the winding corridor to the upper floors in search of suitable quarters. The beauties of the other buildings were repeated in this, and, as usual, I was soon lost in a tour of investigation and discovery.

I finally chose a front room on the third floor, because this brought me nearer to Dejah Thoris, whose apartment was on the second floor of the adjoining building, and it flashed upon me that I could rig up some means of communication whereby she might signal me in case she needed either my services or my protection.

Adjoining my sleeping apartment were baths, dressing rooms, and other sleeping and living apartments, in all some ten rooms on this floor. The windows of the back rooms overlooked an enormous court, which formed the center of the square made by the buildings which faced the four contiguous streets, and which was now given over to the quartering of the various animals belonging to the warriors occupying the adjoining buildings.

While the court was entirely overgrown with the yellow, moss-like vegetation which blankets practically the entire surface of Mars, yet numerous fountains, statuary, benches, and pergola-like contraptions bore witness to the beauty which the court must have presented in bygone times, when graced by the fair-haired, laughing people whom stern and unalterable cosmic laws had driven not only from their homes, but from all except the vague legends of their descendants.

One could easily picture the gorgeous foliage of the luxurious Martian vegetation which once filled this scene with life and color; the graceful figures of the beautiful women, the straight and handsome men; the happy frolicking children—all sunlight, happiness and peace. It was difficult to realize that they had gone; down through the ages of darkness, cruelty, and ignorance, until their hereditary instincts of culture and humanitarianism had risen ascendant once more in the final composite race which now is dominant upon Mars.

My thoughts were cut short by the advent of several young females bearing loads of weapons, silks, furs, jewels, cooking utensils, and casks of food and drink, including considerable loot from the air craft. All this, it seemed, had been the property of the two chieftains I had slain, and now, by the customs of the Tharks, it had become mine. At my direction they placed the stuff in one of the back rooms, and then departed, only to return with a second load, which they advised me constituted the balance of my goods. On the second trip they were accompanied by ten or fifteen other women and youths, who, it seemed, formed the retinues of the two chieftains.

They were not their families, nor their wives, nor their servants; the relationship was peculiar, and so unlike anything known to us that it is most difficult to describe. All property among the green Martians is owned in common by the community, except the personal weapons, ornaments and sleeping silks and furs of the individuals. These alone can one claim undisputed right to, nor may he accumulate more of these than are required for his actual needs. The surplus he holds merely as custodian, and it is passed on to the younger members of the community as necessity demands.

The women and children of a man's retinue may be likened to a military unit for which he is responsible in various ways, as in matters of instruction, discipline, sustenance, and the exigencies of their continual roamings and their unending strife with other communities and with the red Martians. His women are in no sense wives. The green Martians use no word corresponding in meaning with this earthly word. Their mating is a matter of community interest solely, and is directed without reference to natural selection. The council of chieftains of each community control the matter as surely as the owner of a Kentucky racing stud directs the scientific breeding of his stock for the improvement of the whole.

In theory it may sound well, as is often the case with theories, but the results of ages of this unnatural practice, coupled with the community interest in the offspring being held paramount to that of the mother, is shown in the cold, cruel creatures, and their gloomy, loveless, mirthless existence.

It is true that the green Martians are absolutely

virtuous, both men and women, with the exception of such degenerates as Tal Hajus; but better far a finer balance of human characteristics even at the expense of a slight and occasional loss of chastity.

Finding that I must assume responsibility for these creatures, whether I would or not, I made the best of it and directed them to find quarters on the upper floors, leaving the third floor to me. One of the girls I charged with the duties of my simple cuisine, and directed the others to take up the various activities which had formerly constituted their vocations. Thereafter I saw little of them, nor did I care to.

Chapter XIII
ᕬ)ᕬᔑᛁᖳ-ᕭᕬᔐᖵᖵᕀᖳᕐ ᕬᔐᕆ ᕭᕬᕐᕀᕲ

(Love-Making on Mars)

FOLLOWING THE BATTLE with the air ships, the
community remained within the city for several days,
abandoning the homeward march until they could feel
reasonably assured that the ships would not return; for
to be caught on the open plains with a cavalcade of
chariots and children was far from the desire of even so
warlike a people as the green Martians.

During our period of inactivity, Tars Tarkas had
instructed me in many of the customs and arts of war
familiar to the Tharks, including lessons in riding and
guiding the great beasts which bore the warriors. These
creatures, which are known as thoats, are as dangerous
and vicious as their masters, but when once subdued
are sufficiently tractable for the purposes of the green
Martians.

Two of these animals had fallen to me from the
warriors whose metal I wore, and in a short time I could
handle them quite as well as the native warriors. The
method was not at all complicated. If the thoats did
not respond with sufficient celerity to the telepathic
instructions of their riders they were dealt a terrific

blow between the ears with the butt of a pistol, and if they showed fight this treatment was continued until the brutes either were subdued, or had unseated their riders.

In the latter case it became a life and death struggle between the man and the beast. If the former were quick enough with his pistol he might live to ride again, though upon some other beast; if not, his torn and mangled body was gathered up by his women and burned in accordance with Tharkian custom.

My experience with Woola determined me to attempt the experiment of kindness in my treatment of my thoats. First I taught them that they could not unseat me, and even rapped them sharply between the ears to impress upon them my authority and mastery. Then, by degrees, I won their confidence in much the same manner as I had adopted countless times with my many mundane mounts. I was ever a good hand with animals, and by inclination, as well as because it brought more lasting and satisfactory results, I was always kind and humane in my dealings with the lower orders. I could take a human life, if necessary, with far less compunction than that of a poor, unreasoning, irresponsible brute.

In the course of a few days my thoats were the

wonder of the entire community. They would follow me like dogs, rubbing their great snouts against my body in awkward evidence of affection, and respond to my every command with an alacrity and docility which caused the Martian warriors to ascribe to me the possession of some earthly power unknown on Mars.

"How have you bewitched them?" asked Tars Tarkas one afternoon, when he had seen me run my arm far between the great jaws of one of my thoats which had wedged a piece of stone between two of his teeth while feeding upon the moss-like vegetation within our court yard.

"By kindness," I replied. "You see, Tars Tarkas, the softer sentiments have their value, even to a warrior. In the height of battle as well as upon the march I know that my thoats will obey my every command, and therefore my fighting efficiency is enhanced, and I am a better warrior for the reason that I am a kind master. Your other warriors would find it to the advantage of themselves as well as of the community to adopt my methods in this respect. Only a few days since you, yourself, told me that these great brutes, by the uncertainty of their tempers, often were the means of turning victory into defeat, since, at a crucial moment, they might elect to unseat and rend their riders."

"Show me how you accomplish these results," was Tars Tarkas' only rejoinder.

And so I explained as carefully as I could the entire method of training I had adopted with my beasts, and later he had me repeat it before Lorquas Ptomel and the assembled warriors. That moment marked the beginning of a new existence for the poor thoats, and before I left the community of Lorquas Ptomel I had the satisfaction of observing a regiment of as tractable and docile mounts as one might care to see. The effect on the precision and celerity of the military movements was so remarkable that Lorquas Ptomel presented me with a massive anklet of gold from his own leg, as a sign of his appreciation of my service to the horde.

On the seventh day following the battle with the air craft we again took up the march toward Thark, all probability of another attack being deemed remote by Lorquas Ptomel.

During the days just preceding our departure I had seen but little of Dejah Thoris, as I had been kept very busy by Tars Tarkas with my lessons in the art of Martian warfare, as well as in the training of my thoats. The few times I had visited her quarters she had been absent, walking upon the streets with Sola, or investigating the buildings in the near vicinity of the plaza. I had warned them against venturing far from the plaza for fear of the great white apes, whose ferocity I was only too well acquainted with. However, since Woola accompanied them on all their excursions, and as Sola was well armed, there was comparatively little cause for fear.

On the evening before our departure I saw them approaching along one of the great avenues which lead into the plaza from the east. I advanced to meet them, and telling Sola that I would take the responsibility for Dejah Thoris' safekeeping, I directed her to return to her quarters on some trivial errand. I liked and trusted Sola, but for some reason I desired to be alone with Dejah Thoris, who represented to me all that I had left behind upon Earth in agreeable and congenial companionship. There seemed bonds of mutual interest between us as powerful as though we had been born under the same roof rather than upon different planets, hurtling through space some forty-eight million miles apart.

That she shared my sentiments in this respect I was positive, for on my approach the look of pitiful hopelessness left her sweet countenance to be replaced by a smile of joyful welcome, as she placed her little right hand upon my left shoulder in true red Martian salute.

"Sarkoja told Sola that you had become a true

Thark," she said, "and that I would now see no more of you than of any of the other warriors."

"Sarkoja is a liar of the first magnitude," I replied, "notwithstanding the proud claim of the Tharks to absolute verity."

Dejah Thoris laughed.

"I knew that even though you became a member of the community you would not cease to be my friend; 'A warrior may change his metal, but not his heart,' as the saying is upon Barsoom.

"I think they have been trying to keep us apart," she continued, "for whenever you have been off duty one of the older women of Tars Tarkas' retinue has always arranged to trump up some excuse to get Sola and me out of sight. They have had me down in the pits below the buildings helping them mix their awful radium powder, and make their terrible projectiles. You know that these have to be manufactured by artificial light, as exposure to sunlight always results in an explosion. You have noticed that their bullets explode when they strike an object? Well, the opaque, outer coating is broken by the impact, exposing a glass cylinder, almost solid, in the forward end of which is a minute particle of radium powder. The moment the sunlight, even though diffused, strikes this powder it explodes with a violence which nothing can withstand. If you ever witness a night battle you will note the absence of these explosions, while the morning following the battle will be filled at sunrise with the sharp detonations of exploding missiles fired the preceding night. As a rule, however, non-exploding projectiles are used at night."*

While I was much interested in Dejah Thoris' explanation of this wonderful adjunct to Martian warfare, I was more concerned by the immediate problem of their treatment of her. That they were keeping her away from me was not a matter for surprise, but that they should subject her to dangerous and arduous labor filled me with rage.

"Have they ever subjected you to cruelty and ignominy, Dejah Thoris?" I asked, feeling the hot blood of my fighting ancestors leap in my veins as I awaited her reply.

"Only in little ways, John Carter," she answered. "Nothing that can harm me outside my pride. They know that I am the daughter of ten thousand jeddaks, that I trace my ancestry straight back without a break

---

*I have used the word radium in describing this powder because in the light of recent discoveries on Earth I believe it to be a mixture of which radium is the base. In Captain Carter's manuscript it is mentioned always by the name used in the written language of Helium and is spelled in hieroglyphics which it would be difficult and useless to reproduce.

to the builder of the first great waterway, and they, who do not even know their own mothers, are jealous of me. At heart they hate their horrid fates, and so wreak their poor spite on me who stand for everything they have not, and for all they most crave and never can attain. Let us pity them, my chieftain, for even though we die at their hands we can afford them pity, since we are greater than they and they know it."

Had I known the significance of those words "my chieftain," as applied by a red Martian woman to a man, I should have had the surprise of my life, but I did not know at that time, nor for many months thereafter. Yes, I still had much to learn upon Barsoom.

"I presume it is the better part of wisdom that we bow to our fate with as good grace as possible, Dejah Thoris; but I hope, nevertheless, that I may be present the next time that any Martian, green, red, pink, or violet, has the temerity to even so much as frown on you, my princess."

Dejah Thoris caught her breath at my last words, and gazed upon me with dilated eyes and quickening breath, and then, with an odd little laugh, which brought roguish dimples to the corners of her mouth, she shook her head and cried:

"What a child! A great warrior and yet a stumbling little child."

"What have I done now?" I asked, in sore perplexity.

"Some day you shall know, John Carter, if we live; but I may not tell you. And I, the daughter of Mors Kajak, son of Tardos Mors, have listened without anger," she soliloquized in conclusion.

Then she broke out again into one of her gay, happy, laughing moods; joking with me on my prowess as a Thark warrior as contrasted with my soft heart and natural kindliness.

"I presume that should you accidentally wound an enemy you would take him home and nurse him back to health," she laughed.

"That is precisely what we do on Earth," I answered. "At least among civilized men."

This made her laugh again. She could not understand it, for, with all her tenderness and womanly sweetness, she was still a Martian, and to a Martian the only good enemy is a dead enemy; for every dead foeman means so much more to divide between those who live.

I was very curious to know what I had said or done to cause her so much perturbation a moment before and so I continued to importune her to enlighten me.

"No," she exclaimed, "it is enough that you have said it and that I have listened. And when you learn, John Carter, and if I be dead, as likely enough I shall be ere the further moon has circled Barsoom another twelve times, remember that I listened and that I—smiled."

It was all Greek to me, but the more I begged her to explain the more positive became her denials of my request, and, so, in very hopelessness, I desisted.

Day had now given away to night and as we wandered along the great avenue lighted by the two moons of Barsoom, and with Earth looking down upon us out of her luminous green eye, it seemed that we were alone in the universe, and I, at least, was content that it should be so.

The chill of the Martian night was upon us, and removing my silks I threw them across the shoulders of Dejah Thoris. As my arm rested for an instant upon her I felt a thrill pass through every fiber of my being such as contact with no other mortal had even produced; and it seemed to me that she had leaned slightly toward me, but of that I was not sure. Only I knew that as my arm rested there across her shoulders longer than the act of adjusting the silk required she did not draw away, nor did she speak. And so, in silence, we walked the surface of a dying world, but in the breast of one of us at least had been born that which is ever oldest, yet ever new.

I loved Dejah Thoris. The touch of my arm upon her naked shoulder had spoken to me in words I could not mistake, and I knew that I had loved her since the first moment that my eyes had met hers that first time in the plaza of the dead city of Korad.

Chapter XIV

ᔕ ᔕᔕᐸᐧᔭ) ᔕᔮ ᔕᔭᐸ ᔕᐸᔮᔕᔭ

(A Duel to the Death)

MY FIRST IMPULSE was to tell her of my love, and then I thought of the helplessness of her position wherein I alone could lighten the burdens of her captivity, and protect her in my poor way against the thousands of hereditary enemies she must face upon our arrival at Thark. I could not chance causing her additional pain or sorrow by declaring a love which, in all probability she did not return. Should I be so indiscreet, her position would be even more unbearable than now, and the thought that she might feel that I was taking advantage of her helplessness, to influence her decision was the final argument which sealed my lips.

"Why are you so quiet, Dejah Thoris?" I asked. "Possibly you would rather return to Sola and your quarters."

"No," she murmured, "I am happy here. I do not know why it is that I should always be happy and contented when you, John Carter, a stranger, are with me; yet at such times it seems that I am safe and that, with you, I shall soon return to my father's court and feel his strong arms about me and my mother's tears and kisses on my cheek."

"Do people kiss, then, upon Barsoom?" I asked, when she had explained the word she used, in answer to my inquiry as to its meaning.

"Parents, brothers, and sisters, yes; and," she added in a low, thoughtful tone, "lovers."

"And you, Dejah Thoris, have parents and brothers and sisters?"

"Yes."

"And a—lover?"

She was silent, nor could I venture to repeat the question.

"The man of Barsoom," she finally ventured, "does not ask personal questions of women, except his mother, and the woman he has fought for and won."

"But I have fought—" I started, and then I wished my tongue had been cut from my mouth; for she turned even as I caught myself and ceased, and drawing my silks from her shoulder she held them out to me, and without a word, and with head held high, she moved with the carriage of the queen she was toward the plaza and the doorway of her quarters.

I did not attempt to follow her, other than to see that she reached the building in safety, but, directing

Woola to accompany her, I turned disconsolately and entered my own house. I sat for hours cross-legged, and cross-tempered, upon my silks meditating upon the queer freaks chance plays upon us poor devils of mortals.

So this was love! I had escaped it for all the years I had roamed the five continents and their encircling seas; in spite of beautiful women and urging opportunity; in spite of a half-desire for love and a constant search for my ideal, it had remained for me to fall furiously and hopelessly in love with a creature from another world, of a species similar possibly, yet not identical with mine. A woman who was hatched from an egg, and whose span of life might cover a thousand years; whose people had strange customs and ideas; a woman whose hopes, whose pleasures, whose standards of virtue and of right and wrong might vary as greatly from mine as did those of the green Martians.

Yes, I was a fool, but I was in love, and though I was suffering the greatest misery I had ever known I would not have had it otherwise for all the riches of Barsoom. Such is love, and such are lovers wherever love is known.

To me, Dejah Thoris was all that was perfect; all that was virtuous and beautiful and noble and good. I believed that from the bottom of my heart, from the depth of my soul on that night in Korad as I sat cross-legged upon my silks while the nearer moon of Barsoom raced through the western sky toward the horizon, and lighted up the gold and marble, and jeweled mosaics of my world-old chamber, and I believe it today as I sit at my desk in the little study overlooking the Hudson. Twenty years have intervened; for ten of them I lived and fought for Dejah Thoris and her people, and for ten I have lived upon her memory.

The morning of our departure for Thark dawned clear and hot, as do all Martian mornings except for the six weeks when the snow melts at the poles.

I sought out Dejah Thoris in the throng of departing chariots, but she turned her shoulder to me, and I could see the red blood mount to her cheek. With the foolish inconsistency of love I held my peace when I might have plead ignorance of the nature of my offense, or at least the gravity of it, and so have effected, at worst, a half conciliation.

My duty dictated that I must see that she was comfortable, and so I glanced into her chariot and rearranged her silks and furs. In doing so I noted with horror that she was heavily chained by one ankle to the side of the vehicle.

"What does this mean?" I cried, turning to Sola.

"Sarkoja thought it best," she answered, her face betokening her disapproval of the procedure.

Examining the manacles I saw that they fastened with a massive spring lock.

"Where is the key, Sola? Let me have it."

"Sarkoja wears it, John Carter," she answered.

I turned without further word and sought out Tars Tarkas, to whom I vehemently objected to the unnecessary humiliations and cruelties, as they seemed to my lover's eyes, that were being heaped upon Dejah Thoris.

"John Carter," he answered, "if ever you and Dejah Thoris escape the Tharks it will be upon this journey. We know that you will not go without her. You have shown yourself a mighty fighter, and we do not wish to manacle you, so we hold you both in the easiest way that will yet ensure security. I have spoken."

I saw the strength of his reasoning at a flash, and knew that it were futile to appeal from his decision, but I asked that the key be taken from Sarkoja and that she be directed to leave the prisoner alone in future.

"This much, Tars Tarkas, you may do for me in return for the friendship that, I must confess, I feel for you."

"Friendship?" he replied. "There is no such thing, John Carter; but have your will. I shall direct that

Sarkoja cease to annoy the girl, and I myself will take the custody of the key."

"Unless you wish me to assume the responsibility," I said, smiling.

He looked at me long and earnestly before he spoke.

"Were you to give me your word that neither you nor Dejah Thoris would attempt to escape until after we have safely reached the court of Tal Hajus you might have the key and throw the chains into the river Iss."

"It were better that you held the key, Tars Tarkas," I replied.

He smiled, and said no more, but that night as we were making camp I saw him unfasten Dejah Thoris' fetters himself.

With all his cruel ferocity and coldness there was an undercurrent of something in Tars Tarkas which he seemed ever battling to subdue. Could it be a vestige of some human instinct come back from an ancient forbear to haunt him with the horror of his people's ways!

As I was approaching Dejah Thoris' chariot I passed Sarkoja, and the black, venomous look she accorded me was the sweetest balm I had felt for many hours. Lord, how she hated me! It bristled from her so palpably that one might almost have cut it with a sword.

A few moments later I saw her deep in conversation

with a warrior named Zad; a big, hulking, powerful brute, but one who had never made a kill among his own chieftains, and so was still an *o mad*, or man with one name; he could win a second name only with the metal of some chieftain. It was this custom which entitled me to the names of either of the chieftains I had killed; in fact, some of the warriors addressed me as Dotar Sojat, a combination of the surnames of the two warrior chieftains whose metal I had taken, or, in other words, whom I had slain in fair fight.

As Sarkoja talked with Zad he cast occasional glances in my direction, while she seemed to be urging him very strongly to some action. I paid little attention to it at the time, but the next day I had good reason to recall the circumstances, and at the same time gain a slight insight into the depths of Sarkoja's hatred and the lengths to which she was capable of going to wreak her horrid vengeance on me.

Dejah Thoris would have none of me again on this evening, and though I spoke her name she neither replied, nor conceded by so much as the flutter of an eyelid that she realized my existence. In my extremity I did what most other lovers would have done; I sought word from her through an intimate. In this instance it was Sola whom I intercepted in another part of camp.

"What is the matter with Dejah Thoris?" I blurted out at her. "Why will she not speak to me?"

Sola seemed puzzled herself, as though such strange actions on the part of two humans were quite beyond her, as indeed they were, poor child.

"She says you have angered her, and that is all she will say, except that she is the daughter of a jed and the granddaughter of a jeddak and she has been humiliated by a creature who could not polish the teeth of her grandmother's sorak."

I pondered over this report for some time, finally asking,

"What might a sorak be, Sola?"

"A little animal about as big as my hand, which the red Martian women keep to play with," explained Sola.

Not fit to polish the teeth of her grandmother's cat! I must rank pretty low in the consideration of Dejah Thoris, I thought; but I could not help laughing at the strange figure of speech, so homely and in this respect so earthly. It made me homesick, for it sounded very much like "not fit to polish her shoes." And then commenced a train of thought quite new to me. I began to wonder what my people at home were doing. I had not seen them for years. There was a family of Carters in Virginia who claimed close relationship with me; I was supposed to be a great uncle, or something of the kind equally foolish. I could pass anywhere for twenty-five to thirty years of age, and to be a great uncle always seemed the height of incongruity, for my thoughts and feelings were those of a boy. There were two little kiddies in the Carter family whom I had loved and who had thought there was no one on Earth like Uncle Jack; I could see them just as plainly, as I stood there under the moonlit skies of Barsoom, and I longed for them as I had never longed for any mortals before. By nature a wanderer, I had never known the true meaning of the word home, but the great hall of the Carters had always stood for all that the word did mean to me, and now my heart turned toward it from the cold and unfriendly peoples I had been thrown amongst. For did not even Dejah Thoris despise me! I was a low creature, so low in fact that I was not even fit to polish the teeth of her grandmother's cat; and then my saving sense of humor came to my rescue, and laughing I turned into my silks and furs and slept upon the moon-haunted ground the sleep of a tired and healthy fighting man.

We broke camp the next day at an early hour and marched with only a single halt until just before dark. Two incidents broke the tediousness of the march. About noon we espied far to our right what was evidently an incubator, and Lorquas Ptomel directed Tars Tarkas to investigate it. The latter took a dozen warriors, including myself, and we raced across the velvety carpeting of moss to the little enclosure.

It was indeed an incubator, but the eggs were very small in comparison with those I had seen hatching in ours at the time of my arrival on Mars.

Tars Tarkas dismounted and examined the enclosure minutely, finally announcing that it belonged to the green men of Warhoon and that the cement was scarcely dry where it had been walled up.

"They cannot be a day's march ahead of us," he exclaimed, the light of battle leaping to his fierce face.

The work at the incubator was short indeed. The warriors tore open the entrance and a couple of them, crawling in, soon demolished all the eggs with their short-swords. Then remounting we dashed back to join the cavalcade. During the ride I took occasion to ask Tars Tarkas if these Warhoons whose eggs we had destroyed were a smaller people than his Tharks.

"I noticed that their eggs were so much smaller than those I saw hatching in your incubator," I added.

He explained that the eggs had just been placed there; but, like all green Martian eggs, they would grow during the five-year period of incubation until they obtained the size of those I had seen hatching on the day of my arrival on Barsoom. This was indeed an interesting piece of information, for it had always seemed remarkable to me that the green Martian women, large as they were, could bring forth such enormous eggs as I had seen the four-foot infants emerging from. As a matter of fact, the new-laid egg is but little larger than an ordinary goose egg, and as it does not commence to grow until subjected to the light of the sun the chieftains have little difficulty in transporting several hundreds of them at one time from the storage vaults to the incubators.

Shortly after the incident of the Warhoon eggs we halted to rest the animals, and it was during this halt that the second of the day's interesting episodes occurred. I was engaged in changing my riding cloths from one of my thoats to the other, for I divided the day's work between them, when Zad approached me, and without a word struck my animal a terrific blow with his long-sword.

I did not need a manual of green Martian etiquette to know what reply to make, for, in fact, I was so wild with anger that I could scarcely refrain from drawing my pistol and shooting him down for the brute he was; but he stood waiting with drawn long-sword, and my only choice was to draw my own and meet him in fair fight with his choice of weapons or a lesser one.

This latter alternative is always permissible, therefore I could have used my short-sword, my dagger, my hatchet, or my fists had I wished, and been entirely within my rights, but I could not use firearms or a spear while he held only his long-sword.

I chose the same weapon he had drawn because I knew he prided himself upon his ability with it, and I wished, if I worsted him at all, to do it with his own weapon. The fight that followed was a long one and delayed the resumption of the march for an hour. The entire community surrounded us, leaving a clear space about one hundred feet in diameter for our battle.

Zad first attempted to rush me down as a bull might a wolf, but I was much too quick for him, and each time I side-stepped his rushes he would go lunging past me, only to receive a nick from my sword upon his arm or back. He was soon streaming blood from a half dozen minor wounds, but I could not obtain an opening to deliver an effective thrust. Then he changed his tactics, and fighting warily and with extreme dexterity, he tried to do by science what he was unable to do by brute strength. I must admit that he was a magnificent swordsman, and had it not been for my greater endurance and the remarkable agility the lesser gravitation of Mars lent me I might not have been able to put up the creditable fight I did against him.

We circled for some time without doing much damage on either side; the long, straight, needle-like swords flashing in the sunlight, and ringing out upon the stillness as they crashed together with each effective parry. Finally Zad, realizing that he was tiring more than I, evidently decided to close in and end the battle in a final blaze of glory for himself; just as he rushed me a blinding flash of light struck full in my eyes, so that I could not see his approach and could only leap blindly to one side in an effort to escape the mighty blade that it seemed I could already feel in my vitals. I was only partially successful, as a sharp pain in my left shoulder attested, but in the sweep of my glance as I sought to again locate my adversary, a sight met my astonished gaze which paid me well for the wound the temporary blindness had caused me. There, upon Dejah Thoris' chariot stood three figures, for the purpose evidently of witnessing the encounter above the heads of the intervening Tharks. There were Dejah Thoris, Sola, and Sarkoja, and as my fleeting glance swept over them a little tableau was presented which will stand graven in my memory to the day of my death.

As I looked, Dejah Thoris turned upon Sarkoja with the fury of a young tigress and struck something from her upraised hand; something which flashed in the sunlight as it spun to the ground. Then I knew what had blinded me at that crucial moment of the fight, and how Sarkoja had found a way to kill me without herself delivering the final thrust. Another thing I saw, too, which almost lost my life for me then and there, for it took my mind for the fraction of an instant entirely from my antagonist; for, as Dejah Thoris struck the tiny mirror from her hand, Sarkoja, her face livid with hatred and baffled rage, whipped out her dagger and aimed a terrific blow at Dejah Thoris; and then Sola, our dear and faithful Sola, sprang between them; the last I saw was the great knife descending upon her shielding breast.

My enemy had recovered from his thrust and was making it extremely interesting for me, so I reluctantly gave my attention to the work in hand, but my mind was not upon the battle.

We rushed each other furiously time after time, 'til suddenly, feeling the sharp point of his sword at my breast in a thrust I could neither parry nor escape, I threw myself upon him with outstretched sword and with all the weight of my body, determined that I would not die alone if I could prevent it. I felt the steel tear into my chest, all went black before me, my head whirled in dizziness, and I felt my knees giving beneath me.

Chapter XV

𝄞𝄞𝄞 𝄞𝄞𝄞 𝄞𝄞 𝄞𝄞 𝄞𝄞𝄞

(Sola Tells Me Her Story)

WHEN CONSCIOUSNESS returned, and, as I soon learned,
I was down but a moment, I sprang quickly to my feet
searching for my sword, and there I found it, buried to
the hilt in the green breast of Zad, who lay stone dead
upon the ochre moss of the ancient sea bottom. As I
regained my full senses I found his weapon piercing my
left breast, but only through the flesh and muscles which
cover my ribs, entering near the center of my chest and
coming out below the shoulder. As I had lunged I had
turned so that his sword merely passed beneath the
muscles, inflicting a painful but not dangerous wound.

Removing the blade from my body I also regained
my own, and turning my back upon his ugly carcass, I
moved, sick, sore, and disgusted, toward the chariots
which bore my retinue and my belongings. A murmur
of Martian applause greeted me, but I cared not for it.

Bleeding and weak I reached my women, who,
accustomed to such happenings, dressed my wounds,
applying the wonderful healing and remedial agents
which make only the most instantaneous of death blows
fatal. Give a Martian woman a chance and death must

take a back seat. They soon had me patched up so that, except for weakness from loss of blood and a little soreness around the wound, I suffered no great distress from this thrust which, under earthly treatment, undoubtedly would have put me flat on my back for days.

As soon as they were through with me I hastened to the chariot of Dejah Thoris, where I found my poor Sola with her chest swathed in bandages, but apparently little the worse for her encounter with Sarkoja, whose dagger it seemed had struck the edge of one of Sola's metal breast ornaments and, thus deflected, had inflicted but a slight flesh wound.

As I approached I found Dejah Thoris lying prone upon her silks and furs, her lithe form wracked with sobs. She did not notice my presence, nor did she hear me speaking with Sola, who was standing a short distance from the vehicle.

"Is she injured?" I asked of Sola, indicating Dejah Thoris by an inclination of my head.

"No," she answered, "she thinks that you are dead."

"And that her grandmother's cat may now have no one to polish its teeth?" I queried, smiling.

"I think you wrong her, John Carter," said Sola. "I do not understand either her ways or yours, but I am sure the granddaughter of ten thousand jeddaks would never grieve like this over the death of one she considered beneath her, or indeed over any who held but the highest claim upon her affections. They are a proud race, but they are just, as are all Barsoomians, and you must have hurt or wronged her grievously that she will not admit your existence living, though she mourns you dead.

"Tears are a strange sight upon Barsoom," she continued, "and so it is difficult for me to interpret them. I have seen but two people weep in all my life, other than Dejah Thoris; one wept from sorrow, the other from baffled rage. The first was my mother, years ago before they killed her; the other was Sarkoja, when they dragged her from me today."

"Your mother!" I exclaimed. "But, Sola, you could not have known your mother, child."

"But I did. And my father also," she added. "If you would like to hear the strange and un-Barsoomian story come to the chariot tonight, John Carter, and I will tell you that of which I have never spoken in all my life before. And now the signal has been given to resume the march, you must go."

"I will come tonight, Sola," I promised. "Be sure to tell Dejah Thoris I am alive and well. I shall not force myself upon her, and be sure that you do not let her know I saw her tears. If she would speak with me I but await her command."

Sola mounted the chariot, which was swinging into its place in line, and I hastened to my waiting thoat and galloped to my station beside Tars Tarkas at the rear of the column.

We made a most imposing and awe-inspiring spectacle as we strung out across the yellow landscape; the two hundred and fifty ornate and brightly colored chariots, preceded by an advance guard of some two hundred mounted warriors and chieftains riding five abreast and one hundred yards apart, and followed by a like number in the same formation, with a score or more of flankers on either side; the fifty extra mastodons, or heavy draught animals, known as zitidars, and the five or six hundred extra thoats of the warriors running loose within the hollow square formed by the surrounding warriors. The gleaming metal and jewels of the gorgeous ornaments of the men and women, duplicated in the trappings of the zitidars and thoats, and interspersed with the flashing colors of magnificent silks and furs and feathers, lent a barbaric splendor to the caravan which would have turned an East Indian potentate green with envy.

The enormous broad tires of the chariots and the

padded feet of the animals brought forth no sound from the moss-covered sea bottom; and so we moved in utter silence, like some huge phantasmagoria, except when the stillness was broken by the guttural growling of a goaded zitidar, or the squealing of fighting thoats. The green Martians converse but little, and then usually in monosyllables, low and like the faint rumbling of distant thunder.

We traversed a trackless waste of moss which, bending to the pressure of broad tire or padded foot, rose up again behind us, leaving no sign that we had passed. We might indeed have been the wraiths of the departed dead upon the dead sea of that dying planet for all the sound or sign we made in passing. It was the first march of a large body of men and animals I had ever witnessed which raised no dust and left no spoor; for there is no dust upon Mars except in the cultivated districts during the winter months, and even then the absence of high winds renders it almost unnoticeable.

We camped that night at the foot of the hills we had been approaching for two days and which marked the southern boundary of this particular sea. Our animals had been two days without drink, nor had they had water for nearly two months, not since shortly after leaving Thark; but, as Tars Tarkas explained to me, they require but little and can live almost indefinitely upon the moss which covers Barsoom, and which, he told me, holds in its tiny stems sufficient moisture to meet the limited demands of the animals.

After partaking of my evening meal of cheese-like food and vegetable milk I sought out Sola, whom I found working by the light of a torch upon some of Tars Tarkas' trappings. She looked up at my approach, her face lighting with pleasure and with welcome.

"I am glad you came," she said; "Dejah Thoris sleeps and I am lonely. Mine own people do not care for me, John Carter; I am too unlike them. It is a sad fate, since I must live my life amongst them, and I often wish that I were a true green Martian woman, without love and without hope; but I have known love and so I am lost.

"I promised to tell you my story, or rather the story of my parents. From what I have learned of you and the ways of your people I am sure that the tale will not seem strange to you, but among green Martians it has no parallel within the memory of the oldest living Thark, nor do our legends hold many similar tales.

"My mother was rather small, in fact too small to be allowed the responsibilities of maternity, as our chieftains breed principally for size. She was also less cold and cruel than most green Martian women, and caring little for their society, she often roamed the deserted avenues of Thark alone, or went and sat among the wild flowers that deck the nearby hills, thinking thoughts and wishing wishes which I believe I alone among Tharkian women today may understand, for am I not the child of my mother?

"And there among the hills she met a young warrior, whose duty it was to guard the feeding zitidars and thoats and see that they roamed not beyond the hills. They spoke at first only of such things as interest a community of Tharks, but gradually, as they came to meet more often, and, as was now quite evident to both, no longer by chance, they talked about themselves, their likes, their ambitions and their hopes. She trusted him and told him of the awful repugnance she felt for the cruelties of their kind, for the hideous, loveless lives they must ever lead, and then she waited for the storm of denunciation to break from his cold, hard lips; but instead he took her in his arms and kissed her.

"They kept their love a secret for six long years. She, my mother, was of the retinue of the great Tal Hajus, while her lover was a simple warrior, wearing only his own metal. Had their defection from the traditions of the Tharks been discovered both would have paid the penalty in the great arena before Tal Hajus and the assembled hordes.

"The egg from which I came was hidden beneath a great glass vessel upon the highest and most inaccessible of the partially ruined towers of ancient Thark. Once each year my mother visited it for the five long years it lay there in the process of incubation. She dared not come oftener, for in the mighty guilt of her conscience she feared that her every move was watched. During this period my father gained great distinction as a warrior and had taken the metal from several chieftains. His love for my mother had never diminished, and his one ambition in life was to reach a point where he might wrest the metal from Tal Hajus himself, and thus, as ruler of the Tharks, be free to claim her as his own, as well as, by the might of his power, protect the child which otherwise would be quickly dispatched should the truth become known.

"It was a wild dream, that of wresting the metal from Tal Hajus in five short years, but his advance was rapid, and he soon stood high in the councils of Thark. But one day the chance was lost forever, in so far as it could come in time to save his loved ones, for he was ordered away upon a long expedition to the ice-clad south, to make war upon the natives there and despoil them of their furs, for such is the manner of the green Barsoomian; he does not labor for what he can wrest in battle from others.

"He was gone for four years, and when he returned all had been over for three; for about a year after his departure, and shortly before the time for the return of an expedition which had gone forth to fetch the fruits of a community incubator, the egg had hatched. Thereafter my mother continued to keep me in the old tower, visiting me nightly and lavishing upon me the love the community life would have robbed us both of. She hoped, upon the return of the expedition from the incubator, to mix me with the other young assigned to the quarters of Tal Hajus, and thus escape the fate which would surely follow discovery of her sin against the ancient traditions of the green men.

"She taught me rapidly the language and customs of my kind, and one night she told me the story I have told to you up to this point, impressing upon me the necessity for absolute secrecy and the great caution I must exercise after she had placed me with the other young Tharks to permit no one to guess that I was fur-ther advanced in education than they, nor by any sign to divulge in the presence of others my affection for her, or my knowledge of my parentage; and then drawing me close to her she whispered in my ear the name of my father.

"And then a light flashed out upon the darkness of the tower chamber, and there stood Sarkoja, her gleaming, baleful eyes fixed in a frenzy of loathing and contempt upon my mother. The torrent of hatred and abuse she poured out upon her turned my young heart cold in terror. That she had heard the entire story was apparent, and that she had suspected something wrong from my mother's long nightly absences from her quarters accounted for her presence there on that fateful night.

"One thing she had not heard, nor did she know, the whispered name of my father. This was apparent from her repeated demands upon my mother to disclose the name of her partner in sin, but no amount of abuse or threats could wring this from her, and to save me from needless torture she lied, for she told Sarkoja that she alone knew nor would she even tell her child.

"With final imprecations, Sarkoja hastened away to Tal Hajus to report her discovery, and while she was gone my mother, wrapping me in the silks and furs of her night coverings, so that I was scarcely noticeable, descended to the streets and ran wildly away toward the outskirts of the city, in the direction which led to the far south, out toward the man whose protection she might not claim, but on whose face she wished to look once more before she died.

"As we neared the city's southern extremity a sound came to us from across the mossy flat, from the direction of the only pass through the hills which led to the gates, the pass by which caravans from either north or south or east or west would enter the city. The sounds we heard were the squealing of thoats and the grumbling of zitidars, with the occasional clank of arms which announced the approach of a body of warriors. The thought uppermost in her mind was that it was my father returned from his expedition, but the cunning of the Thark held her from headlong and precipitate flight to greet him.

"Retreating into the shadows of a doorway she awaited the coming of the cavalcade which shortly entered the avenue, breaking its formation and thronging the thoroughfare from wall to wall. As the head of the procession passed us the lesser moon swung clear of the overhanging roofs and lit up the scene with all the brilliancy of her wondrous light. My mother shrank further back into the friendly shadows, and from her hiding place saw that the expedition was not that of my father, but the returning caravan bearing the young Tharks. Instantly her plan was formed, and as a great chariot swung close to our hiding place she slipped stealthily in upon the trailing tailboard, crouching low in the shadow of the high side, straining me to her bosom in a frenzy of love.

"She knew, what I did not, that never again after that night would she hold me to her breast, nor was it likely we would ever look upon each other's face again. In the confusion of the plaza she mixed me with the other children, whose guardians during the journey were now free to relinquish their responsibility. We were herded together into a great room, fed by women who had not accompanied the expedition, and the next day we were parceled out among the retinues of the chieftains.

"I never saw my mother after that night. She was imprisoned by Tal Hajus, and every effort, including the most horrible and shameful torture, was brought to bear upon her to wring from her lips the name of my father; but she remained steadfast and loyal, dying at last amidst the laughter of Tal Hajus and his chieftains during some awful torture she was undergoing.

"I learned afterwards that she told them that she had killed me to save me from a like fate at their hands, and that she had thrown my body to the white apes.

Sarkoja alone disbelieved her, and I feel to this day that she suspects my true origin, but does not dare expose me, at the present, at all events, because she also guesses, I am sure, the identity of my father.

"When he returned from his expedition and learned the story of my mother's fate I was present as Tal Hajus told him; but never by the quiver of a muscle did he betray the slightest emotion; only he did not laugh as Tal Hajus gleefully described her death struggles. From that moment on he was the cruelest of the cruel, and I am awaiting the day when he shall win the goal of his ambition, and feel the carcass of Tal Hajus beneath his foot, for I am as sure that he but waits the opportunity to wreak a terrible vengeance, and that his great love is as strong in his breast as when it first transfigured him nearly forty years ago, as I am that we sit here upon the edge of a world-old ocean while sensible people sleep, John Carter."

"And your father, Sola, is he with us now?" I asked.

"Yes," she replied, "but he does not know me for what I am, nor does he know who betrayed my mother to Tal Hajus. I alone know my father's name, and only I and Tal Hajus and Sarkoja know that it was she who carried the tale that brought death and torture upon her he loved."

We sat silent for a few moments, she wrapped in the gloomy thoughts of her terrible past, and I in pity for the poor creatures whom the heartless, senseless customs of their race had doomed to loveless lives of cruelty and of hate. Presently she spoke.

"John Carter, if ever a real man walked the cold, dead bosom of Barsoom you are one. I know that I can trust you, and because the knowledge may someday help you or him or Dejah Thoris or myself, I am going to tell you the name of my father, nor place any restrictions or conditions upon your tongue. When the time comes, speak the truth if it seems best to you. I trust you because I know that you are not cursed with the terrible trait of absolute and unswerving truthfulness, that you could lie like one of your own Virginia gentlemen if a lie would save others from sorrow or suffering. My father's name is Tars Tarkas."

CHAPTER XVI

𐌔𐍃 𐍄𐍃𐍃𐍃𐍃 𐍃𐍃𐍃𐍃𐍃𐍃

(We Plan Escape)

THE REMAINDER of our journey to Thark was uneventful. We were twenty days upon the road, crossing two sea bottoms and passing through or around a number of ruined cities, mostly smaller than Korad. Twice we crossed the famous Martian waterways, or canals, so-called by our earthly astronomers. When we approached these points a warrior would be sent far ahead with a powerful field glass, and if no great body of red Martian troops was in sight we would advance as close as possible without chance of being seen and then camp until dark, when we would slowly approach the cultivated tract, and, locating one of the numerous, broad highways which cross these areas at regular intervals, creep silently and stealthily across to the arid lands upon the other side. It required five hours to make one of these crossings without a single halt, and the other consumed the entire night, so that we were just leaving the confines of the high-walled fields when the sun broke out upon us.

Crossing in the darkness, as we did, I was able to see but little, except as the nearer moon, in her wild and ceaseless hurtling through the Barsoomian heavens, lit up little patches of the landscape from time to time, disclosing walled fields and low, rambling buildings, presenting much the appearance of earthly farms. There were many trees, methodically arranged, and some of them were of enormous height; there were animals in some of the enclosures, and they announced their presence by terrified squealings and snortings as they scented our queer, wild beasts and wilder human beings.

Only once did I perceive a human being, and that was at the intersection of our crossroad with the wide, white turnpike which cuts each cultivated district longitudinally at its exact center. The fellow must have been sleeping beside the road, for, as I came abreast of him, he raised upon one elbow and after a single glance at the approaching caravan leaped shrieking to his feet and fled madly down the road, scaling a nearby wall with the agility of a scared cat. The Tharks paid him not the slightest attention; they were not out upon the warpath, and the only sign that I had that they had seen him was a quickening of the pace of the caravan as we hastened toward the bordering desert which marked our entrance into the realm of Tal Hajus.

Not once did I have speech with Dejah Thoris, as she sent no word to me that I would be welcome at her chariot, and my foolish pride kept me from making any advances. I verily believe that a man's way with women is in inverse ratio to his prowess among men. The weakling and the saphead have often great ability to charm the fair sex, while the fighting man who can face a thousand real dangers unafraid, sits hiding in the shadows like some frightened child.

Just thirty days after my advent upon Barsoom we entered the ancient city of Thark, from whose long-forgotten people this horde of green men have stolen even their name. The hordes of Thark number some thirty thousand souls, and are divided into twenty-five communities. Each community has its own jed and lesser chieftains, but all are under the rule of Tal Hajus, Jeddak of Thark. Five communities make their headquarters at the city of Thark, and the balance are scattered among other deserted cities of ancient Mars throughout the district claimed by Tal Hajus.

We made our entry into the great central plaza early in the afternoon. There were no enthusiastic friendly greetings for the returned expedition. Those who chanced to be in sight spoke the names of warriors or women with whom they came in direct contact, in the formal greeting of their kind, but when it was discovered that they brought two captives a greater interest was aroused, and Dejah Thoris and I were the centers of inquiring groups.

We were soon assigned to new quarters, and the balance of the day was devoted to settling ourselves to the changed conditions. My home now was upon an avenue leading into the plaza from the south, the main artery down which we had marched from the gates of the city. I was at the far end of the square and had an entire building to myself. The same grandeur of architecture which was so noticeable a characteristic of Korad was in evidence here, only, if that were possible, on a larger and richer scale. My quarters would have been suitable for housing the greatest of earthly emperors, but to these queer creatures nothing about a building appealed to them but its size and the enormity of its chambers; the larger the building, the more desirable; and so Tal Hajus occupied what must have been an enormous public building, the largest in the city, but entirely unfitted for residence purposes; the next largest was reserved for Lorquas Ptomel, the next for the jed of a lesser rank, and so on to the bottom of the list of five jeds. The warriors occupied the buildings with the chieftains to whose retinues they belonged; or, if they preferred, sought shelter among any of the thousands of untenanted buildings in their own quarter of town; each community being assigned a certain section of the city. The selection of building had to be made in accordance with these divisions, except in so far as the jeds were concerned, they all occupying edifices which fronted upon the plaza.

When I had finally put my house in order, or rather seen that it had been done, it was nearing sunset, and I hastened out with the intention of locating Sola and her charges, as I had determined upon having speech with Dejah Thoris and trying to impress on her the necessity of our at least patching up a truce until I could find some way of aiding her to escape. I searched in vain until the upper rim of the great red sun was just disappearing behind the horizon and then I spied the ugly head of Woola peering from a second-story window on the opposite side of the very street where I was quartered, but nearer the plaza.

Without waiting for a further invitation I bolted up the winding runway which led to the second floor, and entering a great chamber at the front of the building was greeted by the frenzied Woola, who threw his great carcass upon me, nearly hurling me to the floor; the poor old fellow was so glad to see me that I thought he would devour me, his head split from ear to ear, showing his three rows of tusks in his hobgoblin smile.

Quieting him with a word of command and a caress, I looked hurriedly through the approaching gloom for a sign of Dejah Thoris, and then, not seeing her, I called her name. There was an answering murmur from the far corner of the apartment, and with a couple of quick strides I was standing beside her where she crouched among the furs and silks upon an ancient carved wooden seat. As I waited she rose to her full height and looking me straight in the eye said:

"What would Dotar Sojat, Thark, of Dejah Thoris his captive?"

"Dejah Thoris, I do not know how I have angered you. It was furtherest from my desire to hurt or offend you, whom I had hoped to protect and comfort. Have none of me if it is your will, but that you must aid me in effecting your escape, if such a thing be possible, is not my request, but my command. When you are safe once more at your father's court you may do with me as you please, but from now on until that day I am your master, and you must obey and aid me."

She looked at me long and earnestly and I thought that she was softening toward me.

"I understand your words, Dotar Sojat," she replied, "but you I do not understand. You are a queer mixture of child and man, of brute and noble. I only wish that I might read your heart."

"Look down at your feet, Dejah Thoris; it lies there now where it has lain since that other night at Korad, and where it will ever lie beating alone for you until death stills it forever."

She took a little step toward me, her beautiful hands outstretched in a strange, groping gesture.

"What do you mean, John Carter?" she whispered. "What are you saying to me?"

"I am saying what I had promised myself that I would not say to you, at least until you were no longer a captive among the green men; what from your attitude toward me for the past twenty days I had thought never to say to you; I am saying, Dejah Thoris, that I am yours, body and soul, to serve you, to fight for you, and to die for you. Only one thing I ask of you in return, and that is that you make no sign, either of condemnation or of approbation of my words until you are safe among your own people, and that whatever sentiments you harbor toward me they be not influenced or colored by gratitude; whatever I may do to serve you will be prompted solely from selfish motives, since it gives me more pleasure to serve you than not."

"I will respect your wishes, John Carter, because I understand the motives which prompt them, and I accept your service no more willingly than I bow to your authority; your word shall be my law. I have twice wronged you in my thoughts and again I ask your forgiveness."

Further conversation of a personal nature was prevented by the entrance of Sola, who was much agitated and wholly unlike her usual calm and possessed self.

"That horrible Sarkoja has been before Tal Hajus," she cried, "and from what I heard upon the plaza there is little hope for either of you."

"What do they say?" inquired Dejah Thoris.

"That you will be thrown to the wild calots [dogs] in the great arena as soon as the hordes have assembled for the yearly games."

"Sola," I said, "you are a Thark, but you hate and loathe the customs of your people as much as we do. Will you not accompany us in one supreme effort to escape? I am sure that Dejah Thoris can offer you a home and protection among her people, and your fate can be no worse among them than it must ever be here."

"Yes," cried Dejah Thoris, "come with us, Sola, you will be better off among the red men of Helium than you are here, and I can promise you not only a home with us, but the love and affection your nature craves and which must always be denied you by the customs of your own race. Come with us, Sola; we might go without you, but your fate would be terrible if they thought you had connived to aid us. I know that even that fear would not tempt you to interfere in our escape, but we want you with us, we want you to come to a land of sunshine and happiness, amongst a people who know the meaning of love, of sympathy, and of gratitude. Say that you will, Sola; tell me that you will."

"The great waterway which leads to Helium is but fifty miles to the south," murmured Sola, half to herself; "a swift thoat might make it in three hours; and then to Helium it is five hundred miles, most of the way through thinly settled districts. They would know and they would follow us. We might hide among the great trees for a time, but the chances are small indeed for escape. They would follow us to the very gates of Helium, and they would take toll of life at every step; you do not know them."

"Is there no other way we might reach Helium?" I asked. "Can you not draw me a rough map of the country we must traverse, Dejah Thoris?"

"Yes," she replied, and taking a great diamond from her hair she drew upon the marble floor the first map of

Barsoomian territory I had ever seen. It was crisscrossed in every direction with long straight lines, sometimes running parallel and sometimes converging toward some great circle. The lines, she said, were waterways; the circles, cities; and one far to the northwest of us she pointed out as Helium. There were other cities closer, but she said she feared to enter many of them, as they were not all friendly toward Helium.

Finally, after studying the map carefully in the moonlight which now flooded the room, I pointed out a waterway far to the north of us which also seemed to lead to Helium.

"Does not this pierce your grandfather's territory?" I asked.

"Yes," she answered, "but it is two hundred miles north of us; it is one of the waterways we crossed on the trip to Thark."

"They would never suspect that we would try for that distant waterway," I answered, "and that is why I think that it is the best route for our escape."

Sola agreed with me, and it was decided that we should leave Thark this same night; just as quickly, in fact, as I could find and saddle my thoats. Sola was to ride one and Dejah Thoris and I the other; each of us carrying sufficient food and drink to last us for two days, since the animals could not be urged too rapidly for so long a distance.

I directed Sola to proceed with Dejah Thoris along one of the less frequented avenues to the southern boundary of the city, where I would overtake them with the thoats as quickly as possible; then, leaving them to gather what food, silks, and furs we were to need, I slipped quietly to the rear of the first floor, and entered the courtyard, where our animals were moving restlessly about, as was their habit, before settling down for the night.

In the shadows of the buildings and out beneath the radiance of the Martian moons moved the great herd of thoats and zitidars, the latter grunting their low gutturals and the former occasionally emitting the sharp squeal which denotes the almost habitual state of rage in which these creatures passed their existence. They were quieter now, owing to the absence of man, but as they scented me they became more restless and their hideous noise increased. It was risky business, this entering a paddock of thoats alone and at night; first, because their increasing noisiness might warn the nearby warriors that something was amiss, and also because for the slightest cause, or for no cause at all some great bull thoat might take it upon himself to lead a charge upon me.

Having no desire to awaken their nasty tempers upon such a night as this, where so much depended upon secrecy and dispatch, I hugged the shadows of the buildings, ready at an instant's warning to leap into the safety of a nearby door or window. Thus I moved silently to the great gates which opened upon the street at the back of the court, and as I neared the exit I called softly to my two animals. How I thanked the kind providence which had given me the foresight to win the love and confidence of these wild dumb brutes, for presently from the far side of the court I saw two huge bulks forcing their way toward me through the surging mountains of flesh.

They came quite close to me, rubbing their muzzles against my body and nosing for the bits of food it was always my practice to reward them with. Opening the gates I ordered the two great beasts to pass out, and then slipping quietly after them I closed the portals behind me.

I did not saddle or mount the animals there, but instead walked quietly in the shadows of the buildings toward an unfrequented avenue which led toward the point I had arranged to meet Dejah Thoris and Sola. With the noiselessness of disembodied spirits we moved stealthily along the deserted streets, but not until we were within sight of the plain beyond the city did I commence to breathe freely. I was sure that Sola and Dejah Thoris would find no difficulty in reaching our rendezvous undetected, but with my great thoats I was not so sure for myself, as it was quite unusual for warriors to leave the city after dark; in fact there was no place for them to go within any but a long ride.

I reached the appointed meeting place safely, but as Dejah Thoris and Sola were not there I led my animals into the entrance hall of one of the large buildings. Presuming that one of the other women of the same household may have come in to speak to Sola, and so delayed their departure, I did not feel any undue apprehension until nearly an hour had passed without a sign of them, and by the time another half hour had crawled away I was becoming filled with grave anxiety. Then there broke upon the stillness of the night the sound of an approaching party, which, from the noise, I knew could be no fugitives creeping stealthily toward liberty. Soon the party was near me, and from the black shadows of my entranceway I perceived a score of mounted warriors, who, in passing, dropped a dozen words that fetched my heart clean into the top of my head.

"He would likely have arranged to meet them just without the city, and so—" I heard no more, they had passed on; but it was enough. Our plan had been discovered, and the chances for escape from now on to the fearful end would be small indeed. My one hope now was to return undetected to the quarters of Dejah Thoris and learn what fate had overtaken her, but how to do it with these great monstrous thoats upon my hands, now that the city probably was aroused by the knowledge of my escape was a problem of no mean proportions.

Suddenly an idea occurred to me, and acting on my knowledge of the construction of the buildings of these ancient Martian cities with a hollow court within the center of each square, I groped my way blindly through the dark chambers, calling the great thoats after me. They had difficulty in negotiating some of the doorways, but as the buildings fronting the city's principal exposures were all designed upon a magnificent scale, they were able to wriggle through without sticking fast; and thus we finally made the inner court where I found, as I had expected, the usual carpet of moss-like vegetation which would prove their food and drink until I could return them to their own enclosure. That they would be as quiet and contented here as elsewhere I was confident, nor was there but the remotest possibility that they would be discovered, as the green men had no great desire to enter these outlying buildings, which were frequented by the only thing, I believe, which caused them the sensation of fear—the great white apes of Barsoom.

Removing the saddle trappings, I hid them just within the rear doorway of the building through which we had entered the court, and, turning the beasts loose, quickly made my way across the court to the rear of the buildings upon the further side, and thence to the avenue beyond. Waiting in the doorway of the building until I was assured that no one was approaching, I hurried across to the opposite side and through the first doorway to the court beyond; thus, crossing through court after court with only the slight chance of detection which the necessary crossing of the avenues entailed, I made my way in safety to the courtyard in the rear of Dejah Thoris' quarters.

Here, of course, I found the beasts of the warriors who quartered in the adjacent buildings, and the warriors themselves I might expect to meet within if I entered; but, fortunately for me, I had another and safer method of reaching the upper story where Dejah Thoris should be found, and, after first determining as nearly as possible which of the buildings she occupied, for I had never observed them before from the court side, I took advantage of my relatively great strength and agility and sprang upward until I grasped the sill of a second-story window which I thought to be in the rear of her apartment. Drawing myself inside the room I moved stealthily toward the front of the building, and not until I had quite reached the doorway of her room was I made aware by voices that it was occupied.

I did not rush headlong in, but listened without to assure myself that it was Dejah Thoris and that it was safe to venture within. It was well indeed that I took this precaution, for the conversation I heard was in the low gutturals of men, and the words which finally came to me proved a most timely warning. The speaker was a chieftain and he was giving orders to four of his warriors.

"And when he returns to this chamber," he was saying, "as he surely will when he finds she does not meet him at the city's edge, you four are to spring upon him and disarm him. It will require the combined strength of all of you to do it if the reports they bring back from Korad are correct. When you have him fast bound bear him to the vaults beneath the jeddak's quarters and chain him securely where he may be found when Tal Hajus wishes him. Allow him to speak with none, nor permit any other to enter this apartment before he comes.

There will be no danger of the girl returning, for by this time she is safe in the arms of Tal Hajus, and may all her ancestors have pity upon her, for Tal Hajus will have none; the great Sarkoja has done a noble night's work. I go, and if you fail to capture him when he comes, I commend your carcasses to the cold bosom of Iss."

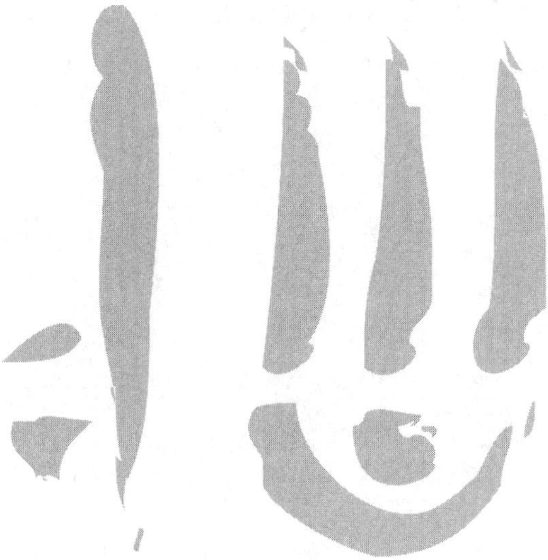
الله

Chapter XVII
ᚠ ᚢᚦᚨᚱᚲ ᚦᚢᚦᚨᛏᚦᛁ

(A Costly Recapture)

As the speaker ceased he turned to leave the apartment by the door where I was standing, but I needed to wait no longer; I had heard enough to fill my soul with dread, and stealing quietly away I returned to the courtyard by the way I had come. My plan of action was formed upon the instant, and crossing the square and the bordering avenue upon the opposite side I soon stood within the courtyard of Tal Hajus.

The brilliantly lighted apartments of the first floor told me where first to seek, and advancing to the windows I peered within. I soon discovered that my approach was not to be the easy thing I had hoped, for the rear rooms bordering the court were filled with warriors and women. I then glanced up at the stories above, discovering that the third was apparently unlighted, and so decided to make my entrance to the building from that point. It was the work of but a moment for me to reach the windows above, and soon I had drawn myself within the sheltering shadows of the unlighted third floor.

Fortunately the room I had selected was untenanted, and creeping noiselessly to the corridor beyond

I discovered a light in the apartments ahead of me. Reaching what appeared to be a doorway I discovered that it was but an opening upon an immense inner chamber which towered from the first floor, two stories below me, to the dome-like roof of the building, high above my head. The floor of this great circular hall was thronged with chieftains, warriors and women, and at one end was a great raised platform upon which squatted the most hideous beast I had ever put my eyes upon. He had all the cold, hard, cruel, terrible features of the green warriors, but accentuated and debased by the animal passions to which he had given himself over for many years. There was not a mark of dignity or pride upon his bestial countenance, while his enormous bulk spread itself out upon the platform where he squatted like some huge devil fish, his six limbs accentuating the similarity in a horrible and startling manner.

But the sight that froze me with apprehension was that of Dejah Thoris and Sola standing there before him, and the fiendish leer of him as he let his great protruding eyes gloat upon the line of her beautiful figure. She was speaking, but I could not hear what she said, nor could I make out the low grumbling of his reply. She stood there erect before him, her head high held, and even at the distance I was from them I could read the scorn and disgust upon her face as she let her haughty glance rest without sign of fear upon him. She was indeed the proud daughter of a thousand jeddaks, every inch of her dear, precious little body; so small, so frail beside the towering warriors around her, but in her majesty dwarfing them into insignificance; she was the mightiest figure among them and I verily believe that they felt it.

Presently Tal Hajus made a sign that the chamber be cleared, and that the prisoners be left alone before him. Slowly the chieftains, the warriors and the women melted away into the shadows of the surrounding chambers, and Dejah Thoris and Sola stood alone before the jeddak of the Tharks.

One chieftain alone had hesitated before departing; I saw him standing in the shadows of a mighty column, his fingers nervously toying with the hilt of his great-sword and his cruel eyes bent in implacable hatred upon Tal Hajus. It was Tars Tarkas, and I could read his thoughts as they were an open book for the undisguised loathing upon his face. He was thinking of that other woman who, forty years ago, had stood before this beast, and could I have spoken a word into his ear at that moment the reign of Tal Hajus would have been over; but finally he also strode from the room, not knowing that he left his own daughter at the mercy of the creature he most loathed.

Tal Hajus arose, and I, half fearing, half anticipating his intentions, hurried to the winding runway which led to the floors below. No one was near to intercept me, and I reached the main floor of the chamber unobserved, taking my station in the shadow of the same column that Tars Tarkas had but just deserted. As I reached the floor Tal Hajus was speaking.

"Princess of Helium, I might wring a mighty ransom from your people would I but return you to them unharmed, but a thousand times rather would I watch that beautiful face writhe in the agony of torture; it shall be long drawn out, that I promise you; ten days of pleasure were all too short to show the love I harbor for your race. The terrors of your death shall haunt the slumbers of the red men through all the ages to come; they will shudder in the shadows of the night as their fathers tell them of the awful vengeance of the green men; of the power and might and hate and cruelty of Tal Hajus. But before the torture you shall be mine for one short hour, and word of that too shall go forth to Tardos Mors, Jeddak of Helium, your grandfather, that he may grovel upon the ground in the agony of his sorrow. Tomorrow the torture will commence; tonight thou art Tal Hajus'; come!"

He sprang down from the platform and grasped her roughly by the arm, but scarcely had he touched her than I leaped between them. My short-sword, sharp and gleaming was in my right hand; I could have plunged it into his putrid heart before he realized that I was upon him; but as I raised my arm to strike I thought of Tars Tarkas, and, with all my rage, with all my hatred, I could not rob him of that sweet moment for which he had lived and hoped all these long, weary years, and so, instead, I swung my good right fist full upon the point of his jaw. Without a sound he slipped to the floor as one dead.

In the same deathly silence I grasped Dejah Thoris by the hand, and motioning to Sola to follow we sped noiselessly from the chamber and to the floor above. Unseen we reached a rear window and with the straps and leather of my trappings I lowered, first Sola and then Dejah Thoris to the ground below. Dropping lightly after them I drew them rapidly around the court in the shadows of the buildings, and thus we returned over the same course I had so recently followed from the distant boundary of the city.

We finally came upon my thoats in the courtyard where I had left them, and placing the trappings upon them we hastened through the building to the avenue beyond. Mounting, Sola upon one beast, and Dejah Thoris behind me upon the other, we rode from the city of Thark through the hills to the south.

Instead of circling back around the city to the northwest and toward the nearest waterway which lay so short a distance from us, we turned to the northeast and struck out upon the mossy waste across which, for two hundred dangerous and weary miles, lay another main artery leading to Helium.

No word was spoken until we had left the city far behind, but I could hear the quiet sobbing of Dejah Thoris as she clung to me with her dear head resting against my shoulder.

"If we make it, my chieftain, the debt of Helium will be a mighty one; greater than she can ever pay you; and should we not make it," she continued, "the debt is no less, though Helium will never know, for you have saved the last of our line from worse than death."

I did not answer, but instead reached to my side and pressed the little fingers of her I loved where they clung to me for support, and then, in unbroken silence, we sped over the yellow, moonlit moss; each of us occupied with his own thoughts. For my part I could not be other than joyful had I tried, with Dejah Thoris' warm body pressed close to mine, and with all our unpassed danger my heart was singing as gaily as though we were already entering the gates of Helium.

Our earlier plans had been so sadly upset that we now found ourselves without food or drink, and I alone was armed. We therefore urged our beasts to a speed that must tell on them sorely before we could hope to sight the ending of the first stage of our journey.

We rode all night and all the following day with only a few short rests. On the second night both we and our animals were completely fagged, and so we lay down upon the moss and slept for some five or six hours, taking up the journey once more before daylight. All the following day we rode, and when, late in the afternoon we had sighted no distant trees, the mark of the great waterways throughout all Barsoom, the terrible truth flashed upon us—we were lost.

Evidently we had circled, but which way it was difficult to say, nor did it seem possible with the sun to guide us by day and the moons and stars by night. At any rate no waterway was in sight, and the entire party was almost ready to drop from hunger, thirst and fatigue. Far ahead of us and a trifle to the right we could distinguish the outlines of low mountains. These we decided to attempt to reach in the hope that from some ridge we might discern the missing waterway. Night fell upon us before we reached our goal, and, almost fainting from weariness and weakness, we lay down and slept.

I was awakened early in the morning by some huge body pressing close to mine, and opening my eyes with a start I beheld my blessed old Woola snuggling close to me; the faithful brute had followed us across that trackless waste to share our fate, whatever it might be. Putting my arms about his neck I pressed my cheek close to his, nor am I ashamed that I did it, nor of the tears that came to my eyes as I thought of his love for me. Shortly after this Dejah Thoris and Sola awakened, and it was decided that we push on at once in an effort to gain the hills.

We had gone scarcely a mile when I noticed that my thoat was commencing to stumble and stagger in a most pitiful manner, although we had not attempted to force them out of a walk since about noon of the preceding day. Suddenly he lurched wildly to one side and pitched violently to the ground. Dejah Thoris and I were thrown clear of him and fell upon the soft moss with scarcely a jar; but the poor beast was in a pitiable condition, not even being able to rise, although relieved of our weight. Sola told me that the coolness of the night, when it fell, together with the rest would doubtless revive him, and so I decided not to kill him, as was my first intention, as I had thought it cruel to leave him alone there to die of hunger and thirst. Relieving him of his trappings, which I flung down beside him, we left the poor fellow to his fate, and pushed on with the one thoat as best we could. Sola and I walked, making Dejah Thoris ride, much against her will. In this way we had progressed to within about a mile of the hills we were endeavoring to reach when Dejah Thoris, from her point of vantage upon the thoat, cried out that she saw a great party of mounted men filing down from a pass in the hills several miles away. Sola and I both looked in the direction she indicated, and there, plainly discernible, were several hundred mounted warriors. They seemed to be headed in a southwesterly direction, which would take them away from us.

They doubtless were Thark warriors who had been sent out to capture us, and we breathed a great sigh of relief that they were traveling in the opposite direction. Quickly lifting Dejah Thoris from the thoat, I commanded the animal to lie down and we three did the same, presenting as small an object as possible for fear of attracting the attention of the warriors toward us.

We could see them as they filed out of the pass, just for an instant, before they were lost to view behind a friendly ridge; to us a most providential ridge; since, had they been in view for any great length of time, they scarcely could have failed to discover us. As what proved to be the last warrior came into view from the pass, he halted and, to our consternation, threw his small but powerful fieldglass to his eye and scanned the sea bottom in all directions. Evidently he was a chieftain, for in certain marching formations among the green men a chieftain brings up at the extreme rear of the column. As his glass swung toward us our hearts stopped in our breasts, and I could feel the cold sweat start from every pore in my body.

Presently it swung full upon us and—stopped. The tension on our nerves was near the breaking point, and I doubt if any of us breathed for the few moments he held us covered by his glass; and then he lowered it and we could see him shout a command to the warriors who had passed from our sight behind the ridge. He did not wait for them to join him, however, instead he wheeled his thoat and came tearing madly in our direction.

There was but one slight chance and that we must take quickly. Raising my strange Martian rifle to my shoulder I sighted and touched the button which controlled the trigger; there was a sharp explosion as the missile reached its goal, and the charging chieftain pitched backward from his flying mount.

Springing to my feet I urged the thoat to rise, and directed Sola to take Dejah Thoris with her upon him and make a mighty effort to reach the hills before the green warriors were upon us. I knew that in the ravines and gullies they might find a temporary hiding place, and even though they died there of hunger and thirst it would be better so than that they fell into the hands of the Tharks. Forcing my two revolvers upon them as a slight means of protection, and, as a last resort, as an escape for themselves from the horrid death which recapture would surely mean, I lifted Dejah Thoris in my arms and placed her upon the thoat behind Sola, who had already mounted at my command.

"Good-bye, my princess," I whispered, "we may meet in Helium yet. I have escaped from worse plights than this," and I tried to smile as I lied.

"What," she cried, "are you not coming with us?"

"How may I, Dejah Thoris? Someone must hold these fellows off for a while, and I can better escape them alone than could the three of us together."

She sprang quickly from the thoat and, throwing

her dear arms about my neck, turned to Sola, saying with quiet dignity: "Fly, Sola! Dejah Thoris remains to die with the man she loves."

Those words are engraved upon my heart. Ah, gladly would I give up my life a thousand times could I only hear them once again; but I could not then give even a second to the rapture of her sweet embrace, and pressing my lips to hers for the first time, I picked her up bodily and tossed her to her seat behind Sola again, commanding the latter in peremptory tones to hold her there by force, and then, slapping the thoat upon the flank, I saw them borne away; Dejah Thoris struggling to the last to free herself from Sola's grasp.

Turning, I beheld the green warriors mounting the ridge and looking for their chieftain. In a moment they saw him, and then me; but scarcely had they discovered me than I commenced firing, lying flat upon my belly in the moss. I had an even hundred rounds in the magazine of my rifle, and another hundred in the belt at my back, and I kept up a continuous stream of fire until I saw all of the warriors who had been first to return from behind the ridge either dead or scurrying to cover.

My respite was short-lived however, for soon the entire party, numbering some thousand men, came charging into view, racing madly toward me. I fired until my rifle was empty and they were almost upon me, and then a glance showing me that Dejah Thoris and Sola had disappeared among the hills, I sprang up, throwing down my useless gun, and started away in the direction opposite to that taken by Sola and her charge.

If ever Martians had an exhibition of jumping, it was granted those astonished warriors on that day long years ago, but while it led them away from Dejah Thoris it did not distract their attention from endeavoring to capture me.

They raced wildly after me until, finally, my foot struck a projecting piece of quartz, and down I went sprawling upon the moss. As I looked up they were upon me, and although I drew my long-sword in an attempt to sell my life as dearly as possible, it was soon over. I reeled beneath their blows which fell upon me in perfect torrents; my head swam; all was black, and I went down beneath them to oblivion.

Chapter XVIII
⊕⧖⧖⊕⧖⧖⧖ ⊕⧖ ⧖⧖⊕⧖⊕⧖⧖

(Chained in Warhoon)

IT MUST HAVE BEEN several hours before I regained consciousness and I well remember the feeling of surprise which swept over me as I realized that I was not dead.

I was lying among a pile of sleeping silks and furs in the corner of a small room in which were several green warriors, and bending over me was an ancient and ugly female.

As I opened my eyes she turned to one of the warriors, saying,

"He will live, O Jed."

"'Tis well," replied the one so addressed, rising and approaching my couch, "he should render rare sport for the great games."

And now as my eyes fell upon him, I saw that he was no Thark, for his ornaments and metal were not of that horde. He was a huge fellow, terribly scarred about the face and chest, and with one broken tusk and a missing ear. Strapped on either breast were human skulls and depending from these a number of dried human hands.

His reference to the great games of which I had

heard so much while among the Tharks convinced me that I had but jumped from purgatory into gehenna.

After a few more words with the female, during which she assured him that I was now fully fit to travel, the jed ordered that we mount and ride after the main column.

I was strapped securely to as wild and unmanageable a thoat as I had ever seen, and, with a mounted warrior on either side to prevent the beast from bolting, we rode forth at a furious pace in pursuit of the column. My wounds gave me but little pain, so wonderfully and rapidly had the applications and injections of the female exercised their therapeutic powers, and so deftly had she bound and plastered the injuries.

Just before dark we reached the main body of troops shortly after they had made camp for the night. I was immediately taken before the leader, who proved to be the jeddak of the hordes of Warhoon.

Like the jed who had brought me, he was frightfully scarred, and also decorated with the breastplate of human skulls and dried dead hands which seemed to mark all the greater warriors among the Warhoons, as well as to indicate their awful ferocity, which greatly transcends even that of the Tharks.

The jeddak, Bar Comas, who was comparatively

young, was the object of the fierce and jealous hatred of his old lieutenant, Dak Kova, the jed who had captured me, and I could not but note the almost studied efforts which the latter made to affront his superior.

He entirely omitted the usual formal salutation as we entered the presence of the jeddak, and as he pushed me roughly before the ruler he exclaimed in a loud and menacing voice,

"I have brought a strange creature wearing the metal of a Thark whom it is my pleasure to have battle with a wild thoat at the great games."

"He will die as Bar Comas, your jeddak, sees fit, if at all," replied the young ruler, with emphasis and dignity.

"If at all?" roared Dak Kova. "By the dead hands at my throat but he shall die, Bar Comas. No maudlin weakness on your part shall save him. O, would that Warhoon were ruled by a real jeddak rather than by a water-hearted weakling from whom even old Dak Kova could tear the metal with his bare hands!"

Bar Comas eyed the defiant and insubordinate chieftain for an instant, his expression one of haughty, fearless contempt and hate, and then without drawing a weapon and without uttering a word he hurled himself at the throat of his defamer.

I never before had seen two green Martian warriors

battle with nature's weapons and the exhibition of animal ferocity which ensued was as fearful a thing as the most disordered imagination could picture. They tore at each other's eyes and ears with their hands and with their gleaming tusks repeatedly slashed and gored until both were cut fairly to ribbons from head to foot.

Bar Comas had much the better of the battle as he was stronger, quicker and more intelligent. It soon seemed that the encounter was done saving only the final death thrust when Bar Comas slipped in breaking away from a clinch. It was the one little opening that Dak Kova needed, and hurling himself at the body of his adversary he buried his single mighty tusk in Bar Comas' groin and with a last powerful effort ripped the young jeddak wide open the full length of his body, the great tusk finally wedging in the bones of Bar Comas' jaw. Victor and vanquished rolled limp and lifeless upon the moss, a huge mass of torn and bloody flesh.

Bar Comas was stone dead, and only the most herculean efforts on the part of Dak Kova's females saved him from the fate he deserved. Three days later he walked without assistance to the body of Bar Comas which, by custom, had not been moved from where it fell, and placing his foot upon the neck of his erstwhile ruler he assumed the title Jeddak of Warhoon.

The dead jeddak's hands and head were removed to be added to the ornaments of his conqueror, and then his women cremated what remained, amid wild and terrible laughter.

The injuries to Dak Kova had delayed the march so greatly that it was decided to give up the expedition, which was a raid upon a small Thark community in retaliation for the destruction of the incubator, until after the great games, and the entire body of warriors, ten thousand in number, turned back toward Warhoon.

My introduction to these cruel and bloodthirsty people was but an index to the scenes I witnessed almost daily while with them. They are a smaller horde than the Tharks but much more ferocious. Not a day passed but that some members of the various Warhoon communities met in deadly combat. I have seen as high as eight mortal duels within a single day.

We reached the city of Warhoon after some three days march and I was immediately cast into a dungeon and heavily chained to the floor and walls. Food was brought me at intervals but owing to the utter darkness of the place I do not know whether I lay there days, or weeks, or months. It was the most horrible experience of all my life and that my mind did not give way to the terrors of that inky blackness has been a wonder to me ever since. The place was filled with creeping, crawling things; cold, sinuous bodies passed over me when I lay down, and in the darkness I occasionally caught glimpses of gleaming, fiery eyes, fixed in horrible intentness upon me. No sound reached me from the world above and no word would my jailer vouchsafe when my food was brought to me, although I at first bombarded him with questions.

Finally all the hatred and maniacal loathing for these awful creatures who had placed me in this horrible place was centered by my tottering reason upon this single emissary who represented to me the entire horde of Warhoons.

I had noticed that he always advanced with his dim torch to where he could place the food within my reach and as he stooped to place it upon the floor his head was about on a level with my breast. So, with the cunning of a madman, I backed into the far corner of my cell when next I heard him approaching and gathering a little slack of the great chain which held me in my hand I waited his coming, crouching like some beast of prey. As he stooped to place my food upon the ground I swung the chain above my head and crashed the links with all my strength upon his skull. Without a sound he slipped to the floor, stone dead.

Laughing and chattering like the idiot I was fast becoming I fell upon his prostrate form my fingers feeling for his dead throat. Presently they came in contact with a small chain at the end of which dangled a number of keys. The touch of my fingers on these keys brought back my reason with the suddenness of thought. No longer was I a jibbering idiot, but a sane, reasoning man with the means of escape within my very hands.

As I was groping to remove the chain from about my victim's neck I glanced up into the darkness to see six pairs of gleaming eyes fixed, unwinking, upon me. Slowly they approached and slowly I shrank back from the awful horror of them. Back into my corner I crouched holding my hands, palms out, before me, and stealthily on came the awful eyes until they reached the dead body at my feet. Then slowly they retreated but this time with a strange grating sound and finally they disappeared in some black and distant recess of my dungeon.

Chapter XIX
(ᏩᏒᏣᏣᏡᏆᏇᏌᏠ ᏡᏒ ᏣᏒᏓ ᏔᏔᏐᏣᏒᏔ)

(Battling in the Arena)

SLOWLY I REGAINED my composure and finally essayed again to attempt to remove the keys from the dead body of my former jailer. But as I reached out into the darkness to locate it I found to my horror that it was gone. Then the truth flashed on me; the owners of those gleaming eyes had dragged my prize away from me to be devoured in their neighboring lair; as they had been waiting for days, for weeks, for months, through all this awful eternity of my imprisonment to drag my dead carcass to their feast.

For two days no food was brought me, but then a new messenger appeared and my incarceration went on as before, but not again did I allow my reason to be submerged by the horror of my position.

Shortly after this episode another prisoner was brought in and chained near me. By the dim torch light I saw that he was a red Martian and I could scarcely await the departure of his guards to address him. As their retreating footsteps died away in the distance, I called out softly the Martian word of greeting, kaor.

"Who are you who speaks out of the darkness?" he answered.

"John Carter, a friend of the red men of Helium."

"I am of Helium," he said, "but I do not recall your name."

And then I told him my story as I have written it here, omitting only any reference to my love for Dejah Thoris. He was much excited by the news of Helium's princess and seemed quite positive that she and Sola could easily have reached a point of safety from where they left me. He said that he knew the place well because the defile through which the Warhoon warriors had passed when they discovered us was the only one ever used by them when marching to the south.

"Dejah Thoris and Sola entered the hills not five miles from a great waterway and are now probably quite safe," he assured me.

My fellow prisoner was Kantos Kan, a padwar (lieutenant) in the navy of Helium. He had been a member of the ill-fated expedition which had fallen into the hands of the Tharks at the time of Dejah Thoris' capture, and he briefly related the events which followed the defeat of the battleships.

Badly injured and only partially manned they had limped slowly toward Helium, but while passing near the city of Zodanga, the capital of Helium's hereditary enemies among the red men of Barsoom, they had been attacked by a great body of war vessels and all but the craft to which Kantos Kan belonged were either destroyed or captured. His vessel was chased for days by three of the Zodangan war ships but finally escaped during the darkness of a moonless night.

Thirty days after the capture of Dejah Thoris, or about the time of our coming to Thark, his vessel had reached Helium with about ten survivors of the original crew of seven hundred officers and men. Immediately seven great fleets, each of one hundred mighty war ships, had been dispatched to search for Dejah Thoris, and from these vessels two thousand smaller craft had been kept out continuously in futile search for the missing princess.

Two green Martian communities had been wiped off the face of Barsoom by the avenging fleets, but no trace of Dejah Thoris had been found. They had been searching among the northern hordes, and only within the past few days had they extended their quest to the south.

Kantos Kan had been detailed to one of the small one-man fliers and had had the misfortune to be discovered by the Warhoons while exploring their city.

The bravery and daring of the man won my greatest respect and admiration. Alone he had landed at the city's boundary and on foot had penetrated to the buildings surrounding the plaza. For two days and nights he had explored their quarters and their dungeons in search of his beloved princess only to fall into the hands of a party of Warhoons as he was about to leave, after assuring himself that Dejah Thoris was not a captive there.

During the period of our incarceration Kantos Kan and I became well acquainted, and formed a warm personal friendship. A few days only elapsed, however, before we were dragged forth from our dungeon for the great games. We were conducted early one morning to an enormous amphitheater, which instead of having been built upon the surface of the ground was excavated below the surface. It had partially filled with debris so that how large it had originally been was difficult to say. In its present condition it held the entire twenty thousand Warhoons of the assembled hordes.

The arena was immense but extremely uneven and unkempt. Around it the Warhoons had piled building stone from some of the ruined edifices of the ancient city to prevent the animals and the captives from escaping into the audience, and at each end had been constructed cages to hold them until their turns came to meet some horrible death upon the arena.

Kantos Kan and I were confined together in one of the cages. In the others were wild calots, thoats, mad zitidars, green warriors, and women of other hordes, and many strange and ferocious wild beasts of Barsoom which I had never before seen. The din of their roaring, growling and squealing was deafening and the formidable appearance of any one of them was enough to make the stoutest heart feel grave forebodings.

Kantos Kan explained to me that at the end of the day one of these prisoners would gain freedom and the others would lie dead about the arena. The winners in the various contests of the day would be pitted against each other until only two remained alive; the victor in the last encounter being set free, whether animal or man. The following morning the cages would be filled with a new consignment of victims, and so on throughout the ten days of the games.

Shortly after we had been caged the amphitheater began to fill and within an hour every available part of the seating space was occupied. Dak Kova, with his jeds and chieftains, sat at the center of one side of the arena upon a large raised platform.

At a signal from Dak Kova the doors of two cages were thrown open and a dozen green Martian females were driven to the center of the arena. Each was given a dagger and then, at the far end, a pack of twelve calots, or wild dogs were loosed upon them.

As the brutes, growling and foaming, rushed upon the almost defenseless women I turned my head that I might not see the horrid sight. The yells and laughter of the green horde bore witness to the excellent quality of the sport and when I turned back to the arena, as Kantos Kan told me it was over, I saw three victorious calots, snarling and growling over the bodies of their prey. The women had given a good account of themselves.

Next a mad zitidar was loosed among the remaining dogs, and so it went throughout the long, hot, horrible day.

During the day I was pitted against first men and then beasts, but as I was armed with a long-sword and always outclassed my adversary in agility and generally in strength as well, it proved but child's play to me. Time and time again I won the applause of the bloodthirsty multitude, and toward the end there were cries that I be taken from the arena and be made a member of the hordes of Warhoon.

Finally there were but three of us left, a great green

warrior of some far northern horde, Kantos Kan, and myself. The other two were to battle and then I to fight the conqueror for the liberty which was accorded the final winner.

Kantos Kan had fought several times during the day and like myself had always proven victorious, but occasionally by the smallest of margins, especially when pitted against the green warriors. I had little hope that he could best his giant adversary who had mowed down all before him during the day. The fellow towered nearly sixteen feet in height, while Kantos Kan was some inches under six feet. As they advanced to meet one another I saw for the first time a trick of Martian swordsmanship which centered Kantos Kan's every hope of victory and life on one cast of the dice, for, as he came to within about twenty feet of the huge fellow he threw his sword arm far behind him over his shoulder and with a mighty sweep hurled his weapon point foremost at the green warrior. It flew true as an arrow and piercing the poor devil's heart laid him dead upon the arena.

Kantos Kan and I were now pitted against each other but as we approached to the encounter I whispered to him to prolong the battle until nearly dark in the hope that we might find some means of escape. The horde evidently guessed that we had no hearts to fight each other and so they howled in rage as neither of us placed a fatal thrust. Just as I saw the sudden coming of dark I whispered to Kantos Kan to thrust his sword between my left arm and my body. As he did so I staggered back clasping the sword tightly with my arm and thus fell to the ground with his weapon apparently protruding from my chest. Kantos Kan perceived my coup and stepping quickly to my side he placed his foot upon my neck and withdrawing his sword from my body gave me the final death blow through the neck which is supposed to sever the jugular vein, but in this instance the cold blade slipped harmlessly into the sand of the arena. In the darkness which had now fallen none could tell but that he had really finished me. I whispered to him to go and claim his freedom and then look for me in the hills east of the city, and so he left me.

When the amphitheater had cleared I crept stealthily to the top and as the great excavation lay far from the plaza and in an untenanted portion of the great dead city I had little trouble in reaching the hills beyond.

Chapter XX
ᐯᐃ ᔑᐃᑊ ᐊᔑᔑᐅᐸᑕᐃᔑᑊᐃᑊ ᔑᐊᑊᐃᔑᐃᑊᔅ

(In the Atmosphere Factory)

FOR TWO DAYS I waited there for Kantos Kan, but as
he did not come I started off on foot in a northwesterly
direction toward a point where he had told me lay the
nearest waterway. My only food consisted of vegetable
milk from the plants which gave so bounteously of this
priceless fluid.

Through two long weeks I wandered, stumbling
through the nights guided only by the stars and hiding
during the days behind some protruding rock or among
the occasional hills I traversed. Several times I was
attacked by wild beasts; strange, uncouth monstrosities
that leaped upon me in the dark, so that I had ever to
grasp my long-sword in my hand that I might be ready
for them. Usually my strange, newly acquired telepathic
power warned me in ample time, but once I was down
with vicious fangs at my jugular and a hairy face pressed
close to mine before I knew that I was even threatened.

What manner of thing was upon me I did not know,
but that it was large and heavy and many-legged I could
feel. My hands were at its throat before the fangs had
a chance to bury themselves in my neck, and slowly I

forced the hairy face from me and closed my fingers, vise-like, upon its windpipe.

Without sound we lay there, the beast exerting every effort to reach me with those awful fangs, and I straining to maintain my grip and choke the life from it as I kept it from my throat. Slowly my arms gave to the unequal struggle, and inch by inch the burning eyes and gleaming tusks of my antagonist crept toward me, until, as the hairy face touched mine again, I realized that all was over. And then a living mass of destruction sprang from the surrounding darkness full upon the creature that held me pinioned to the ground. The two rolled growling upon the moss, tearing and rending one another in a frightful manner, but it was soon over and my preserver stood with lowered head above the throat of the dead thing which would have killed me.

The nearer moon, hurtling suddenly above the horizon and lighting up the Barsoomian scene, showed me that my preserver was Woola, but from whence he had come, or how found me, I was at a loss to know. That I was glad of his companionship it is needless to say, but my pleasure at seeing him was tempered by anxiety as to the reason of his leaving Dejah Thoris. Only her death I felt sure, could account for his absence from her, so faithful I knew him to be to my commands.

By the light of the now brilliant moons I saw that he was but a shadow of his former self, and as he turned from my caress and commenced greedily to devour the dead carcass at my feet I realized that the poor fellow was more than half starved. I, myself, was in but little better plight but I could not bring myself to eat the uncooked flesh and I had no means of making a fire. When Woola had finished his meal I again took up my weary and seemingly endless wandering in quest of the elusive waterway.

At daybreak of the fifteenth day of my search I was overjoyed to see the high trees that denoted the object of my search. About noon I dragged myself wearily to the portals of a huge building which covered perhaps four square miles and towered two hundred feet in the air. It showed no aperture in the mighty walls other than the tiny door at which I sank exhausted, nor was there any sign of life about it.

I could find no bell or other method of making my presence known to the inmates of the place, unless a small round role in the wall near the door was for that purpose. It was of about the bigness of a lead pencil and thinking that it might be in the nature of a speaking tube I put my mouth to it and was about to call into it when a voice issued from it asking me whom I might be, where from, and the nature of my errand.

I explained that I had escaped from the Warhoons and was dying of starvation and exhaustion.

"You wear the metal of a green warrior and are followed by a calot, yet you are of the figure of a red man. In color you are neither green nor red. In the name of the ninth day, what manner of creature are you?"

"I am a friend of the red men of Barsoom and I am starving. In the name of humanity open to us," I replied.

Presently the door commenced to recede before me until it had sunk into the wall fifty feet, then it stopped and slid easily to the left, exposing a short, narrow corridor of concrete, at the further end of which was another door, similar in every respect to the one I had just passed. No one was in sight, yet immediately we passed the first door it slid gently into place behind us and receded rapidly to its original position in the front wall of the building. As the door had slipped aside I had noted its great thickness, fully twenty feet, and as it reached its place once more after closing behind us, great cylinders of steel had dropped from the ceiling behind it and fitted their lower ends into apertures countersunk in the floor.

A second and third door receded before me and slipped to one side as the first, before I reached a large inner chamber where I found food and drink set out upon a great stone table. A voice directed me to satisfy my hunger and to feed my calot, and while I was thus engaged my invisible host put me through a severe and searching cross-examination.

"Your statements are most remarkable," said the voice, on concluding its questioning, "but you are evidently speaking the truth, and it is equally evident that you are not of Barsoom. I can tell that by the conformation of your brain and the strange location of your internal organs and the shape and size of your heart."

"Can you see through me?" I exclaimed.

"Yes, I can see all but your thoughts, and were you a Barsoomian I could read those."

Then a door opened at the far side of the chamber and a strange, dried up, little mummy of a man came toward me. He wore but a single article of clothing or adornment, a small collar of gold from which depended upon his chest a great ornament as large as a dinner plate set solid with huge diamonds, except for the exact center which was occupied by a strange stone, an inch in diameter, that scintillated nine different and distinct rays; the seven colors of our earthly prism and two beautiful rays which, to me, were new and nameless. I cannot describe them any more than you could describe red to a blind man. I only know that they were beautiful in the extreme.

The old man sat and talked with me for hours, and the strangest part of our intercourse was that I could read his every thought while he could not fathom an iota from my mind unless I spoke.

I did not apprise him of my ability to sense his mental operations, and thus I learned a great deal which proved of immense value to me later and which I would never have known had he suspected my strange power, for the Martians have such perfect control of their mental machinery that they are able to direct their thoughts with absolute precision.

The building in which I found myself contained the machinery which produces that artificial atmosphere which sustains life on Mars. The secret of the entire process hinges on the use of the ninth ray, one of the beautiful scintillations which I had noted emanating from the great stone in my host's diadem.

This ray is separated from the other rays of the sun by means of finely adjusted instruments placed upon the roof of the huge building, three-quarters of which is used for reservoirs in which the ninth ray is stored. This product is then treated electrically, or rather certain proportions of refined electric vibrations are incorporated with it, and the result is then pumped to the five principal air centers of the planet where, as it is released, contact with the ether of space transforms it into atmosphere.

There is always sufficient reserve of the ninth ray stored in the great building to maintain the present Martian atmosphere for a thousand years, and the only fear, as my new friend told me, was that some accident might befall the pumping apparatus.

He led me to an inner chamber where I beheld a battery of twenty radium pumps any one of which was equal to the task of furnishing all Mars with the atmosphere compound. For eight hundred years, he told me, he had watched these pumps which are used alternately a day each at a stretch, or a little over twenty-four and one-half Earth hours. He has one assistant who divides the watch with him. Half a Martian year, about three hundred and forty-four of our days, each of these men spend alone in this huge, isolated plant.

Every red Martian is taught during earliest childhood the principles of the manufacture of atmosphere, but only two at one time ever hold the secret of ingress to the great building, which, built as it is with walls a hundred and fifty feet thick, is absolutely unassailable, even the roof being guarded from assault by air craft by a glass covering five feet thick.

The only fear they entertain of attack is from the green Martians or some demented red man, as all Barsoomians realize that the very existence of every form of life of Mars is dependent upon the uninterrupted working of this plant.

One curious fact I discovered as I watched his thoughts was that the outer doors are manipulated by telepathic means. The locks are so finely adjusted that the doors are released by the action of a certain combination of thought waves. To experiment with my new-found toy I thought to surprise him into revealing this combination and so I asked him in a casual manner how he had managed to unlock the massive doors for me from the inner chambers of the building. As quick as a flash there leaped to his mind nine Martian sounds, but as quickly faded as he answered that this was a secret he must not divulge.

From then on his manner toward me changed as though he feared that he had been surprised into divulging his great secret, and I read suspicion and fear in his looks and thoughts, though his words were still fair.

Before I retired for the night he promised to give

me a letter to a nearby agricultural officer who would help me on my way to Zodanga, which he said, was the nearest Martian city.

"But be sure that you do not let them know you are bound for Helium as they are at war with that country. My assistant and I are of no country, we belong to all Barsoom and this talisman which we wear protects us in all lands, even among the green men—though we do not trust ourselves to their hands if we can avoid it," he added.

"And so good-night, my friend," he continued, "may you have a long and restful sleep—yes, a long sleep."

And though he smiled pleasantly I saw in his thoughts the wish that he had never admitted me, and then a picture of him standing over me in the night, and the swift thrust of a long dagger and the half formed words, "I am sorry, but it is for the best good of Barsoom."

As he closed the door of my chamber behind him his thoughts were cut off from me as was the sight of him, which seemed strange to me in my little knowledge of thought transference.

What was I to do? How could I escape through these mighty walls? Easily could I kill him now that I was warned, but once he was dead I could no more escape, and with the stopping of the machinery of the great plant I should die with all the other inhabitants of the planet—all, even Dejah Thoris were she not already dead. For the others I did not give the snap of my finger, but the thought of Dejah Thoris drove from my mind all desire to kill my mistaken host.

Cautiously I opened the door of my apartment and, followed by Woola, sought the inner of the great doors. A wild scheme had come to me; I would attempt to force the great locks by the nine thought waves I had read in my host's mind.

Creeping stealthily through corridor after corridor and down winding runways which turned hither and thither I finally reached the great hall in which I had broken my long fast that morning. Nowhere had I seen my host, nor did I know where he kept himself by night.

I was on the point of stepping boldly out into the room when a slight noise behind me warned me back into the shadows of a recess in the corridor. Dragging Woola after me I crouched low in the darkness.

Presently the old man passed close by me, and as he entered the dimly lighted chamber which I had been about to pass through I saw that he held a long thin dagger in his hand and that he was sharpening it upon a stone. In his mind was the decision to inspect the radium pumps, which would take about thirty minutes, and then return to my bed chamber and finish me.

As he passed through the great hall and disappeared down the runway which led to the pump room, I stole stealthily from my hiding place and crossed to the great door, the inner of the three which stood between me and liberty.

Concentrating my mind upon the massive lock I hurled the nine thought waves against it. In breathless expectancy I waited, when finally the great door moved softly toward me and slid quietly to one side. One after the other the remaining mighty portals opened at my command and Woola and I stepped forth into the darkness, free, but little better off than we had been before, other than that we had full stomachs.

Hastening away from the shadows of the formidable pile I made for the first crossroad, intending to strike the central turnpike as quickly as possible. This I reached about morning and entering the first enclosure I came to I searched for some evidences of a habitation.

There were low rambling buildings of concrete barred with heavy impassable doors, and no amount of hammering and hallooing brought any response. Weary and exhausted from sleeplessness I threw myself upon the ground commanding Woola to stand guard.

Some time later I was awakened by his frightful growlings and opened my eyes to see three red Martians standing a short distance from us and covering me with their rifles.

"I am unarmed and no enemy," I hastened to explain. "I have been a prisoner among the green men and am on my way to Zodanga. All I ask is food and rest for myself and my calot and the proper directions for reaching my destination."

They lowered their rifles and advanced pleasantly toward me placing their right hands upon my left shoulder, after the manner of their custom of salute, and asking me many questions about myself and my wanderings. They then took me to the house of one of them which was only a short distance away.

The buildings I had been hammering at in the early morning were occupied only by stock and farm produce, the house proper standing among the grove of enormous trees, and, like all red-Martian homes, had been raised at night some forty or fifty feet from the ground on a large round metal shaft which slid up or down within a sleeve sunk in the ground, and was operated by a tiny radium engine in the entrance hall of the building. Instead of bothering with bolts and bars for their dwellings, the red Martians simply run them up out of harm's way during the night. They also have private means for lowering or raising them from the ground without if they wish to go away and leave them.

These brothers, with their wives and children, occupied three similar houses on this farm. They did no work themselves, being government officers in charge. The labor was performed by convicts, prisoners of war, delinquent debtors and confirmed bachelors who were too poor to pay the high celibate tax which all red-Martian governments impose.

They were the personification of cordiality and hospitality and I spent several days with them, resting and recuperating from my long and arduous experiences.

When they had heard my story—I omitted all reference to Dejah Thoris and the old man of the atmosphere plant—they advised me to color my body to more nearly resemble their own race and then attempt to find employment in Zodanga, either in the army or the navy.

"The chances are small that your tale will be believed until after you have proven your trustworthiness and won friends among the higher nobles of the court. This you can most easily do through military service, as we are a warlike people on Barsoom," explained one of them, "and save our richest favors for the fighting man."

When I was ready to depart they furnished me with

a small domestic bull thoat, such as is used for saddle purposes by all red Martians. The animal is about the size of a horse and quite gentle, but in color and shape an exact replica of his huge and fierce cousin of the wilds.

The brothers had supplied me with a reddish oil with which I anointed my entire body and one of them cut my hair, which had grown quite long, in the prevailing fashion of the time, square at the back and banged in front, so that I could have passed anywhere upon Barsoom as a full-fledged red Martian. My metal and ornaments were also renewed in the style of a Zodangan gentleman, attached to the house of Ptor, which was the family name of my benefactors.

They filled a little sack at my side with Zodangan money. The medium of exchange upon Mars is not dissimilar from our own except that the coins are oval. Paper money is issued by individuals as they require it and redeemed twice yearly. If a man issues more than he can redeem, the government pays his creditors in full and the debtor works out the amount upon the farms or in mines, which are all owned by the government. This suits everybody except the debtor as it has been a difficult thing to obtain sufficient voluntary labor to work the great isolated farm lands of Mars, stretching as they do like narrow ribbons from pole to pole, through wild stretches peopled by wild animals and wilder men.

When I mentioned my inability to repay them for their kindness to me they assured me that I would have ample opportunity if I lived long upon Barsoom, and bidding me farewell they watched me until I was out of sight upon the broad white turnpike.

Chapter XXI
ゟ҈ ゟ҈ ⰅⰔⰕ ⰅⰔⰕ ゟ҈ⰊⰋ
(An Air Scout for Zodanga)

As I proceeded on my journey toward Zodanga many strange and interesting sights arrested my attention, and at the several farm houses where I stopped I learned a number of new and instructive things concerning the methods and manners of Barsoom.

The water which supplies the farms of Mars is collected in immense underground reservoirs at either pole from the melting ice caps, and pumped through long conduits to the various populated centers. Along either side of these conduits, and extending their entire length, lie the cultivated districts. These are divided into tracts of about the same size, each tract being under the supervision of one or more government officers.

Instead of flooding the surface of the fields, and thus wasting immense quantities of water by evaporation, the precious liquid is carried underground through a vast network of small pipes directly to the roots of the vegetation. The crops upon Mars are always uniform, for there are no droughts, no rains, no high winds, and no insects, or destroying birds.

On this trip I tasted the first meat I had eaten since

leaving Earth—large, juicy steaks and chops from the well-fed domestic animals of the farms. Also I enjoyed luscious fruits and vegetables, but not a single article of food which was exactly similar to anything on Earth. Every plant and flower and vegetable and animal has been so refined by ages of careful, scientific cultivation and breeding that the like of them on Earth dwindled into pale, gray, characterless nothingness by comparison.

At a second stop I met some highly cultivated people of the noble class and while in conversation we chanced to speak of Helium. One of the older men had been there on a diplomatic mission several years before and spoke with regret of the conditions which seemed destined ever to keep these two countries at war.

"Helium," he said, "rightly boasts the most beautiful women of Barsoom, and of all her treasures the wondrous daughter of Mors Kajak, Dejah Thoris, is the most exquisite flower.

"Why," he added, "the people really worship the ground she walks upon and since her loss on that ill-starred expedition all Helium has been draped in mourning.

"That our ruler should have attacked the disabled fleet as it was returning to Helium was but another of his awful blunders which I fear will sooner or later compel Zodanga to elevate a wiser man to his place.

"Even now, though our victorious armies are sur-rounding Helium, the people of Zodanga are voicing their displeasure, for the war is not a popular one, since it is not based on right or justice. Our forces took advantage of the absence of the principal fleet of Helium on their search for the princess, and so we have been able easily to reduce the city to a sorry plight. It is said she will fall within the next few passages of the further moon."

"And what, think you, may have been the fate of the princess, Dejah Thoris?" I asked as casually as possible.

"She is dead," he answered. "This much was learned from a green warrior recently captured by our forces in the south. She escaped from the hordes of Thark with a strange creature of another world, only to fall into the hands of the Warhoons. Their thoats were found wandering upon the sea bottom and evidences of a bloody conflict were discovered nearby."

While this information was in no way reassuring, neither was it at all conclusive proof of the death of Dejah Thoris, and so I determined to make every effort possible to reach Helium as quickly as I could and carry to Tardos Mors such news of his granddaughter's possible whereabouts as lay in my power.

Ten days after leaving the three Ptor brothers I arrived at Zodanga. From the moment that I had come in contact with the red inhabitants of Mars I had noticed that Woola drew a great amount of unwelcome attention to me, since the huge brute belonged to a species which is never domesticated by the red men. Were one to stroll down Broadway with a Numidian lion at his heels the effect would be somewhat similar to that which I should have produced had I entered Zodanga with Woola.

The very thought of parting with the faithful fellow caused me so great regret and genuine sorrow that I put it off until just before we arrived at the city's gates; but then, finally, it became imperative that we separate. Had nothing further than my own safety or pleasure been at stake no argument could have prevailed upon me to turn away the one creature upon Barsoom that had never failed in a demonstration of affection and loyalty; but as I would willingly have offered my life in the service of her in search of whom I was about to challenge the unknown dangers of this, to me, mysterious city, I could not permit even Woola's life to threaten the success of my venture, much less his momentary happiness, for I doubted not he soon would forget me. And so I bade the poor beast an affectionate farewell, promising him, however, that if I came through my adventure in safety that in some way I should find the means to search him out.

He seemed to understand me fully, and when I pointed back in the direction of Thark he turned sorrowfully away, nor could I bear to watch him go; but resolutely set my face toward Zodanga and with a touch of heartsickness approached her frowning walls.

The letter I bore from them gained me immediate entrance to the vast, walled city. It was still very early in the morning and the streets were practically deserted. The residences, raised high upon their metal columns, resembled huge rookeries, while the uprights themselves presented the appearance of steel tree trunks. The shops as a rule were not raised from the ground nor were their doors bolted or barred, since thievery is practically unknown upon Barsoom. Assassination is the ever-present fear of all Barsoomians, and for this reason alone their homes are raised high above the ground at night, or in times of danger.

The Ptor brothers had given me explicit directions for reaching the point of the city where I could find living accommodations and be near the offices of the government agents to whom they had given me letters. My way led to the central square or plaza, which is a characteristic of all Martian cities.

The plaza of Zodanga covers a square mile and is bounded by the palaces of the jeddak, the jeds, and other members of the royalty and nobility of Zodanga, as well as by the principal public buildings, cafés, and shops.

As I was crossing the great square lost in wonder and admiration of the magnificent architecture and the gorgeous scarlet vegetation which carpeted the broad lawns I discovered a red Martian walking briskly toward me from one of the avenues. He paid not the slightest attention to me, but as he came abreast I recognized him, and turning I placed my hand upon his shoulder, calling out:

"Kaor, Kantos Kan!"

Like lightning he wheeled and before I could so much as lower my hand the point of his long-sword was at my breast.

"Who are you?" he growled, and then as a backward leap carried me fifty feet from his sword he dropped the point to the ground and exclaimed, laughing,

"I do not need a better reply, there is but one man upon all Barsoom who can bounce about like a rubber ball. By the mother of the further moon, John Carter, how came you here, and have you become a Darseen that you can change your color at will?

"You gave me a bad half minute my friend," he continued, after I had briefly outlined my adventures since parting with him in the arena at Warhoon. "Were my name and city known to the Zodangans I would shortly be sitting on the banks of the lost sea of Korus with my revered and departed ancestors. I am here in the interest of Tardos Mors, Jeddak of Helium, to discover the whereabouts of Dejah Thoris, our princess. Sab Than, prince of Zodanga, has her hidden in the city and has fallen madly in love with her. His father, Than Kosis, Jeddak of Zodanga, has made her voluntary marriage to his son the price of peace between our countries, but Tardos Mors will not accede to the demands and has sent word that he and his people would rather look upon the dead face of their princess than see her wed to any than her own choice, and that personally he would prefer being engulfed in the ashes of a lost and burning Helium to joining the metal of his house with that of Than Kosis. His reply was the deadliest affront he could have put upon Than Kosis and the Zodangans, but his people love him the more for it and his strength in Helium is greater today than ever.

"I have been here three days," continued Kantos Kan, "but I have not yet found where Dejah Thoris is imprisoned. Today I join the Zodangan navy as an air scout and I hope in this way to win the confidence of Sab Than, the prince, who is commander of this division of the navy, and thus learn the whereabouts of Dejah Thoris. I am glad that you are here, John Carter, for I know your loyalty to my princess and two of us working together should be able to accomplish much."

The plaza was now commencing to fill with people going and coming upon the daily activities of their duties. The shops were opening and the cafés filling with early morning patrons. Kantos Kan led me to one of these gorgeous eating places where we were served entirely by mechanical apparatus. No hand touched the food from the time it entered the building in its raw state until it emerged hot and delicious upon the tables before the guests, in response to the touching of tiny buttons to indicate their desires.

After our meal, Kantos Kan took me with him to the headquarters of the air-scout squadron and introducing me to his superior asked that I be enrolled as a member of the corps. In accordance with custom an examination was necessary, but Kantos Kan had told me to have no fear on this score as he would attend to that part of the matter. He accomplished this by taking my order for examination to the examining officer and representing himself as John Carter.

"This ruse will be discovered later," he cheerfully explained, "when they check up my weights, measurements, and other personal identification data, but it will be several months before this is done and our mission should be accomplished or have failed long before that time."

The next few days were spent by Kantos Kan in teaching me the intricacies of flying and of repairing the dainty little contrivances which the Martians use for this purpose. The body of the one-man air craft is about sixteen feet long, two feet wide and three inches thick, tapering to a point at each end. The driver sits on top of this plane upon a seat constructed over the small, noiseless radium engine which propels it. The medium of buoyancy is contained within the thin metal walls of the body and consists of the eighth Barsoomian ray, or ray of propulsion, as it may be termed in view of its properties.

This ray, like the ninth ray, is unknown on Earth, but the Martians have discovered that it is an inherent property of all light no matter from what source it emanates. They have learned that it is the solar eighth ray which propels the light of the sun to the various planets, and that it is the individual eighth ray of each planet which "reflects," or propels the light thus obtained out into space once more. The solar eighth ray would be absorbed by the surface of Barsoom, but the Barsoomian eighth ray, which tends to propel light from Mars into space, is constantly streaming out from the planet constituting a force of repulsion of gravity which when confined is able to lift enormous weights from the surface of the ground.

It is this ray which has enabled them to so perfect aviation that battleships far outweighing anything known upon Earth sail as gracefully and lightly through the thin air of Barsoom as a toy balloon in the heavy atmosphere of Earth.

During the early years of the discovery of this ray many strange accidents occurred before the Martians learned to measure and control the wonderful power they had found. In one instance, some nine hundred years before, the first great battleship to be built with eighth ray reservoirs was stored with too great a quantity of the rays and she had sailed up from Helium with five hundred officers and men, never to return.

Her power of repulsion for the planet was so great that it had carried her far into space, where she can be seen today, by the aid of powerful telescopes, hurtling through the heavens ten thousand miles from Mars; a tiny satellite that will thus encircle Barsoom to the end of time.

The fourth day after my arrival at Zodanga I made my first flight, and as a result of it I won a promotion which included quarters in the palace of Than Kosis.

As I rose above the city I circled several times, as I had seen Kantos Kan do, and then throwing my engine into top speed I raced at terrific velocity toward the south, following one of the great waterways which enter Zodanga from that direction.

I had traversed perhaps two hundred miles in a little less than an hour when I descried far below me a party of three green warriors racing madly toward a small figure on foot which seemed to be trying to reach the confines of one of the walled fields.

Dropping my machine rapidly toward them, and circling to the rear of the warriors, I soon saw that the object of their pursuit was a red Martian wearing the metal of the scout squadron to which I was attached. A short distance away lay his tiny flier, surrounded by the tools with which he had evidently been occupied in repairing some damage when surprised by the green warriors.

They were now almost upon him; their flying mounts charging down on the relatively puny figure at terrific speed, while the warriors leaned low to the right, with their great metal-shod spears. Each seemed striving to be the first to impale the poor Zodangan and in another moment his fate would have been sealed had it not been for my timely arrival.

Driving my fleet air craft at high speed directly behind the warriors I soon overtook them and without diminishing my speed I rammed the prow of my little flier between the shoulders of the nearest. The impact sufficient to have torn through inches of solid steel, hurled the fellow's headless body into the air over the head of his thoat, where it fell sprawling upon the moss. The mounts of the other two warriors turned squealing in terror, and bolted in opposite directions.

Reducing my speed I circled and came to the ground at the feet of the astonished Zodangan. He was warm in his thanks for my timely aid and promised that my day's work would bring the reward it merited, for it was none other than a cousin of the jeddak of Zodanga whose life I had saved.

We wasted no time in talk as we knew that the warriors would surely return as soon as they had gained control of their mounts. Hastening to his damaged machine we were bending every effort to finish the needed repairs and had almost completed them when we saw the two green monsters returning at top speed from opposite sides of us. When they had approached within a hundred yards their thoats again became unmanageable and absolutely refused to advance further toward the air craft which had frightened them.

The warriors finally dismounted and hobbling their animals advanced toward us on foot with drawn long-swords. I advanced to meet the larger, telling the Zodangan to do the best he could with the other. Finishing my man with almost no effort, as had now from much practice become habitual with me, I hastened to return to my new acquaintance whom I found indeed in desperate straits.

He was wounded and down with the huge foot of his antagonist upon his throat and the great long-sword raised to deal the final thrust. With a bound I cleared the fifty feet intervening between us, and with outstretched point drove my sword completely through the body of the green warrior. His sword fell, harmless, to the ground and he sank limply upon the prostrate form of the Zodangan.

A cursory examination of the latter revealed no mortal injuries and after a brief rest he asserted that he felt fit to attempt the return voyage. He would have to pilot his own craft, however, as these frail vessels are not intended to convey but a single person.

Quickly completing the repairs we rose together into the still, cloudless Martian sky, and at great speed and without further mishap returned to Zodanga.

As we neared the city we discovered a mighty concourse of civilians and troops assembled upon the plain before the city. The sky was black with naval vessels and private and public pleasure craft, flying long streamers of gay-colored silks, and banners and flags of odd and picturesque design.

My companion signaled that I slow down, and running his machine close beside mine suggested that we approach and watch the ceremony, which, he said, was for the purpose of conferring honors on individual officers and men for bravery and other distinguished service. He then unfurled a little ensign which denoted that his craft bore a member of the royal family of Zodanga, and together we made our way through the maze of low-lying air vessels until we hung directly over the jeddak of Zodanga and his staff. All were mounted upon the small domestic bull thoats of the red Martians, and their trappings and ornamentation bore such a quantity of gorgeously colored feathers that I could not but be struck with the startling resemblance the concourse bore to a band of the red Indians of my own Earth.

One of the staff called the attention of Than Kosis to the presence of my companion above them and the ruler motioned for him to descend. As they waited for the troops to move into position facing the jeddak the two talked earnestly together, the jeddak and his staff occasionally glancing up at me. I could not hear their conversation and presently it ceased and all dismounted, as the last body of troops had wheeled into position before their emperor. A member of the staff advanced toward the troops, and calling the name of a soldier commanded him to advance. The officer then recited the nature of the heroic act which had won the approval of the jeddak, and the latter advanced and placed a metal ornament upon the left arm of the lucky man.

Ten men had been so decorated when the aide called out, "John Carter, air scout!"

Never in my life had I been so surprised, but the habit of military discipline is strong within me, and I dropped my little machine lightly to the ground and advanced on foot as I had seen the others do. As I halted before the officer, he addressed me in a voice audible to the entire assemblage of troops and spectators.

"In recognition, John Carter," he said, "of your remarkable courage and skill in defending the person of the cousin of the jeddak Than Kosis and, singlehanded, vanquishing three green warriors, it is the pleasure of our jeddak to confer on you the mark of his esteem."

Than Kosis then advanced toward me and placing an ornament upon me, said:

"My cousin has narrated the details of your wonderful achievement, which seems little short of miraculous, and if you can so well defend a cousin of the jeddak how much better could you defend the person of the jeddak himself. You are therefore appointed a padwar of The Guards and will be quartered in my palace hereafter."

I thanked him, and at his direction joined the members of his staff. After the ceremony I returned my machine to its quarters on the roof of the barracks of the air-scout squadron, and with an orderly from the palace to guide me I reported to the officer in charge of the palace.

Chapter XXII
ๆ ย์นิีัั อุเออ๊ด
(I Find Dejah)

THE MAJOR-DOMO to whom I reported had been given instructions to station me near the person of the jeddak, who, in time of war, is always in great danger of assassination, as the rule that all is fair in war seems to constitute the entire ethics of Martian conflict.

He therefore escorted me immediately to the apartment in which Than Kosis then was. The ruler was engaged in conversation with his son, Sab Than, and several courtiers of his household, and did not perceive my entrance.

The walls of the apartment were completely hung with splendid tapestries which hid any windows or doors which may have pierced them. The room was lighted by imprisoned rays of sunshine held between the ceiling proper and what appeared to be a ground-glass false ceiling a few inches below.

My guide drew aside one of the tapestries, disclosing a passage which encircled the room, between the hangings and the walls of the chamber. Within this passage I was to remain, he said, so long as Than Kosis was in the apartment. When he left I was to follow. My only duty was to guard the ruler and keep out of sight as much as possible. I would be relieved after a period of four hours. The major-domo then left me.

The tapestries were of a strange weaving which gave the appearance of heavy solidity from one side, but from my hiding place I could perceive all that took place within the room as readily as though there had been no curtain intervening.

Scarcely had I gained my post than the tapestry at the opposite end of the chamber separated and four soldiers of The Guard entered, surrounding a female figure. As they approached Than Kosis the soldiers fell to either side and there standing before the jeddak and not ten feet from me, her beautiful face radiant with smiles, was Dejah Thoris.

Sab Than, Prince of Zodanga, advanced to meet her, and hand in hand they approached close to the jeddak. Than Kosis looked up in surprise, and, rising, saluted her.

"To what strange freak do I owe this visit from the Princess of Helium, who, two days ago, with rare consideration for my pride, assured me that she would prefer Tal Hajus, the green Thark, to my son?"

Dejah Thoris only smiled the more and with the

roguish dimples playing at the corners of her mouth she made answer:

"From the beginning of time upon Barsoom it has been the prerogative of woman to change her mind as she listed and to dissemble in matters concerning her heart. That you will forgive, Than Kosis, as has your son. Two days ago I was not sure of his love for me, but now I am, and I have come to beg of you to forget my rash words and to accept the assurance of the Princess of Helium that when the time comes she will wed Sab Than, Prince of Zodanga."

"I am glad that you have so decided," replied Than Kosis. "It is far from my desire to push war further against the people of Helium, and, your promise shall be recorded and a proclamation to my people issued forthwith."

"It were better, Than Kosis," interrupted Dejah Thoris, "that the proclamation wait the ending of this war. It would look strange indeed to my people and to yours were the Princess of Helium to give herself to her country's enemy in the midst of hostilities."

"Cannot the war be ended at once?" spoke Sab Than. "It requires but the word of Than Kosis to bring peace. Say it, my father, say the word that will hasten my happiness, and end this unpopular strife."

"We shall see," replied Than Kosis, "how the people of Helium take to peace. I shall at least offer it to them."

Dejah Thoris, after a few words, turned and left the apartment, still followed by her guards.

Thus was the edifice of my brief dream of happiness dashed, broken, to the ground of reality. The woman for whom I had offered my life, and from whose lips I had so recently heard a declaration of love for me, had lightly forgotten my very existence and smilingly given herself to the son of her people's most hated enemy.

Although I had heard it with my own ears I could not believe it. I must search out her apartments and force her to repeat the cruel truth to me alone before I would be convinced, and so I deserted my post and hastened through the passage behind the tapestries toward the door by which she had left the chamber. Slipping quietly through this opening I discovered a maze of winding corridors, branching and turning in every direction.

Running rapidly down first one and then another of them I soon became hopelessly lost and was standing panting against a side wall when I heard voices near me. Apparently they were coming from the opposite side of the partition against which I leaned and presently I made out the tones of Dejah Thoris. I could not hear the words but I knew that I could not possibly be mistaken in the voice.

Moving on a few steps I discovered another passageway at the end of which lay a door. Walking boldly forward I pushed into the room only to find myself in a small antechamber in which were the four guards who had accompanied her. One of them instantly arose and accosted me, asking the nature of my business.

"I am from Than Kosis," I replied, "and wish to speak privately with Dejah Thoris, Princess of Helium."

"And your order?" asked the fellow.

I did not know what he meant, but replied that I was a member of The Guard, and without waiting for a reply from him I strode toward the opposite door of the antechamber, behind which I could hear Dejah Thoris conversing.

But my entrance was not to be so easily accomplished. The guardsman stepped before me, saying,

"No one comes from Than Kosis without carrying an order or the password. You must give me one or the other before you may pass."

"The only order I require, my friend, to enter where I will, hangs at my side," I answered, tapping my longsword; "will you let me pass in peace or no?"

For reply he whipped out his own sword, calling to

the others to join him, and thus the four stood, with drawn weapons, barring my further progress.

"You are not here by the order of Than Kosis," cried the one who had first addressed me, "and not only shall you not enter the apartments of the Princess of Helium but you shall go back to Than Kosis under guard to explain this unwarranted temerity. Throw down your sword; you cannot hope to overcome four of us," he added with a grim smile.

My reply was a quick thrust which left me but three antagonists and I can assure you that they were worthy of my metal. They had me backed against the wall in no time, fighting for my life. Slowly I worked my way to a corner of the room where I could force them to come at me only one at a time, and thus we fought upward of twenty minutes; the clanging of steel on steel producing a veritable bedlam in the little room.

The noise had brought Dejah Thoris to the door of her apartment, and there she stood throughout the conflict with Sola at her back peering over her shoulder. Her face was set and emotionless and I knew that she did not recognize me, nor did Sola.

Finally a lucky cut brought down a second guardsman and then, with only two opposing me, I changed my tactics and rushed them down after the fashion of my fighting that had won me many a victory. The third fell within ten seconds after the second, and the last lay dead upon the bloody floor a few moments later. They were brave men and noble fighters, and it grieved me that I had been forced to kill them, but I would have willingly depopulated all Barsoom could I have reached the side of my Dejah Thoris in no other way.

Sheathing my bloody blade I advanced toward my Martian princess, who still stood mutely gazing at me without sign of recognition.

"Who are you, Zodangan?" she whispered. "Another enemy to harass me in my misery?"

"I am a friend," I answered, "a once cherished friend."

"No friend of Helium's princess wears that metal," she replied, "and yet the voice! I have heard it before; it is not—it cannot be—no, for he is dead."

"It is, though, my Princess, none other than John Carter," I said. "Do you not recognize, even through paint and strange metal, the heart of your chieftain?"

As I came close to her she swayed toward me with outstretched hands, but as I reached to take her in my arms she drew back with a shudder and a little moan of misery.

"Too late, too late," she grieved. "O my chieftain that

was, and whom I thought dead, had you but returned one little hour before—but now it is too late, too late."

"What do you mean, Dejah Thoris?" I cried. "That you would not have promised yourself to the Zodangan prince had you known that I lived?"

"Think you, John Carter, that I would give my heart to you yesterday and today to another? I thought that it lay buried with your ashes in the pits of Warhoon, and so today I have promised my body to another to save my people from the curse of a victorious Zodangan army."

"But I am not dead, my princess. I have come to claim you, and all Zodanga cannot prevent it."

"It is too late, John Carter, my promise is given, and on Barsoom that is final. The ceremonies which follow later are but meaningless formalities. They make the fact of marriage no more certain than does the funeral cortege of a jeddak again place the seal of death upon him. I am as good as married, John Carter. No longer may you call me your princess. No longer are you my chieftain."

"I know but little of your customs here upon Barsoom, Dejah Thoris, but I do know that I love you, and if you meant the last words you spoke to me that day as the hordes of Warhoon were charging down upon us, no other man shall ever claim you as his bride.

You meant them then, my princess, and you mean them still! Say that it is true."

"I meant them, John Carter," she whispered. "I cannot repeat them now for I have given myself to another. Ah, if you had only known our ways, my friend," she continued, half to herself, "the promise would have been yours long months ago, and you could have claimed me before all others. It might have meant the fall of Helium, but I would have given my empire for my Tharkian chief."

Then aloud she said: "Do you remember the night when you offended me? You called me your princess without having asked my hand of me, and then you boasted that you had fought for me. You did not know, and I should not have been offended; I see that now. But there was no one to tell you, what I could not, that upon Barsoom there are two kinds of women in the cities of the red men. The one they fight for that they may ask them in marriage; the other kind they fight for also, but never ask their hands. When a man has won a woman he may address her as his princess, or in any of the several terms which signify possession. You had fought for me, but had never asked me in marriage, and so when you called me your princess, you see," she faltered, "I was hurt, but even then, John Carter, I did not repulse you, as I should have done, until you made it doubly worse by taunting me with having won me through combat."

"I do not need ask your forgiveness now, Dejah Thoris," I cried. "You must know that my fault was of ignorance of your Barsoomian customs. What I failed to do, through implicit belief that my petition would be presumptuous and unwelcome, I do now, Dejah Thoris; I ask you to be my wife, and by all the Virginian fighting blood that flows in my veins you shall be."

"No, John Carter, it is useless," she cried, hopelessly, "I may never be yours while Sab Than lives."

"You have sealed his death warrant, my princess—Sab Than dies."

"Nor that either," she hastened to explain. "I may not wed the man who slays my husband, even in self-defense. It is custom. We are ruled by custom upon Barsoom. It is useless, my friend. You must bear the sorrow with me. That at least we may share in common. That, and the memory of the brief days among the Tharks. You must go now, nor ever see me again. Good-bye, my chieftain that was."

Disheartened and dejected, I withdrew from the room, but I was not entirely discouraged, nor would

I admit that Dejah Thoris was lost to me until the ceremony had actually been performed.

As I wandered along the corridors, I was as absolutely lost in the mazes of winding passageways as I had been before I discovered Dejah Thoris' apartments.

I knew that my only hope lay in escape from the city of Zodanga, for the matter of the four dead guardsmen would have to be explained, and as I could never reach my original post without a guide, suspicion would surely rest on me so soon as I was discovered wandering aimlessly through the palace.

Presently I came upon a spiral runway leading to a lower floor, and this I followed downward for several stories until I reached the doorway of a large apartment in which were a number of guardsmen. The walls of this room were hung with transparent tapestries behind which I secreted myself without being apprehended.

The conversation of the guardsmen was general, and awakened no interest in me until an officer entered the room and ordered four of the men to relieve the detail who were guarding the Princess of Helium. Now, I knew, my troubles would commence in earnest and indeed they were upon me all too soon, for it seemed that the squad had scarcely left the guardroom before one of their number burst in again breathlessly, crying that they had found their four comrades butchered in the antechamber.

In a moment the entire palace was alive with people. Guardsmen, officers, courtiers, servants, and slaves ran helter-skelter through the corridors and apartments carrying messages and orders, and searching for signs of the assassin.

This was my opportunity and slim as it appeared I grasped it, for as a number of soldiers came hurrying past my hiding place I fell in behind them and followed through the mazes of the palace until, in passing through a great hall, I saw the blessed light of day coming in through a series of larger windows.

Here I left my guides, and, slipping to the nearest window, sought for an avenue of escape. The windows opened upon a great balcony which overlooked one of the broad avenues of Zodanga. The ground was about thirty feet below, and at a like distance from the building was a wall fully twenty feet high, constructed of polished glass about a foot in thickness. To a red Martian escape by this path would have appeared impossible, but to me, with my earthly strength and agility, it seemed already accomplished. My only fear was in being detected before darkness fell, for I could not make the leap in broad daylight while the court below and the avenue beyond were crowded with Zodangans.

Accordingly I searched for a hiding place and finally found one by accident, inside a huge hanging ornament which swung from the ceiling of the hall, and about ten feet from the floor. Into the capacious bowl-like vase I sprang with ease, and scarcely had I settled down within it than I heard a number of people enter the apartment. The group stopped beneath my hiding place and I could plainly overhear their every word.

"It is the work of Heliumites," said one of the men.

"Yes, O Jeddak, but how had they access to the palace? I could believe that even with the diligent care of your guardsmen a single enemy might reach the inner chambers, but how a force of six or eight fighting men could have done so unobserved is beyond me. We shall soon know, however, for here comes the royal psychologist."

Another man now joined the group, and, after making his formal greetings to his ruler, said:

"O mighty Jeddak, it is a strange tale I read in the dead minds of your faithful guardsmen. They were felled not by a number of fighting men, but by a single opponent."

He paused to let the full weight of this announcement

impress his hearers, and that his statement was scarcely credited was evidenced by the impatient exclamation of incredulity which escaped the lips of Than Kosis.

"What manner of weird tale are you bringing me, Notan?" he cried.

"It is the truth, my Jeddak," replied the psychologist. "In fact the impressions were strongly marked on the brain of each of the four guardsmen. Their antagonist was a very tall man, wearing the metal of one of your own guardsmen, and his fighting ability was little short of marvelous for he fought fair against the entire four and vanquished them by surpassing skill and superhuman strength and endurance. Though he wore the metal of Zodanga, my Jeddak, such a man was never seen before in this or any other country upon Barsoom.

"The mind of the Princess of Helium whom I have examined and questioned was a blank to me, she has perfect control, and I could not read one iota of it. She said that she witnessed a portion of the encounter, and that when she looked there was but one man engaged with the guardsmen; a man whom she did not recognize as ever having seen."

"Where is my erstwhile savior?" spoke another of the party, and I recognized the voice of the cousin of Than Kosis, whom I had rescued from the green warriors.

"By the metal of my first ancestor," he went on, "but the description fits him to perfection, especially as to his fighting ability."

"Where is this man?" cried Than Kosis. "Have him brought to me at once. What know you of him, cousin? It seemed strange to me now that I think upon it that there should have been such a fighting man in Zodanga, of whose name, even, we were ignorant before today. And his name too, John Carter, who ever heard of such a name upon Barsoom!"

Word was soon brought that I was nowhere to be found, either in the palace or at my former quarters in the barracks of the air-scout squadron. Kantos Kan, they had found and questioned, but he knew nothing of my whereabouts, and as to my past, he had told them he knew as little, since he had but recently met me during our captivity among the Warhoons.

"Keep your eyes on this other one," commanded Than Kosis. "He also is a stranger and likely as not they both hail from Helium, and where one is we shall sooner or later find the other. Quadruple the air patrol, and let every man who leaves the city by air or ground be subjected to the closest scrutiny."

Another messenger now entered with word that I was still within the palace walls.

"The likeness of every person who has entered or left the palace grounds today has been carefully examined," concluded the fellow, "and not one approaches the likeness of this new padwar of the guards, other than that which was recorded of him at the time he entered."

"Then we will have him shortly," commented Than Kosis contentedly, "and in the meanwhile we will repair to the apartments of the Princess of Helium and question her in regard to the affair. She may know more than she cared to divulge to you, Notan. Come."

They left the hall, and, as darkness had fallen without, I slipped lightly from my hiding place and hastened to the balcony. Few were in sight, and choosing a moment when none seemed near I sprang quickly to the top of the glass wall and from there to the avenue beyond the palace grounds.

CHAPTER XXIII

𖤍)(𝑓)ⁱ)ᴤ 𝒬𝄂 𝄐𝄐ᵏ 𝑓𝄐𝄐

(Lost in the Sky)

WITHOUT EFFORT at concealment I hastened to the vicinity of our quarters, where I felt sure I should find Kantos Kan. As I neared the building I became more careful, as I judged, and rightly, that the place would be guarded. Several men in civilian metal loitered near the front entrance and in the rear were others. My only means of reaching, unseen, the upper story where our apartments were situated was through an adjoining building, and after considerable maneuvering I managed to attain the roof of a shop several doors away.

Leaping from roof to roof, I soon reached an open window in the building where I hoped to find the Heliumite, and in another moment I stood in the room before him. He was alone and showed no surprise at my coming, saying he had expected me much earlier, as my tour of duty must have ended some time since.

I saw that he knew nothing of the events of the day at the palace, and when I had enlightened him he was all excitement. The news that Dejah Thoris had promised her hand to Sab Than filled him with dismay.

"It cannot be," he exclaimed. "It is impossible!

Why no man in all Helium but would prefer death to the selling of our loved princess to the ruling house of Zodanga. She must have lost her mind to have assented to such an atrocious bargain. You, who do not know how we of Helium love the members of our ruling house, cannot appreciate the horror with which I contemplate such an unholy alliance.

"What can be done, John Carter?" he continued. "You are a resourceful man. Can you not think of some way to save Helium from this disgrace?"

"If I can come within sword's reach of Sab Than," I answered, "I can solve the difficulty in so far as Helium is concerned, but for personal reasons I would prefer that another struck the blow that frees Dejah Thoris."

Kantos Kan eyed me narrowly before he spoke.

"You love her!" he said. "Does she know it?"

"She knows it, Kantos Kan, and repulses me only because she is promised to Sab Than."

The splendid fellow sprang to his feet, and grasping me by the shoulder raised his sword on high, exclaiming:

"And had the choice been left to me I could not have chosen a more fitting mate for the first princess of Barsoom. Here is my hand upon your shoulder, John Carter, and my word that Sab Than shall go out at the point of my sword for the sake of my love for Helium, for Dejah Thoris, and for you. This very night I shall try to reach his quarters in the palace."

"How?" I asked. "You are strongly guarded and a quadruple force patrols the sky."

He bent his head in thought a moment, then raised it with an air of confidence.

"I only need to pass these guards and I can do it," he said at last. "I know a secret entrance to the palace through the pinnacle of the highest tower. I fell upon it by chance one day as I was passing above the palace on patrol duty. In this work it is required that we investigate any unusual occurrence we may witness, and a face peering from the pinnacle of the high tower of the palace was, to me, most unusual. I therefore drew near and discovered that the possessor of the peering face was none other than Sab Than. He was slightly put out at being detected and commanded me to keep the matter to myself, explaining that the passage from the tower led directly to his apartments, and was known only to him. If I can reach the roof of the barracks and get my machine I can be in Sab Than's quarters in five minutes; but how am I to escape from this building, guarded as you say it is?"

"How well are the machine sheds at the barracks guarded?" I asked.

"There is usually but one man on duty there at night upon the roof."

"Go to the roof of this building, Kantos Kan, and wait me there."

Without stopping to explain my plans I retraced my way to the street and hastened to the barracks. I did not dare to enter the building, filled as it was with members of the air-scout squadron, who, in common with all Zodanga, were on the lookout for me.

The building was an enormous one, rearing its lofty head fully a thousand feet into the air. But few buildings in Zodanga were higher than these barracks, though several topped it by a few hundred feet; the docks of the great battleships of the line standing some fifteen hundred feet from the ground, while the freight and passenger stations of the merchant squadrons rose nearly as high.

It was a long climb up the face of the building, and one fraught with much danger, but there was no other way, and so I essayed the task. The fact that Barsoomian architecture is extremely ornate made the feat much simpler than I had anticipated, since I found ornamental ledges and projections which fairly formed a perfect ladder for me all the way to the eaves of the building. Here I met my first real obstacle. The eaves projected nearly twenty feet from the wall to which I clung, and though I encircled the great building I could find no opening through them.

The top floor was alight, and filled with soldiers engaged in the pastimes of their kind; I could not, therefore, reach the roof through the building.

There was one slight, desperate chance, and that I decided I must take—it was for Dejah Thoris, and no man has lived who would not risk a thousand deaths for such as she.

Clinging to the wall with my feet and one hand, I unloosened one of the long leather straps of my trappings at the end of which dangled a great hook by which air sailors are hung to the sides and bottoms of their craft for various purposes of repair, and by means of which landing parties are lowered to the ground from the battleships.

I swung this hook cautiously to the roof several times before it finally found lodgment; gently I pulled on it to strengthen its hold, but whether it would bear the weight of my body I did not know. It might be barely caught upon the very outer verge of the roof, so that as my body swung out at the end of the strap it would slip off and launch me to the pavement a thousand feet below.

An instant I hesitated, and then, releasing my grasp upon the supporting ornament, I swung out into space at the end of the strap. Far below me lay the brilliantly lighted streets, the hard pavements, and death. There was a little jerk at the top of the supporting eaves, and a nasty slipping, grating sound which turned me cold with apprehension; then the hook caught and I was safe.

Clambering quickly aloft I grasped the edge of the eaves and drew myself to the surface of the roof above. As I gained my feet I was confronted by the sentry on duty, into the muzzle of whose revolver I found myself looking.

"Who are you and whence came you?" he cried.

"I am an air scout, friend, and very near a dead one, for just by the merest chance I escaped falling to the avenue below," I replied.

"But how came you upon the roof, man? No one has landed or come up from the building for the past hour. Quick, explain yourself, or I call the guard."

"Look you here, sentry, and you shall see how I came and how close a shave I had to not coming at all," I answered, turning toward the edge of the roof, where, twenty feet below, at the end of my strap, hung all my weapons.

The fellow, acting on impulse of curiosity, stepped

to my side and to his undoing, for as he leaned to peer over the eaves I grasped him by his throat and his pistol arm and threw him heavily to the roof. The weapon dropped from his grasp, and my fingers choked off his attempted cry for assistance. I gagged and bound him and then hung him over the edge of the roof as I myself had hung a few moments before. I knew it would be morning before he would be discovered, and I needed all the time that I could gain.

Donning my trappings and weapons I hastened to the sheds, and soon had out both my machine and Kantos Kan's. Making his fast behind mine I started my engine, and skimming over the edge of the roof I dove down into the streets of the city far below the plane usually occupied by the air patrol. In less than a minute I was settling safely upon the roof of our apartment beside the astonished Kantos Kan.

I lost no time in explanations, but plunged immediately into a discussion of our plans for the immediate future. It was decided that I was to try to make Helium while Kantos Kan was to enter the palace and dispatch Sab Than. If successful he was then to follow me. He set my compass for me, a clever little device which will remain steadfastly fixed upon any given point on the surface of Barsoom, and bidding each other farewell we rose together and sped in the direction of the palace which lay in the route which I must take to reach Helium.

As we neared the high tower a patrol shot down from above, throwing its piercing searchlight full upon my craft, and a voice roared out a command to halt, following with a shot as I paid no attention to his hail. Kantos Kan dropped quickly into the darkness, while I rose steadily and at terrific speed raced through the Martian sky followed by a dozen of the air-scout craft which had joined the pursuit, and later by a swift cruiser carrying a hundred men and a battery of rapid-fire guns. By twisting and turning my little machine, now rising and now falling, I managed to elude their search-lights most of the time, but I was also losing ground by these tactics, and so I decided to hazard everything on a straightaway course and leave the result to fate and the speed of my machine.

Kantos Kan had shown me a trick of gearing, which is known only to the navy of Helium, that greatly increased the speed of our machines, so that I felt sure I could distance my pursuers if I could dodge their pro-jectiles for a few moments.

As I sped through the air the screeching of the bullets around me convinced me that only by a miracle could I escape, but the die was cast, and throwing on full speed

I raced a straight course toward Helium. Gradually I left my pursuers further and further behind, and I was just congratulating myself on my lucky escape, when a well-directed shot from the cruiser exploded at the prow of my little craft. The concussion nearly capsized her, and with a sickening plunge she hurtled downward through the dark night.

How far I fell before I regained control of the plane I do not know, but I must have been very close to the ground when I started to rise again, as I plainly heard the squealing of animals below me. Rising again I scanned the heavens for my pursuers, and finally making out their lights far behind me, saw that they were landing, evidently in search of me.

Not until their lights were no longer discernible did I venture to flash my little lamp upon my compass, and then I found to my consternation that a fragment of the projectile had utterly destroyed my only guide, as well as my speedometer. It was true I could follow the stars in the general direction of Helium, but without knowing the exact location of the city or the speed at which I was traveling my chances for finding it were slim.

Helium lies a thousand miles southwest of Zodanga, and with my compass intact I should have made the trip, barring accidents, in between four and five hours. As it turned out, however, morning found me speeding over a vast expanse of dead sea bottom after nearly six hours of continuous flight at high speed. Presently a great city showed below me, but it was not Helium, as that alone of all Barsoomian metropolises consists in two immense circular walled cities about seventy-five miles apart and would have been easily distinguishable from the altitude at which I was flying.

Believing that I had come too far to the north and west, I turned back in a southeasterly direction, passing during the forenoon several other large cities, but none resembling the description which Kantos Kan had given me of Helium. In addition to the twin-city formation of Helium, another distinguishing feature is the two immense towers, one of vivid scarlet rising nearly a mile into the air from the center of one of the cities, while the other, of bright yellow and the same height, marks her sister.

Chapter XXIV

𝄞𝄢𝄡𝄢 𝄞𝄢𝄡𝄢𝄣𝄢 𝄞𝄡𝄢𝄣𝄢 𝄠 𝄞𝄡𝄢𝄣𝄢

(Tars Tarkas Finds a Friend)

ABOUT NOON I PASSED low over a great dead city of ancient Mars, and as I skimmed out across the plain beyond I came full upon several thousand green warriors engaged in a terrific battle. Scarcely had I seen them than a volley of shots was directed at me, and with the almost unfailing accuracy of their aim my little craft was instantly a ruined wreck, sinking erratically to the ground.

I fell almost directly in the center of the fierce combat, among warriors who had not seen my approach so busily were they engaged in life and death struggles. The men were fighting on foot with long-swords, while an occasional shot from a sharpshooter on the outskirts of the conflict would bring down a warrior who might for an instant separate himself from the entangled mass.

As my machine sank among them I realized that it was fight or die, with good chances of dying in any event, and so I struck the ground with drawn long-sword ready to defend myself as I could.

I fell beside a huge monster who was engaged with three antagonists, and as I glanced at his fierce face, filled with the light of battle, I recognized Tars Tarkas the Thark. He did not see me, as I was a trifle behind him, and just then the three warriors opposing him, and whom I recognized as Warhoons, charged simultaneously. The mighty fellow made quick work of one of them, but in stepping back for another thrust he fell over a dead body behind him and was down and at the mercy of his foes in an instant. Quick as lightning they were upon him, and Tars Tarkas would have been gathered to his fathers in short order had I not sprung before his prostrate form and engaged his adversaries. I had accounted for one of them when the mighty Thark regained his feet and quickly settled the other.

He gave me one look, and a slight smile touched his grim lip as, touching my shoulder, he said,

"I would scarcely recognize you, John Carter, but there is no other mortal upon Barsoom who would have done what you have for me. I think I have learned that there is such a thing as friendship, my friend."

He said no more, nor was there opportunity, for the Warhoons were closing in about us, and together we fought, shoulder to shoulder, during all that long, hot afternoon, until the tide of battle turned and the remnant of the fierce Warhoon horde fell back upon their thoats, and fled into the gathering darkness.

Ten thousand men had been engaged in that titanic struggle, and upon the field of battle lay three thousand dead. Neither side asked or gave quarter, nor did they attempt to take prisoners.

On our return to the city after the battle we had gone directly to Tars Tarkas' quarters, where I was left alone while the chieftain attended the customary council which immediately follows an engagement.

As I sat awaiting the return of the green warrior I heard something move in an adjoining apartment, and as I glanced up there rushed suddenly upon me a huge and hideous creature which bore me backward upon the pile of silks and furs upon which I had been reclining. It was Woola—faithful, loving Woola. He had found his way back to Thark and, as Tars Tarkas later told me, had gone immediately to my former quarters where he had taken up his pathetic and seemingly hopeless watch for my return.

"Tal Hajus knows that you are here, John Carter," said Tars Tarkas, on his return from the jeddak's quarters; "Sarkoja saw and recognized you as we were returning. Tal Hajus has ordered me to bring you before him tonight. I have ten thoats, John Carter; you may take your choice from among them, and I will accompany you to the nearest waterway that leads to Helium.

Tars Tarkas may be a cruel green warrior, but he can be a friend as well. Come, we must start."

"And when you return, Tars Tarkas?" I asked.

"The wild calots, possibly, or worse," he replied. "Unless I should chance to have the opportunity I have so long waited of battling with Tal Hajus."

"We will stay, Tars Tarkas, and see Tal Hajus tonight. You shall not sacrifice yourself, and it may be that tonight you can have the chance you wait."

He objected strenuously, saying that Tal Hajus often flew into wild fits of passion at the mere thought of the blow I had dealt him, and that if ever he laid his hands upon me I would be subjected to the most horrible tortures.

While we were eating I repeated to Tars Tarkas the story which Sola had told me that night upon the sea bottom during the march to Thark.

He said but little, but the great muscles of his face worked in passion and in agony at recollection of the horrors which had been heaped upon the only thing he had ever loved in all his cold, cruel, terrible existence.

He no longer demurred when I suggested that we go before Tal Hajus, only saying that he would like to speak to Sarkoja first. At his request I accompanied him to her quarters, and the look of venomous hatred she cast upon me was almost adequate recompense for any future misfortunes this accidental return to Thark might bring me.

"Sarkoja," said Tars Tarkas, "forty years ago you were instrumental in bringing about the torture and death of a woman named Gozava. I have just discovered that the warrior who loved that woman has learned of your part in the transaction. He may not kill you, Sarkoja, it is not our custom, but there is nothing to prevent him tying one end of a strap about your neck and the other end to a wild thoat, merely to test your fitness to survive and help perpetuate our race. Having heard that he would do this on the morrow, I thought it only right to warn you, for I am a just man. The river Iss is but a short pilgrimage, Sarkoja. Come, John Carter."

The next morning Sarkoja was gone, nor was she ever seen after.

In silence we hastened to the jeddak's palace, where we were immediately admitted to his presence; in fact, he could scarcely wait to see me and was standing erect upon his platform glowering at the entrance as I came in.

"Strap him to that pillar," he shrieked. "We shall see who it is dares strike the mighty Tal Hajus. Heat the irons; with my own hands I shall burn the eyes from his head that he may not pollute my person with his vile gaze."

"Chieftains of Thark," I cried, turning to the assembled council and ignoring Tal Hajus, "I have been a chief among you, and today I have fought for Thark shoulder to shoulder with her greatest warrior. You owe me, at least, a hearing. I have won that much today. You claim to be just people—"

"Silence," roared Tal Hajus. "Gag the creature and bind him as I command."

"Justice, Tal Hajus," exclaimed Lorquas Ptomel. "Who are you to set aside the customs of ages among the Tharks."

"Yes, justice!" echoed a dozen voices, and so, while Tal Hajus fumed and frothed, I continued.

"You are a brave people and you love bravery, but where was your mighty jeddak during the fight today? I did not see him in the thick of battle; he was not there. He rends defenseless women and little children in his lair, but how recently has one of you seen him fight with men? Why, even I, a midget beside him, felled him with a single blow of my fist. Is it of such that the Tharks fashion their jeddaks? There stands beside me now a great Thark, a mighty warrior and a noble man. Chieftains, how sounds, Tars Tarkas, Jeddak of Thark?"

A roar of deep-toned applause greeted this suggestion.

"It but remains for this council to command, and Tal Hajus must prove his fitness to rule. Were he a brave man he would invite Tars Tarkas to combat, for he does not love him, but Tal Hajus is afraid; Tal Hajus, your jeddak, is a coward. With my bare hands I could kill him, and he knows it."

After I ceased there was tense silence, as all eyes were riveted upon Tal Hajus. He did not speak or move, but the blotchy green of his countenance turned livid, and the froth froze upon his lips.

"Tal Hajus," said Lorquas Ptomel in a cold, hard voice, "never in my long life have I seen a jeddak of the Tharks so humiliated. There could be but one answer to this arraignment. We wait it." And still Tal Hajus stood as though petrified.

"Chieftains," continued Lorquas Ptomel, "shall the jeddak, Tal Hajus, prove his fitness to rule over Tars Tarkas?"

There were twenty chieftains about the rostrum, and twenty swords flashed high in assent.

There was no alternative. That decree was final, and so Tal Hajus drew his long-sword and advanced to meet Tars Tarkas.

The combat was soon over, and, with his foot upon the neck of the dead monster, Tars Tarkas became jeddak among the Tharks.

His first act was to make me a full-fledged chieftain with the rank I had won by my combats the first few weeks of my captivity among them.

Seeing the favorable disposition of the warriors toward Tars Tarkas, as well as toward me, I grasped the opportunity to enlist them in my cause against Zodanga. I told Tars Tarkas the story of my adventures, and in a few words had explained to him the thought I had in mind.

"John Carter has made a proposal," he said, addressing the council, "which meets with my sanction. I shall put it to you briefly. Dejah Thoris, the Princess of Helium, who was our prisoner, is now held by the jeddak of Zodanga, whose son she must wed to save her country from devastation at the hands of the Zodangan forces.

"John Carter suggests that we rescue her and return her to Helium. The loot of Zodanga would be magnificent, and I have often thought that had we an alliance with the people of Helium we could obtain sufficient assurance of sustenance to permit us to increase the size and frequency of our hatchings, and thus become

unquestionably supreme among the green men of all
Barsoom. What say you?"

It was a chance to fight, an opportunity to loot, and
they rose to the bait as a speckled trout to a fly.

For Tharks they were wildly enthusiastic, and before
another half hour had passed twenty mounted messengers were speeding across dead sea bottoms to call the
hordes together for the expedition.

In three days we were on the march toward Zodanga,
one hundred thousand strong, as Tars Tarkas had been
able to enlist the services of three smaller hordes on the
promise of the great loot of Zodanga.

At the head of the column I rode beside the great
Thark while at the heels of my mount trotted my
beloved Woola.

We traveled entirely by night, timing our marches so
that we camped during the day at deserted cities where,
even to the beasts, we were all kept indoors during the
daylight hours. On the march Tars Tarkas, through
his remarkable ability and statesmanship, enlisted fifty
thousand more warriors from various hordes, so that,
ten days after we set out we halted at midnight outside
the great walled city of Zodanga, one hundred and fifty
thousand strong.

The fighting strength and efficiency of this horde

of ferocious green monsters was equivalent to ten times their number of red men. Never in the history of Barsoom, Tars Tarkas told me, had such a force of green warriors marched to battle together. It was a monstrous task to keep even a semblance of harmony among them, and it was a marvel to me that he got them to the city without a mighty battle among themselves.

But as we neared Zodanga their personal quarrels were submerged by their greater hatred for the red men, and especially for the Zodangans, who had for years waged a ruthless campaign of extermination against the green men, directing special attention toward despoiling their incubators.

Now that we were before Zodanga the task of obtaining entry to the city devolved upon me, and directing Tars Tarkas to hold his forces in two divisions out of earshot of the city, with each division opposite a large gateway, I took twenty dismounted warriors and approached one of the small gates that pierced the walls at short intervals. These gates have no regular guard, but are covered by sentries, who patrol the avenue that encircles the city just within the walls much as our metropolitan police patrol their beats.

The walls of Zodanga are seventy-five feet in height and fifty feet thick. They are built of enormous blocks of carborundum, and the task of entering the city seemed, to my escort of green warriors, an impossibility. The fellows who had been detailed to accompany me were of one of the smaller hordes, and therefore did not know me.

Placing three of them with their faces to the wall and arms locked, I commanded two more to mount to their shoulders, and a sixth I ordered to climb upon the shoulders of the upper two. The head of the topmost warrior towered over forty feet from the ground.

In this way, with ten warriors, I built a series of three steps from the ground to the shoulders of the topmost man. Then starting from a short distance behind them I ran swiftly up from one tier to the next, and with a final bound from the broad shoulders of the highest I clutched the top of the great wall and quietly drew myself to its broad expanse. After me I dragged six lengths of leather from an equal number of my warriors. These lengths we had previously fastened together, and passing one end to the topmost warrior I lowered the other end cautiously over the opposite side of the wall toward the avenue below. No one was in sight, so, lowering myself to the end of my leather strap, I dropped the remaining thirty feet to the pavement below.

I had learned from Kantos Kan the secret of opening

these gates, and in another moment my twenty great fighting men stood within the doomed city of Zodanga.

I found to my delight that I had entered at the lower boundary of the enormous palace grounds. The building itself showed in the distance a blaze of glorious light, and on the instant I determined to lead a detachment of warriors directly within the palace itself, while the balance of the great horde was attacking the barracks of the soldiery.

Dispatching one of my men to Tars Tarkas for a detail of fifty Tharks, with word of my intentions, I ordered ten warriors to capture and open one of the great gates while with the nine remaining I took the other. We were to do our work quietly, no shots were to be fired and no general advance made until I had reached the palace with my fifty Tharks. Our plans worked to perfection. The two sentries we met were dispatched to their fathers upon the banks of the lost sea of Korus, and the guards at both gates followed them in silence.

CHAPTER XXV

𐌀𐌎𐌋 𐌕𐌉𐌀𐌀𐌋𐌉𐌔𐌇 𐌀𐌋 𐌚𐌀𐌔𐌀𐌔𐌇𐌀

(The Looting of Zodanga)

As THE GREAT GATE where I stood swung open my fifty Tharks, headed by Tars Tarkas himself, rode in upon their mighty thoats. I led them to the palace walls, which I negotiated easily without assistance. Once inside, however, the gate gave me considerable trouble, but I finally was rewarded by seeing it swing upon its huge hinges, and soon my fierce escort was riding across the gardens of the jeddak of Zodanga.

As we approached the palace I could see through the great windows of the first floor into the brilliantly illuminated audience chamber of Than Kosis. The immense hall was crowded with nobles and their women, as though some important function was in progress. There was not a guard in sight without the palace, due, I presume, to the fact that the city and palace walls were considered impregnable, and so I came close and peered within.

At one end of the chamber, upon massive golden thrones encrusted with diamonds, sat Than Kosis and his consort, surrounded by officers and dignitaries of state. Before them stretched a broad aisle lined on either side with soldiery, and as I looked there entered this aisle at the far end of the hall, the head of a procession which advanced to the foot of the throne.

First there marched four officers of the jeddak's Guard bearing a huge salver on which reposed, upon a cushion of scarlet silk, a great golden chain with a collar and padlock at each end. Directly behind these officers came four others carrying a similar salver which supported the magnificent ornaments of a prince and princess of the reigning house of Zodanga.

At the foot of the throne these two parties separated and halted, facing each other at opposite sides of the aisle. Then came more dignitaries, and the officers of the palace and of the army, and finally two figures entirely muffled in scarlet silk, so that not a feature of either was discernible. These two stopped at the foot of the throne, facing Than Kosis. When the balance of the procession had entered and assumed their stations Than Kosis addressed the couple standing before him. I could not hear the words, but presently two officers advanced and removed the scarlet robe from one of the figures, and I saw that Kantos Kan had failed in his mission, for it was Sab Than, Prince of Zodanga, who stood revealed before me.

Than Kosis now took a set of the ornaments from one of the salvers and placed one of the collars of gold about his son's neck, springing the padlock fast. After a few more words addressed to Sab Than he turned to the other figure, from which the officers now removed the enshrouding silks, disclosing to my now comprehending view Dejah Thoris, Princess of Helium.

The object of the ceremony was clear to me; in another moment Dejah Thoris would be joined forever to the Prince of Zodanga. It was an impressive and beautiful ceremony, I presume, but to me it seemed the most fiendish sight I had ever witnessed, and as the ornaments were adjusted upon her beautiful figure and her collar of gold swung open in the hands of Than Kosis I raised my long-sword above my head, and, with the heavy hilt, I shattered the glass of the great window and sprang into the midst of the astonished assemblage. With a bound I was on the steps of the platform beside Than Kosis, and as he stood riveted with surprise I brought my long-sword down upon the golden chain that would have bound Dejah Thoris to another.

In an instant all was confusion; a thousand drawn swords menaced me from every quarter, and Sab Than sprang upon me with a jeweled dagger he had drawn from his nuptial ornaments. I could have killed him as easily as I might a fly, but the age-old custom of Barsoom stayed my hand, and grasping his wrist as the dagger flew toward my heart I held him as though in a vise and with my long-sword pointed to the far end of the hall.

"Zodanga has fallen," I cried. "Look!"

All eyes turned in the direction I had indicated, and there, forging through the portals of the entranceway rode Tars Tarkas and his fifty warriors on their great thoats.

A cry of alarm and amazement broke from the assemblage, but no word of fear, and in a moment the soldiers and nobles of Zodanga were hurling themselves upon the advancing Tharks.

Thrusting Sab Than headlong from the platform, I drew Dejah Thoris to my side. Behind the throne was a narrow doorway and in this Than Kosis now stood facing me, with drawn long-sword. In an instant we were engaged, and I found no mean antagonist.

As we circled upon the broad platform I saw Sab Than rushing up the steps to aid his father, but, as he raised his hand to strike, Dejah Thoris sprang before him and then my sword found the spot that made Sab

Than jeddak of Zodanga. As his father rolled dead upon the floor the new jeddak tore himself free from Dejah Thoris' grasp, and again we faced each other. He was soon joined by a quartet of officers, and, with my back against a golden throne, I fought once again for Dejah Thoris. I was hard pressed to defend myself and yet not strike down Sab Than and, with him, my last chance to win the woman I loved. My blade was swinging with the rapidity of lightning as I sought to parry the thrusts and cuts of my opponents. Two I had disarmed, and one was down, when several more rushed to the aid of their new ruler, and to avenge the death of the old.

As they advanced there were cries of "The woman! The woman! Strike her down; it is her plot. Kill her! Kill her!"

Calling to Dejah Thoris to get behind me I worked my way toward the little doorway back of the throne, but the officers realized my intentions, and three of them sprang in behind me and blocked my chances for gaining a position where I could have defended Dejah Thoris against any army of swordsmen.

The Tharks were having their hands full in the center of the room, and I began to realize that nothing short of a miracle could save Dejah Thoris and myself, when I saw Tars Tarkas surging through the crowd of pigmies that swarmed about him. With one swing of his mighty long-sword he laid a dozen corpses at his feet, and so he hewed a pathway before him until in another moment he stood upon the platform beside me, dealing death and destruction right and left.

The bravery of the Zodangans was awe-inspiring, not one attempted to escape, and when the fighting ceased it was because only Tharks remained alive in the great hall, other than Dejah Thoris and myself.

Sab Than lay dead beside his father, and the corpses of the flower of Zodangan nobility and chivalry covered the floor of the bloody shambles.

My first thought when the battle was over was for Kantos Kan, and leaving Dejah Thoris in charge of Tars Tarkas I took a dozen warriors and hastened to the dungeons beneath the palace. The jailers had all left to join the fighters in the throne room, so we searched the labyrinthine prison without opposition.

I called Kantos Kan's name aloud in each new corridor and compartment, and finally I was rewarded by hearing a faint response. Guided by the sound, we soon found him helpless in a dark recess.

He was overjoyed at seeing me, and to know the meaning of the fight, faint echoes of which had reached his prison cell. He told me that the air patrol had captured him before he reached the high tower of the palace, so that he had not even seen Sab Than.

We discovered that it would be futile to attempt to cut away the bars and chains which held him prisoner, so, at his suggestion I returned to search the bodies on the floor above for keys to open the padlocks of his cell and of his chains.

Fortunately among the first I examined I found his jailer, and soon we had Kantos Kan with us in the throne room.

The sounds of heavy firing, mingled with shouts and cries, came to us from the city's streets, and Tars Tarkas hastened away to direct the fighting without. Kantos Kan accompanied him to act as guide, the green warriors commencing a thorough search of the palace for other Zodangans and for loot, and Dejah Thoris and I were left alone.

She had sunk into one of the golden thrones, and as I turned to her she greeted me with a wan smile.

"Was there ever such a man!" she exclaimed. "I know that Barsoom has never before seen your like. Can it be that all Earth men are as you? Alone, a stranger, hunted, threatened, persecuted, you have done in a few short months what in all the past ages of Barsoom no man has ever done: joined together the wild hordes of the sea bottoms and brought them to fight as allies of a red Martian people."

"The answer is easy, Dejah Thoris," I replied smiling. "It was not I who did it, it was love, love for Dejah Thoris, a power that would work greater miracles than this you have seen."

A pretty flush overspread her face and she answered, "You may say that now, John Carter, and I may listen, for I am free."

"And more still I have to say, ere it is again too late," I returned. "I have done many strange things in my life, many things that wiser men would not have dared, but never in my wildest fancies have I dreamed of winning a Dejah Thoris for myself—for never had I dreamed that in all the universe dwelt such a woman as the Princess of Helium. That you are a princess does not abash me, but that you are you is enough to make me doubt my sanity as I ask you, my princess, to be mine."

"He does not need to be abashed who so well knew the answer to his plea before the plea was made," she replied, rising and placing her dear hands upon my shoulders, and so I took her in my arms and kissed her.

And thus in the midst of a city of wild conflict,

filled with the alarms of war; with death and destruction reaping their terrible harvest around her, did Dejah Thoris, Princess of Helium, true daughter of Mars, the God of War, promise herself in marriage to John Carter, Gentleman of Virginia.

Chapter XXVI

꙳꙼꙾ (꙳꙼꙾꙼꙾ ꙳꙼ ꙾꙼꙾

(Through Carnage to Joy)

SOMETIME LATER Tars Tarkas and Kantos Kan returned to report that Zodanga had been completely reduced. Her forces were entirely destroyed or captured, and no further resistance was to be expected from within. Several battleships had escaped, but there were thousands of war and merchant vessels under guard of Thark warriors.

The lesser hordes had commenced looting and quarreling among themselves, so it was decided that we collect what warriors we could, man as many vessels as possible with Zodangan prisoners and make for Helium without further loss of time.

Five hours later we sailed from the roofs of the dock buildings with a fleet of two hundred and fifty battleships, carrying nearly one hundred thousand green warriors, followed by a fleet of transports with our thoats.

Behind us we left the stricken city in the fierce and brutal clutches of some forty thousand green warriors of the lesser hordes. They were looting, murdering, and fighting amongst themselves. In a hundred places they had applied the torch, and columns of dense smoke were rising above the city as though to blot out from the eye of heaven the horrid sights beneath.

In the middle of the afternoon we sighted the scarlet and yellow towers of Helium, and a short time later a great fleet of Zodangan battleships rose from the camps of the besiegers without the city, and advanced to meet us.

The banners of Helium had been strung from stem to stern of each of our mighty craft, but the Zodangans did not need this sign to realize that we were enemies, for our green Martian warriors had opened fire upon them almost as they left the ground. With their uncanny marksmanship they raked the on-coming fleet with volley after volley.

The twin cities of Helium, perceiving that we were friends, sent out hundreds of vessels to aid us, and then began the first real air battle I had ever witnessed.

The vessels carrying our green warriors were kept circling above the contending fleets of Helium and Zodanga, since their batteries were useless in the hands of the Tharks who, having no navy, have no skill in naval gunnery. Their small-arm fire, however, was most effective, and the final outcome of the engagement was strongly influenced, if not wholly determined, by their presence.

At first the two forces circled at the same altitude, pouring broadside after broadside into each other. Presently a great hole was torn in the hull of one of the immense battle craft from the Zodangan camp; with a lurch she turned completely over, the little figures of her crew plunging, turning and twisting toward the ground a thousand feet below; then with sickening velocity she tore after them, almost completely burying herself in the soft loam of the ancient sea bottom.

A wild cry of exultation arose from the Heliumite squadron, and with redoubled ferocity they fell upon the Zodangan fleet. By a pretty maneuver two of the vessels of Helium gained a position above their adversaries, from which they poured upon them from their keel bomb batteries a perfect torrent of exploding bombs.

Then, one by one, the battleships of Helium succeeded in rising above the Zodangans, and in short time a number of the beleaguering battleships were drifting hopeless wrecks toward the high scarlet tower of greater Helium. Several others attempted to escape, but they were soon surrounded by thousands of tiny individual fliers, and above each hung a monster battleship of

Helium ready to drop boarding parties upon their decks.

Within but little more than an hour from the moment the victorious Zodangan squadron had risen to meet us from the camp of the besiegers the battle was over, and the remaining vessels of the conquered Zodangans were headed toward the cities of Helium under prize crews.

There was an extremely pathetic side to the surrender of these mighty fliers, the result of an age-old custom which demanded that surrender should be signalized by the voluntary plunging to earth of the commander of the vanquished vessel. One after another the brave fellows, holding their colors high above their heads, leaped from the towering bows of their mighty craft to an awful death.

Not until the commander of the entire fleet took the fearful plunge, thus indicating the surrender of the remaining vessels, did the fighting cease, and the useless sacrifice of brave men come to an end.

We now signaled the flagship of Helium's navy to approach, and when she was within hailing distance I called out that we had the Princess Dejah Thoris on board, and that we wished to transfer her to the flagship that she might be taken immediately to the city.

As the full import of my announcement bore in

upon them a great cry arose from the decks of the flagship, and a moment later the colors of the Princess of Helium broke from a hundred points upon her upper works. When the other vessels of the squadron caught the meaning of the signals flashed them they took up the wild acclaim and unfurled her colors in the gleaming sunlight.

The flagship bore down upon us, and as she swung gracefully to and touched our side a dozen officers sprang upon our decks. As their astonished gaze fell upon the hundreds of green warriors, who now came forth from the fighting shelters, they stopped aghast, but at sight of Kantos Kan, who advanced to meet them, they came forward, crowding about him.

Dejah Thoris and I then advanced, and they had no eyes for other than her. She received them gracefully, calling each by name, for they were men high in the esteem and service of her grandfather, and she knew them well.

"Lay your hands upon the shoulder of John Carter," she said to them, turning toward me, "the man to whom Helium owes her princess as well as her victory today."

They were very courteous to me and said many kind and complimentary things, but what seemed to impress them most was that I had won the aid of the fierce

Tharks in my campaign for the liberation of Dejah Thoris, and the relief of Helium.

"You owe your thanks more to another man than to me," I said, "and here he is; meet one of Barsoom's greatest soldiers and statesmen, Tars Tarkas, Jeddak of Thark."

With the same polished courtesy that had marked their manner toward me they extended their greetings to the great Thark, nor, to my surprise, was he much behind them in ease of bearing or in courtly speech. Though not a garrulous race, the Tharks are extremely formal, and their ways lend themselves amazingly to dignified and courtly manners.

Dejah Thoris went aboard the flagship, and was much put out that I would not follow, but, as I explained to her, the battle was but partly won; we still had the land forces of the besieging Zodangans to account for, and I would not leave Tars Tarkas until that had been accomplished.

The commander of the naval forces of Helium promised to arrange to have the armies of Helium attack from the city in conjunction with our land attack, and so the vessels separated and Dejah Thoris was borne in triumph back to the court of her grandfather, Tardos Mors, Jeddak of Helium.

In the distance lay our fleet of transports, with the thoats of the green warriors, where they had remained during the battle. Without landing stages it was to be a difficult matter to unload these beasts upon the open plain, but there was nothing else for it, and so we put out for a point about ten miles from the city and began the task.

It was necessary to lower the animals to the ground in slings and this work occupied the remainder of the day and half the night. Twice we were attacked by parties of Zodangan cavalry, but with little loss, however, and after darkness shut down they withdrew.

As soon as the last thoat was unloaded Tars Tarkas gave the command to advance, and in three parties we crept upon the Zodangan camp from the north, the south and the east.

About a mile from the main camp we encountered their outposts and, as had been prearranged, accepted this as the signal to charge. With wild, ferocious cries and amidst the nasty squealing of battle-enraged thoats we bore down upon the Zodangans.

We did not catch them napping, but found a well-entrenched battle line confronting us. Time after time we were repulsed until, toward noon, I began to fear for the result of the battle.

The Zodangans numbered nearly a million fighting men, gathered from pole to pole, wherever stretched their ribbon-like waterways, while pitted against them were less than a hundred thousand green warriors. The forces from Helium had not arrived, nor could we receive any word from them.

Just at noon we heard heavy firing all along the line between the Zodangans and the cities, and we knew then that our much-needed reinforcements had come.

Again Tars Tarkas ordered the charge, and once more the mighty thoats bore their terrible riders against the ramparts of the enemy. At the same moment the battle line of Helium surged over the opposite breast-works of the Zodangans and in another moment they were being crushed as between two millstones. Nobly they fought, but in vain.

The plain before the city became a veritable shambles ere the last Zodangan surrendered, but finally the carnage ceased, the prisoners were marched back to Helium, and we entered the greater city's gates, a huge triumphal procession of conquering heroes.

The broad avenues were lined with women and children, among which were the few men whose duties necessitated that they remain within the city during the battle. We were greeted with an endless round of applause and showered with ornaments of gold, platinum, silver, and precious jewels. The city had gone mad with joy.

My fierce Tharks caused the wildest excitement and enthusiasm. Never before had an armed body of green warriors entered the gates of Helium, and that they came now as friends and allies filled the red men with rejoicing.

That my poor services to Dejah Thoris had become known to the Heliumites was evidenced by the loud crying of my name, and by the loads of ornaments that were fastened upon me and my huge thoat as we passed up the avenues to the palace, for even in the face of the ferocious appearance of Woola the populace pressed close about me.

As we approached this magnificent pile we were met by a party of officers who greeted us warmly and requested that Tars Tarkas and his jeds with the jeddaks and jeds of his wild allies, together with myself, dismount and accompany them to receive from Tardos Mors an expression of his gratitude for our services.

At the top of the great steps leading up to the main portals of the palace stood the royal party, and as we reached the lower steps one of their number descended to meet us. He was an almost perfect specimen of manhood; tall, straight as an arrow, superbly muscled and with the carriage and bearing of a ruler of men. I did not need to be told that he was Tardos Mors, Jeddak of Helium.

The first member of our party he met was Tars Tarkas and his first words sealed forever the new friendship between the races.

"That Tardos Mors," he said, earnestly, "may meet the greatest living warrior of Barsoom is a priceless honor, but that he may lay his hand on the shoulder of a friend and ally is a far greater boon."

"Jeddak of Helium," returned Tars Tarkas, "it has remained for a man of another world to teach the green warriors of Barsoom the meaning of friendship; to him we owe the fact that the hordes of Thark can understand you; that they can appreciate and reciprocate the sentiments so graciously expressed."

Tardos Mors then greeted each of the green jeddaks and jeds, and to each spoke words of friendship and appreciation.

As he approached me he laid both hands upon my shoulders.

"Welcome, my son," he said; "that you are granted, gladly, and without one word of opposition, the most precious jewel in all Helium, yes, on all Barsoom, is sufficient earnest of my esteem."

We were then presented to Mors Kajak, Jed of lesser Helium, and father of Dejah Thoris. He had followed close behind Tardos Mors and seemed even more affected by the meeting than had his father.

He tried a dozen times to express his gratitude to me, but his voice choked with emotion and he could not speak, and yet he had, as I was to later learn, a reputation for ferocity and fearlessness as a fighter that was remarkable even upon warlike Barsoom. In common with all Helium he worshipped his daughter, nor could he think of what she had escaped without deep emotion.

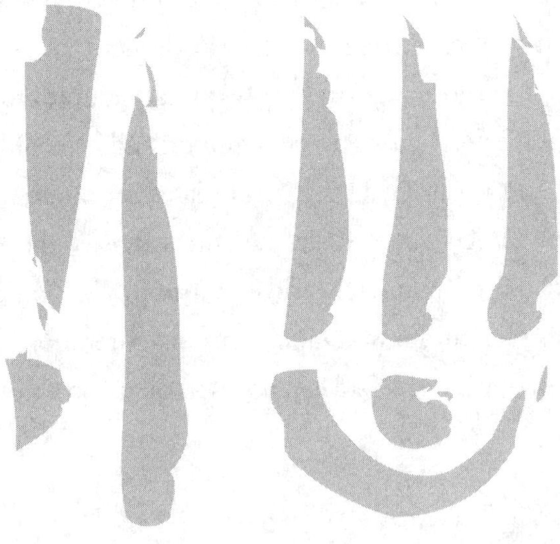

Chapter XXVII
⟨⟨glyphs⟩⟩
(From Joy to Death)

FOR TEN DAYS the hordes of Thark and their wild allies were feasted and entertained, and, then, loaded with costly presents and escorted by ten thousand soldiers of Helium commanded by Mors Kajak, they started on the return journey to their own lands. The Jed of lesser Helium with a small party of nobles accompanied them all the way to Thark to cement more closely the new bonds of peace and friendship.

Sola also accompanied Tars Tarkas, her father, who before his chieftains had acknowledged her as his daughter.

Three weeks later, Mors Kajak and his officers, accompanied by Tars Tarkas and Sola, returned upon a battleship that had been dispatched to Thark to fetch them in time for the ceremony which made Dejah Thoris and John Carter one.

For nine years I served in the councils and fought in the armies of Helium as a prince of the house of Tardos Mors. The people seemed never to tire of heaping honors upon me, and no day passed that did not bring some new proof of their love for my princess, the incomparable Dejah Thoris.

In a golden incubator upon the roof of our palace lay a snow-white egg. For nearly five years ten soldiers of the jeddak's Guard had constantly stood over it, and not a day passed when I was in the city that Dejah Thoris and I did not stand hand in hand before our little shrine planning for the future, when the delicate shell should break.

Vivid in my memory is the picture of the last night as we sat there talking in low tones of the strange romance which had woven our lives together and of this wonder which was coming to augment our happiness and fulfill our hopes.

In the distance we saw the bright-white light of an approaching airship, but we attached no special significance to so common a sight. Like a bolt of lightning it raced toward Helium until its very speed bespoke the unusual.

Flashing the signals which proclaimed it a dispatch bearer for the jeddak, it circled impatiently awaiting the tardy patrol boat which must convoy it to the palace docks.

Ten minutes after it touched at the palace a message

called me to the council chamber, which I found filling with the members of that body.

On the raised platform of the throne was Tardos Mors, pacing back and forth with tense-drawn face. When all were in their seats he turned toward us.

"This morning," he said, "word reached the several governments of Barsoom that the keeper of the atmosphere plant had made no wireless report for two days, nor had almost ceaseless calls upon him from a score of capitals elicited a sign of response.

"The ambassadors of the other nations asked us to take the matter in hand and hasten the assistant keeper to the plant. All day a thousand cruisers have been searching for him until, just now one of them returns bearing his dead body, which was found in the pits beneath his house horribly mutilated by some assassin.

"I do not need to tell you what this means to Barsoom. It would take months to penetrate those mighty walls, in fact the work has already commenced, and there would be little to fear were the engine of the pumping plant to run as it should and as they all have for hundreds of years; but the worst, we fear, has happened. The instruments show a rapidly decreasing air pressure on all parts of Barsoom—the engine has stopped."

"My gentlemen," he concluded, "we have at best three days to live."

There was absolute silence for several minutes, and then a young noble arose, and with his drawn sword held high above his head addressed Tardos Mors.

"The men of Helium have prided themselves that they have ever shown Barsoom how a nation of red men should live, now is our opportunity to show them how they should die. Let us go about our duties as though a thousand useful years still lay before us."

The chamber rang with applause and as there was nothing better to do than to allay the fears of the people by our example we went our ways with smiles upon our faces and sorrow gnawing at our hearts.

When I returned to my palace I found that the rumor already had reached Dejah Thoris, so I told her all that I had heard.

"We have been very happy, John Carter," she said, "and I thank whatever fate overtakes us that it permits us to die together."

The next two days brought no noticeable change in the supply of air, but on the morning of the third day breathing became difficult at the higher altitudes of the rooftops. The avenues and plazas of Helium were filled with people. All business had ceased. For the most part the people looked bravely into the face of their unalterable doom. Here and there, however, men and women gave way to quiet grief.

Toward the middle of the day many of the weaker commenced to succumb and within an hour the people of Barsoom were sinking by thousands into the unconsciousness which precedes death by asphyxiation.

Dejah Thoris and I with the other members of the royal family had collected in a sunken garden within an inner courtyard of the palace. We conversed in low tones, when we conversed at all, as the awe of the grim shadow of death crept over us. Even Woola seemed to feel the weight of the impending calamity, for he pressed close to Dejah Thoris and to me, whining pitifully.

The little incubator had been brought from the roof of our palace at request of Dejah Thoris and now she sat gazing longingly upon the unknown little life that now she would never know.

As it was becoming perceptibly difficult to breathe Tardos Mors arose, saying,

"Let us bid each other farewell. The days of the greatness of Barsoom are over. Tomorrow's sun will look down upon a dead world which through all eternity must go swinging through the heavens peopled not even by memories. It is the end."

He stooped and kissed the women of his family, and laid his strong hand upon the shoulders of the men.

As I turned sadly from him my eyes fell upon Dejah Thoris. Her head was drooping upon her breast, to all appearances she was lifeless. With a cry I sprang to her and raised her in my arms.

Her eyes opened and looked into mine.

"Kiss me, John Carter," she murmured. "I love you! I love you! It is cruel that we must be torn apart who were just starting upon a life of love and happiness."

As I pressed her dear lips to mine the old feeling of unconquerable power and authority rose in me. The fighting blood of Virginia sprang to life in my veins.

"It shall not be, my princess," I cried. "There is, there must be some way, and John Carter, who has fought his way through a strange world for love of you, will find it."

And with my words there crept above the threshold of my conscious mind a series of nine long forgotten sounds. Like a flash of lightning in the darkness their full purport dawned upon me—the key to the three great doors of the atmosphere plant!

Turning suddenly toward Tardos Mors as I still clasped my dying love to my breast, I cried,

"A flier, Jeddak! Quick! Order your swiftest flier to the palace top. I can save Barsoom yet."

He did not wait to question, but in an instant a guard was racing to the nearest dock and though the air was thin and almost gone at the rooftop they managed to launch the fastest one-man, air-scout machine that the skill of Barsoom had ever produced.

Kissing Dejah Thoris a dozen times and commanding Woola, who would have followed me, to remain and guard her, I bounded with my old agility and strength to the high ramparts of the palace, and in another moment I was headed toward the goal of the hopes of all Barsoom.

I had to fly low to get sufficient air to breathe, but I took a straight course across an old sea bottom and so had to rise only a few feet above the ground.

I traveled with awful velocity for my errand was a race against time with death. The face of Dejah Thoris hung always before me. As I turned for a last look as I left the palace garden I had seen her stagger and sink upon the ground beside the little incubator. That she had dropped into the last coma which would end in death, if the air supply remained unreplenished, I well knew, and so, throwing caution to the winds, I flung overboard everything but the engine and the compass, even to my ornaments, and lying on my belly along the deck with one hand on the steering wheel and the other pushing the speed lever to its last notch I split the thin air of dying Mars with the speed of a meteor.

An hour before dark the great walls of the atmosphere plant loomed suddenly before me, and with a sickening thud I plunged to the ground before the small door which was withholding the spark of life from the inhabitants of an entire planet.

Beside the door a great crew of men had been laboring to pierce the wall, but they had scarcely scratched the flint-like surface, and now most of them lay in the last sleep from which not even air would awaken them.

Conditions seemed much worse here than at Helium, and it was with difficulty that I breathed at all. There were a few men still conscious, and to one of these I spoke.

"If I can open these doors is there a man who can start the engines?" I asked.

"I can," he replied, "if you open quickly. I can last but a few moments more. But it is useless, they are both dead and no one else upon Barsoom knew the secret of these awful locks. For three days men crazed with fear have surged about this portal in vain attempts to solve its mystery."

I had no time to talk, I was becoming very weak and it was with difficulty that I controlled my mind at all.

But, with a final effort, as I sank weakly to my knees I hurled the nine thought waves at that awful thing before me. The Martian had crawled to my side and with staring eyes fixed on the single panel before us we waited in the silence of death.

Slowly the mighty door receded before us. I attempted to rise and follow it but I was too weak.

"After it," I cried to my companion, "and if you reach the pump room turn loose all the pumps. It is the only chance Barsoom has to exist tomorrow!"

From where I lay I opened the second door, and then the third, and as I saw the hope of Barsoom crawling weakly on hands and knees through the last doorway I sank unconscious upon the ground.

Chapter XXVIII

ᎭᏎ ᎡᏎᎢᎮ ᎭᎫᏉᎮᎮᏎᏎ ᏫᎭᎢᎮ

(At the Arizona Cave)

IT WAS DARK when I opened my eyes again. Strange, stiff garments were upon my body; garments that cracked and powdered away from me as I rose to a sitting posture.

I felt myself over from head to foot and from head to foot I was clothed, though when I fell unconscious at the little doorway I had been naked. Before me was a small patch of moonlit sky which showed through a ragged aperture.

As my hands passed over my body they came in contact with pockets and in one of these a small parcel of matches wrapped in oiled paper. One of these matches I struck, and its dim flame lighted up what appeared to be a huge cave, toward the back of which I discovered a strange, still figure huddled over a tiny bench. As I approached it I saw that it was the dead and mummified remains of a little old woman with long black hair, and the thing it leaned over was a small charcoal burner upon which rested a round copper vessel containing a small quantity of greenish powder.

Behind her, depending from the roof upon rawhide

thongs, and stretching entirely across the cave, was a row of human skeletons. From the thong which held them stretched another to the dead hand of the little old woman; as I touched the cord the skeletons swung to the motion with a noise as of the rustling of dry leaves.

It was a most grotesque and horrid tableau and I hastened out into the fresh air; glad to escape from so gruesome a place.

The sight that met my eyes as I stepped out upon a small ledge which ran before the entrance of the cave filled me with consternation.

A new heaven and a new landscape met my gaze. The silvered mountains in the distance, the almost stationary moon hanging in the sky, the cacti-studded valley below me were not of Mars. I could scarce believe my eyes, but the truth slowly forced itself upon me—I was looking upon Arizona from the same ledge from which ten years before I had gazed with longing upon Mars.

Burying my head in my arms I turned, broken, and sorrowful, down the trail from the cave.

Above me shone the red eye of Mars holding her awful secret, forty-eight million miles away.

Did the Martian reach the pump room? Did the vitalizing air reach the people of that distant planet in time to save them? Was my Dejah Thoris alive, or did her beautiful body lie cold in death beside the tiny golden incubator in the sunken garden of the inner courtyard of the palace of Tardos Mors, the jeddak of Helium?

For ten years I have waited and prayed for an answer to my questions. For ten years I have waited and prayed to be taken back to the world of my lost love. I would rather lie dead beside her there than live on Earth all those millions of terrible miles from her.

The old mine, which I found untouched, has made me fabulously wealthy; but what care I for wealth!

As I sit here tonight in my little study overlooking the Hudson, just twenty years have elapsed since I first opened my eyes upon Mars.

I can see her shining in the sky through the little window by my desk, and tonight she seems calling to me again as she has not called before since that long dead night, and I think I can see, across that awful abyss of space, a beautiful black-haired woman standing in the garden of a palace, and at her side is a little boy who puts his arm around her as she points into the sky toward the planet Earth, while at their feet is a huge and hideous creature with a heart of gold.

I believe that they are waiting there for me, and something tells me that I shall soon know.